TALES from THAC

A COLLECTION OF SHORT STORIES AND NOVELLAS

F.P. SPIRIT, K.J. FOGLEMAN

SHANNON PEMRICK

T.P. DORAN, J.L. PRICE

Thanks to Tim for creating the world of Thac, and for being kind enough to be part of this anthology of authors. Also, thanks to Kathryn, Jeff, Shannon, and Erik for participating in this ambitious endeavor. Finally, thanks to our friends and families for their support in the creation of this book.

Table of Contents

Thac is a relatively small isle in the larger world of Arinthar. The mainland of Laurentia, for instance, could fit nearly fifty islands the size of Thac within its wide borders. Yet despite its insignificant size, many important events have occurred on this western isle. Seven hundred years ago, the Mad Emperor Naradon founded and ruled the third great human empire from the shores of Thac. His reach extended well into the great forest and the blasted plains. Five hundred years ago, the Elf/Human wars were fought here, driving the Galinthral elves into the depths of the Ruanaiaith, never to be seen again. One hundred and fifty years ago, the Thrall Masters' powerful armies overran the isle. Yet their bid for world domination was stopped there as well. Thus, the tiny island has many stories to share, in many cases its influence extending even beyond its own borders...

- Lady Lara Stealle, High Wizard of Penwick

The Emerald Blade

F.P. Spirit

The Emerald Blade

The coastal waters shone a crystal blue, clear enough to see one's reflection. The sun had reached its zenith in the sky, its golden rays warming the afternoon breeze. Lush jade treetops lined the shore on the eastern horizon. To the untrained eye, the scene appeared idyllic, but Gilis Stinvich knew better—these were pirate waters.

"What'cha broodin' 'bout, Gil?"

Harget Fitzwin. The lanky man swabbed the deck just a few feet away.

"Who says I'm broodin'?" Gil fired back as he finished knotting a line to a belaying pin.

The tall man's face split into a toothy grin. "I've been sailin' wit'cha long enough to knows when you's broodin'."

Gil had met Harget nearly fifteen years ago on a ship out of Palt. The two had struck up a fast friendship and had been inseparable ever since. There wasn't a nautical mile along the north coast they hadn't sailed together.

Gil snorted in response. "Fine, I'm broodin'. Ya just had to go and sign us up on this merchantman bound south."

Harget's face sank at the jab. "I said I was sorry. How was I supposed to know our last ship would leave Kaniron without us?"

Gil scowled at his tall friend. "Aye, you go on a bender, and we miss the only ship in port with a navigator that can thread the Vortex."

Harget visibly shuddered at the mention of the giant storm.

The Vortex was actually two storms—twin maelstroms that sat on the coast north of Kaniron. Spawned by some unfathomable magic, they never moved or died out. A thin path of calm existed where the pair buffeted each other, but only the most experienced of navigators could traverse it safely.

Harget blessed himself with the sign of Zesstara, the goddess of the sea, before speaking again. "I—thought I was doin' us a favor—figured it was better than takin' the long way 'round the Vortex."

Gil continued to glare at his friend, then finally shrugged. Harget, empty-headed as he was, obviously meant well. "I think I'd have preferred the extra week to traveling through pirate waters."

Harget gave him another toothy grin. "You need to learn to relax there, Gilly. The odds of us runnin' into pirates is probably slim at best."

Gil narrowed an eye at his optimistic friend, but any reply he might have had was abruptly interrupted.

"Ship astern!" came a shout from the crow's nest above.

Gil let out an angry breath as he fixed Harget with a stare that screamed "I told you so."

Harget glanced nervously toward the rear of the vessel, his voice catching in his throat. "J-jus' 'cause there's another ship, don't mean its pirates."

Gil let out a rude laugh. "Ha! In these waters? The sun must be gettin' to you if you think it's anything else."

Across the deck, the rest of the crew had all frozen in place. The captain came rushing out of his cabin and vaulted up the stairs to the quarterdeck. He hurried to the rear rail and pulled out a spyglass. The air was thick with tension as the entire crew drifted toward the back of the vessel.

A few moments passed before the captain spun about. He briskly strode back across the deck, barking out orders as he went. "Unfurl all the sails! Get the wind at our backs! Ready the cannons!"

"Is it pirates, captain?" a youthful sailor asked nervously.

The captain gave him a brief nod as he marched by. "Aye. Dasati."

Harget gulped as he glanced at Gil. "Dasati? What does that mean?"

Gil's mouth flattened into a tense line. "It means we're being chased by the deadliest pirate clan on the high seas."

The merchantman cleaved through the blue coastal waters like a fox on the run, but it was no match for the pirate vessel. The three-masted galleon slowly gained on them 'til they could see its colors—an ebon stingray on a field of white. As it drew closer, they could read the name etched across its deep brown hull—*Dark Halo*.

There was a brief exchange of cannon fire as the vessels drew alongside each other, but the pirates were expert marksmen. They took out the couple of guns the merchantman carried in a few shots. After that, things moved quickly. The Dark Halo drew beside them, and hooked lines were used to draw the ships together. Fighting broke out at the starboard rail as groups of brigands swung across to engage the crew.

Gil and Harget were among those assigned to protect the cargo hatch. They stood there now, swords in hand, though neither was very good with them.

Harget squealed in terror as one of the sailors went down to a pirate's blade. "We're gonna die here, Gilly! I jus' knows it."

Gil cast a sidelong glance at his quaking friend. "Get behind me, Har. You're no good to anyone with that pig-sticker."

Harget grimaced as he shuffled behind him. "I'm—I'm sorry, Gil. It's my fault we're in this mess."

Gil shrugged, not taking his eyes off the fighting. "No use blamin' yerself now. What's done is done."

The sailor in front of Gil fell to another brigand's blade. The pirate withdrew his sword, then set his sights on Gil. A wicked grin split his grizzled face as he slowly advanced on him.

Gil held his blade up stiffly, but he knew it was a lost cause. It wouldn't be long now till both he and Harget were food for the fishes.

Just then a commanding voice boomed over the fracas. "Dasati, fall back!"

As one, the brigands halted in their tracks and withdrew a few steps.

Gil's heart pounded in his throat. By some miracle, he and Harget had been spared from immediate death. But who was their mysterious benefactor, and what did he want?

The rest of the crew appeared as confused as Gil. They all watched with growing apprehension as a lone figure crossed over on a plank from the pirate vessel.

The newcomer was a squat, powerfully built buccaneer wearing a green coat and tricorne hat. Thick red hair covered most of his lower face and draped across his broad shoulders. The lone brigand strode with the utmost confidence onto the main deck. He finally stopped near the mainmast and glanced around 'til his eyes fell upon Gil.

"Where's your captain?" the pirate asked in that same deep, commanding tone.

The question caught Gil completely by surprise. Before he knew it, he was pointing up at the quarterdeck.

"I'm the captain." The captain of the merchant vessel cautiously descended the stairs from the upper deck. His eyes darted around carefully as he approached the lone brigand, but no one accosted him. He drew within a few feet of the man, then stopped, his voice amazingly firm for the situation. "What are you planning on doing with us?"

The squat buccaneer regarded him carefully before speaking. "That depends. You travel our waters without paying tribute."

The captain arched a single eyebrow, somehow finding the nerve to scoff at the newcomer. "Pay tribute? To pirates?"

"He's gonna get us all killed for sure," Harget whispered frantically. Gil hushed him with a wave of his hand.

The buccaneer appeared unfazed by the remark. "Pirate is such a harsh word. These waters are ours by the grace of Zesstara. Those who see the wisdom of this have an accord with us. Those who do not are trespassers and are dealt with accordingly."

Those last words sounded like a death sentence. Unable to control himself, Harget squealed so loud that Gil had to clamp a hand over his mouth.

The blood drained from the captain's face, yet he still managed to stand his ground. "So, do you mean to slaughter us all, then?"

A deathly silence fell over the deck as the squat pirate mulled over their fate. Gil felt beads of sweat form on his brow and trickle down the side of his face. After what seemed like an eternity, the red-haired buccaneer spoke again. "I will give you one chance to prove your worth. Face me in single combat and the rest of your crew will be spared."

Harget pulled Gil's hand away from his mouth. "Does this mean we ain't gonna die?"

Gil hushed him again as the captain responded. "And what of my ship?"

A round of evil laughter broke out among the pirates, but the lone brigand silenced it with a single gesture. His expression remained stony. "If you win, you and your ship can go on its way."

The captain eyed him with clear disbelief. "And I'm supposed to take your word for it?"

"I don't see as you have much choice," the brigand rumbled.

"Do you really think he'd let us go?" Harget whispered in Gil's ear.

"Shhh." Gil waved him off.

The captain swept his gaze around the deck. He clearly did not believe the pirate, but truly had little choice in the matter. "Very well."

He drew his sword and fell into a fighting stance, waving the brigand forward. "Let's have at it, then."

Murmurs went through the crowd as both pirates and sailors made room for the two combatants. A hush fell over the crew as the squat buccaneer drew his sword.

The light of the afternoon sun glinted off what appeared to be a blunt-edged blade. As if that wasn't curious enough, the blade was painted vivid green and decorated with violet lotus flowers.

"Is this some sorta joke?" Harget whispered, mirroring Gil's own astonishment. Yet their skepticism quickly died as nervous murmurs spread among the crew.

"The Emerald Blade."

"It's the Emerald Blade."

"No one's ever beaten him."

The captain visibly paled, but managed to hold his ground. The Emerald Blade set himself into a casual fighting stance, then waved the captain forward in turn. The captain eyed him uncertainly at first, but then set his jaw and lunged at the brigand. The squat man parried the captain's blade with relative ease. The captain had obvious skill, but the pirate's defenses were very solid.

The battle exploded into a whirling dance of flashing blades. Both men moved with amazing grace and dexterity. Lunges, feints, parries, and counters were all executed with expert skill. Parries were met with counter-parries. Counters were met with reverse-counters.

Gil had never seen anything like it. Both men seemed evenly matched until the Emerald Blade executed a lightning-fast move. He caught the captain's blade with his own, then abruptly sidestepped. In one swift motion, he was through the captain's defenses and his blunt-edged sword slammed into the man's midriff.

The captain doubled over in pain as the wind was knocked out of him. Had it been an actual blade, he would have been cloven in half.

The captain's sword clattered to the deck as he fell to his knees. Cheers rang out amongst the pirates, but quickly subsided as the Emerald Blade placed the tip of his sword underneath the captain's chin. "Do you yield?"

Tears of pain streamed from the captain's eyes as he stared up at the man who had bested him. The brigand prodded him with the tip of his blunt sword. "Do you yield?"

The captain nodded fervently as he gasped his response. "Yes… yes… I yield…"

"Good," the pirate said simply as he sheathed his strange sword. The Emerald Blade then turned on his heel, his deep voice void of emotion as he strode back toward his ship. "Give them the lifeboats. Make sure no one is left aboard."

A short while later, Gil and Harget found themselves in a long boat filled with a good portion of the crew. Three other long boats with the rest of the crew floated not far from them. The four boats had made it nearly halfway to the distant shore when the sound of cannon fire exploded behind them.

Harget nearly jumped out of his seat. "They're firin' on us!"

Gil spun around to see their ship in flames. "Easy, Har. It's not us they're firin' on."

The entire boat had stopped rowing. Everyone watched as the roaring fire overtook their vacated ship. In mere minutes, what was left of the charred hull had sunk beneath the waters.

After the last volley, the pirate ship set sail. Gil watched the dark vessel as it receded toward the horizon, thankful to still be alive.

The Emerald Blade let out a deep sigh as he trudged into his large cabin. Bright light flooded in from the array of windows at the back of the room. A long mahogany table stood in front of those windows, surrounded by a mismatched set of ornate chairs. A globe sat on a circular stand in a corner next to a tall bookcase. A plush cupboard bed was set into the opposite wall beside an elaborate mahogany wardrobe.

The broad-shouldered man doffed his green coat and hat, then unbuckled his sword belt. He briefly ran his hands over the decorative scabbard before hanging it on a stand next to the wardrobe.

Weariness washed over the Emerald Blade—yet it was not a failing of the body. He had barely broken a sweat during his duel with the other ship's captain. Rather, the fatigue he felt was more of the spirit.

He had only been a pirate now for a couple of years, and the captain of this ship for maybe half of that. Yet it was not what he had wanted of his life. In fact, it was the polar opposite of what his life had been before.

"One must flow with the current of the river," the stout man reminded himself as he plodded over to the row of windows. A line of miniature bonsai and dwarf lotus trees stretched along the wide sill. Some were a lush green, others grew small red berries, and a few bloomed with pale pink and violet flowers.

A watering can and small spade lay just underneath the sill. The weary man grabbed them, his mood picking up as he meticulously tended to each plant. When he was done, he put down his gardening tools, and turned to face the long table.

The rich mahogany surface was barely visible under the charts and books strewn across its length. The man's eyes flitted across the parchments and tomes lain there, finally settling on a map of the vast mainland, Laurentia.

Bold lettering paralleled the shore on the southwest side of the great continent. *The Pirate Coast.* It was the unofficial home of the thirteen clans of the pirate nation. The pirate coast stretched five hundred miles along the shore, all the way from Kaniron down to Isandor.

Isandor. The stout man's eyes drifted to the country that stretched across the southern end of Laurentia. Images flashed through his mind of a life that used to be.

Rows and rows of armored warriors lined up in front of him in perfect formation.

A robust man with surprisingly gentle eyes astride a magnificent throne.

An impulsive young boy with a mop of thick black hair, barely old enough to hold the wooden training sword in his small hands.

A sudden knock on the door interrupted his melancholy thoughts. "Captain?"

The Emerald Blade cleared his throat while wiping the stray moisture from his eyes. "Ahem. Come in, Mr. Siithe!"

The first mate of the *Dark Halo* stepped through the door. "Beggin' yer pardon, Captain. We scoured the ship from top to bottom and took anything of possible value."

"What cargo were they carrying?" the captain rumbled.

The first mate listed off a number of items they found in the hold, which included food stuffs, kegs of wine and ale, a few small chests filled with silver and gold coins, and a variety of lesser-valued items. In the middle of his tally, another knock came at the door.

"Come in!" the captain bellowed once more.

The cook entered the cabin carrying a steaming tankard in his hands. He scurried over to the captain and gingerly held it out to him, a stray eye going to the first mate as he did so. "Your—drink, Sir."

A thin smile split the captain's thick red beard as he took the tankard. He lifted it to his lips, blew on it, then took a brief sip. His smile spread wider, a faint sigh escaping his lips. "Ah, that's excellent. Thank you."

"You're welcome, Captain." The cook beamed as he turned to leave. His gaze strayed once again to the first mate as he scurried back out of the cabin.

Mr. Siithe watched the cook go with a single eyebrow raised. His glance briefly passed over the steaming mug, but otherwise he made no comment. The captain seated himself in an ornate chair and waved for the first mate to go on while he continued to sip from his tankard.

Mr. Siithe finished his litany of items they'd procured from the merchant ship. When he was done, the captain sat forward and placed his tankard aside. "Is everyone off the ship?"

"Just as you ordered, Sir." Mr. Siithe nodded. "What about the ship itself?"

The captain gently stroked his beard as he mulled over the fate of the merchant vessel. "It's rather slow… and it can't hold more than two cannons on either side…"

His mouth wrinkled as he reached a decision. "Put some distance between us and sink her."

Mr. Siithe grinned. "Aye, Captain."

The captain reached for his tankard again as the door slammed behind his first mate. He took another sip as his eyes went back to the large map in front of him.

"What an awful way to drink one's tea," he murmured to himself.

Once a proud nation, the Saricordi's lands had been poisoned and broken during the fall of the Baleful Moon. With the world in complete disarray, no one would take in a displaced people. They survived only by the grace of Zesstara, the goddess granting them dominion over the seas.

The clans of the Saricordi built a fleet of ships that stopped and demanded tribute of all those who traversed their watery territory. Unfortunately, their claim to the seas was disputed by most of the world. Thus, the clans took to force in order to gain what was rightfully theirs, and were soon labeled pirates of the coast.

With their questionable standing, the clans hid their homes from the rest of the world. Thus, the *Dark Halo* now glided through a well-hidden water cave that connected the seas to Loch Dasati.

The Emerald Blade stood at the prow of the ship, trusting his navigator to steer them through the dark, narrow waters of the cave. A flat smile graced his lips when they finally re-emerged into the sunlight. It was not exactly home, but it was still quite beautiful.

Before them stretched a long blue lake, its calm waters like some vast mirror seated in the earth. Its surface perfectly reflected the tall, craggy peaks that surrounded the loch on all four sides. Over on the western shore sat a comely town nestled at the foot of one of those peaks. It was *Renere*, home now for more than a thousand years to the Dasati clan.

Long docks jutted out from Renere into the still waters of the loch. A number of tall ships were moored there. The Emerald Blade recognized each and every one of them: *The Black Cat, Red Cry, Honors Break, Blood Tears,* and the flagship of the fleet, the *Midnight Manta.* A few ships were missing from their berths, but they were most likely out patrolling the open waters.

The Emerald Blade remained at the prow as the *Dark Halo* pulled into port. The docks bustled with activity. Plunder was offloaded from the moored ships, replaced with supplies for further voyages. Folks milled about at the edge of town—it was always an event when the ships came in.

The Emerald Blade's eyes were drawn to a group of young teens chasing each other around the docks. They were still young enough to enjoy play, but only a few years from being inducted into a crew.

"Ahoy there, Captain," a voice called from below.

The Emerald Blade glanced down to see a tall man staring up at him from the pier. Garbed in a blue coat with gold buttons and trim, the man had a commanding presence. *Tharne Ozden.*

Tharne was the Lord Captain of the Dasati. A hard man, he was merciless to his enemies, but fair to his men and those who surrender to him. He was a man the Emerald Blade could respect.

"Greetings to you, Captain Ozden," the Emerald Blade replied.

Once the gangplank was lowered, Tharne made his way up onto the ship. Keen brown eyes darted across the deck from a well-weathered face. A sparse beard and mustache decorated the lower half of his features. Long locks of frayed brown hair overlaid the collar of his blue long coat.

Tharne strode over to join the captain as he surveyed the spoils waiting to be unloaded. "It seems you brought back a good haul."

The Emerald Blade shrugged. "We did our best."

Tharne laughed heartily, placing an arm around the stout captain's shoulders. "Don't sell yourself short, my friend. Your 'best' is typically better than most," he dropped his voice, "and a sight less bloody, I dare say."

The Emerald Blade merely nodded at the compliment. "Life is too short as it is. Why end that which will be gone tomorrow anyway?"

Tharne let out a sigh. "I wish you could teach that wisdom to the rest of my captains." He headed back toward the gangplank, pausing at the top. "Anyway, when you are done here, I was wondering if you would join me for a drink? There's a small matter I'd like to discuss with you."

"Will there be tea?" the Emerald Blade asked hopefully.

A knowing smile crossed Tharne's face. "Yes, my friend, there will be tea."

"Then I'll be there," the Emerald Blade responded.

Tharne gave him a brief wave, then disembarked the ship.

Outwardly, the Emerald Blade remained stoic, but something about Tharne's invitation made him feel uneasy. He sensed something more behind Tharne's invitation than just a simple discussion. Still, he didn't perceive anything threatening. Tharne had always been rather good to him. Two years ago, without knowing anything about him, Tharne had given him a place on his crew. A year later, it was Tharne who promoted him to captain.

Once the *Dark Halo* was unloaded, the Emerald Blade left the ship. At the edge of town, he passed by the group of teens who had been running around the docks. Two young women led the band—one with long black hair and a light tan complexion, the other nearly the twin of the first, except that her hair was light brown. He immediately recognized them as Kortiama and Solais—Tharne's daughters.

Tharne had no children of his own, but adopted and raised the girls, nonetheless. The Emerald Blade respected that. Family was extremely important to him. In fact, his own nephew would be about the same age as them by now.

The girls suddenly darted away from the rest. The one wasn't watching where she was going and nearly collided with him. The Emerald Blade caught her just in time.

Completely unfazed, Kortiama peered up at him with her dark bright eyes. Her smile lit her entire face. "Thanks for the assist, Captain." Before he could respond, she was off again, the other teens chasing after them.

"Korti, that isn't just any captain—that's the Emerald Blade, you idiot!" he heard Solais admonish.

"Is it? He's shorter in person." Kortiama glanced over her shoulder and gave him another dazzling smile.

The Emerald Blade chuckled to himself. *Tharne's daughters are certainly full of energy.*

A wave of homesickness abruptly washed over him. This Kortiama reminded him of his nephew. He continued to watch until the teens disappeared down the crowded docks. The stout man let out a long sigh and continued onward into town.

***

For the Lord Captain of the Dasati, Tharne Ozden's house was a modest dwelling. Set behind a short fence on a busy street corner, the two-story home was lined with tall-paned windows. A wide porch wrapped around the front of the house, with a hexagonal tower rising over one end. A dormer jutted out of the roof next to the tower, which in turn was capped with a widow's peak.

The inside of the house was not overly large. The first floor consisted merely of a center hallway, parlor, library, dining room, and kitchen. If there was anything ornate about the interior, it was the décor. Rich blue satin drapes framed the windows. The parlor contained a matching sofa and chairs arrayed in front of a wide fireplace. The dining room set was made of a vibrant cherry wood and had seating for twelve. A large cherrywood desk sat in the middle of the library surrounded by four walls of matching cherrywood bookcases. Trinkets lined most of those shelves with a few books scattered here and there.

Tharne turned out to be a gracious host. His cook had prepared a small afternoon repast of seafood delicacies for the two men. The conversation remained mundane, however, until they adjourned to the library.

Tharne sat behind his ornate desk, holding a glass of brandy in one hand. As promised, the Emerald Blade had been provided with a delicious cup of peppermint tea. Tharne sent all his servants home, leaving the two men alone with their drinks.

The Lord Captain took a sip from his brandy, then carefully laid the glass on his desk. His lips pursed as he fixed his guest with a curious gaze. "We've known each other for over two years now. How do you judge me?"

The Emerald Blade felt a tingling sensation in the center of his brow. Again, it was not threatening, but he sensed the need to be cautious here. He took another sip of tea, then responded in a measured tone. "I believe you to be a man of your word."

The corners of Tharne's mouth upturned slightly at the compliment. "More so, I'd wager, than when you first signed on."

The Emerald Blade finished another sip. "That is a wager you would win."

Tharne broke out into a full grin. He grabbed his glass, sat back, and finished his brandy. When he was done, he wiped his mouth with his sleeve. "I'm not blind, you know. I can tell you're not happy."

The Emerald Blade's brow twinged again. "Happiness is relative.

Is a stone happy sitting in the sun? Is the water happy, lapping against the shore?"

Tharne let out a hearty laugh. "There you go again, waxing philosophical. If I didn't know any better, I'd say you used to be one of those priests from Isandor."

A brief flash of anger welled up inside the Emerald Blade at the mention of the Isandorian priesthood. He quickly pushed it back down, his voice remaining even. "That is a wager I'm afraid you would lose."

Tharne sat forward again, his eyes narrowing. "You know, I've been watching you for some time now."

The twinging turned to pulsing in the Emerald Blade's brow.

"You follow a strict code of honor. You never draw a real sword, and you handle that blunt-edged one like an expert."

The Emerald Blade continued to calmly sip his tea, though the pulsing in his head had become pounding.

"And the decorations on the blade, the violet lotus flowers—that is the mark of the House Kazari, first family of the finest clan of Shin Tauri clan warriors in Isandor."

The pounding had now migrated to the Emerald Blade's heart. Still, he managed to keep a calm demeanor. "That is a great compliment you pay me. To be compared to the premier warrior clan of Isandor is praise indeed."

Tharne sat even farther forward, his voice dropping to a whisper. "It's also interesting that you appeared about a month after the King of Isandor's assassination. In fact, it was only a couple of weeks after Isandor's greatest general, Draigo Kazari, was driven out by the priesthood."

Anger rose inside the Emerald Blade again, but he immediately quelled it. His eyes dipped slightly as he mapped his exit route from the house. "You seem to know a lot about Isandor and this General—Draigo, was it?"

The side of Tharne's mouth drifted upward. He waved a hand to the books on the shelves behind him. "These are all on the art of war. I'm a student of the craft, and General Draigo is a master tactician. As for my knowledge of Isandor, news gets around if you have the ear for it."

The Emerald Blade grunted as he slowly put down his tea. "Hmm, I see. And these speculations of yours—have you shared them with anyone else?"

Tharne's eyes danced with amusement. "Do you seriously think anyone else in this town reads, let alone cares about the politics of other nations?"

The Emerald Blade abruptly gave up the idea of running. His hand carefully edged toward the sword at his side.

Tharne, however, was quite observant. He caught the slight movement and immediately sat back with his hands up. "Hold on, my friend. There's no need for that. If I'd wanted trouble, I wouldn't be sitting here alone with you now."

The Emerald Blade eyed him for a few moments, then withdrew his hand from his sword hilt. "So, what is it you want?"

Tharne's mouth twisted sideways. He grabbed the bottle of brandy on his desk, and poured himself another glass. He then downed the whole thing in one long gulp. After letting out a slight gasp, Tharne put the glass down and wiped his sleeve across his mouth. "Ah, I needed that."

His gaze turned back to his guest. Tharne's expression appeared earnest, yet there was a twinge of desperation in his eyes. "The truth is, General Draigo, or not, you are still one of my best captains—and one of the few I trust."

Draigo Kazari weighed Tharne's words carefully. He sensed the ring of truth behind them. He was also curious as to Tharne's motivation for bringing this up now. Still, he had not been ready to reveal his secret past to anyone. In the end, he decided to let this play out and see where it went.

Draigo met Tharne's gaze evenly. "Trust has to go both ways."

Tharne pursed his lips. "Indeed. You're aware of my family situation?"

Draigo responded with a curt nod. "Your older brother, Rikton, feels he should be head of the Dasati."

An ironic smile crossed Tharne's lips. He slowly got up, clasped his hands behind his back, and started to pace. "Aye, that's the truth of it. The only thing keeping my head from a pike right now is my wits and my dead brother's wife."

Liadha Rowan, the dark witch of the Ramulos clan—the widowed bride of Tharne's eldest brother, the Pirate Warlord Eboneye. Liadha wielded a power blacker than the night. Every pirate in every clan feared her, even Tharne's brother, Rikton.

"Liadha is a powerful ally," Draigo agreed, still wondering where this was all going.

A hollow laugh escaped Tharne's lips. "She's just using me to further her own dark ends." He stopped pacing and faced Draigo, his expression turning solemn. "I know your secret—now I'm going to entrust you with mine."

Thirteen years ago, the pirate warlord, Eboneye, united the clans of the coast. He led them across the seas in a full-scale invasion of the wealthy city of Penwick. The clans sustained huge losses during that long, bloody raid, and in the end were driven out. Eboneye had fallen as well, but not before producing an heir—a girl born during the siege. Moreover, he named her next Lord Captain of the Dasati when she came of age.

Rikton had railed against the decree, thinking himself next in line. Yet he had been a supporter of the costly raid, in direct violation of the mandates of Zesstara. Tharne, who had been against the invasion from the very start, was chosen acting Lord Captain in his stead. However, not all agreed with Tharne's selection, and thus a rift formed within the Dasati.

The rift left Eboneye's heir in a precarious position. If anything were to befall her before coming of age, the title of Lord Captain would again come into question. Hence, Liadha hid the baby to keep her out of harm's way.

Tharne let out a huge sigh as he sat back down and poured himself another brandy. For the first time that evening, Draigo noted the dark circles under his eyes. As Tharne downed another glass, a thought came to Draigo.

"Your daughters, Kortiama and Solais, they'd be about the same age as Eboneye's daughter."

Tharne put down his glass and fixed an eye on him. "Aye, they would be."

Any unease Draigo felt abruptly drained out of him. He had been right to admire this man. All this time, he'd been carrying a heavy burden. Draigo's voice was soft when he spoke. "Do they know?"

Tharne shook his head. "When we returned to Renere, Liadha secreted Korti to the orphanage amid a group of newly stolen waifs. A few years later, I adopted her along with Solais. So, only a few of us know her true heritage."

Draigo's lips flattened into a line. "Hmm. I imagine your brother suspects."

Tharne's mouth twisted sideways. "He does indeed, but he won't touch either for fear of never finding the mandate."

Draigo nodded thoughtfully. The mandates of Zesstara were more than just a set of abstract rules from the goddess. The lord captain of each clan possessed a mystical item from the goddess herself that signified their right to lead.

Tharne chuckled softly in his chair. "My dear brother had this house ransacked more times than I can count, but he never found it"—he leaned forward, his eyes glowing with intensity—"nor will he. No one will see it again, until the day of…"

The sudden slam of a door interrupted him before he could finish.

"Captain Tharne! Captain Tharne!" A young voice cried, the name accompanied by the sound of running feet.

Tharne shot out of his seat, his face filled with concern. "In here, lad!"

Draigo spun around as a young teen entered from the hall. Tall and lanky, he recognized him as one of the youths who had been chasing Kortiama and Solais around the docks.

The lad leaned forward, his breath coming in short ragged bursts. "It's Korti… she's gone… up to… the Ghoul's Den…"

Tharne rushed from behind his desk across the room. He grasped the boy by the collar, yanked him up straight, and spat a single angry word. "What?"

Terror filled the boy's eyes as he choked out his response. "It… it was Capt'n Rikton. He said… the ebon eye was up there…"

Draigo let out a soft whistle. The ebon eye—the legacy of

Tharne's brother. The size and shape of a human eye, it was that black artifact that had given him the power to unite the clans.

"Blast Rikton! He knows that place is dangerous." Tharne shuddered with anger. All of sudden, his face fell. He dropped the youth, rushed to his desk, and frantically rummaged through it.

A few moments later, Tharne stood back and slammed the desk closed with exasperation. "Damn that Solais, it's gone!"

Draigo narrowed an eye him. "What's gone?"

"A dispel magic scroll," Tharne sighed with exasperation. He fixed his gaze on the young teen. "When did they leave?"

The youth coughed as he rubbed his sore neck. "A little while ago, Capt'n."

"Right," Tharne nodded, his brow furrowing into deep creases. "Stay put, I've got a few more questions for you." He grabbed Draigo by the arm and dragged him into the hall. Draigo could see the fear in his eyes as Tharne whispered a single phrase to him. "Go get your real sword."

Draigo had not drawn a real blade since leaving Isandor. The Shin Tauri code of honor demanded that one's true blade only be drawn in defense of king, country, or matters of life and death. Based on Tharne's reaction, this seemed to be the latter.

For the first time in nearly two years, Draigo pulled out his true blade from its hiding place aboard the *Dark Halo*. The former general paused a moment. Mixed emotions played through his mind as he again held the emerald sheath adorned with violet lotus flowers. Visions of his old life briefly flashed through his mind, ending with an image of his impetuous nephew. Kortiama reminded him so much of the lad.

Kortiama!

The thought of the young woman's peril roused Draigo from his musings. He swiftly fastened the sheath to his belt, then headed from the cabin and disembarked the *Dark Halo*. He found Tharne waiting for him with a pair of horses at the end of the dock.

"Just us?" Draigo asked as he vaulted onto his mount.

"'Fraid so," Tharne said, his expression grim. "I'll explain on the way."

The duo set off at a gallop, soon leaving Renere behind. There was little time to talk as they raced along the shores of Loch Dasati. At the south end, a winding path led up from the valley. Tharne explained the rest to Draigo as they climbed to the top of the southernmost peak.

"At the summit lies the Villa Dasati, the former home of my brother and his wife."

"Eboneye and Liadha," Draigo clarified.

"Aye, the same." Tharne nodded. "After Berngal died, Liadha sealed the place with dark magic. There's a barrier around the house proper that only one of her own blood can break."

Draigo pressed his lips together. "Hmm. May I ask why?"

Tharne let out a hollow laugh. "It was sort of a red herring for Rikton. She knew he'd be searching for the mandate, and what better place than my brother's home?"

"That makes sense." Draigo noted the haunted look in Tharne's eyes. "I'm guessing there's more to I,t though."

"There is." Tharne's expression darkened further. "Rikton sent a few expeditions up here. Almost no one came back."

Draigo arched a single eyebrow. "Liadha left more than just a barrier behind."

"Indeed." Tharne grimaced. "Ghostly creatures patrol the grounds, killing anyone that gets too close." He paused a moment, his voice growing soft. "I declared the place off limits, but that didn't help much. Young folks saw it as a challenge—nicknamed it the Ghoul's Den. Those that wanted to prove themselves would spend the night up there. Some lived to tell the tale,"—his voice caught in his throat—"Some did not…"

Draigo felt a wrenching in his gut. In his time as a general, he had grown accustomed to loss, but losing someone so young was never easy. Still, something nagged at the back of his mind. "Why didn't you just ask Liadha to get rid of the creatures?"

Tharne sighed with exasperation. "I did. She told me I needed better control over my people."

"Hmm, that seems a bit harsh," Draigo rumbled.

"Have you met my sister-in-law?" The side of Tharne's mouth twisted upward.

"Can't say I have, nor that I want to," Draigo responded with equal irony. "Still, your niece seems quite spirited. How is it she never came up here before?"

Tharne let out a short laugh. "Thankfully, I got a bit smarter with age"—he leaned toward him in the saddle—"I had magic wards put around the villa to stop folks from entering. Of course, anyone adept at magic, or with the right scroll, can still bypass them."

"Ah, so that's what the girls stole from your study." Draigo nodded with understanding.

"Aye." Tharne signed once more. "Between the girls and Rikton, they've managed to outflank me. My dear brother has been flashing a 'magic' amulet around town that's supposed to bypass the barrier."

Draigo frowned. "Is that possible?"

"Not even remotely." Tharne shook his head. "Blood magic is the hardest to break."

Draigo's brow creased. Tharne was probably right. If the amulet was that powerful, Rikton would have used it already to gain entrance to the villa.

Tharne's expression grew pained. "He bragged he was going to use it to claim our brother's greatest treasure, the ebon eye itself— but it was all a ruse to tempt my niece and her crew. Sure enough, they fell for it. They nicked the amulet off him and took off for the villa shortly thereafter."

Draigo only knew Kortiama from afar. While she did appear somewhat impulsive, he couldn't fathom why she would put herself, and her friends, in so much danger. All at once, it dawned on him. "She wants to get the ebon eye before Rikton does—for your sake."

Tharne hung his head. "Aye. I'm afraid so. If my brother were truly to find the ebon eye, he would wrest control of the clan from me, mandate or not."

Tharne's head was bowed, but Draigo could sense how torn he was over his niece's misguided attempt to protect him. Draigo made up his mind then and there. He would do all in his power to save this heroic, if rash, young lady—even if it cost him his very life.

It was nearing sunset when Draigo caught his first glimpse of their destination. Before them laid a huge walled villa, half fortress and half palatial estate. The tiled roof was definitely orange, but even the smooth walls shone blood-red in the rays of the setting sun.

A feeling of foreboding washed over him as they spurred their horses forward. "Remind me again why it's just the two of us?"

Tharne grimaced as they closed on the villa. "Anyone who knows anything about magic is sure to realize the amulet's a fake. If they were to see Korti enter the house, they'd know for certain she's Liadha's heir."

That secret won't do her much good if she's dead, Draigo thought. Still, saying as much wouldn't do any good at this point.

When they reached the villa, the wards were down, as Tharne had surmised. The main gate stood wide open before them. The riders galloped straight through, but reigned in immediately beyond. A wide courtyard spread out before them, the entire place bathed in an eerie silence. Withered trees stood scattered around the yard, with not a single bird or animal in sight. What was once probably a lush garden lay across the yard, now overgrown with weeds and thickets.

The villa itself appeared rather ominous. Despite the falling night, the windows remained dark. A cold wind kicked up behind them, adding to the feeling of dread.

Without a word, the duo spurred their mounts across the yard. There was no sign of the teens or their horses, but the front door lay partially open. As they drew up in front of the villa, shouts emanated from somewhere inside.

"That sounds like Solais!" Tharne cried in dismay.

Both men leapt off their mounts, drawing their blades as they ran for the house. They slowed only to push against the door, which creaked eerily as it swung inward.

The inside of the villa was pitch black, the sun now set behind the mountains. The shouts had stopped as well, the house grown deathly silent. Draigo felt an unnatural chill in the air. Goosebumps formed on his arms despite his firm resolve.

A dim light suddenly sprang up around them. Tharne held a solitary lantern in his off hand.

A wide foyer extended around them, its ceiling hidden in the darkness above. A black and white checkered floor extended across the room past two side entrances. A circular stairwell rose on either side of the back wall, then met at a long landing before climbing out of sight.

Draigo noted this all in an instant, his eyes riveted to the bodies scattered around the room. A pair of ghostly black-robed figures hovered above the two in the center. More ghost-like forms dragged the rest out of sight.

"Korti! Solais!" Tharne cried, his voice filled with anguish. He charged past Draigo straight for the two downed girls.

The hovering figures turned their attention toward them. No faces could be seen inside those thick hoods, but a skeletal hand reached for Draigo as he lashed out with his sword. The hand grazed his arm as the blade passed through it. It met little resistance, yet the figure recoiled, nonetheless. A horrible screech emanated from beneath its hood before it spun around and fled up into the darkness.

Draigo's shoulder felt ice-cold at the point where the figure had touched him. He shook off a momentary wave of weariness as Tharne drove off the second creature. "What were those things?"

"Wraiths," Tharne hissed.

Wraiths? That explained why his blade went through it. Wraiths were like ghosts—they could pass through solid objects and vice-versa.

Draigo planted himself over the two girls as Tharne bent down to check on them. He could sense their energy, though it seemed rather weak.

"How are they?" he asked while scanning the darkness above and around them.

"They're alive"—Tharne breathed a sigh of relief—"which is more than I can say if those wraiths latch unto us. If they do, they'll drain your life-force in a matter of minutes."

That was why Draigo suddenly felt so weary. *How do you fight something that you can't touch and can't let touch you?* Still, he had felt something when he swiped at it. *Maybe it has to turn semi-solid in order to attack?*

Years of training and battle experience formulated into a strategy in his mind. "Quick, stand back-to-back around the girls," Draigo urged his companion. "Don't swing at a wraith until it reaches for you."

Tharne grumbled as he stood and turned his back to Draigo. "I just hope you know what you're doing."

The two men waited wordlessly, eyes fixed on the edge of the darkness. Abruptly, a wraith reappeared, hurtling at them with frightening speed.

"Here it comes again!" Draigo warned.

"And the other one!" Tharne hissed.

A quick glance over his shoulder confirmed the second wraith was diving at them. Draigo tilted his head so he could see each creature out of the corner of an eye.

"Wait for it." Draigo cautioned. The wraiths were almost within striking distance.

"Wait for it," Draigo repeated. Skeletal hands appeared from under each wraith's robe.

"Now!" Draigo shouted.

He swung at the dark figure, his blade connecting with something almost solid. The wraith flinched backward and uttered an inhuman scream. Its body shook, then abruptly evaporated. All that lingered was its fiendish cry that also faded after a few moments.

Draigo glanced behind him just in time to see the second wraith retreating back into the darkness.

"Dragon dung!" Tharne swore. "The blasted thing got me!"

"Keep your guard up," Draigo warned. As the words left his lips, two more wraiths came flying down at them.

"How many of these things are there?" Tharne cried in frustration.

"As many as there are," Draigo responded in a matter-of-fact tone. "Now concentrate."

They repeated the same tactic. This time both wraiths dissolved into nothingness.

"Wah-hoo!" Tharne cried with exultation. "Take that, you bilge rat!"

"Concentrate," Draigo admonished as two more wraiths swooped down toward them. At the same time, a third one flew in from the side.

"Now that's just not playing fair!" Tharne protested.

"Just focus on one of them," Draigo directed his companion.

"What about the third?" Tharne griped.

"I'll take care of it."

"You better!"

They used the same strategy. Draigo dispatched the nearest wraith with one slice, then immediately swung about. Of the two remaining creatures, one retreated to the shadows, but the other had latched onto Tharne.

Draigo caught the creature with a vicious upswing. It shrieked, but clung tenaciously to Tharne. In the blink of an eye, the expert swordsman changed directions, bringing his blade down on the stubborn wraith.

Finally, the creature let go its grip. It arched its back and let out a horrific scream as it dispersed into oblivion.

In the meantime, Tharne had visibly paled. The tall pirate staggered where he stood. "I—I don't feel so good. I think—I need to sit down."

Draigo helped the man to the floor next to the two passed-out girls. Just as he had seated Tharne, two more wraiths came flying down at them from opposite sides.

Draigo firmly planted himself between the two girls and Tharne. With a deep breath, he stilled his mind in the way of the Shin Tauri. His breathing slowed, and with it the world around him. He could feel his spirit. The energy surged out from his abdomen and into his arms and legs.

The wraiths must have sensed it as well. They came straight for him, ignoring the figures on the ground at his feet. The creatures drew within striking distance, two bony skeletal hands reaching for his still form.

All at once, Draigo lashed out. With seemingly impossible speed, he sent his blade spinning in complete circular arc. It sliced through first creature, then continued on, slashing through the next. Both wraiths recoiled, their twin shrieks echoing through the room as they disappeared into nothingness.

Draigo breathed a heavy sigh, hoping that was the last of them. "Is it over?" Tharne mumbled at his feet.

Draigo's response died on his lips. Something huge floated at the edge of the darkness—something that made the hair on his neck stand on end.

A giant, black-robed creature glided into the light. Easily ten feet tall, it looked similar to the other wraiths, but this one wore no hood. Its skeletal head was uncovered except for a dark crown. Two glowing yellow eyes fixed themselves on him, sending a chill up Draigo's spine.

"Wraith Lord..." Tharne mumbled beneath his feet. "Worse than... a broadside from a Man of War..."

Draigo didn't doubt Tharne's words. The wraiths were dangerous enough, but this thing looked like it could decimate an entire crew.

The wraith lord came toward them, but unlike the others, it did not rush. It seemed quite sure of itself. Draigo could sense the energy the creature exuded. From what he could feel, it had every right to be confident.

Retreating would have been the best course of action, but moving Tharne and the girls was out of the question. With no other recourse, Draigo took a firm stand in front of the downed pirate and his daughters. *This will take everything I have. Hopefully it's enough.*

The Shin Tauri master slowed his breath, then reached inside to find his spirit. A low hum came from his throat as he brought the energy forth. The sound slowly rose in crescendo as the energy coursed up through his arms. It expanded out into his blade, the air around it catching fire. Yellow flames danced up and down the shaft, yet that wasn't all—trails of intense blue lightning arced between the flames.

The giant wraith paused at the sight of the brilliant sword, but a second later resumed its inexorable march toward them. It closed to within a few yards, then lashed out with frightening speed.

Draigo was ready for it. He side-stepped the great skeletal hand and sliced through its wrist with his flaming blade.

A petrifying wail echoed through the foyer. As Draigo recoiled, another giant hand swatted at him. He managed to deflect it with his blade, but the large fingers grazed him nonetheless.

A tingling sensation, like ice-cold daggers shot up his arms. Draigo's eyes grew heavy. They nearly closed all the way until he shook himself alert. *This is no time to nap.*

The wraith lord must have sensed his weakness. It drew closer, its long arms growing more insistent.

Draigo was hard pressed to keep those giant hands at bay. Thankfully, they recoiled from his flaming blade, but neither could he land a decisive strike without being touched. The creature slowly drove him back. If he wasn't careful, he would trip over Tharne or the girls, and that would be the end for all of them.

If one path doesn't work, try another. The words crystalized a desperate plan in Draigo's mind. As the next giant hand reached for him, he drove it back, then dove beneath it.

Tucking and rolling, Draigo came up behind the hands still on the move. Blade beside him, he strafed it across the wraith's body as he ran past.

A terrifying scream burst from the huge wraith. Draigo turned around in time to see it shake in agony, yet it did not disappear as he had hoped. Instead, it set its sights on the three prone figures in front of it.

The weakened lord captain stared up at the huge wraith towering over him. With a herculean effort, he forced himself to his feet. Barely able to stand, Tharne cursed the dark creature. "Do your worst, you bloody ghoul—you won't have my girls!"

Draigo knew he'd never reach them in time. There was only one way he might save them. The Shin Tauri master sheathed his sword.

Tharne's eyes went wide with disbelief. "What in the seven hells are you doing?"

Ignoring Tharne's cry, Draigo slowed his breath and gathered his spirit. The energy coursed through him, flowing to all his limbs at once.

The giant hands had nearly closed on Tharne when Draigo grasped his sword hilt. In a movement almost too fast to see, he shot across the intervening space, drew his sword, and sliced through the wraith lord in a single devastating strike.

The creature halted in its tracks. It floated there for a moment, mere inches away from Tharne. Suddenly, it arched its back and let out a bloodcurdling shriek. Its huge form shook, then without warning exploded in all directions.

Draigo shielded his eyes. When he finally uncovered them, the wraith lord was gone.

The night was clear outside the northernmost tower of the Villa Dasati. Draigo stood at a tall window looking out over the loch far below. The lights of Renere twinkled brilliantly along the western shore. The glow extended out onto the lake where a half-dozen ships were moored.

"It's beautiful, isn't it?" Tharne asked in a hushed voice. He drew up next to him, still somewhat hobbled from their encounter with the wraiths.

"Indeed," Draigo rumbled gently. The stout man glanced behind him at the two four-poster beds that occupied this room. Kortiama laid quietly in one while Solais tossed fitfully in the other. From what he could feel, their energy levels had begun to recover. "They should wake up sometime tomorrow."

Tharne nodded, his expression grateful. "Thank Zesstara for that"—his brow furrowed—"though Korti is going to have a tough time dealing with the deaths of her friends."

After the battle they had searched the rest of the villa. The wraiths were all gone, but they had found the bodies of the other teens—all completely drained of their life force.

Draigo closed his eyes and grimaced. "As a war veteran, I've had some experience dealing with grief. If you want, I can stay up here and counsel the both of them."

Tharne smiled at him appreciatively. "Thank you, my friend. I can never repay you for all you have done, but I have an idea that might benefit both of us."

"Oh?" Draigo lifted both eyebrows.

Tharne glanced back out the window. The lights of Renere still twinkled off in the distance. "As I said before, I know you are not thrilled with the pirate life. What if I told you there was a way you could retire?"

Draigo pressed his lips together. "I'm listening."

"You know of the *Day of Choosing?*"

"I've heard of it," Draigo admitted. Once every three years, during the time of the harvest moon, there came a day of great celebration amongst the clans—the *Day of Choosing*. That day, those youths who had come of age would be chosen to join a ship's crew.

Tharne gazed at Draigo, a haunted look in his eyes. "Four years from now, Korti will be of age. It is then she will be revealed to all as the new Lord Captain. Rikton will surely call for a *Grand Choosing*."

"Hmm." Draigo nodded thoughtfully. "He will challenge her for the title."

Tharne's grimace was so pronounced that Draigo could feel his pain. "Yes. It is well within his rights. No one will be able to intervene, not me, not Liadha." Tharne's voice sounded hollow. "It will be a slaughter. No one can stand against my brother with a blade—no one except perhaps you."

Draigo suddenly understood where Tharne was headed with this. "You want me to train her."

"Aye." Tharne closed his eyes and nodded. "So, what if I were to tell folks the Emerald Blade died saving me and my girls?"

"Go on," Draigo rumbled, his curiosity piqued.

"I'll put up the wards again and tell folks the place is off limits— only my family and the caretaker will be allowed up here."

"Caretaker?" Draigo raised an eyebrow.

"The simple gardener, Iro." Tharne's mouth twisted sideways.

Draigo breathed a deep sigh. "Trade my sword in for a hoe? That would be heavenly."

Tharne chuckled softly to himself. "You are a strange man, my friend."

Draigo shrugged. "To each his own. So, how are you going to cover the fact that Korti took down the barrier?"

Tharne's smirk widened. "My brother's already seen to that—I'll just blame it on the amulet."

They had found the worthless piece of jewelry on Kortiama. Tharne now hefted it in his hand. "As long as no one else sees this, they won't be able to say it's not real."

"Rikton will know," Draigo reminded him.

Tharne casually flipped the amulet between his fingers. "That changes nothing. He won't openly attack them without the mandate."

Draigo pressed his lips together and nodded. "Fair enough. Still, now that the barrier's down, what's to stop him from coming up here to look for it?"

"Absolutely nothing. He's part of my family, and he's welcome up here *anytime*—at least, that's what I'll tell him." Tharne winked.

Draigo nodded appreciatively. If Rikton thought there was nothing to hide here, he would most likely lose interest. "That'll take the wind out of his sails."

Tharne's mouth spread into a grin. "Indeed, my friend. Indeed."

Grand Choosing

Shannon Pemrick

Haunted
Chapter 1

A darkness surrounded Kortiama, one so thick not even her lantern could penetrate. Eyes darting about, her breathing came in short, ragged gasps, her heart racing. Her nose flared out, taking in the musty smell surrounding her. A cold sensation rushed past her back. She spun around, holding back a scream.

A blood-curdling shriek filled the air, then it was cut short. *Lathara? No, it can't be.*

"Korti, run! Get the others out and run!" a young man shouted before he cried out in pain. Silence.

"Regarn? Regarn?" No, he couldn't be gone. "Trevis! Trevis, where are you?"

More silence.

Kortiama tugged on the arm of her sister, who lay in a heap on the ground, her wild mane of hair curtaining her face. Still breathing, her skin was pale and cold, as if the life had been sucked out of her. "Solais, get up. We have to go. This was a mistake."

Air moved in a brisk current behind her. Kortiama spun around, desperately trying to find what had taken her friends. Her pulse pounded in her ears, making it hard to think. Why had she done this? She knew it was unsafe. And yet—

A cold, dark, foreboding presence sent a chill up her spine. Kortiama turned to face a floating figure in a dark billowing cloak. A large boney hand reached for her, coming within mere inches of her skin. Unable to move a muscle, she let out a chilling scream.

Kortiama's eyes snapped open as she shot upright. Her breaths came shallow and hard, sweat dripping from all over her. Her fingers clutched soft sheets. She was no longer in a dark room. Instead, she sat in the large four-post bed in her room, bright morning light filtering in through a tall arched window. Tears streamed down her cheeks and she pulled her knees to her chest. Her long raven hair spilled around them.

It was a dream… but at the same time it wasn't. The recurring nightmare wouldn't leave her, forcing her to relive that fateful mistake from three years ago, over and over. She knew the villa was dangerous at the time. That was why they needed a ward-breaking spell to get in. Yet she couldn't let her ambitious uncle Rikton get his hands on the Mandate—the one item that would give him power over the Dasati. Even as a child, she'd learned what kind of ruin that would bring to their clan.

Still, as a foolish child, she thought her little group of orphan misfits could handle it. They were a capable bunch—unfortunately, not capable enough.

The door to her room flew open and heavy feet rushed in. "Korti? Korti, are you okay?" Soft hands touched her shoulders. "Korti, I could hear the screams from the other room."

Kortiama lifted her head, her cheeks tear-stained as she gazed at her sister Solais. Aside from the mane of light-brown hair, she looked remarkably like Korti. She had a similar tan complexion, with deep brown eyes and even the same round-shaped face.

The two of them were the only ones to have survived the massacre, and only because Tharne and the Emerald Blade had come to rescue them—only the rescue had come at a cost, the Emerald Blade's life. Afterwards, Kortiama discovered the Mandate hadn't even been at the villa. It'd been a ruse by Rikton, and another example of her poor decision-making.

Some leader I am.

Solais stroked her head. "It was that nightmare again, wasn't it?"

Kortiama nodded, struggling to find her voice. She feared any quaver in it would only make her sound more pathetic.

"You need to let it go, Korti," her sister said, gently taking her by her shoulders. "It wasn't your fault."

"It was," Kortiama insisted. "I was our leader. Everyone looked to me for direction. They trusted me. And I got them all killed."

Solais fixed her with a hard stare. "We followed you because we believed in you—and your goal. I'm the one who stole the barrier-canceling scroll from Uncle Tharne. You didn't even know he had it. I chose to follow you. We all knew the dangers and what the cost might be."

Kortiama's shoulders slumped. Knowing her friends had made those choices of their own accord didn't absolve her of the guilt. It ate away at her every day. They were all supposed to make it to the day of choosing and be placed on one of the grand ships. They were to do their clan proud and be the best privateers in all the clans—at least one of them becoming a ship's captain. That was the dream they all shared. But now only she and Solais would see that day come.

With a reluctant sigh, Kortiama pulled herself out of bed and dressed. Solais left to do the same, knowing no words would help at this point.

Kortiama pulled out a white low-shouldered blouse with long, flowing sleeves, and dark pants. A black underbust corset complimented the shirt, though it took a moment for her to lace up on her own. While difficult, it wasn't impossible for Kortiama, due to years of practice.

She then rummaged for her favorite boots, finding them tucked away in a corner. After pulling them tight up to her knees, Kortiama went about brushing her hair, staring out one of the tall arched windows of her tower. The villa below, constructed of smooth limestone with terracotta roof tiles, sprawled across a manicured plateau. Another tower stood on the south side of the home. A fortified wall surrounded the grounds, adding a fortress feel to the estate.

Craggy mountaintops secluded her home to the east, while a forest and hills bordered the villa to the west. The sparkling waters of the loch shone beyond the treetops. Renere, the home port of the Dasati, sprawled along the western shore with a number of tall ships moored at its docks.

She loved her little town, but like all in her clan, she yearned to be out on the water. Of course, until the day of the choosing, she would be confined to sailing skiffs in the loch.

Kortiama's brushing stopped, realization dawning on her. Today was her birthday, and that meant the next choosing was only a few months away. She and Solais had missed the last one due to the unfortunate event at the villa. This meant Kortiama could finally be chosen for one of the great ships of the Dasati, and sail with the rest of her clan.

Renewed vigor hastened her routine, the nightmare soon becoming a distant memory.

When she exited her room, Solais was just leaving hers as well. She'd dressed in leather pants and a cropped white blouse, the sleeves long and hanging low off her shoulders, accentuating her slender, muscular frame. A bright red bandana now pulled her hair out of her eyes, a failed attempt to control her wild mane.

"Feeling better and ready to take on the day?" Solais asked.

Kortiama nodded, and Solais' face broke out in a wide grin before latching onto Kortiama. "Good. Can't have my baby sister all gloomy on her birthday."

Kortiama's nose scrunched as she swatted at Solais. "Must you call me that? You're only three months older than me."

Solais winked. "Still makes me older."

She and Solais weren't blood sisters. Both had been orphaned as babies during the largest raid in Dasati history. Lord Captain Eboneye, who had united the thirteen clans, led the raid on Penwick. It'd been long and grueling, with casualties on many fronts. But the feared man held the city, until their goddess' favor ran out—or so it was claimed.

Kortiama and Solais grew up together, alongside other children orphaned by that event, until Captain Tharne adopted both of them.

Solais grabbed Kortiama's wrist and dragged her toward the stairs. "C'mon, I'm sure Eyro has breakfast waiting."

Kortiama nodded, smiling, and followed her sister down the winding stone staircase. When they made it to the bottom of the tower, a faint savory smell teased their noses. *Solais was right, Eyro has been busy this morning.*

Solais and Kortiama strolled down the hall, past several rooms and a large library. The villa seemed unnecessarily large, consisting of over twenty rooms between the first and second floors. Kortiama wasn't entirely sure why it need to be so big. To her knowledge, the original owner never utilized even half the rooms. *Power, most likely.*

They made it to the large foyer, descending one of the two curving stairs. Their boots clicked on the tiled black and white marble floor. Before entering the room where the smell wafted from, Kortiama stopped in front of a double portrait hanging between the stairs depicting an imposing couple. The man was garbed in a fancy, dark long coat and white shirt, with a red sash tied at the waist. An eye patch, grizzled dark beard, and scars enhanced his menacing visage, though it was the woman in the painting that was even more frightening.

Her sable hair and porcelain skin framed coal-black eyes so dark one would swear they'd steal your soul. The elegant black grown and intricately woven hair did nothing to hide the ominous aura that was perfectly captured of this fearsome woman.

These two were none other than Bernal "Eboneye" Ozden and his wife, Liadha Rowan, a powerful witch of the Ramulos clan. The estate had once belonged to them, until Liadha abandoned it after Eboneye's death. That was how it fell into the state Kortiama and her friends had come to, before it had been purged of the dark horrors.

Solais rested her arm on Kortiama's shoulder. "I still say you look a lot like her."

Kortiama tapped her finger against pursed lips. They did share many similarities, something others had pointed out when Liadha made the occasional visit to the clan to see her former brother-by-marriage. "Maybe. But I still say you look like Eboneye."

Her sister crossed her arms and puffed out her chest, arrogance radiating off of her. "Maybe I am his long-lost daughter, after all."

The two shared a glance and then doubled over in laughter. It wasn't uncommon for children to pretend to be the fabled pirate's lost heir. Who wouldn't want to be related to such a man, and possibly have the blood right to lead the clan?

"Korti, Solais, are you two finally downstairs?" came a masculine voice.

"Yes, Eyro," they responded in unison.

A portly older man with weathered yellow-tan skin emerged from the adjacent room. He wore a simple robe, something he called a kimono. A gray beard framed his gentle features, long gray hair flowed behind his back, though the morning sun peeking through the nearby windows reflected off the bald spot atop his head where his hair had receded, threatening to make Koriama enter a fit of giggles. Solais, on the other hand, didn't contain herself.

His dark eyes crinkled in the corners as he chuckled, his smile deepening the few wrinkles he had. "From the sounds of it, you both are ready to get into trouble, and all before you've had your morning tea."

Oi, tea! Kortiama swore this man bled the stuff with how much he drank it. She smiled at him. "We're not getting into any trouble…" She winked. "Yet."

Eyro laughed some more, resting a hand on his round belly. "Ah, of course. Now, before you two go causing havoc in town, come and have breakfast."

He ushered them into the adjacent room, where food was prepared and laid out for the taking. Kortiama's eyes went wide. *So much.* They had bread and cheese, fish of several varieties, berries, a whole chicken, rice, eggs, and more. There were also several cups, and a tea pot waiting in the center. It all made her mouth water. "Eyro, what is all this?"

He rested his hand on her shoulder. "We can't have our lady of honor miss a basic meal in the morning, now, can we?"

Kortiama twirled a lock of hair. "You didn't need to go through the trouble, but thank you."

He'd gone to this length for Solais' birthday as well, so she shouldn't have been surprised.

"Tharne should be joining us any minute." He pushed her to

a chair. "Now sit, and I'll pour you tea. I sense you've had a rough morning."

Solais was all too eager to claim her seat and dig into the grandiose meal. Kortiama, however, took a little more time, seating herself and watching as Eyro lifted the porcelain tea pot and poured a pale green liquid into tiny round cups. She smiled her thanks when he handed her one. The light floral scent wafted up to her nose, along with the steam. Kortiama wasn't overly fond of tea, but she knew better than to refuse, or else Eyro would go on some long speech about how good it was for one's soul… or something like that.

She glanced around the spread of food, looking for something in particular. A smile formed on her lips when she found the small bowl filled with a golden liquid near the tea pot. Kortiama snatched up the container and dipped a spoon in, scooping it into her tea cup.

When she'd added enough, she slipped the spoon into her mouth, savoring the sweet stickiness left behind on the spoon, before stirring her tea. While the tea had a light smell, she knew this tea tended to taste bitter, so honey was great to remedy that. Of course, one glance at Eyro showed the pointed disapproving look he gave her. He didn't like that she altered the tea, but rarely did he stop her.

Kortiama lifted the cup to her lips, blowing on it for a moment to cool, before taking a sip. Her shoulders relaxed as the warm liquid entered her throat, the sweetened floral taste doing wonders on her tongue. Another sip reduced much of the lingering tension inside her. One thing Eyro was right about, tea did help calm her.

"Do not underestimate the power of tea," Eyro said before drinking his.

Solais rolled her eyes and continued to tear into some chicken and bread she'd helped herself to. Kortiama took another sip before breaking into a loaf of bread and taking some cheese to go with it, as well as snatching up a few berries, to start herself off.

Not two bites into her breakfast, the clomping of heavy footsteps on stone came from the foyer. A moment later, a tall man garbed in a long dark coat entered the room. The hard expression on his face softened as he laid eyes on Kortiama and Solais. "I see my girls are up and ready for the day."

"Morning, Uncle Tharne," they greeted.

Tharne Ozden let out a deep sigh and removed his hat, his dark, wiry hair remaining tied in place at the nape of his neck. "Would it kill you two to call me 'Father' for once?"

The two giggled, while Eyro let out a boisterous laugh. Tharne had visited the orphanage many times before adopting them. He was so kind and caring, all the children called him uncle. When he'd adopted Kortiama and Solais, they'd been so used to calling him by one name, it continued to stick.

That didn't mean Kortiama didn't see him as her father, though. After everything he'd done for her, she wouldn't see him as anything less.

Tharne sat down at the table with them, setting his hat down. "I see you two have already begun to eat without me."

Solais tore into some more chicken. "Not our fault you're late."

Their father let out a heavy sigh. "A Lord Captain's duties never cease, even in the wee hours of the morning."

After Eboneye's death, a new leader for the Dasati had to be chosen. Most assumed the title would fall to Rikton, as he was Eboneye's next-oldest younger brother. But Liadha claimed that upon Eboneye's last breath, he'd named his youngest brother Lord Captain—Tharne.

The decision had ruffled more than a few feathers in the clan. Some thought Rikton was better suited for the position. Others doubted the claim, since Tharne couldn't prove he had the Mandate. The Mandate of the Seas were powerful symbols bestowed upon the Saricordi by their goddess Zesstara. Thirteen mandates in all, one for each clan. They served as proof one had the right to lead a clan. Still, Tharne had enough backing to hold his claim to the Dasati—for now.

While Rikton only postured about taking the clan under his rightful rule, everyone knew he would eventually make a true attempt. Kortiama wasn't sure how he would do so, but she'd back her uncle in any way she could to ensure the clan didn't fall into Rikton's filthy hands.

Eyro leaned back in his seat. "You need to learn to slow down,

Tharne. Drink some tea—take a stroll in the garden—feel the sun on your face. It won't do anyone any good if you're dead."

Tharne grunted and partook in the feast before them. "Thanks, oh *wise* man, I'll reflect on that advice."

Solais and Kortiama laughed.

Tharne peered at the two of them. "So, Korti, Solais, Eyro told me yesterday your training is going well. Care to tell me more?"

Kortiama pursed her lips. What was there to say? Eyro, while a caretaker of this villa, had some unusual skill. This seemingly harmless man knew all manner of tactics and fighting techniques, and how to use them. Of course, he'd never fight with any real weapon. Most of the time he'd beat the crap out of her and Solais with a broom. It was as annoying as it was embarrassing. Still, beyond getting their asses whooped, he'd taught them how to properly wield different blades, allowing them to make the choice of style on their own.

She and Solais ended up picking vastly different styles to hone, each with their unique challenges and advantages.

A wicked grin spread across Kortiama's face when she thought of something. "Solais finally learned to block attacks, instead of just trying to beat them into submission."

Her sister's mouth fell open. "Korti!"

Tharne's head flew back as he laughed. "Did she now? I was wondering when she'd learn the pointy end of a blade could be turned on her if she wasn't careful."

Solais' face went red, her face scrunching as she pointed at Kortiama. "Well, Korti now cheats to win!"

Kortiama's mouth twisted as it fell open. "I do not!"

"Yes you do." Solais tossed her hair to the side as if imitating Kortiama. "I'm Korti, I'm so beautiful, look at me. I can't fight with my toothpick of a weapon, so I fling spells everywhere to force a win."

Korti glared at her sister. "At least I'm smart enough to use magic!"

The two of them continued casting verbal jabs at each other. The longer it went on, the more Kortiama found herself actually irritated with her sister. They felt more like personal insults than just fun jabs.

Eyro sighed. "Both of you are like raging rivers, eager to overpower each other. You should be like streams, complementing the other's flow to make one harmonized force."

Both girls stopped and stared at the older gentlemen.

"Okay…" Kortiama drawled. "Not sure what a river has to do with any of this."

Eyro, however, didn't respond. Instead, he wore that all-too-familiar, knowing smile as he sipped his tea. Yet before she could call him on it, Solais interrupted them.

"Dad," her sister whined, "Tell Korti she can't use magic in our fights!"

Korti turned to defend herself, but Tharne's gaze was not on Solais. He seemed to be peering off in the distance, rubbing his temples as he muttered to himself. "Of course she uses magic."

Kortiama's brow rose. "What's that supposed to mean?"

Their father took a deep breath and leveled his eyes at them. "Using magic in a fight isn't cheating. You'll find out on the waters that you'll run into opponents of various skills. Some are like Liadha, where all they use is magic, and many others will be like Solais and me, fighting fiercely with our blades. Then you'll come against individuals who will do what Korti has done—mix magic in with their sword style."

Solais sat back in her seat, crossing her arms and letting out a displeased *hmph*. Kortiama couldn't stop herself from sticking her tongue out at her sister in triumph.

"Speaking of Liadha," Tharne began, "We should be expecting her to dock rather soon." His eyes darted to Kortiama. "Korti, I want you to be the one to meet her when she arrives."

Kortiama's brow rose. "Not that I don't want to, but why me? We all know she's going to expect you."

"On a normal day, yes. But seeing as she's coming specifically to see you today, we will make an exception."

That brought a small smile to Kortiama's face. As scary as the woman was, she always treated her and Solais well. Even though she was no longer considered family, that didn't stop her from acting like it with them and Tharne.

"Besides, Eyro needs me to help get this place in order before your birthday celebration, so take your time coming back." He looked to Solais. "We'd like your help as well, Solais. It's only fair, since Korti helped with your celebration."

Her sister let out a heavy sigh. "Yeah, okay."

Tharne nodded, and the four of them fell into more casual conversation while eating. Near the end, Tharne abruptly stopped and a far-off gaze came to his eyes. Then he nodded. "That was Liadha. The Dark Rider should be coming in soon."

Kortiama pushed out of her seat. "Then I'd best get down there quick, so she's not waiting."

Without another word, she rushed out the front doors and into the expansive courtyard. Large maple and oak trees stood tall and scattered about, shading patches of grass to invite one to sit and rest under them. Tended gardens of flowers, fruits, and vegetables grew in long rows. Her feet clomped on a wooden bridge stretched over a pool of water, little fish swimming among the lily pads and reeds. A bullfrog croaked and then leapt into the water in fright.

Kortiama's memories threatened to bring back the vision of this place's former condition, dead and overgrown, but the serenity its current state brought onto her prevented that from happening.

Eyro did so well tending to the villa grounds. She didn't know where Tharne found the man—he wasn't from the clan—but no one could have brought this place back to life like he had.

She passed a sandy patch with tall stones, tiny manicured plants, and grooves deliberately drawn into the loose, gravelly surface. Eyro called it a zen garden—something he'd added to the courtyard with Tharne's permission. Kortiama had never heard of them until then. It was a strange setup, but Eyro insisted the placement had purpose, and every time he changed the lines, it was done for reasons understood only by him. *He's such a strange man.* Though as odd as he may be, Kortiama enjoyed his company. While Tharne had become her father figure, Eyro filled that older, doting uncle or even grandfather void.

Kortiama ran out the front gate, noting the usual hum of arcane energy wasn't present. Since Tharne had arrived only a little while ago, it made sense that he'd have removed the protective barrier that went up every night. A "precaution," the two of them called it. They didn't want anyone from the village wandering up here and causing trouble.

Kortiama cut tight around the wall and down over the ridge to the village, avoiding, with practiced ease, all manner of wards still in place. There were many of them, ranging from illusionary wrong turns to pitfalls and more. It wasn't the easiest route, but it certainly was the fastest.

Kortiama made it to the docks just as the Dark Rider pulled into port. The large vessel proudly flew the colors of the Ramulos clan, an amber sea horse on a field of deep azure. Staring at the flag made Kortiama's fingers tingle; laying eyes on such a powerful symbol did that to her. The Ramulos were not a clan you wanted to cross paths with.

Lady Captain Cassala was a prime example. Not only was she a powerful witch with a small but loyal coven, Cassala was the same age as Kortiama, and she'd already become a captain after only three short years of sailing. She also happened to be a kind of cousin of Kortiama's, as she was Liadha's niece.

And then there was Liadha. A witch of immense power, her aunt was one of the most feared and respected leaders across all the clans. No one dared to cross that woman. *Made her the perfect wife for Eboneye.*

Kortiama aspired to be even half as amazing as either of these women.

She did her best not to fidget as she leaned on a crate, waiting for Liadha to disembark. She didn't need to be scolded for being impatient. In reality, she was just excited. Liadha didn't visit as often as she used to, and Kortiama enjoyed her aunt's company. She'd also taught her a thing or two about the basics of magic, which had prompted her efforts to combine it with swordplay.

The plank of the Dark Rider slammed down on the dock, and a woman nearly identical to the painting in the villa immediately strode down. She exuded confidence, her long sable hair moving about her as if it has a will of its own. A rumor in the clan said she could kill ten men at once with it. Kortiama wasn't sure how true the claim was, but given Liadha's fearsome reputation, Kortiama wouldn't outright dismiss the possibility.

The dock hands were quick to move out of the witch's way, her coal eyes scanning the area. Kortiama pushed away from the crates and rushed toward the ship. "Aunt Liadha!"

The witch pinned her eyes on Kortiama and her menacing expression melted into a warm, welcoming one. She held out her arms and smiled. "My Korti."

The two embraced. When Kortiama pulled away, Liadha touched her face. "Look at you. You've grown on me again."

"I haven't changed since I last saw you."

"I beg to differ." Liadha rubbed her thumb on Kortiama's cheek. "And you've got a spot of dirt on your face. Honestly, you're not doing well convincing me Tharne doesn't have you living in squalor."

Kortiama laughed. "I promise, I want for nothing, thanks to him."

"Good. That had better be the case. You deserve nothing less." Her aunt glanced around. "Did he not accompany you?"

Kortiama shook her head. "No. He's helping Eyro with prepping for my party up at the villa."

"Good, about time he's useful."

Her aunt's gaze drifted away. Kortiama glanced the same way when the woman's face grew hard. A man in a long, dark coat and feathered hat approached them, his boots hitting hard on the wooden planks of the dock. He had tanned, weathered skin, salt-stained dark hair, and a scraggly beard. A scowl etched in his scarred face, his dark eyes sending a chill down Kortiama's spine. She masked her fear; she wouldn't let it show in front of him.

"Rikton," Liadha greeted, her voice chilling.

"I was told ye had docked, Liadha," Rikton said. "Seems that claim is true."

Liadha arched a single eyebrow at him. "I wouldn't be here if it weren't."

Rikton eyed the woman. "It's unusual you didn't give advance notice."

Liadha laughed, a rather dry one. "Why would I need to do that?" She placed her hand on Kortiama's shoulder. "After all, I'm here because of our dear Korti."

Rikton's cold eyes snapped to Kortiama. She forced the sweetest smile she could. "It's my birthday today, remember, Uncle? You were invited up to the villa to celebrate with us."

Her uncle's lip curled. "Yes. Well, I do have important duties to deal with. So try not to hold it against me, girl, if I don't show up."

Kortiama continue her sweetness act. "I wouldn't dream of it, Uncle."

His lips twitched and he spun on his heels, leaving without saying another word. Kortiama stuck her tongue out at his back. The gods knew she hated that man. As much as he terrified her at times, she would never let him see it.

She had no doubt that he wouldn't show, a fact that did little to disappoint her. Though her adopted uncle, Rikton had never been afraid to show how much he didn't like her. He detested all children, but she and Solais always seemed to get the worst of it.

"Not going to show the old fool where he really stands?" Liadha asked, not looking at Kortiama. Liadha didn't like him any more than Kortiama. From what she understood, the two of them never got along, which made Rikton's sudden appearance here all the more strange. *Why do I feel like he's up to something?*

Kortiama shook her head, more to clear her mind than in response to her aunt. "I promised Uncle Tharne I'd behave, and not start something with Uncle Rikton." She grinned at her aunt. "Now, finishing something is another story."

A semi-malicious grin spread across Liadha's lips. It send a startling chill through Kortiama, reminding her just how dangerous her aunt could appear. "I can give you a few tips on how to end one of those, if you'd like."

The expression soon disappeared, and a far-too-kind smile replaced it. "Now, let us head to the villa and see what kind of chaos Tharne has concocted."

Birthright
Chapter 2

By the time the villa came into view from the road, the sun had reached its zenith. The heat followed the light in the sky, making Korti want nothing more than to rest under the shade of a tree in the courtyard, or rush back down the mountain to dive into the lake.

"Liadha," she started, "I want to thank you for allowing Solais and me to stay in the villa whenever we want."

Liadha narrowed an eye at her. "How many times am I going to have to tell you to stop thanking me about that? I'm just glad this place is finding use again." Her gaze turned back to the trail in front of them. "From what Tharne tells me, the caretaker he hired has done an adequate job bringing the place back to life, and even added a few extra touches of his own." Her face darkened. "He better hope that I approve of them."

Korti gulped, not wanting to think what her aunt would do if she didn't. She decided to steer the conversation away from Eyro's improvements. "Are you okay with coming up here?"

Even though Liadha had made visits to Renere before, this would be the first time Kortiama knew her to set foot inside the villa since Eboneye's death.

Liadha peered at Korti once more, obviously amused with her niece's concern. "Yes. In fact, I've been meaning to for a while now, but just haven't had the time."

Liadha's reaction quelled any further concerns Korti might have had. She should have known better. Her aunt was a strong woman, the strongest woman she knew, in fact.

The two entered the courtyard and Liadha gazed about, taking everything in. Kortiama, on the other hand, noticed the villa was a little *too* quiet.

The horses came to a halt and the pair dismounted. Kortiama's senses remained on edge as they tied the equines to a nearby hitching post so they wouldn't go after Eyro's carefully tended work.

Suddenly, something small hit her arm. And then before she knew it, several people of various ages popped out from hiding in the gardens and tossed more small objects at her. "Get her!"

Kortiama jumped back, using her horse's rear as a partial shield. The projectiles didn't hurt, and one ended up splattering on her cheek. She wiped it away and licked her finger. *Mmm, that tasted good.*

She snatched up several of the berries that had fallen to the ground and tossed them back at her "attackers." Liadha had stepped well aside, watching the "battle" with a bemused expression. Korti wondered if she had known about this beforehand, or had merely sensed it with her magic.

Eventually the berry attack ended, and all the kids Kortiama had been playing with slipped out of their tactical spaces. Liadha chuckled. "Friends of yours, Korti?"

She nodded. "Other orphans Solais and I grew up with. I'm glad you all could make it."

"We wouldn't miss it for anything," one of the older boys, a little younger than Kortiama, declared.

"We wanted to have fun with you!" a little girl, maybe seven in age, proclaimed.

"And we were told there was food," another boy said.

Kortiama laughed. While she and Solais had been close with Regarn, Trevis, and Lathara, they still had other friends at the orphanage. She was happy they'd all come for her big day.

"Well then, your guests are obviously all here. I suppose we should make sure Tharne hasn't burnt down the villa, shall we?" Liadha gestured to the front door.

Amused chuckles rumbled through the orphans, and everyone headed for the building. Kortiama caught her aunt gazing around again. Somewhat concerned, she voiced a tentative question. "Do you like what Eyro has done?"

Liadha turned to face her niece and slowly nodded. "Yes. I don't remember a time the courtyard looked this beautiful." Her voice grew distant. "Perhaps Berngal and I should have had a caretaker long ago."

Kortiama felt relieved and saddened at the same time. It wasn't often Eboneye's name was used in the village. But when Liadha did, it always carried a bittersweet tinge to it. Those in the village tried to claim Liadha's and Eboneye's marriage was nothing but a political move. Kortiama could believe some of that was true; it wasn't an uncommon practice. But the way Liadha's demeanor changed when he came up in conversation, even for an instant, told Kortiama her aunt did care for the pirate king in her own way.

The orphans ran into the foyer, stopping short to gaze around in awe. They rarely ever came up here.

"Uncle Tharne, Eyro, Solais, I'm back!" Kortiama called out.

A moment later, Solais poked her head around the entryway to the gathering room. "You stay there, we're not done. Hi, Aunt Liadha."

Kortiama's lips twisted. *How could they not be done yet?*

"Sol, can we help?" one of the younger orphans asked.

She nodded. "Extra hands are welcome."

The little ones cheered and rushed inside. The older orphans were far calmer in abandoning Kortiama. She expected Liadha to go with them, but when Kortiama glanced her aunt's way, she'd wandered over to the painting that hung between the curving stairs. Kortiama joined her.

"I'm surprised to see this still here," Liadha murmured. She reached over, her hand running along the frame of the large portrait.

Kortiama's voice grew hushed. "It didn't feel right to remove it."

"The frame is different." Liadha noted softly.

Kortiama nodded. "It hadn't withstood the state the villa had fallen into, so Tharne had a new one made. This one should last much longer."

"That's good to hear." Liadha replied, though her voice sounded a million miles away.

Silence fell between them. After a few moments, Liadha turned her gaze to Kortiama, her eyes fixed on her niece.

Those deep, dark eyes seemed to burrow into her, suddenly making her very uncomfortable. Kortiama nervously rubbed her arm. "Something the matter, Aunt Liadha?"

Her aunt shook her head, the hint of a smile appearing on her lips. "No. I'm just taking in the kind of woman you've grown into. Contrary to my earlier concerns, Tharne appears to have done well raising you and Solais. I expect many great things from you."

Kortiama's brow spiked. Why had Liadha been concerned about Tharne adopting her? She wasn't sure how she was supposed to take that.

Liadha's eyes fell to the common room, a coldness falling over her face. Kortiama turned to see Tharne standing in the foyer.

"I see you haven't burnt down this place… yet," Liadha said.

Tharne chuckled. "It's good to see you too, Liadha. I'm glad you could make it."

Her aunt placed a hand on Kortiama's shoulder. "You know I wouldn't miss today."

Kortiama glanced between the two. She got the feeling there was more to their words, though she couldn't be sure. "Uncle, will there be anyone else coming up here?"

His eyes drifted to her and he grinned. "Everyone arrived before you had. The orphans just decided they wanted to surprise you in their own way."

Excitement bubbled up inside her. "You mean we can start now?"

Her father gestured to the common room. She squealed and rushed in. Before her, friends and family gathered around a larger table filled with food and objects all wrapped up in various ways. They cheered on her entry, bringing an even bigger smile to her face. She felt so lucky to have them all.

Kortiama leaned on the table to get a good look at the feast that had been prepared. It was much like this morning, but a few extra surprises were added, like cooked eel and other fish from the sea, and colorful round balls and fun shapes on some other plates. She didn't know what those were, but they were neat.

There was also a honey cake, one of Kortiama's favorites.

Then there were the wrapped items. Nothing fancy, most cloth or leather, but not a single one was the same size—she guessed them to be gifts. Though, one thing that did draw her eye was a wooden ship. Kortiama lifted it up and carefully inspected it, finding the name of the ship—*Midnight Manta*. That was the Dasati flagship. *So much detail!* Each rope, piece of wood, even paint had its place and purpose. As she played with it, she found that even the door to the captain's chambers worked. It was beautifully detailed inside. In fact, so was the cargo hold.

A great big smile spread over her face. "Who made this? It's amazing!"

Rague, the helmsman of the Midnight Manta, and a close friend of the family, claimed the credit. Kortiama couldn't begin to imagine the work that went into this, or the time. She thanked him profusely.

After a few more moments of admiring, she set it back down on the table. That would go in her room for sure. Her eyes scanned everything before her. "I don't know if I should tell everyone to eat, or find out what's been gifted to me."

She received a chorus of different answers, making her laugh. But Solais' answer was hard to ignore, given that she had slammed her hands down on the table. "Before you do anything, taste those sticky treats."

Kortiama pursed her lips and then pointed to the colorful balls and shapes she'd noticed before. "These things?"

Solais nodded. "Eyro had us working hard on making those."

"Hard?" Tharne said. "You had the easy part, shaping them. I had to worry about Eyro breaking my hand with that mallet."

"Shaping them isn't as easy as you think," Solais muttered. "I mean, just look at your face I tried to make with it."

Kortiama looked over the treats. "You made his face?"

Her sister pointed to a plate with a rather large, multi-colored shape. Sure enough, it looked like a face attempt. Not that it turned out to be one—it looked more like a misshapen blob, though Kortiama could make out the pink beard she'd attempted with one of the colors.

Tharne grimaced when Kortiama lifted the plate for everyone to see. "That's my face?"

Laughter filled the villa.

Tharne let out a heavy sigh. "Just eat your treat."

"Not yet." Eyro stepped up. In his hands he carried two more of these treats, both pink. "I have these special ones for the two of you."

Solais cocked her head. "Both of us?"

Eyro grinned. "I didn't have the supplies to make it for you on your day, so I made one for each of you now." He handed the two young women each a ball.

Kortiama held her ball, noting the springy texture as she lightly squeezed it. "But what are they?" Kortiama asked.

"A treat from my homeland." Eyro said with a wink.

Solais and Kortiama looked at each other and then bit into the unusual treat. Kortiama's teeth sunk easily into a part of the treat before hitting something solid. She bit down more, the familiar sweet taste of strawberry tickling her tongue. Shredding through the entire treat, Kortiama chewed the sticky, springy confection. Her brow twisted as she processed the unusual texture mixed with sweet zing on her tongue.

"This is so good!" Solais gushed.

Kortiama nodded. "It's different, but it's good."

Eyro continued to smile, his hands folding into the long sleeves of his kimono. "I knew you'd enjoy it."

Kortiama pointed to the feast and treats. "Everyone needs to get in on this. No need to wait around."

Her guests were all too happy to take their share, breaking into some kegs Tharne set up. Unsurprisingly, the orphans got their hands on the sweeter treats first. The only time they were this spoiled was when Tharne brought them treats and trinkets from his journeys out on the waters. He was a tough leader, a reputation that was well-deserved, but it was no secret he had a soft spot for the children in the clan.

Kortiama finished off her treat and licked her fingers clean before washing it down with a mug of ale. Eyro scolded her for not savoring the treat properly with tea. Kortiama swiftly reminded him—her birthday, her rules. He sighed, made one more comment, and then let her be, opting to go introduce himself to Liadha. The stern woman had chosen to stand away from the rest of the partygoers to observe the celebration.

Kortiama grew apprehensive for a moment, but once the two engaged in a polite conversation about the villa, Kortiama tuned it out and focused on the gifts that had been left for her. She wasn't hungry enough to indulge in too much of the feast yet; she was still rather full from the large breakfast she'd had earlier.

While there weren't many gifts on the table, there were more than she expected. At most, she figured maybe one or two from Tharne and Solais. Kortiama chose a small, long, wrapped item. Removing the cloth wrap revealed a spyglass of remarkable quality. She lifted it into her hands, turning it in several directions to give it a good inspection, before aiming it out a nearby window. Just as she hoped for a quality piece, the details of the nearby mountainside became easier to see. That is, until Solais jumped in front of it.

Kortiama yelped and jumped back. Her eyes narrowed at her sister, who grinned like a coyote while the room filled with laughter. Kortiama snapped the sectional parts in on each other and set the spyglass down, digging in to more gifts.

Gift after gift, she opened them, each just as nice as the last. When Kortiama got to the last of them, she was left a little confused. Her family hadn't claimed credit for any of the gifts she'd opened.

Solais giggled and held out her hand, revealing a small wrapped item. "We didn't forget, promise."

Kortiama glanced to Eyro, who also held a gift now, something long and thin. She smirked. Of course they'd hold onto them. Wouldn't be them if they didn't pick on her, even on her birthday.

She took the wrapped item from Solais, finding it to be rather light. Kortiama carefully unwrapped it, afraid she might break something if she were too rough. She inhaled a sharp breath, her eyes widening when she revealed a sparkling hairpin made of gold. A ship riding the waves had been carved and shaped into the large metal ring, the thin needle used to keep the hair in shaped like spyglass. The light peeking through the windows danced over the gem-facet accents.

"Solais… this is…" She was a loss for words.

Her sister smiled. "Thought it'd be good to keep your hair tamed while out on the sea."

Kortiama snorted. "Speak for yourself."

Solais' eyes squinted as a wide smile spread over her face before she assisted Kortiama with pulling her hair back and pinning it.

One of the younger orphan girls ran up to her. "You look pretty with it, Korti."

"Thank you, Chiro." Kortiama noticed something in the young girl's hands. It wasn't wrapped, and appeared to be made out of beads. "What do you have there?"

"Your gift from us!"

Her brow spiked. "Us?"

The little girl pointed to the rest of the orphans. One of the teens stepped up. "We couldn't afford much, so we all came together to give you something special."

Kortiama's heart swelled. "You didn't have to."

Chiro held up her hand. Kortiama accepted the gift, watching the small beaded bracelet fall into her palm. She looked it over, smiling. Not only was it made from beads, but it also had three large sea shells. She cocked her head when she noticed the sea shells had letters written on them—R, T, L. "Is this…"

The boy from before nodded. "This way, they can still sail with you, like you all had planned."

Kortiama's chest constricted, tears welling up in her eyes. She couldn't get it onto her wrist fast enough. Once it was, she held the bracelet close to her chest. This would never come off.

Solais poked her cheek, grinning. "Don't start crying on us now."

Warmth spread over Kortiama's face. "I'm not going to cry!"

Her sister laughed and then moved away when Liadha and Tharne approached. Her father didn't have anything, but her aunt did. She, too, had a small gift.

"It's from us both," Tharne said, when Liadha handed the gift over.

"But it's mostly from me," Liadha said, giving him a sidelong glance.

Tharne grunted. "Don't go taking all the credit."

Kortiama laughed as they bickered, and began unwrapping the gift. Hidden within the cloth was an amulet in the shape of their family crest. A wide grin came to her face. She should have known. Solais got a gift like this too, a belt buckle. Kortiama clipped the necklace around her neck, the amulet sitting perfectly on her chest. Though, what perplexed Kortiama about this gift was the combined nature of it. *There's no way it's just an amulet if Liadha is also claiming half the ownership.*

A wicked smile spread over Liadha's lips. "I see that thoughtful look. My part of the gift is the enchantment on that amulet. Give it two taps in the middle."

Kortiama pursed her lips and then did so. A moment after she did, a tingling sensation rippled over her skin, then nothing. Kortiama's brow furrowed and she went to ask her aunt about it, but stopped when she noticed many of her party guests looking in all directions, as if searching for something.

Even Solais looked. "Where did she go?"

"I didn't go anywhere," Kortiama said.

Her sister gasped and jumped back, her eyes wide. Tharne let out a boisterous laugh, though it was Liadha who spoke. "It's an invisibility spell. It will only work once a day, and only lasts an hour."

"So use it wisely," Tharne said, his eyes darting to the witch. "That's quite the enchantment Liadha is entrusting you with."

Liadha shrugged, her eyes dancing with dark amusement. "I expect her not to use it wisely. It'll keep you on your toes."

Tharne glowered at her. Kortiama laughed, unable to contain herself. It was always interesting seeing these two in the same room together.

She tapped the amulet again, assuming that would break the spell prematurely. She was right.

Kortiama gave her aunt and then her father a tight hug. "Thank you."

Liadha rubbed her head affectionately, the thinnest of smiles crossing her lips. Eyro then approached, offering his gift. "One last one, Korti."

She accepted it, noting the light nature of the long gift. She didn't open it right away, her mind thinking about what it could possibly be. *Wait, what did Eyro give Solais for her day?* When the memory dawned on her, she eagerly removed the linen wrapping.

A wide smile came her face when she looked down at the rapier in her hands. She dropped the cloth and pulled it out of its scabbard. The silver metal gleamed, and the ornate handle wrapped around her hand, protecting it well.

Kortiama flourished the pointed blade and stabbed the air, the weapon light and weighted, just as she'd hoped. *Such fine craftsmanship.*

Eyro chuckled. "I think she likes it!"

Solais grabbed Kortiama's shoulders and peered over her. "Let me see your fancy stick."

She pulled away and gave her older sister a pointed look. "This *stick* will bleed you dry if you're not careful."

Solais grinned. "In your dreams, baby sister." She clapped her hands together. "But we should put that through its paces. What do you say?"

Some of the other orphans looked rather excited at the prospect, and even some of the adults looked intrigued. Kortiama looked to Tharne and Liadha for permission.

Liadha merely shrugged. Tharne crossed his arms and nodded. "Just don't go overboard."

Kortiama wrapped her arms around him. "Thank you!"

She ran outside, the other orphans charging after her. Solais veered off for the tower, needing to get her weapons. Eyro assisted with setting up, retrieving some practice weapons for the smaller or less-proven children. Kortiama chose to do a quick warmup to get used to the weapon. It had far better balancing and weight than the one she'd been using all this time.

Solais returned a little while later. "Okay, who is up first?"

One of the ship captains stepped up, drawing the cutlass strapped to his hip. "I'd like to test Korti. Make sure she's ready for life on the ships."

Kortiama smirked, flourishing her rapier. "Have at you, then."

Steel clashed with steel as Solais went at it with a ship's captain. Her ferocious attack kept the experienced man on his toes, but she wasn't gaining much ground otherwise. Kortiama watched with keen interest. The sparring turned into a small tournament of sorts, and now Solais and the captain were the only ones left. Kortiama had done well herself, but ultimately the experience of her last opponent overpowered her.

While unhappy she'd been beaten, Kortiama would use it as a lesson to become better. There wouldn't be second chances when fighting a true enemy.

The captain disarmed one of Solais' hands, following up quickly with a hard blow to her other hand. Solais managed to hold strong on her weapon, but the fight was now over. With her weapon too far out to take a defensive position, the captain slipped in and leveled his blade with Solais' throat. "I win."

Solais' face twisted in her displeasure, but after a moment of defiance, she sighed and relented. "Yeah, you win."

The man chuckled and patted her shoulder while the others around applauded. He looked to Tharne. "You've done well with them, Tharne. We need more with their skills on the ships. Just be careful, we might steal them from under ya in during the choosing."

Tharne grunted, his arms crossed. "We'll see about that."

Liadha looked up at the sky, now painted in hues of red and orange with the setting sun. "It's late. It may be best to call it a day."

Some of the younger orphans groaned and protested, saying they were having too much fun to leave. Kortiama promised that she'd come and play with them tomorrow, which cheered them up. She then said goodbye to everyone, thanking them for all the gifts and for coming.

Liadha drew up next to her as Kortiama waved to her retreating guests. "Korti, Tharne and I have something important to discuss with you."

Kortiama cocked her head. *What could they possibly want to talk about?* She nodded and followed her aunt back into the house, Tharne drawing up behind her.

The procession didn't escape Solais' eye, but Eyro stopped her. "I need your help cleaning up."

"But where are they going?" Solais asked.

Eyro's expression remained stoic. "They have something to discuss between themselves."

Yet Solais remained adamant. "But why? Why can't I be included? I didn't get any special secret meeting on my birthday."

Kortiama pressed her lips together as she followed Liadha up one of the foyer stairs to the second level. Solais was right, nothing like this happened for her, so what was going on?

Her aunt led her to Tharne's study on the second floor, Tharne closing the door behind them. Kortiama's fingers curled. The air felt a little too tense. Or was that just her nerves?

Liadha stared out the window at the landscape below. When the room remained silent for a little longer than Kortiama was comfortable, she spoke up. "So, you wanted to talk to me about something?"

Her aunt was quiet for a moment longer. "Did you know, at the time of the raid on Penwick, I was with child?"

Kortiama's brow knitted. *That's a strange question.* "I'd heard mention of it now and then. Most said something happened during the raid and you lost it."

Liadha continued to peer out the window. "What else have you heard?"

She thought for a moment, still confused. "Some have claimed the child wasn't lost at all, but instead hidden away."

Liadha nodded, finally turning from the window, but she didn't look at Kortiama still. "Do you know why that would be?"

"Um." Kortiama couldn't begin to wonder why Liadha would hide a child, let alone lie about something like that.

"For her safety." Liadha finally answered for her.

Tightness formed in Kortiama's stomach. "Her?"

Her aunt turned her gaze onto Kortiama, a hollowed, haunted expression masking her face. "The night Berngal met his end, our daughter came into this world. She was small, but strong. With his final breath, he placed the Dasati mandate on her—an infant not even hours old. That would have most certainly damned her to death if I allowed anyone to know."

Kortiama watched her aunt closely, the knot in her stomach tightening.

Liadha closed her eyes for a moment before continuing. "So I lied about her death and smuggled her into an orphanage to be raised away from me. To grow in secret to ensure she lived to fulfill the destiny her father placed on her."

Kortiama's fingers twitched at her side, her mind racing as she thought through the ramifications of what her aunt had just told her. "An orphanage? The orphanage Solais and I grew up in? You can't mean…"

The witch's eyes bore into her, and slowly, realization dawned on her. Kortiama pointed a shaky hand at herself. "M–me?"

Liadha nodded. Kortiama let out a weak laugh. "You're joking, right?"

They have to be joking. She looked to Tharne, who had an unsettling, stoic expression. *They're not…*

Her eyes darted between the two of them as she tried to process this. Liadha was her mother? She'd been so doting whenever she came to visit, but Kortiama always assumed that was what an aunt should do. Now she could see it was Liadha's way of being her mother from afar.

And then there was Tharne, who really was her uncle, and not just by the name he'd crafted for all the orphans. And that meant Rikton was her blood uncle, too. She swallowed hard. This was too much.

"She's what?" A familiar voice cried.

All eyes fell on the window, where Solais peeked in, her eyes wide. There was no doubt she heard that all, too.

"Solais, what are you doing?" Tharne snapped.

The ferocity of his tone startled her. Solais' grip faltered and she gasped when she fell back. Kortiama's pulse raced. *She'll die if she falls from that height!*

Liadha reacted quickly, muttering an incantation and pointing to Solais with a single finger. Then, Solais ceased to fall, her body now suspended in the air.

The wild-haired young woman looked around. "Wow, that was close. Thanks, Aunt Liadha."

"Solais? Solais, where are you?" Eyro called from somewhere in the house.

Tharne opened the door and ducked out. "We've got her. She was too slippery for even you."

Eyro sighed. "Sorry, Captain."

"It's fine, we'll deal with it."

Liadha opened the window and brought Solais in. The moment the young woman's feet touched the floor, Liadha looked over her, a terrifying aura leaking out of her. "What do you think you were doing?"

Solais, her eyes tight, stuck out her chin in defiance. "It wasn't fair Korti got some secret special meeting with all of you. So I wanted to find out what it was about, and because Eyro was so busy keeping me away from the door, I scaled the wall to spy and get information. That's what I do."

Tharne sighed, pinching his nose. "She's not wrong."

Solais' eyes sparkled. "But not even I could have predicted this amazing news." She faced Kortiama. "Korti, this is fantastic! It's— why do you look unhappy?"

All eyes fell on Kortiama once again. It didn't help the turning in her gut as she tried to wrap her mind around all this. She leaned against the wall and rubbed her face. "It's not that I'm unhappy. I'm just... trying to process this."

"What is there to process?" her sister asked. "We used to pretend we were Eboneye's lost heir when we were kids."

Kortiama let out a tight sigh. "Pretending is one thing, but to actually be them?"

Her eyes fell to the ground. "I thought I knew my life. I didn't have parents to call my own. Either they died or didn't want me. I was adopted with my best friend by the Lord Captain and raised as his own. I now had a family to call mine. But now…"

Kortiama ran her hands through her hair. "Now I'm finding out that was all a lie. Nothing I knew was…"

She hid her face in her hands, her emotions getting to be too much for her.

Tharne approached and placed his hands on her shoulders. "We did it to protect you, Korti. Taking you in as my own would ensure you'd be safe. I took in Solais so you two could grow up together—and to keep you safer. Rikton would have killed you without a second thought if he knew the truth."

Kortiama's hand fell to her side, though she struggled to meet his gaze. "I know you did… I just…"

Her shoulders sagged. She didn't even know how to put this all into words.

Liadha crossed her arms. "Korti, you're going to have to accept this as your new normal. We don't have time to waste. There's a lot to go over so you're ready for the choosing."

"Liadha, slow down," Tharne said. "There's no harm in giving her more time to take this in."

"How is this going to be revealed to the clan?" Solais asked.

Tharne pulled away from Kortiama, drawing her attention. "A Grand Choosing will be called in place of the standard choosing, and Korti will be presented as Eboneye's daughter, and the new Lord Captain."

That's only three months away! Kortiama's mind raced, her thoughts jumping in different directions trying to think of all the things she'd have to learn. Was it even possible to be ready to take over the Dasati in that short a time?

"Great, we can get Korti ready in time, no problem." Solais sounded far too confident about this for Kortiama's liking. She tried to catch her sister's eye, but Solais' gaze was firmly fixed on Liadha. "Excuse me, Aunt Liadha, but there's something I don't understand. You said you put Korti in the orphanage to later be adopted by Tharne for her protection"—she placed her hands on her hips—

"but you're the infamous Witch of the Seas. There's no way her life would have been in danger with you around."

Kortiama's brow ticked up. That was a good point. All heads turned to Liadha, who stood there, her eyes closed. Silence pervaded the room until she finally responded. When she did, her voice was low. "Her life would be in constant danger, even with my protection."

Liadha opened her eyes and leveled them at Solais. Nothing menacing dwelled there. No, instead Kortiama saw respect within them, as if Solais' questioning had earned her points with the witch. "There was also the matter of her taking over the Dasati when she came of age. If she were raised by me, the entire clan would think I was controlling her. After what happened with Berngal…" Liadha sighed and shook her head, her eyes filled with regret. "It was better this way."

Solais crossed her arms, her lips pursed. "Then why not raise Korti as a Ramulos instead? You didn't have any obligation to keep her as part of the clan."

The corner of Liadha's eyes tightened. Kortiama sensed the build-up of ominous magic in the air. *Leave it to Solais to push things too far.* Kortiama almost stepped in at that point, but then Liadha's face relaxed, the sudden spike of magic in the air fading away.

"I owed it to Berngal," Liadha replied in a cold tone.

Kortiama knew the conversation was over at that point. Solais' probing had irritated the witch for some reason.

Solais accepted the answer rather easily, most likely because she sensed the same thing as Kortiama. She turned to face Kortiama, flourishing with an unneeded bow. "Well, influenced or not, I know where my loyalty lies. Let me be the first to pledge my allegiance to our new Lord Captain."

Intense heat rushed to Kortiama's cheeks, and her hands balled up tight against her hips. "That's not funny, Solais!"

Her sister gave a goofy grin. "Sure it is, because you won't lighten up."

Kortiama's gaze fell again. "I'm just processing."

Tharne place a firm hand on her shoulder again. "And we'll give you tonight to do that. Tomorrow we can go over what needs to be covered in the next three months before we tell the clan. It won't hurt to wait. And if you have questions between now and then, ask them. There's nothing to hide here."

Kortiama nodded, thankful he respected the time she needed.

Liadha was the first to leave, but not before passing Kortiama a spine-shivering intense look. Kortiama had seen the witch give this to others, but never to her. She couldn't deny, the longer the stare lasted, the harder it was to stave off her fear.

"Don't take too long, Korti," Liadha warned. Her gaze shifted to Tharne, the dark expression not letting up, and then she left.

Solais passed Kortiama a concerned glance before leaving. Tharne was the last to follow. He looked back at her for a moment, his expression pained.

"Uncle Tharne," Kortiama said, before he could close the door behind him. He halted and listened. "You're still my father."

Tharne turned to look at her, his eyes wider than before.

"I may be Eboneye's daughter by blood, but you're the one who raised me." She licked her lips. "So, I don't want you to think anything changes, because it doesn't."

He smiled, moisture brimming his eyes. Kortiama sensed both joy and pride radiating of him, even at this distance. "Thank you."

A Sister's Gift
Chapter 3

Kortiama leaned against a tree, watching Renere far below. *So much hustle and excitement.* Soon the ships would leave, and the grand event would commence. Of course, none of the clans knew just how important—yet. Kortiama wasn't quite sure she comprehended its importance. Since the reveal on her birthday three months ago, she had struggled with the truth. Add to that everything Tharne and Liadha had taught her in preparation for taking over the clan, and it was a wonder she could breathe at all. She was barely an adult, with no experience sailing a large ship, let alone captaining one. How in all Arinthar was she supposed to gain the support of and lead an entire clan?

The more these questions looped through Kortiama's head, the further away the simpler days of carefree fun and pretending seemed. *What was I thinking, dreaming of a responsibility like this?*

The crunching of footsteps behind her caught her attention. Kortiama ripped her gaze away to see Solais approaching. "Is it time?"

Her sister had given her the space to think before they headed down to meet with Tharne. Solais had been one of Kortiama's most crucial supports during this time of adjustment. She thought her sister may get jealous after a while and pull away, but the opposite occurred. Solais was more determined than ever to be her anchor during this storm.

"Almost," Solais said. "Before we go, I want to give you something. I think it'll help get you through tonight." She rubbed the back of her neck. "Of course, as I was walking down here, I realized I left it in the tower. I figured we could both just go up there instead of me running back."

Kortiama shook her head. That was just like Solais. "Only because it's you."

Her sister smiled and then took off up the path. "Great, race ya there!"

"Hey!" Kortiama chased after Solais, mindful of the protective wards and traps. She cleared over a few fallen trees and bulging rocks with ease, yet Solais remained several strides ahead.

Kortiama's lungs burned by the time she and Solais made it back to the villa. Her sister maintained her lead as they raced through the courtyard, making it to the front entrance and into the foyer first. She taunted Kortiama for a brief moment, though it hadn't been that much of a win, then rushed up the stairs to their tower. Kortiama remained hot on her heels up the winding staircase.

She nearly ran into her sister, who had stopped short on the landing of the top floor. "What gives?"

Solais spun around and held up a bandana. "It's a surprise, so you need to wear this."

Kortiama's brow spiked, but she took the cloth and wrapped it around her head, doing her best to cover her eyes. She saw the shadow movement of Solais' hand waving in front of her, making her laugh. "The secret is safe. Can we please get to the surprise? We're going to be late if we dawdle too long."

Solais took Kortiama's hand and pulled her into a room. Her sister positioned her to face a specific way and then took a step back. A moment passed in silence.

Kortiama's brow spiked again. "Can I take this blind off yet?"

"Nope, not yet." Solais' voice sounded a little too far away for her liking.

"Where are you?" she asked.

"Getting your gift."

A muscle twitched in Kortiama's neck. Something didn't feel right. "You'd better not be pulling a trick on me."

Solais laughed, her voice carrying farther than before. "Would I do that to you?"

"Yes."

Silence fell in the tower. Kortiama shifted her weight between her legs, impatience growing stronger. "Solais, are you done yet?"

Silence.

Her lips pressed into a tight line. "Solais?"

Silence.

Kortiama pulled her blindfold off and looked around. She stood in her room of the tower—alone. A door below slammed shut, echoing up the stairs. She took slow steps out of the room, her boots clicking on the stone floor. Kortiama looked down the winding staircase. "Solais?"

The sound of something heavy dragging across the floor below carried up the tower. Kortiama's shoulders tensed as she flew down the stairs. She knew her sister was acting strange. She should have been more careful.

Kortiama reached the landing and crashed into the wooden door. She fell to the ground, rolling in pain. "The hell?"

Climbing back to her feet, Kortiama tried to open the door, only it wouldn't budge. She reached into a pocket and procured a key, sticking it into the keyhole and turning it. She tried the door again— no luck. *This isn't right.* The door to the tower could only be locked from the inside.

She yanked on the pull ring, pushed as hard as she could, but still the door wouldn't move. Kortiama pounded on the door. "Solais, this isn't funny! Let me out."

"I'm not playing a game, Korti," Solais said on the other side. She exhaled hard, and something heavy hit the door. "I'm doing this to protect you."

Kortiama's brow furrowed. "What are you talking about?"

"You haven't been the only one learning these past few months.

I've done my own training. I've scoured for every bit of information I could find to ensure I could effectively stand by your side. And I found one. A challenge for your position."

A challenge? Could someone challenge her claim? How would they gain control of the Mandate? Kortiama wasn't even sure where to find it. Tharne had warned her she'd have three years from the announcement or the birthright claim wouldn't matter.

"The challenge is a duel to the death."

Kortiama swallowed, the muscles in her neck tightening. *Is that true? Why didn't Tharne warn me?*

"But I'm not about to stand by and watch you fight that," Solais continued. "I'm the better fighter. You're good, Korti, but we both know I was born to swing a blade. And you can have someone duel in your stead." She took a heavy breath. "We both know Rikton won't stand for your birthright claim. He'll challenge you, and I'll be there to fight him."

Kortiama placed her hand on the door. "Solais, you don't have to do this. We can face him together."

Her sister's voice lowered. Kortiama thought she caught a slight quake to it. "I won't fail you. I promise."

"Solais!" Kortiama cried out when her sister ran off. Silence was the only thing to respond. She hit the wooden door with a clenched fist. "Dammit, Solais. You're such a fool."

Her hands fell to her sides. Solais wasn't the only one, though. Kortiama should have known her sister would pull something like this. As vicious of a fighter as Solais was, she didn't lack intelligence. She was the mastermind behind nearly all of the schemes their little band of misfits had perpetrated. And she was always the one to get them out when they got into hot water.

Kortiama wasn't like her sister; she didn't have the same ferocious fighting spirit. She didn't know how to create brilliant schemes. Kortiama's hands balled into a fist. *But I'm not an idiot.* She had charm, and grace, and knew how to use them. She thought of the big picture, when Solais thought only of the obstacle in front of her. Solais was a good fighter, but she wasn't the best in the clan—not yet. Her focus on winning Kortiama's place as clan leader blinded her to that fact. *Not that Solais would ever admit she's not the best fighter as it is.*

Eyes darting about, Kortiama looked for a less obvious way to escape. She was at the tower's lowest point. She peered out the nearby window, but she was still too far up to jump. She looked again at the door. Could she muster enough strength to move whatever was blocking it? *I'm not strong, but…* Her eyes wandered up the stairs. If she got a good enough start and braced herself, maybe she could budge whatever was blocking the door. She might even topple it over if Solais had picked something tall and top heavy. *Worth a shot.*

Kortiama rushed up the stairs, going about two levels' worth. Taking a deep breath, she sprinted down, praying she didn't lose her balance. When the door came into sight, she braced herself for impact.

Excruciating pain shot through her shoulder when it collided with the door. Kortiama fell back on the ground, holding her injured arm. *Ow… Nice going, Korti. That didn't work…* The door hadn't budged at all.

Slowly, she got to her feet, working out the pain by rolling her shoulder. She took an annoyed breath and kicked the door with her heel before pacing. *Think, Korti. Think.* She had to get creative.

She stopped dead. *Wait. Magic!* After she'd accepted her fate as the new Lord Captain, Kortiama had worked with Liadha on honing her arcane abilities, improving her mana reservoir and control. In an unexpected way, it helped her accept her duty little by little over the last few months. Maybe it was because it helped her get closer to her mother—learn just a little more of what she was missing. Or maybe it was because it allowed Kortiama to understand her heritage better.

He fist clenched. That reasoning didn't matter. *Now that practice is going to ensure Solais doesn't face this alone.*

Question was, did she have the right spell at her disposal to help her in this moment?

Kortiama ran the limited spell list through her mind. *I could disguise myself—Korti, how the hell would that help?* She shook the thought from her head and skipped over her non-combative spells.

She had a lightning spell that wouldn't help her much. Then there was a scorching fire spell. *Yeah, that should work.* This spell should easily destroy the door. It was also the most powerful spell she had in her arsenal.

Kortiama took a deep breath and backed up. She didn't need to be too close and get burned in the process. She focused inward, searching for the dormant energy within her. Something sparked, and she grabbed it, willing it out and muttering an incantation. She lifted her fingers, and the moment the incantation finished, a warm glow enveloped her fingers before a hot ray of fire shot toward the door.

The fire slammed into the wood surface, spreading across it quickly and then dying just as fast. Kortiama lowered her hand and her heart sank at the sight of the still-standing door. The spell had only blackened the surface. "Dammit…"

That should have worked. *Now what am I going to do?*

Kortiama began to pace, thinking about her spells again. She needed something with the same force, but more concentrated. She halted in her tracks. *Wait, what about…* It couldn't hurt to try that one. Combined with the damage the previous spell created, it might just work.

She backed up farther than the first spell. The force this one created could seriously injure her if she didn't put enough distance between her and the door.

Once far enough up the stairs to still see the door, but protected some by the stone walls, Kortiama drew up the energy needed again and muttered the incantation. She lifted her fingers, and arcane energy leapt from three of her fingers and careened toward the door like fast-moving arrows.

Kortiama ducked behind the wall, crouching down and covering her head just as the arcane bolts collided with the door. A resounding *crack* echoed loudly through the staircase. While she'd done her best to protect them, her ears rang from the deafening volume.

When things finally calmed in her head, she peered around the stone walls of the tower. Splinters lay strewn about the floor, three sizable holes now broken into the door. While they weren't large enough for a person to fit through, Kortiama could see the large chest Solais had used to block the door. *Well, that worked, sort of.* She'd get an earful from Eyro and Tharne for the destruction, but they'd understand once they heard her story.

Kortiama picked her way over to the damaged barrier to inspect it. As she thought, she wouldn't be able to squeeze through, but the fire spell had weakened the wood, so a few swift kicks should allow her to change that.

She struck the damaged surface a few times before a large portion broke off. *That should be enough.* Kortiama squeezed through the narrow gap, contorting herself around the chest. *Sorry, Solais, but I win.*

Now free, she took a deep breath and then sprinted out of the villa for the village.

Grand Choosing
Chapter 4

Dark waves crashed against Kortiama's skiff. The full moon shone brightly in the clear sky above, guiding her way. By the time she'd reached the village, the ships had long sailed for the secluded area where the choosing took place. Still, not all hope was lost. The choosing had been off-limits to the children before they'd come of age, but Kortiama and her band had learned the whereabouts of the grand event and found a way to sneak in.

Sailing there wasn't much of an issue, but the wards had always been troublesome. Of course, combined heads, and some help from Liadha, had always gotten them through the traps and they'd been able to witness the choosing many times without being caught. *Liadha…* Kortiama still wrestled with things. Everything the witch had done for her now made sense. But could she rightfully call Liadha her mother? *Though it is nice to know I'm related to such a strong and powerful woman.*

The grand ships of all the other clans came into view, drawing her attention back to the matter at hand. Lanterns illuminated the decks of the vessels she sailed past, but few crew members manned the decks. Instead, they stood watching one ship in the middle, the only one lit up in its entirety, and full of life—the Dasati's flagship, the *Midnight Manta*. Kortiama ground her teeth together. *It's already started.*

She pushed her skiff on toward the main vessel, noting the different flags flying on ships. Not all were Dasati. Tharne had warned her that for a Grand Choosing, more than just the Dasati would be present. And from the look of the number of ships anchored, he hadn't exaggerated. Archite, Fleckeri, Poruso—all thirteen clans were present for such an event.

Kortiama made it to the Midnight Manta, but now she needed to find a way to get up. She couldn't expect any help from above, so she'd need to rely on herself and any tools at her disposal in her skiff. Kortiama rummaged through the sailing supplies at the bottom of her boat, finding climbing hooks. *Perfect.* Hooks in hand, and sure she had her rapier, she made haste up the side of the wooden vessel.

When she made it to the top, she climbed over the railing and tried to see over the massive crowd on deck. *Where is Solais?* She needed to know the state her sister was in. Was she okay? Was she winning? Did Rikton pull any dirty tricks to ensure a win and rip her sister away from Kortiama forever? She couldn't tell. Too many stood taller than her, and that wasn't okay. *I need to get closer.*

Kortiama had no qualms about pushing her way through or demanding passage, especially when some didn't care to listen. Kortiama knew the faces of these ones—Rikton loyalists. They'd follow him to the ends of Arinthar if he demanded it—but she wouldn't be deterred. Kortiama would prove she could handle her birthright claim, no matter the odds stacked against her.

When she finally found herself on the inner edge of the dueling circle, her breath caught at the sight of the massive buccaneer looming there. *Solais is fighting him?* Kortiama's heart raced, her breath coming short as her eyes darted around for her sister's wild mane, yet she didn't see Solais. No—instead, a familiar older gentleman stood before the imposing figure—one who'd always greeted her with a smile and offered her tea every chance he got. His breath appeared heavy, his sword drawn, the kindness she knew replaced with hardened purpose. *Wait... that weapon!*

Eyro didn't carry just any sword, he wielded a katana—an ornate green katana. Only one man she ever knew wielded such a blade, and he had never drawn it. *It can't be… Eyro can't be—*

The hulking buccaneer swung his sword. Kortiama gasped as her beloved gardener dodged with surprising speed and sliced into the man with two quick strikes. The challenger howled in pain, but wasn't deterred.

"Don't fail me," a familiar voice said from the other side of the wide circle.

Kortiama spied her uncle Rikton, his eyes fixed on the man fighting her champion. She wasn't surprised. She knew Rikton wouldn't fight himself, but that didn't matter. While she didn't know where Solais was, Eyro had put his life on the line for her. She wouldn't allow her uncle to win.

Kortiama rested her hand on the hilt of her rapier and held her head high, her voice ringing out above the din of the crowd. "Emerald Blade, you know what you must do."

Her words carried a tone of authority that surprised even her, drawing the attention of every onlooker. A ripple of astonished chatter coursed through the crowd. She suspected that may happen the moment she spoke his old name. If his weapon hadn't been a dead giveaway before, not many could deny the deceased privateer was back from the dead.

Even his opponent gave pause, his eyes now reflecting his uncertainty. The Emerald Blade had never lost a fight.

Eyro turned his head just enough to look at her and nod, his eyes burning with a fighter's spirit despite his fatigue. "Aye, Captain. As you command."

All these years, Kortiama had believed the Emerald Blade was dead. She blamed herself for that. Her foolishness had led to his demise, just like the others. But here he was—had always been. Her beloved gardener; the man who loved tea far too much and taught her how to properly wield a blade.

He'd never left. He'd stood by her side, guiding her in so many ways. And now, she repaid that by believing he'd defend her honor.

Rikton's face pulled into a haughty sneer as he looked her way.

"Aw, the sea-legless little girl playin' capt'n finally decided to show up. You're too late, girlie." His eyes focused on his lackey. "He ain't no fabled Emerald Blade. Just an' old man. Kill 'im quick-like, I ain't got all day."

Kortiama's hands balled into tight fists, her shoulders squaring. She wouldn't allow her uncle to intimidate her in any way.

Eyro's stance changed—not a lot to the untrained eye, but Kortiama knew him—knew how he fought. He was going in for the kill. Rikton's champion came in for another swing, and Eyro ducked and rolled out of the way, using the momentum to propel him forward and take two quick strikes at his opponent. Blood spattered across the ship's deck, yet the two attacks seemed to do nothing to the hulking man as he raged and took another swing for Eyro.

Her champion ducked, though narrowly dodged, his balance thrown off. A knot formed in Kortiama's stomach. This was too stressful for her liking. As much as she trusted in the skill of the legendary Emerald Blade, she'd never actually seen him fight. He was said to be undefeated until the day at the villa, but what kind of opponents had he faced in his time? Could he kill a mountain? Or would a mountain crush a gemmed blade? *Oh great, I'm talking like him now.*

Rikton's champion landed a heavy blow on Eyro. Kortiama's hand flew up to her mouth as he went flying across the deck. All manner of reactions came from the crowd—some excited, some surprised or worried.

Rikton's lips spread into a sick, toothy grin. "Finish 'im. Teach this *Emerald Blade* he should have just stayed dead, where he belonged."

A deep, guttural chuckle came from his hulking champion and lifted his sword to swing down a deadly strike.

No… No… No! This couldn't happen to him. "Emerald Blade—"

"Don't worry, Captain." Eyro drew to his feet even as his opponent swung, his posture strong, showing his sureness. "I promised I'd defend your honor. And I intend to keep that promise."

He took a breath and then his whole body went still, his eyes closing. Kortiama's heart raced. What was he doing? How would what he was doing win her this duel—the very duel that would decide her fate as leader of the Dasati clan?

Eyro exhaled, and then in nary a blink, he disappeared. A ripple of unfamiliar energy whisked past Kortiama, though she was too focused to register what it could have been. Rikton's champion's blade slammed into the wooden deck, the force so great it cracked and splintered the wood. Then suddenly, Eyro reappeared behind the man, his sword extended as if he'd struck. Kortiama watched crimson liquid drip from his blade. *What did he just do?*

Her champion dragged the blade over his poised leg, wiping the blood from it, and then sheathed his weapon. Rikton's champion collapsed on the ground, his body separating into two parts where the blade had cleaved him through. Blood and viscera covered the deck, the pungent odor of bile filling the air.

Everything went still. Not a sound could be heard, save for the waves lapping against the boats. *Is it… over?* Numbness fell over Kortiama as she tried to process what had just happened.

Eyro let out a heavy breath. "The Lord Captain's honor remains. Her birthright claim is held."

A deafening uproar enveloped the ship. Some cheers, some not so much. Yet Kortiama couldn't care less. She rushed over to Eyro just as he collapsed to one knee. She placed a soft hand on his shoulder and bent down. "Are you alright?"

He chuckled. "I may be old, but I'm still a warrior, my dear Korti. Don't you worry about me now. Address the clan and take your title with honor."

She nodded. "You have some explaining to do after, though."

Eyro snickered and gave a curt nod in response.

Kortiama took a deep, calming breath, then stood up straight and rested her hand on the hilt of her rapier. "Clans of the Saricordi. I am Kortiama Ozden. Daughter of Eboneye Ozden and Liadha Rowan. Just before his—"

"Ye really think anyone believes yer the daughter o' my brother, girlie?" Rikton chuckled and then spit on the deck. "A scrawny, unproven brat like yerself?"

"Captain Liadha uttered it from her own lips." A devilish smirk spread across Kortiama's mouth. "But, if you'd like to challenge her claim, Rikton, I'm sure I could find her."

"No need," came a familiar voice from the crowd. Onlookers practically jumped out of the way of Liadha as she approached the inner circle. Her sable eyes dead set on Rikton, the promise of death for his insolence clear for anyone to see. "And here I thought you didn't have any balls, Rikton. Must have swiped them from the filth you scatter around under the docks, to even think of challenging me."

The darkness in her eyes deepened, and Kortiama swore she caught traces of arcane forming on the witch's fingers. "But if you really wish to repeat that challenge and test yourself again me, I won't stop you. I'd be more than happy to wipe the seas clean of your pitiful existence."

Rikton blanched, his throat bobbing several times as he fought his fear of the dreaded woman.

Murmurs flowed through the onlooking crowd. Some were just as fearful as Rikton, while others were excited to watch the captain be put in his place.

"Eboneye placed the Mandate on me before he died," Kortiama continued, drawing attention back to her. She needed to ensure she wouldn't be ignored. "He named Tharne as acting captain until I came of age. That day is here, even after a combat trial."

"One ye didn't win yerself." Rikton's eyes snapped to her, his lip curling into a sneer. "Why would anyone follow an unproven li'l girl who needed another to fight in her stead?" His eyes flicked to Eyro, who now struggled to his feet. "A gardener, who claims to be a man said to have perished several years ago. Ye expect me—"

"You expect me to believe your claim would have been any more valid, had your champion won?" Kortiama held her head high. She wouldn't allow her uncle to undermine her.

Murmurs picked up in the crowd, and she continued. "You didn't even have the backbone to fight my champion yourself. I would have, had I not been inconveniently delayed. But you"—she snorted—"you stood here like a coward, instead of facing the Emerald Blade yourself."

More murmuring around her. Some agreed with her, while others argued about Kortiama's claim of Rikton's cowardice.

Kortiama placed a hand on Eyro's shoulder. "The Emerald Blade never died. He merely offered his alliance and guidance, choosing to go with a false death story of his own fruition."

She really hoped that was true, or at least close enough to it that the truth wouldn't come back to bite her. Making this up as she went wasn't easy for her. Staying strong and confident under the dark gaze of her uncle was tough as it was.

"What Captain Kortiama claims is true." Eyes fell behind her to the new voice calling out. Kortiama turned to see Tharne forcing his way through the cluster of people. *Uncle Tharne… When had he gotten here? Had he been here the whole time and decided to watch? Was this a plan between him and Eyro?*

Tharne glanced Liadha's way for only a brief moment. "Not that Liadha hasn't already confirmed as much. Kortiama is Eboneye's blood daughter, and rightful Captain of the Dasati." His eyes leveled with Rikton, a deadly glint in his eye. "Any disloyalty to our lady captain will be met with swift justice."

An eruption of supportive cheers took Kortiama by surprise, though she did her best to mask it. She did not expect that kind of reaction. Rikton had one thing right, Eyro fighting in her stead did not do well to strengthen her claim. She would always have Tharne's support, and Liadha's, which subsequently meant the whole Ramulos clan, but that wouldn't be enough to keep the Dasatis in order.

Her eyes scanned the onlookers to take in who else supported her, finding most were well-known supporters of Tharne. Whether they merely offered their support to her because of him, or because they truly backed her, it didn't matter. She'd prove herself to them, and in turn, they'd help her keep order among her people.

Rikton looked about, taking in her supporters. From the disgusted look on his face, he did not expect this reaction, either. He ground his teeth and spat on the ground, spinning on his heels. "She ain't no capt'n o' mine."

Her brooding uncle stalked away. He wasn't the only one, though. More captains, those known to be loyal to Rikton, followed suit. From a quick count, Kortiama calculated half the ship captains were with him. This was going to make her life that much harder.

Tharne took a step forward to reprimand the retreating captains, but Kortiama stopped him with a firm hand. He glanced at her, his brow cocked, and she held up her other hand, finger extended, in response. Muttering the same incantation she had to puncture the tower door, and summoning the energy to do so, a single bolt of arcane leapt from her finger and slammed into the back of Rikton's head.

The older man stumbled, but didn't fall. His hat flew off in a way-ward direction. He snarled and snapped his gaze back at Kortiama. Before he could bite out a retort, she beat him to it. "A warning, Rikton. I'm not some harmless little girl. You cross me, and you will regret it." She gave pointed looks to the other insubordinate captains. "That goes for all of you."

Her uncle watched her for a moment, and Kortiama swore she caught a flash of respect cross the man's eyes. "Be careful who ye trust, lassie." He retrieved his hat, then nodded toward Liadha. "I'd wager ye haven't been told half o' the truth by that one."

Rikton placed his hat back on his head, then spun on his heel and stormed off. Kortiama's brow furrowed. What had he meant by that? She snuck a quick look at her mother, but Liadha's dark eyes were fixed on Rikton, her expression stone cold. Korti felt a brief shiver run up her spine, but then she shook the question away. More than likely, he was trying to get under her skin.

Liadha joined her side, placing a hand on her head. "Not bad for a beginner. Your execution could use some work, but nothing that can't be easily fixed."

Kortiama smiled. The praise was much appreciated in such a tense moment.

The witch's eyes leveled with Tharne. "You're late."

Her uncle let out a deep sigh and shook his head. "Yes. I was waylaid by Isandor ships."

"Well, isn't that convenient." No one could miss the dark tone on Liadha's words. Kortiama agreed with her. Isandor caused problems with their ships every now and then, but the timing was too good.

Tharne placed both hands on Kortiama's shoulders. "I'm sorry it happened. Are you okay?"

She opened her mouth to speak, but Eyro spoke quicker. "Oh sure, ask if she's okay when I'm the one who did all the fighting against that ugly brute." He grinned and waved Tharne off as the tall captain reached out to him. "No, I'm fine. Don't need any assistance at all."

Kortiama chuckled and rushed over to her precious gardener, offering her shoulder to lean on. "Thank you for standing in for me, Eyro. Though, I'm surprised it was you."

Tharne scratched the side of his head. "Aye. I had prepared to step in as your champion myself."

Kortiama placed a finger on the side of her cheek. "Well, I'd expected to see Solais. She's the one who locked me in the tower so she could fight on my behalf, after finding out about the challenge somehow."

Tharne's eyes widened. "She did what?"

Kortiama looked around, looking for Solais. *Where could she possibly be? There's no way she wouldn't have been able to get here on her own if she missed the boat leaving the village.*

Eyro chuckled. "Solais is crafty, but she hasn't mastered the ways of a fox yet."

Both Kortiama and Tharne looked at him, their brow furrowed.

Eyro smirked. "How do you think she found out about the Grand Choosing to begin with? Such information just doesn't lie about for anyone to see."

The creases in Kortiama's brow deepened. "You told her?"

"Told her? No." He laughed as he shook his head. "But I may have left a certain book lying about for her to find. And made sure she overheard Tharne and me discussing it one day prior to leaving a trail."

"But why?"

"To test what she would do." He nodded slowly, stroking his beard. "She did what I suspected, and thus I was forced to step in before she got herself killed." He shook his head again and murmured to himself, "The reckless girl."

Is that why I can't find her? Korti frowned, her hands going to her waist. "What did you do with her, Eyro?"

"Knocked her unconscious and locked her in the broom closet!"

Kortiama almost fell over. He looked so damned proud of himself about that fact, too.

Tharne shook his head. "Well, that solves that part of the mystery. But, if Eyro didn't let you out, Korti, how did you escape the tower? Knowing Solais, she was sure to make that difficult on you."

Kortiama scratched the side of her face and managed a weak smile. "Yeah, about that. Um… we need a new door to the tower. I may have… blown it apart?"

Her uncle stared at her with a blank face for a moment, then hid his face in his hand and let out a deep sigh. "Of course…"

Liadha stifled an amused chuckle while Eyro grinned widely. "That's our Korti."

Kortiama's attention waned when she heard the voice of her sister, pushing her way through people. Everyone turned just as Solais burst through into the circle. She looked around, eyes wide. "Where is Korti?"

Her eyes fell on her younger sister. "You're alive!"

Solais rushed to Kortiama and wrapped her up in a tight, back-crushing hug. The uncharacteristic behavior took Kortiama by surprise. It didn't take long for her older sister to snap back to her senses and let go. "I'm, uh, glad you're okay, Korti.

She spotted Rikton's dead champion over Kortiama's shoulder and then whined. "Aw man. I missed seeing him get run through? Who did it?"

Kortiama snickered. "The same person who locked you in the closet."

Her sister's eyes fell on Eyro. "You?"

The old gardener smiled. "Me."

Solais crossed her arms and huffed, muttering mostly to herself, "I wanted to be the one to stick it to Rikton. Why'd you have to steal all the fun?"

This got most of the people laughing, including those hanging around and listening in.

Tharne shook his head. "We should get back to the village. With so many captains siding with Rikton, there's much to discuss."

Kortiama patted Eyro's shoulder. "And we can get you some healing and tea for a job well done."

Eyro hummed, his eyes squinting. "Tea sounds heavenly."

"And you owe me some explanations."

"Ah, yes. And you shall have them." He gestured to the quarter deck. "But first we must get home to do so, don't we, Captain?"

Warm excitement bubbled up through Kortiama. This was her big moment. Everything she'd trained for—everything she'd dreamed of since she was a child. It was now here. "Helmsman!"

A scraggly fellow with a gnarly bearded peered over the quarter deck railing. "Aye, Capt'n?"

At least he was showing her some respect. Only time would tell if it stuck as she fought to prove herself rightful leader of her people. "Unfurl the sails and hoist the anchor. We're setting sail."

A toothy grin spread over his weathered face. "Where to?"

"The best place for us to revel in drink after a night like tonight."

The deck erupted with cheers and the helmsman nodded. "Aye, Capt'n."

Kortiama hoped he understood that meant home. But if not, she'd roll with the fallout of her vague order.

Liadha left the Dark Rider in the hand of her first mate, opting to stay with Kortiama, and Eyro refused to go rest in the captain's quarters, claiming he wanted fresh air. Kortiama chose not to fight his stubbornness and worked with Tharne and Solais to assist the rest of the crew.

While she'd managed to hold onto her birthright this day, Kortiama knew she had a long road ahead of her. Rikton and his followers were going to buck her at every turn. The next few years would not be easy, but she'd prove to them in any way she could that she was fit to be Lord Captain of the Dasati.

Price of Honor

F.P. Spirit

When You Least Expect It
Chapter 1

The wave crashed over Seishin's head before he could catch his breath. His lungs burned; his body ached to draw in air. Yet if he did, it would not be the life-giving ether that filled his lungs.

Spots appeared before his eyes. He began to feel light-headed. Let go, Seishin, a small voice sounded inside his head. Let go. It will be easier that way.

Seishin nearly listened to the voice, but something inside him railed against it. No. I will not. Not when so many are depending on me.

He screwed his mouth shut even tighter, but the urge to breathe continued to grow. Just when he thought his lungs would burst, the water around him finally subsided.

The young Shin Tauri was at the beach, or perhaps more accurately, in it. Sand covered him all the way up to his neck. The late morning sun beat down on his matted mop of thick black hair. The sounds of the sea permeated the background.

"That's what ya get for tryin' to woo one of our own!" The ugly mug of a hulking pirate stared down at him.

A second large raider smacked the first on the arm. "Now don't go pickin' on him, Narl. He did it all for love!"

Both men chortled with glee at his expense. Still, they were not wrong.

Seishin had been an idiot. He had let his feelings get in the way of the most important task of his entire life. As the next wave came crashing over his head, he remembered where it all went wrong.

Seishin sat in the midst of a dingy tavern, the smoke-filled air reeking of rum and ale. Dim light filtered down from overhead fixtures and sconces that lined the wood-framed walls. The dozen or so tables scattered around the place sat empty as the tavern's seedier denizens engaged in a typical drunken brawl.

"Tell me you don't you miss this life?"

A lean young man sat across from him, an ironic smile on his boyish face. He wore the brown and scarlet tunic of an Isandor soldier. Tobin had been Seishin's best friend during his time in the army. They had been inseparable until Seishin's abrupt discharge two months ago.

Seishin shrugged. "I do miss some things. This is not one of—" He abruptly ducked as something flew over his head. A glass smashed into the wall behind him.

"Now this is getting out of hand." Tobin rose from his seat and pulled a short wooden rod from his belt. The corner of his mouth lifted as he gazed at Seishin. "Want to lend a hand for old time's sake?"

Seishin stood and pulled a similar rod from his belt. Without another word, the two of them waded into the fray.

Seishin wedged himself between a pair of combatants, catching one in the knee with his foot, while slamming the butt of his rod into the other's face. A swift elbow to the chin finished the first man. Both fell to the floor, out cold.

Tobin grinned. "I see you haven't lost your touch."

Seishin shrugged once more. "Guess it's in my blood."

Seishin stemmed from an ancient clan known as the Kazari. They had been Isandor's finest Shin Tauri warriors before a tragedy in the nation's capital a couple of months ago. What followed included the discharge of every Kazari from the army.

Tobin appraised the fighting around them. "It's getting worse. We'd better split up if we're going to stop this."

The two men exchanged a nod, then went in opposite directions.

Seishin swept through the crowd, disabling one rowdy brawler after another. It was exhilarating. He hadn't felt this alive since the loss of his commission.

Seishin had trained his entire life to be a Shin Tauri warrior. He had felt lost after his discharge, but a few weeks ago he was given a new purpose. The Queen herself had tasked him with finding his missing uncle, Draigo. The former head of the army, Draigo might be the only one who could set things right in Isandor.

As Seishin broke through the crowd, all other thoughts were driven from his mind. A striking young woman with long raven hair stood alone at the bar. Garbed in black with a frilly white shirt, she casually twirled a thin pointed blade in the one hand, while dangling a bottle of rum in the other.

A rough-dressed sailor nearly twice her size leered at the young woman menacingly from a few feet away. The muscles in his arms bulged as he brandished a long, jagged-edged sailing knife.

The woman did not appear the least intimidated. A mischievous grin adorned her lightly tanned face as she carefully circled around her opponent. She moved with an almost cat-like grace—not a stride too long, and not a drop spilled from her bottle. She finally stopped and casually taunted the hulking sailor. "So, are you all talk and no action?"

The big man moved with a speed that belied his size; Seishin found himself too far away when the sailor lunged for her. He started forward, but halted as the young woman elegantly side-stepped the brute.

She could have easily run him through, but instead chose to slam the butt of her sword into the back of his neck. The big man fell head-first into the bar as the young woman danced away with a quick swig of rum.

A bell-like laugh escaped her lips. "Ha! You'll have to do better than that."

Two sailors near Seishin stopped their fighting and glared at the woman.

"She can't do that to one of us!"

"Let's get 'er!"

Seishin intercepted the duo before they had taken a couple of steps. He caught the first in the gut with his club, doubling him over. He then used the man's back to vault over to his companion. Seishin landed a flying kick directly into the second man's torso. The sailor went flying into a nearby table, not to get up again. Seishin then finished off the first sailor with a quick chop to the back of his neck.

The young woman eyed him with a strange expression, then gave him a quick smile. Despite the frantic situation, Seishin found himself smiling back.

"Slippery one, ain't ya?" Over at the bar, the huge sailor had recovered. He rubbed the back of his neck with a large-hammed hand. "Jus' ya wait 'til I get me hands on ya—"

He lunged at the woman with surprising speed, but again she proved too fast for him. The brute went flying into the crowd, taking down at least five other brawlers with him. Everyone nearby stopped fighting at that point, their attention riveted on the battle at the bar.

If this keeps up, they'll do my job for me, Seishin thought with wry amusement. Deciding to see how things played out, he placed himself in a strategic position to keep any others from intervening.

The big man slowly rose to his feet, shoving a few onlookers out of the way. His balance seemed slightly off as he turned and growled at the waiting woman.

An impish smile decorated her perfectly round face. "Is that all you've got, you bilge rat?"

The brute's face turned bright red as he lunged at her yet again. This time he was not even close. She agilely twirled out of the way as he slammed into the bar.

Crack!

He hit the bar with such force that the wood split all the way down to its base. The huge man groaned, then slumped to the floor, unmoving.

The feisty young woman laughed again, then took another swig from her bottle. She lowered it, her deep brown eyes fixing on Seishin. A warm smile crossed her lips as she sheathed her blade. "Thanks for the assist."

Seishin swept his eyes around the tavern. The brawl had come to an end, so he shrugged and joined the woman at the bar. "You're welcome."

The corner of her mouth quirked upward as she smoothed out her shirt and pants. "That move you used was quite spectacular. Tell me, where did you learn it?"

A slight blush rose to Seishin's cheeks. "Oh, that was just a little something my uncle taught me."

The woman leaned back against the bar and tapped her chin with a slender pair of fingers. "Your uncle, huh? He must be an amazing warrior. Shin Tauri, I assume?"

Seishin gave her a quick nod. "It runs in the family."

She twirled a strand of long raven hair as she gazed at him. "Well, you're not so bad yourself. You seem quite adept with that little rod of yours…" She trailed off with a lilting laugh.

Seishin didn't know quite how to respond to that. Thankfully, he was saved from having to by Tobin.

"Alright, alright, show's over folks!" His lean friend stepped in and shooed away any remaining spectators. At the same time, the town guardsmen dragged away the downed sailors.

Tobin glanced from Seishin to the swordswoman and then back again. "We'll take care of the rest. Why don't you escort your new 'friend' out of here?" He leaned in and whispered in Seishin's ear, "You two make a cute couple."

Tobin gave him a sly wink before leaving to help the remaining town guards. Seishin shifted his weight uncomfortably as he returned his gaze to the intriguing young woman.

She was impressive, yet there was more to her than her good looks and dry wit. He could sense a power within her. She did a marvelous job of masking it, but Seishin had noticed it flare up during her battle with the large sailor.

The woman took another sip from her bottle, then she, too, gave him a sly wink. "Well, since we're 'friends' now, I'll let you escort me out of here." She stood and laced her arms through his.

This time, Seishin's cheeks burned with embarrassment. He waited as she took another sip from her bottle. She tilted her head, a dazzling smile lighting her entire face. "Lead the way, escort."

That look practically melted Seishin's insides. He didn't trust himself to speak again until they made it outside. The tangy smell of salt water filled the cool night air. Seishin took a deep breath to calm himself, then asked a careful question. "Um… if you don't mind… ma'am… what led to the drawing of blades?"

The young woman pushed him away, her jaw set and her hands on her hips. What little remained of her rum jostled around in the bottle. "Do I look like a ma'am to you?"

Seishin was caught off guard by her abrupt change in temperament. He sputtered until her expression relaxed, replaced with a mischievous grin. "It's Korti—and you can have all your questions answered while you escort me home."

Before Seishin could utter another word, Korti laced her arm through his again and dragged him down the street. "You know, you're really not good at this whole escort thing, but that's okay"— she winked at him again— "I'll show you the ropes."

Seishin didn't know what to make of this vibrant young woman. As quick to anger as she was to laughter, she posed an intriguing mystery to him. He listened with rapt attention as she retold the story of what started the barfight.

"That huge lug thought his size entitled him to anything he wanted, including my posterior." She laughed gaily as she slapped herself on the rump.

Seishin's eyes followed her motion, but immediately shifted away, his cheeks turning warm again.

Korti must have noticed his discomfort. An impish smile played across her lips. "Why, Mr. Shin Tauri, I do believe I've embarrassed you."

Seishin felt himself flush even further. He dropped his gaze and replied in a soft voice, "It's Seishin—my name is Seishin."

"Say—shin." Korti rolled the name around on her tongue. After a moment she gave him a firm nod. "I like it."

Seishin gazed up in time to catch her sizing him up. She smiled again, but there was a strange intensity in her eyes. She gently bit her lower lip, then peered away and returned to her story.

"Anyway, I told the big oaf he had two seconds to remove his hand from my backside or I would cut it off. When he didn't, I threw my drink in his face."

A thin smile crossed Seishin's lips. "I guess that didn't deter him."

Korti shook her head. "No, not at all. He tried to grab me, so I hit him on the head with the empty glass. It didn't seem to faze him much, but it gave me time to put some distance between us—and liberate the bottle of course."

Seishin's brow creased. "The bottle of rum?"

Korti cocked her head to one side. "Well you didn't expect me to waste it now, did you?"

Seishin shook his head. This Korti had an interesting set of priorities.

"Anyway, the big oaf pulled out a knife, so I drew my blade. You saw the rest from there…"

Seishin nodded thoughtfully. The way she handled herself during that battle spoke volumes to her proficiency with a blade. He also found it quite interesting that she fought without drawing any blood. "You could have easily run him through at least three times by my count."

Korti's face darkened. "Trust me, I was sorely tempted. You have no idea how difficult it is to be a woman sailor. Half the men I sail with don't take me seriously."

Seishin felt a keen sense of sympathy for her plight. "I think I understand. Because of my family name, no one took me seriously at first, either. I was constantly challenged, having to prove my skill at every turn."

Korti eyed him for a moment, but then her expression relaxed. "Maybe you do, at that." She lowered her eyes. "Still, my mentor would have my head if I used my blade so callously."

"I think our mentors are very similar," Seishin noted wryly. He cleared his throat and recited in a stiff tone, "The Shin Tauri code demands that blood only be drawn in defense of king, country, or matters of life and death."

Korti let out a long whistle. "And you live by that standard?"

Seishin sighed. "I try to, but the truth is, it's not an easy code to live by. I've found myself tempted as well, especially with the politics in Isandor as of late."

A frown crossed Korti's brow as she continued to hold his gaze. "So, does this mean you don't think any less of me?"

She appeared to be hanging on his approval. Seishin couldn't fathom why his opinion mattered to her at all. Still, her apparent need for his support engendered a feeling of closeness within him. "Not in the slightest. I think it's remarkable that you showed so much restraint."

Korti's face lit up with that same dazzling smile. She laced her arm through his again and snuggled her head against his shoulder.

A warm glow surged throughout Seishin's body. He felt elated. They walked on like that in silence until Korti turned them down a side street.

"So then, Seishin, you mentioned something about politics. Is that why you're here in this backwater part of Isandor?"

Seishin winced at the sudden question. He had been so content just moments ago. Now all his inner turmoil came rushing back to the surface.

Korti read the expression on his face perfectly. "It is, isn't it? This has to do with the fall of the Kazari."

Seishin let out a deep sigh. "It's a long story…"

Korti tilted her head to one side, her lips spreading into a winsome smile. "I've got time."

Seishin's heart thumped in his chest. There was just no denying this woman when she looked at him like that. Knowing he had already lost the battle, he proceeded to tell her his tale.

"You're right. The Kazari have fallen out of favor thanks to the schemes of the priesthood. They've been trying to take over the country ever since the King was assassinated. That's why the Queen created a council in the first place—not only to help run things, but also to keep the priesthood in check."

Korti's face took on a faraway expression. "Hmm, it definitely sounds like there's dissension in the ranks."

Seishin eyed her with curiosity. "That sounds like the voice of experience."

Korti swung her gaze back to him, a thin smile on her lips. "You could say that. Not everyone gets along—aboard ship."

Seishin felt there was more behind her words than she let on. Still, she seemed reluctant to talk about it, so he decided to go on with his tale. "Anyway, a couple of months ago, a member of the Isandor council was assassinated. They blamed my father for the death."

Korti's eyes narrowed. "Let me guess—your father is a high-ranking Kazari official."

"Another council member, and the head of our clan." Seishin nodded, again impressed with her keen mind. "Not only did they throw him in prison, but they used it as an excuse to kick every Kazari out of the military." Seishin's gut wrenched as he said those words. He knew he sounded bitter, but his wounds were still fresh from being discharged from the service.

Thankfully, Korti didn't seem to mind. She squeezed his arm and gave him a knowing look. "Politics at its finest. Trust me, Seishin, I more than understand."

Somehow her words made him feel better. He gave her a small smile. She returned the expression, biting her lower lip once more. The heat rose to Seishin's cheeks as they continued to stare at each other. Korti flushed as well, then broke off her gaze. "So, your father's in prison and you're all the way out here in Islen."

The corner of Seishin's mouth lifted slightly. There was no getting anything past her. Still, this part was a sensitive subject, so he kept his response necessarily vague. "I'm looking for my uncle."

Korti gave him a curt nod as they turned another corner. "I see. You think he can help with your father's current situation."

"I hope so," Seishin answered with a short sigh. "He had a lot of influence in the capital before he left."

Korti arched a single eyebrow. "It sounds like you have a lot of faith in him."

"I do," Seishin admitted with a wan smile. "He taught me more than just the blade. Everything I know about truth, honor, and the way of the Shin Tauri, I owe to him."

"Those are rare commodities these days," Korti murmured. Her mood grew pensive. She let go of his arm and folded her own across her chest.

Seishin cast a puzzled stare at the distant young woman. "Did I say something wrong?"

She slowly spun her gaze around. "What? No." She shook her head and smiled. "I'm envious is all. He sounds like quite the mentor."

A sheepish smile spread across his face as he grasped the back of his neck. "He would always tell me, 'Being a Shin Tauri is about more than just using your body. It's what is in your mind and heart that counts.'" He intoned the last in a perfect imitation of his uncle's deep, rumbling voice.

Korti cocked her head to one side, her eyes widening ever so slightly. "That's funny. Our gardener would say almost the same exact thing—except about swordplay in general, of course."

Seishin chuckled at the thought of a gardener giving advice on the use of the sword. The corner of his mouth quirked upward. "Well then, your gardener is very wise."

Korti seemed to be half-listening, her attention far away once more.

Seishin cleared his throat. "So, Korti, what's your story? Sailing run in the family?"

She started as if being woken from a dream, then peered at him and laughed. "Oh, you could say that. It goes back quite a few generations, in fact. My father was a sailor, as was his father, and his father's father before him. In fact, both my uncles are sailors."

"Your father is deceased?" Seishin asked softly.

A rueful smile adorned Korti's face. "It happened before I was born, so I never actually met him"—her expression turned wistful—"but he loved the sea as much as I do. The salt air, the wind in your face, the freedom to go wherever you want—that's what sailing is truly about."

The passion with which she described the sea took his breath away. "I've never heard anyone explain it quite like that. It sounds wonderful."

Korti grinned, her smile lighting up the night around them. "Oh, it is. There is nothing quite like the sea. She can be difficult at times, but her beauty is undeniable."

"I can see that," Seishin said, staring directly into her bright dark eyes.

Korti stopped and held his stare, her hands going to her hips. "Can you now?"

"Most definitely," Seishin nodded, absolutely mesmerized by this vibrant young woman.

They held each other's gaze until the side of Korti's mouth twisted upward. "Well now, didn't you turn out to be the charmer."

She laced her arm back through his and leaned in close as she led him around another corner. They walked quietly arm-in-arm for the next few blocks, until Korti drew to a sudden halt. She had stopped in front of a large dwelling with a wide porch. A sign over the entrance read the Inn of the Swan.

Korti let go of his arm and gazed up at him. "Well, Seishin, this is where I'm staying."

She moved in closer and placed her hands on his chest. "You know, you didn't turn out to be such a bad escort after all."

A warm feeling rose in Seishin's chest. Something had passed between them this night, an implicit understanding of one another. Seishin found it both comforting and enticing.

Korti's eyes glinted as she reached up and pulled his head down toward hers. Their lips met. It was soft and warm, and sent sparks throughout his entire being.

A long kiss ensued, ending when she pulled back and gazed up into his eyes. "Mmm, that was nice. We should do this more."

She pulled him down again and their lips intertwined.

Captive Heart
Chapter 2

Seishin spent much of the next few weeks in Islen with Korti. She was bold and carefree, the complete opposite of how he had been raised. He had never felt quite so alive as when he was with her. Yet her past remained a mystery. She would only say she had grown tired of sailing and intended to stay on dry land for a while.

Seishin hadn't completely forgotten about his mission. However, finding information on his missing uncle proved difficult. It had been nearly ten years since Draigo had left the capital in search of the King's assassins. Seishin's only lead was that he had headed for the Pirate Coast.

A thousand-mile stretch of land just north of Isandor, the Pirate Coast was the home of the thirteen clans of the pirate nation. Without some clue as to Draigo's specific destination, seeking him out would be like looking for a needle in a haystack. After three weeks, they finally found a veteran who had seen Draigo. He remembered the ex-general passing through Islen on his way north, toward the small port of Korsol.

When Seishin told Korti he had to leave, she insisted on coming with him. "It's not like I'm doing anything around here. Plus, it sounds like it might be fun."

Unfortunately, it turned out to be anything but fun. When they arrived at Korsol, they found it under attack. Screams and shouts echoed across the small town from the direction of the docks. As they drew closer, they could hear the ring of steel on steel.

The village had one long pier. A battle raged up and down its length, between a platoon of Isandor soldiers and a band of rough-looking pirates. A tall vessel stood at the other end of the dock—a three-masted galleon, its long hull sitting low in the water. Numerous gun ports lined its length. He could just make out the ominous name that decorated its bow from here—Midnight Manta.

Korti rushed into the fray before he could stop her. "I've got to end this before someone gets hurt!"

Seishin took off after her, drawing his blades as he went. Still a few strides behind Korti, all he could do was watch as she barreled into the frantic melee.

Without warning, Korti leapt the last few feet and brought the butt of her sword down on the back of a soldier's neck. The unsuspecting man slumped to the dock, out cold.

Seishin froze in place, not believing what he had just seen. The soldier's opponent seemed equally confused. Yet as his gaze fixed on Korti, the color drained from his face.

"Leave this town alone!" Korti growled in a fierce voice.

"Y-yes, ma'am!" the pirate stuttered. He backed away two steps, then spun on his heel and bolted down the docks.

Seishin stared blankly after the pirate as he dashed toward the vessel at the end of the pier. When he returned his gaze to Korti, she was no longer there. Seishin swept his eyes around the dock. He finally spied her in the midst of it all, attacking both soldiers and pirates alike.

Still confused, Seishin launched himself into the fray to intercept her. A pirate got in his way, but he easily caught the man's blade with a counter-parry. He swept it out of the way and ran the pirate through with his other blade.

A second pirate blocked his path, but Seishin out-maneuvered him with a swift feint. He followed it with a parry and a backspin slice. The pirate went down.

A pair of combatants now stood in his path, but moments later the soldier fell. A slim figure stood over the man, a long-curved blade in either hand.

Seishin froze. Aside from the mane of light-brown hair that spilled over her bright red bandana, the slender pirate looked remarkably like Korti. She had a similar complexion, with deep brown eyes and even the same round-shaped face.

A thin smirk graced the raider's lips as she stared back at Seishin. He could feel power exuding from her as she stepped over the soldier's body. Without warning, she rushed him.

The young warrior immediately found himself hard pressed. The raider's twin blades flickered almost faster than the eye could see. It took every ounce of his skill to hold her back, her swords slashing from angles he didn't think humanly possible.

The style she used was not all that unfamiliar. It was almost as if she'd had Shin Tauri training, although some of her movements were quite unorthodox. Still, he adjusted his defense, and slowly, but inexorably, fought her to a standstill. Seishin then launched an offensive of his own.

Four blades flashed back and forth in intricate patterns as each struggled to gain the advantage. Slash, parry, feint, counter—she matched him move for move. It took all of his concentration to keep up with this incredible swordswoman.

Doubts began to creep into his mind on whether he could win this battle. Sweat poured down his brow, threatening to impede his vision. If that happened, he'd be dead for sure.

"Stop!"

The loud scream reverberated across the docks. All at once, the fighting up and down the pier came to a halt. Even his fierce opponent pulled back in mid-strike. All eyes turned toward the source of that cry.

Korti stood on the other side of the battle, her gaze firmly fixed on Seishin. Their eyes met for a moment, and he thought he detected a glimmer of regret in them. Abruptly, her countenance hardened.

"Dasati, fall back!" she cried in a tone that brooked no quarter.

Seishin watched in awe as every pirate along the dock unquestioningly obeyed her command. As one, they disengaged from the battle and made for the end of the wharf.

Seishin's opponent obeyed her as well, but not before taking one last swipe at him. It was a quick flick of the blade, which he easily knocked away.

"It's been fun! Kill you later," the swordswoman called over her shoulder as she, too, retreated down the dock.

The soldiers gave chase, but Seishin stayed rooted to the spot. *Korti's a pirate.* He had wondered about her mysterious past, but nothing about her fit the stereotypical pirate mold. She certainly wasn't bloodthirsty. Still, all the pirates had listened to her without question, which meant she wasn't just any pirate.

She's a pirate captain! The realization felt like ice cold water being splashed in his face.

Down the dock, the pirate vessel suddenly let loose a volley. Seishin watched in horror as the troops scattered, but when the shell struck, it merely exploded into a cloud of thick fog.

The incident shattered Seishin's paralysis. *Korti's not a killer.*

Despite being a pirate leader, she had shown mercy at every turn. It proved to him that deep down inside, she was still the same woman he had met back in Islen—the woman he had come to care for these last few weeks.

The realization spurred him into action. There was a skiff tied to the dock just below. If he hurried, he could make it before the fog rolled past him. In three great strides, he reached the edge of the dock and launched himself into the small boat.

A quick flick of his blade sliced the line. He grabbed the oars just as the thick white cloud blanketed over him. Seishin rowed as hard as he could, but the unnaturally dense fog forced him to struggle with each stroke. He silently prayed he was going in the right direction.

After a few tense minutes, he passed out of the thick bank of fog. The tall hull of a retreating vessel rose out of the thinning mists before him.

A slight breeze blew across the bay. Seishin hoisted his small sail and the skiff took off across the water. Within minutes he had nearly caught up to the ship, but when he saw the name across the bow his blood ran cold. The words clearly read Blood Tears.

A chill ran up Seishin's spine. I've been chasing the wrong ship!

He frantically scanned the nearby waters. A vessel nearly the twin of this one sailed across the bay about five hundred yards to starboard. That has to be Korti's!

Seishin grabbed the lines and had just brought the skiff about when he heard a loud boom. The water around him exploded, upending his tiny boat and sending him flying head first into the murky depths.

Seishin should have been dead twice over by his count. The cannon fire didn't kill him. Instead, he had been fished out of the water by the crew of the Blood Tears. Amazingly, they also didn't kill him. They tied him up and brought him before their captain, a man named Rikton.

Garbed all in black, the tall pirate appeared quite intimidating. His scraggly hair and craggy features added to his harsh appearance. Yet, the amount of power the man radiated is what truly unnerved Seishin. It rivaled anyone he had ever met, with the possible exception of his uncle, Draigo.

Rikton seemed quite interested as to why Seishin chased them down on his own. It amused him further when Korti marched aboard and demanded Seishin be handed over to her. Rikton taunted her, guessing at the relationship between her and the 'Isandorian.'

Korti then surprised everyone by declaring that Seishin "be put to the slow death—a fitting lesson for any buffoon who chooses to chase after me." Her words cut Seishin like a knife.

Rikton remanded him into Korti's custody. They brought Seishin to the pirates' village and chained him to the wall of a dungeon cell. He had not seen Korti since.

"Seishin, you're a fool!"

A tiny amount of light filtered in from one small window high above. A single torch anchored to the opposite wall barely augmented it. Korti stepped into the dim circle of light and leveled a glare at him that could have seared through armor. "What were you thinking, following me like that? Do you have any idea the position you've put me in?"

Korti's slim frame shook with anger. She crossed her arms and squeezed her eyes tight as she struggled with her emotions.

Seishin did not speak. Instead he watched silently as the woman he had come to care for, the same woman who had declared his death sentence, stood only a few feet away. Dark shadows played across her features in the flickering torchlight.

After a long silence, Korti drew herself up and threw back her shoulders. "I am Kortiama Ozden, daughter of Berngal Ozden—the man the world knew as the dread pirate Eboneye. I am, further, Lord Captain of the Dasati tribe of the Clans of the Coast."

The leader of a pirate clan? Eboneye's daughter? The blood in Seishin's veins turned to ice. The woman he knew simply as Korti was in reality the daughter of the most infamous pirate warlord in history.

Eboneye had united the thirteen clans. He led them on a path of destruction along the coast and across the sea. Had he not met an untimely death, there is no telling how much devastation he would have wreaked on the world of Arinthar.

Not trusting himself to speak, Seishin grappled in silence with his emotions. Until this moment, he still believed the Korti he knew existed somewhere inside this woman. Now he realized it was all a lie.

His lack of response seemed to add to Korti's anger. She began to pace back and forth, her hands waving around wildly as she spoke.

"I am responsible for my entire clan—nearly four-thousand of them. They look to me for leadership. As it stands, I can barely hold them together. They are fractured and at constant odds. On top of that, I am surrounded by sharks like Rikton just waiting to tear me down. My every move is watched—my every decision questioned."

Seishin half-heard her rant. *What have I done? My father, the Queen, they were all counting on me. How could I have screwed up so badly?*

Korti halted in front of him, her hands on her hips, her eyes burning into him. "A liaison with a Shin Tauri from Isandor would be the end of my rule. It would be the end of my people. If warmongers like Rikton were to seize control, they would be dragged into a war that would spill carnage up and down the coast. None would survive unscathed—not the Dasati, not the other clans, not Isandor."

Her words wrenched Seishin out of his self-loathing. *Is she serious? Is she really trying to prevent a war instead of starting one?*

Seishin stared into her eyes until the anger there dissipated. She looked away from him, her voice faltering. "I—I cannot do that to my people." She folded her arms across her chest and hung her head. She looked worn out.

Seishin began to have second thoughts. Perhaps it hadn't all been a lie. Maybe there was a trace of his Korti in this pirate captain after all. Seishin understood honor and responsibility only too well. It had been ingrained in him since he was a lad. This Kortiama had to do what was best for her people.

"I understand." He forced himself to say the words, though they left a bitter taste in his mouth.

Kortiama did not respond. Mixed emotions played across her face as if two facets warred with each other on the inside. Abruptly her countenance reddened, and she spun toward him. "Do you? Do you? You understand nothing!"

She grabbed the front of his tunic, her eyes burning with anger, her face mere inches away. Then, without so much as a word, she grasped the back of his neck and kissed him hard on the lips.

It was a passionate, desperate kiss that went on 'til they were almost breathless. Seishin lost himself in it—the taste of her lips, the smell of her skin, the heat that coursed through his entire body.

As quickly as it started, the kiss ended. Korti let go of his tunic and drew away, the flush of her face still evident.

The Lord Captain of the Dasati absently straightened her outfit, her eyes never leaving his. When she spoke, her voice was hollow, as if the life had been drained from her. "You are to be put to death in the morning—buried up to your neck in the sand and left to drown in the tide."

Seishin said nothing. He no longer blamed her. She was only doing what was best for her people. He only wished he had the chance to do the same for his.

Yet Korti could not quite abide his silence. Her cheeks turned flaming red as her frustration burst forth. "You brought this on yourself. I cannot stop it"—she caught herself, her voice dropping to a whisper—"even were it my heart's greatest desire."

An ironic smile spread across Seishin's face. Somewhere deep down inside, she did still care for him—not that it mattered. He would be put to death, his mission over. He would fail his family and his country. Still, it was his own fault. He pushed down his bubbling emotions and spoke three soft words.

"I forgive you."

Kortiama's eyes went wide. A sharp gasp escaped her lips. She stared at him for a long while, faint traces of moisture appearing in the corners of her eyes. When she spoke, her words were just above a whisper. "Oh, Seishin—if only I could forgive myself."

With that, the young Lady Captain of pirates whirled on her heel and fled through the cell door. It clanged firmly shut behind her, leaving him alone in that dim cell.

As promised, the next morning Seishin found himself buried up to his neck in sand. Low tide had passed, and now the waves inched their way up the beach toward him. Based on their progress, he would probably be dead in little more than an hour. He had tried to make peace with his fate, but couldn't quite come to terms with how miserably he had botched things.

Father, I'm sorry I failed you.

Kortiama stood a short distance off, her arms folded, and her gaze turned away. A tall, broad-shouldered man hovered beside her, garbed in a blue coat with gold buttons and trim. A sparse brown and grey beard decorated his well-weathered features. The man had a strong air about him, but Seishin noted a hint of sympathy in his keen brown eyes.

On the opposite side of Korti stood the swordswoman he had faced in Korsol—the one who bore a striking resemblance to her.

In stark contrast to the tall man, the swordswoman wore a hard demeanor, but it was not directed at Seishin. Instead, she stared with open hostility at the group across from his sandy tomb.

Captain Rikton waited there, flanked on either side by a hulking raider. A wide-brimmed hat shadowed his eyes, but did little to hide his craggy features. A wicked grin spread between his thin mustache and scraggly greyish-brown beard.

"Nothin' so fine as a drowned Shin Tauri first thing in the mornin'," Rikton chortled at the group across from him.

Kortiama chose not to respond, her frame remaining rigid. Yet her female companion was not so forgiving. "Shut your piehole, Rikton, before I come over there and shut it for you."

She took a step forward, her hands straying to her weapon hilts. Korti put out a staying hand, forcing her companion to halt her advance. Seishin could barely hear Korti's words over the sound of the crashing surf.

"Not here, Solais. Not now."

Solais shrugged, her lips curling to one side. "You're lucky, Rikton. Thanks to Kortiama, you get to live another day."

The wicked smile never left Rikton's lips. "The day we do cross blades, lassie, ye better hope yer swords are as sharp as yer tongue."

The tall man next to Korti had been silent up until now. He breathed a long sigh at Rikton. "Why must you constantly foster dissension between us, brother? Don't the Dasatis have enough problems as it is?"

Seishin raised an eyebrow. *The man next to Korti is Rikton's brother?*

Rikton glared at his brother and scowled. "Aye, Tharne, n' we wouldn't have under a strong hand."

Tharne merely shook his head, but Korti didn't let the slight go unchallenged. "You mean under your hand, Uncle."

Seishin nearly choked. *Rikton is Korti's uncle?*

A chuckle escaped Rikton's lips. "Aye, if it comes ta that."

Korti squared her shoulders as she held the older pirate's stare. "It won't, Uncle. I can promise you that."

Seishin's mind spun at the sudden revelation. Rikton and Tharne were both Korti's uncles. Yet where Tharne supported her, Rikton vehemently opposed her. And I thought my family had issues.

Rikton and Kortiama continued to stare each other down, the tension between them so thick it could be cut with a knife. Rikton finally broke the silence with a snarl. "What kind o' pirate uses smoke spells in their cannon?"

Kortiama rolled her eyes. "We're not pirates, Uncle—and it's called strategy. It's a better distraction."

Rikton spat on the ground in front of him. "Bah! Don't be lecturin' me, lass. I knows our history better than ye. Since the fall of the baleful moon, the Saricordi have had ta fend fer themselves. No one raised a hand ta help us—not even the high n' mighty Ralnai."

He flicked a hand under his bearded chin toward the heavens. "Only by the grace o' Zesstara and the power o' the mandates did we survive. Still, we was forced ta take tribute as we could, in blood n' coin if it came ta it."

Rikton drew his sword and spun the tip around in small circles. "So, we be called pirates and raiders, by the gen'teel folk o' the lands. We use fire in our cannon n' these ta make our point. We don't need no stinkin' distractions…"

Solais drew her own blades, but Kortiama stepped in front of her, again blocking her advance. The Lord Captain of the Dasati leveled an acid glare at her uncle. "They can call us what they want, but we're not barbarians—and my father used smoke in the taking of Penwick itself, if you recall."

The corner of Rikton's mouth twisted sideways. "I'll give ya this, ya got yer father's spirit, lass, if not his stomach. But don't ya be tellin' me about Penwick. I was there, n' sure Berngal used smoke, but he also burnt nearly half the city ta the ground."

A smug expression crossed Kortiama's face. "And what good did it do him? In the end he lost almost half our people, as well as his own life. The other clans will never follow us again."

Rikton scowled at her—she had obviously struck a nerve. "Aye, but at least they won't be laughin' at us."

Kortiama leveled a finger at him, her voice as hard as stone. "And your way, they don't respect us. The clan is flourishing, we've lost almost no one in these last few months, and our coffers are fuller than they have been in years. So what if we don't leave a trail of blood behind us in every raid?"

Rikton shook his head in disgust. "Bah! You'll ne'er be a true pirate captain."

He motioned toward Seishin with his sword. "Why don't ya just take yer Shin Tauri boy-toy here n' run off together. Leave the plunderin' n' pillagin' to real pirates."

Korti's cheeks flushed a brilliant red. "Neanderthal…" she spat under her breath. She shifted her gaze toward Seishin. Her eyes locked with his, the hardness draining from them.

Seishin saw everything in those eyes, from passion to regret to self-loathing. The myriad of emotions left him breathless. *If only we weren't from two different worlds.* Unfortunately, she was pirate royalty, and he would soon be dead. There was no use dwelling on what would never be.

Korti held his gaze for a moment more, then spun on her heel and stormed up the beach. Solais followed her, but Tharne lingered behind.

Rikton called after them. "Why rush off so quick, dear? Don't ya want to see him take his last breath?" A hollow laugh escaped his lips as he turned his attention to his brother. "Shouldn't ya be goin' and consolin' yer darlin' niece?"

Tharne leveled a hard glare at his brother. "Must you persist at this?" He waved a hand at Seishin. "Is that the work of someone who's weak?"

Rikton cast a glance at Seishin and chuckled. "I have ta admit, I didn't expect her ta go so far. Maybe she's got a bit of her old man in her after all."

He said it as if it were a blessing, but Seishin knew it to be a curse. The blood of Eboneye had caused her to turn on him. How long would it be before it led her people down the path of ruin?

Tharne edged closer to his brother. "She's stronger than you think." He lowered his voice. Seishin could barely hear him over the sound of the crashing surf. "Come with me now. Talk to her. If you still believe she's too weak to rule, then I'll tell what I know about the whereabouts of the mandate."

Rikton squinted at Tharne. "After all these years? What are you playin' at, brother?"

Tharne breathed a heavy sigh. "I'm just tired, brother—tired of all this infighting. The Dasati need unity."

"Aye, on that we agree." Rikton gave him a curt nod. He eyed Tharne for a few more moments, then swung his head toward Seishin. "What of this cur?"

Tharne waved a dismissive hand at Seishin. "Leave the boy to his fate."

Gee, thanks, Seishin thought. He had judged Tharne to be more of a gentleman than the rest. As it turned out, he was just another callous pirate.

Rikton appeared to be mulling over his brother's offer. He shifted his gaze between Seishin and Tharne a few times before addressing his men. "Ya two stay here. Make sure the job gets done right—even if ya have to help it along yerselves."

Rikton crossed a finger over his neck and flashed an evil grin at Seishin. He then took off up the beach with Tharne after Kortiama. His malicious laugh still rang through the air as he disappeared.

The two hulking pirates loomed over Seishin, but did not carry out Rikton's threat. Instead they enjoyed watching the tide come in and slowly cover his head.

Living Legend
Chapter 3

"Seishin. Seishin—wake up, boy."

Seishin's eyes slowly fluttered open. He lay on a soft surface, staring up into a clear blue sky. The sounds of the sea still surrounded him, as did the smell of salt air. His clothes felt wet, and he itched from sand in places he didn't want to think about. He tried to sit up, but began coughing as water spilled out of his mouth.

"Slowly," the cool voice chided.

Seishin bent forward and coughed out more water. In between fits, his gaze fell on two bodies down by the water's edge. Rikton's men! The two hulking pirates lay unmoving in the sand, from all appearances dead.

It abruptly dawned on Seishin that he should be as well. Yet somehow, he was still alive and no longer buried up to his neck in the sand.

Seishin spun around to see a lean, grey-robed man crouched next to him. A pair of steel-blue eyes watched him intently from beneath a mop of short, straight black hair. There was an intelligence behind those eyes that belied the man's youthful appearance.

"Do I…" Seishin tried to speak, but stopped as more water spilled from his mouth. After another coughing fit, he tried again. "Do I have you—to thank for my rescue?"

The grey-robed man arched an eyebrow at him. "That remains to be seen. Can you move? We really shouldn't stay here much longer."

Seishin responded with a curt nod. He attempted to lift himself from the sand, but a wave of dizziness overtook him.

"Easy there." The grey-robed man leaned forward to catch him. The movement jostled his neatly combed hair, revealing the tip of a pointed ear.

Seishin's mouth fell open. The "man" wasn't a man at all. He's an elf! Elves were extremely rare here at the southern end of the continent. They seldom left their woodland cities in the great forest far to the north.

After a few moments, Seishin found his voice. "Who—are you?"

The corner of the elf's mouth curved upward. He peered over his shoulder. "He doesn't know who I am."

Seishin gazed where the elf looked, but there was no one there.

The elf slowly shook his head. "Yes, you're right. This generation of bards is sorely lacking."

Seishin's brow furrowed. Who in Arinthar is he talking to?

The elf swung his gaze back to Seishin. "Let's just say I knew your great, great, great, great grandfather."

"My great, great—" Seishin's eyes went wide as it dawned on him to whom the elf referred. His ancestor, Tibarn, was something of a legend. He and his comrades had defeated the Thrall Masters, ending a deadly war in the western isles. Seishin knew the stories by heart and memorized the names of all Tibarn's companions. One in particular was an elven wizard named…

"Aldurin?"

A wry smile spread across the elf's lips. "The same."

Seishin's mouth went dry. Aldurin? Truly? But the Thrall Wars had ended nearly a hundred and fifty years ago! Still, he could sense the elf's power—the subtle but unmistakable aura of a well-trained magic user.

Aldurin glanced over his shoulder as Seishin struggled with the startling revelation. "Yes, yes. I'm sure he's aware that elves are long-lived." He paused a moment as if listening to someone speak.

Seishin strained his ears, but could hear nothing.

Aldurin shook his head, his expression one of exasperation. "Yes, I'll be sure to explain to him how I found him."

Seishin felt completely baffled. *Does he have some sort of invisible companion, or is he just plain nuts?* He opened his mouth to speak, but Aldurin motioned him silent.

"There will be time for questions later. Right now, we need to move"—the corner of his mouth lifted once more—"unless you want to spend more time with your pirate friends?"

Seishin's thoughts immediately drifted to Korti. She obviously regretted all that happened, but had sentenced him to death nonetheless. His mind then turned to Rikton. The thought of the malevolent pirate sent shivers up his spine. *There's nothing left for me here.*

"No, that's alright. Let's go," Seishin said with a wan smile.

Aldurin led them at a brisk pace along the beach. About a half-mile up the shoreline, they reached a rocky outcropping. Two horses waited behind it, hitched to some large pieces of driftwood.

The duo mounted and rode away, swiftly leaving the beach behind. Yet many questions continued to burn in Seishin's mind.

The strange elf who claimed to be Aldurin led them through a high rocky pass and into the forest beyond. The trees were thick and the ground steep here along the mountainside. No discernable path laid before them, but the elf never wavered, leading them unerringly through the woods.

Seishin rode along in silence. *How can I be sure this elf is Aldurin?*

Most of Arinthar knew of Tibarn. Wielder of the Shin Tauri blade, he defeated the mightiest of creatures in the Thrall Masters' armies. That decisive victory brought the Thrall Wars to an end. Tibarn settled down on his return to Isandor, but his thirst for adventure eventually drew him away again. The last time, he never returned, both he and the blade lost to antiquity.

Yet, the blade was a symbol of their family's strength. Thus, Seishin's clan kept its loss a closely guarded secret. As far as any outsider knew, the blade was still entombed at the shrine in their ancestral home. That gave Seishin an idea. He cleared his throat to speak, but Aldurin interrupted him.

"Renere—the home of the Dasati." The elf nudged his head to their right.

Seishin peered in that direction. The sparkling waters of a crystal blue lake shone through a break in the trees. A town sprawled along the western shore below them, with a number of tall ships moored at its docks.

Seishin blinked. It was hard to believe he had been held captive there only this morning. Once again, he caught himself thinking about Korti. He mentally berated himself. *Let it go, Seishin. She's made her choice more than clear.*

The town and lake disappeared from sight as they entered another rocky pass. Still, try as he might, he could not get the visage of the enticing young woman out of his mind. He shook his head in disgust. *I must have a death wish.*

A short while later, they exited the ravine and rode down into a lush green woodland. Aldurin reined in his mount and shook his head. "No, I don't think we were followed."

Seishin's brow furrowed at the oddly phrased statement. "Are you talking to me?"

"Shh," the elf hushed him. He cocked his head to the side as if listening to someone, or something. A few moments later, he let out an exasperated huff. "Do you think I'm an amateur at this? I cleared our tracks with a gust of wind—they won't know what direction to look."

Seishin stifled a laugh. Whoever he was talking to definitely liked sassing him.

A satisfied expression crossed Aldurin's face. "Apology accepted." He swung his mount around and fixed his steel-blue gaze on Seishin. "Now is the time for questions."

Seishin took a deep breath. The answer to his next query should tell him whether this elf is Aldurin. "First, where does the Shin Tauri blade reside?"

The elf arched an eyebrow at him. "Hmm, that is a trick question. Most would say it lies in your family shrine, but as we both know, they would be wrong."

Seishin felt the tension drain from his shoulders. Only the real Aldurin would be privy to that information.

Aldurin exhaled a deep sigh. "The truth is, I've spent many a generation searching for that blade. Unfortunately, I've yet to find a lead that hasn't gone dry." He swung his horse around and flicked the reins, motioning for Seishin to follow. The young man urged his own mount into a slow trot next to the elven wizard's.

Aldurin regarded him with shrewd stare. "Now that that's out of the way, I suppose you'll want to know how I found you."

Seishin cocked his head to one side and shrugged. "That was one of my questions."

Aldurin pursed his lips together. "The truth is, I wasn't so much looking for you as I was visiting your uncle."

Seishin's eyes went wide. "You mean Uncle Draigo?"

"The same." Aldurin nodded, the corner of his mouth lifting slightly.

"Where is he?" Seishin sat forward in his saddle, hardly daring to breath.

Aldurin snorted, his amusement with the young man quite apparent. "Where do you think we're headed now?"

A sudden wave of elation washed over the young Shin Tauri. He hadn't completely botched his mission after all. By some weird twist of fate, his encounter with the pirates had set him on the path to his missing uncle.

"I am not being pompous!" Aldurin burst out all of a sudden.

Seishin watched with growing amusement as the elf engaged in a heated argument with his "invisible" friend. Aldurin grew silent afterwards. Seishin prudently decided to leave the elf in peace.

Midday came and passed as they continued their journey. Brilliant sunlight filtered down through the overhead canopy of rustling leaves. With the hills behind them, the smell of the sea disappeared from the air. The strong scent of pine now took its place. The path they followed split just ahead. Aldurin led them down the right fork—south along the coast.

The elven wizard seemed in decent spirits once again. Seishin decided to try his luck with another question. "You still never explained how you found me."

"No, I did not," Aldurin agreed. He raised a hand as Seishin opened his mouth to retort. "Before I get accused again of being pompous,"—he cast a spurious glance off to one side—"I can tell you that I am not altogether unfamiliar with these parts. And I may have some friends in high places—friends that might not necessarily want to see you die."

Seishin's brow knit into a single line. Friends in high places—on the Pirate Coast? His heart suddenly leapt in his chest. "Do you mean Korti?"

Aldurin raised a single eyebrow. "Not Kortiama. Tharne."

As fast as Seishin's emotions had risen, they came crashing down again. Tharne? Korti's uncle? Seishin vividly remembered the last words Tharne's had said. Leave the boy to his fate. That certainly didn't sound like someone concerned with his well-being.

Seishin stared skeptically at Aldurin, his tone filled with suspicion. "Why would Tharne even care whether I live or die?"

Instead of immediately answering, Aldurin stared intently at him. Seishin felt more and more uncomfortable, as if the elf could see into his very soul. "What you really want to know is why doesn't Kortiama?"

Ouch. Aldurin had indeed seen right through him. Seishin could feel the blood rush to his cheeks. He hung his head and responded in a soft voice. "You're right. I'm just being stupid."

Aldurin continued to hold his stare, then abruptly swiveled in his saddle. "I'm not being too hard on him." He paused a moment as if listening to a silent conversation. "Yes, I know he's just a boy, but if he's not careful, that girl will be the death of him."

Those words sent a chill up Seishin's spine. Aldurin was not wrong. He had nearly died this day because of Korti. Part of him knew she was bad for him, but he'd be lying if he said he didn't still feel something for her.

Aldurin had turned his gaze back toward Seishin. The young man gave him a wan smile. "I know there can never be anything between us."

Aldurin's eyes practically bore into him. "See that you don't forget it again."

The elven wizard spurred his horse onward. Seishin clamped his mouth shut and followed suit. He had more questions than answers, but realized he would learn nothing more from the elf right now.

The duo rode together in silence through the afternoon countryside. Seishin's emotions were in complete disarray. He fell back on his training, using his breath to quiet his mind.

Late that afternoon they turned west, back toward the mountain range they'd previously crossed farther north. Aldurin led them through a well-hidden gorge, then along a winding path that led up the mountainside.

It was nearing dusk when the two riders reached the summit. Below them, Seishin spied that same lake they'd passed before—Loch Dasati, the pirates called it. They were south of it now, but the lights from Renere were clearly visible along the western shore.

"We're almost there," Aldurin announced in a flat tone that discouraged conversation.

Seishin merely nodded. His inner turmoil had abated somewhat, but he still felt foolish for getting his hopes up earlier.

Large boulders and outcroppings blocked their way, but Aldurin expertly weaved through them. Abruptly, the craggy mountaintop gave way to a wide plateau. In its center stood a sprawling villa that appeared to be half estate and half walled fortress. The tiled roof shone bright orange, but even the smooth walls appeared blood-red in the rays of the setting sun.

The sight filled Seishin with a sense of foreboding. "Uncle Draigo is there?"

Aldurin responded with a soft chuckle. "It's cozier than it looks."

They stopped just outside the main gate. Seishin could sense energy coursing along the length of the walls. He also felt the magic buildup as Aldurin cast a quick spell. Moments later, the energy surrounding the place disappeared and the main gate swung open.

A wide courtyard spread out before them. Even in the vanishing light, Seishin could see the beautiful trees and lush garden across the yard. It reminded him very much of his family's courtyard back home.

Warm lights sprang from the villa itself, helping to further ease his tension. A solitary figure stood framed in the doorway. Seishin could sense the person's energy even from here. It felt huge, but also familiar. He dismounted and slowly approached the stocky silhouette. As he drew closer, the setting sun revealed the face of his long-missing uncle.

"Uncle Draigo." Seishin murmured the name, still not believing his eyes.

"Seishin, my boy," Draigo's deep voice rumbled in reply.

All at once, the dam holding back Seishin's feelings burst. He threw himself at the stout man, his arms encircling his uncle's bulky frame. Strong arms enveloped him in turn, making him almost wince. Tears welled in the young man's eyes, his throat thick with emotion. "It's good to see you, Uncle."

"It's good to see you, too," Draigo said, his deep voice cracking ever so slightly.

"You nearly didn't see him at all," Aldurin's voice sounded from behind them. "Had I arrived any later, I would be bringing you his corpse."

"Ah, Aldurin, jovial as ever," Draigo noted in a dry tone.

The ex-general stood back and grasped Seishin by the shoulders. "You do look like you've had a rough time. Come on in and we'll get you a change of clothes—and some hot tea."

Draigo wrapped a sturdy arm around his nephew and led him into the villa. A wide foyer stretched out before them, its rich tiled floor made of black and white marble. A circular stairwell rose on either side of the back wall.

Between the stairs hung a double portrait of a rather imposing couple. The man wore a fancy long coat, his grim countenance enhanced by an eye patch and dark beard. The woman's fine black gown and intricately woven hair did little to offset her ominous expression. Still, there was something familiar about her.

Seishin halted and squinted at the painting. "Is that Korti's mother?"

"It is," his uncle rumbled.

"Then that would make the man…"

"…Eboneye," Draigo finished for him.

Seishin mulled over his uncle's response. "Then that would make this…"

"…Eboneye's villa." Draigo stared at him with a stoic expression.

The revelation left Seishin speechless. He finally found his voice only to stutter. "How… when…"

"You left out where and why," Aldurin interrupted. The elven wizard watched him with obvious amusement. All of a sudden, his smile faded. "I was not being rude!" Aldurin exclaimed over his shoulder. Another one-sided squabble ensued.

Seishin stepped closer to his uncle and whispered, "Does he do this often?"

"Yes," Draigo murmured, his eyes rolling to the sky. "It's part of his charm."

Seishin was hard pressed to stifle his laughter.

Aldurin's quarrel finally ended with the wizard storming off into the next room. Seishin exchanged a glance with his uncle and then followed the irate elf. They entered a large area the size of a small tavern. A couch and some plush chairs created a cozy nook around an open hearth. A long mahogany dining table stood at the other end of the room.

Aldurin had parked himself in a chair by the fire. Draigo brought Seishin a fresh robe, and once he had changed, he rejoined the others. His uncle had set out a tray of hot tea. Seishin peered at the ex-general as he poured him a cup. The years had aged him. The top of his head now bare, his remaining hair and beard had turned a dark gray.

As the trio sat around the fire, Draigo explained how he ended up in this place. It all began with his search for the king's assassins. Posing as a pirate, Draigo infiltrated the Dasati. He swiftly rose through the ranks, gaining a reputation as the Emerald Blade.

Seishin's eyes widened. "I've heard of that pirate. It's said he never killed anyone, only using a blunt blade to disable his opponents."

"None of those battles were a matter of honor," his uncle stated in a pragmatic tone.

Draigo continued to play his role, but found no evidence of pirate involvement in the assassination. Yet before leaving the Pirate Coast, he got drawn into the feud between Rikton, Tharne, and Kortiama. Rikton was set on becoming Lord Captain of the Dasati, and Korti stood in his way. To save her from certain death, Draigo took on the mantle of both her mentor and champion.

After hearing the entire twisted tale, Seishin felt a deep sense of remorse. Like Korti, his uncle had put the needs of others above his own wants and desires. It was an honorable way to live, but it came with a steep price.

His story finished, Draigo now rose from his seat. "If you two will excuse me, I'll go check on dinner."

Silence fell over the room as the ex-general left them alone. Aldurin had been quietly brooding through Draigo's entire story. The eccentric elf now sat back in his chair, his eyes closed and his hands steepled together.

Seishin stared at the fireplace, the dancing shadows cast by its light magnifying his sullen mood. He had been childish and selfish. He silently swore from this day forward to place honor above his own needs and desires. The young man continued to brood until Draigo announced that dinner was served.

Seishin hadn't eaten since the previous night and found himself ravenous. His uncle had always been a good cook, but the feast he now laid before them was almost fit for a king. It consisted of a hearty soup, two whole chickens, potatoes, a host of other vegetables, three types of fruit pies, and more hot tea of course.

Seishin dug into the meal as if he hadn't eaten for a week. Forty-five minutes later, nearly every plate on the table sat empty. His appetite sated, Seishin sat back, feeling much better about things in general.

A soft chuckle drew his attention to Uncle Draigo. He watched his nephew with clear amusement. "It appears you still like my cooking."

Seishin's face grew warm with embarrassment. "I have to admit, it's even better than I remembered."

"That's good to know." A thin smile crossed Draigo's lips as he poured them all more tea. Once done, the he took a sip and cleared his throat. "So then, my boy, care to tell us how you ended up in this mess?"

Seishin sat up in his seat and met Draigo's gaze evenly. "Actually, Uncle, I came here looking for you."

Draigo's brows knit into a line. "Me? Why? What's happened?"

Seishin swiftly relayed his mission. He told them about the assassination in the capital and how his father had been blamed for it. He also detailed the dismissal of the Kazari and their replacement with members of the priesthood.

Aldurin exchanged a knowing glance with Draigo. "Sounds like a coup."

Draigo's expression remained grim. "Go on."

Seishin set his jaw and continued. "Ever since he joined the council, the High Priest has been advocating an alliance with Parthos. They've managed to hold him in check 'til now, but with Father out of the way, the Queen has been overruled."

Aldurin cast a glance to one side. "Yes, yes, I'm well aware Parthos is an aggressor nation—ask anyone from Thac or the northern mainland." He steepled his hands together in front of his chin and mused aloud, "Just what game is this priest playing at?"

"Hmm," Draigo mused. "He's probably selling it as a counter to the pirate raids. The Isandor army is one of the best. Still, they are out of their element against sea-based assaults, and Parthos does have one of the strongest navies in Arinthar."

Seishin gave his uncle a curt nod. "It's got the entire west coast of Isandor scared."

Draigo's eyes narrowing even further. "How is the Queen doing?"

Seishin shook his head. "Not good. Without the Kazari, things on the coast are getting worse, but she's more worried about the capital. If Parthos gains a foothold in Isandor, the government as we know it could completely collapse."

Seishin sat forward in his seat. "That's why she sent me to find you. She needs you back there now more than ever."

"Hmm. I see," Draigo rumbled, his expression growing pensive. "Unfortunately, my return might cause even more problems."

Seishin's mouth fell open. He stared at his uncle with disbelief. Those were the last words he expected to hear from Isandor's most decorated general.

"How so?" Aldurin asked before Seishin could find his voice.

Draigo breathed a deep sigh. "It had been my responsibility to protect the king. Ultimately, his death was my fault, a fact the priesthood broadcast all across Isandor."

"What was that?" Aldurin cast a glance over his shoulder. "Oh yes, I quite agree." He turned his gaze back to Draigo. "Dragon dung."

A thin smile momentarily crossed the ex-general's lips. "Perhaps, but the priesthood has many followers, all who solemnly believed that I should step down at the time. It nearly split the country in two."

Seishin's mouth hung open. He had been rather young at the time, and didn't remember any of that. Yet his uncle appeared quite adamant in his belief that he might make things worse. What could he possibly say to change his mind?

Thankfully, once again, Aldurin came to the rescue. "Be that as it may, that was nearly a decade ago. As things currently stand, the Queen might lose everything without your support."

"Hmm." Draigo sat back and gingerly stroked his beard.

The intervening silence kept Seishin on the edge of his seat. He had no idea what would happen to Isandor without his uncle.

After what seemed like forever, Draigo finally responded. "You are right, as always, my old friend." He shifted his gaze to Seishin. "Very well, I will return to Isandor with you."

Seishin sighed with relief. It felt as if a great weight had been lifted off his shoulders.

After dinner, the trio discussed their next steps. Draigo needed a few days to set things in order. The villa had to be closed up, and Tharne should be informed of his departure. Seishin solemnly agreed.

A short while later, Draigo escorted his nephew to a guest room.

The chamber lay atop the northernmost tower of the Villa Dasati. A large four-posted bed with matching dresser and wardrobe furnished the room. Two tall arched windows stood in the wall opposite the entrance.

Seishin peered out one of the windows at the loch far below. The lights of Renere twinkled brilliantly along the western shore, bathing over the ships that were moored at the docks. Unwittingly, Seishin's mind wandered to Korti.

"It's beautiful, isn't it?" Draigo's soft voice sounded beside him.

"Yes, she is." Seishin nodded absently.

His uncle's soft chuckle brought him back from his musings. Seishin felt stupid yet again. "Sorry, uncle. I shouldn't be thinking…"

"…about Kortiama," Draigo finished for him.

A wan smile crossed Seishin's lips. "Am I that transparent?"

"Like glass." His uncle's eyes sparkled with amusement.

Seishin sighed. Would he ever get her out of his head? He and Korti were over. Plain and simple.

A strong hand grasped him by the shoulder. "It's alright, my boy. Love is like a river—it flows where it will."

Seishin nearly jumped out of his skin. "What? Who said anything about love?"

Draigo fixed him with a knowing stare. Once again Seishin felt bared to his very soul. His eyes fell to the floor. "I am pathetic. I need to learn to control my heart instead of the other way around."

His uncle chuckled once more. "If you do, my boy, you'd be the first."

Dagger in the Night
Chapter 4

ldurin left early the next day, after a cryptic discussion with his invisible friend. Seishin spent the rest of the day helping Draigo ready the place for his departure. That evening, his uncle headed into town to see Tharne, after telling Seishin not to wait up for him.

The young man felt uneasy being left alone in what once was Eboneye's villa. The place was huge, consisting of nearly twenty rooms between the first and second floors alone. That didn't include the two towers on the north and south sides of the villa. One of the rooms turned out to be a sizable library. Seishin perused it for a good book to read, settling on one entitled A History of the Saricordi.

According to Draigo, the pirate clans once went by that name. They had been a proud nation of craftsmen and warriors.

Night had fallen as Seishin curled up in front of the fire with his book and a cup of tea. It began to rain outside; the occasional crash of lightning punctuated the pitter-patter of drops against the house. Seishin became so engrossed in his book that he grew deaf to the repetitive sounds. Thus, he nearly jumped out of his seat when the front door creaked open.

Years in the army had taught him to keep at least one weapon close at hand. Seishin grabbed it now and carefully pulled the long-curved sword from its sheath. Outside, the rain had turned into a torrential downpour. The roar masked his steps as he silently padded toward the foyer.

A pair of dim wall sconces barely illuminated the entrance hall. Seishin froze at the sight of a shadow standing in the open doorway. A sudden crash of lightning revealed the shape to be a figure in a dark cloak.

Seishin almost rushed the dark figure, but something held him back. The aura he sensed seemed somehow familiar. All at once, the figure dropped its hood.

Seishin's mouth fell open. "Korti?"

The young Lord Captain of Pirates stepped into the dim light, but her eyes were not focused on him. "What am I doing here?" she murmured under her breath. Her voice sounded hollow.

She dropped her cloak and slowly walked past him, her eyes sweeping around the room. "Tharne told me about his plan. He said you were most likely up here at the villa."

Korti stopped, her eyes settling on the large portrait hanging on the wall. Seishin sheathed his weapon and walked up to stand beside her.

She wrapped her arms around her slim frame and shivered ever so slightly. "I've tried to live up to his legacy—to make them both proud of me. I was even willing to let you die…"

She lifted her chin and peered up at him, black circles showing beneath her eyes. It appeared as if she had been crying.

Seishin felt torn inside. She looked so beautiful and yet so forlorn. She had nearly had him killed. Still, he had brought that on himself. He shook his head and sighed. "Korti, what are you doing here?"

A shade of a smile crossed her lips. "I've been asking myself that same question. I know it's a bad idea, my coming up here. I probably shouldn't have"—she paused and placed a hand on his arm—"but for some reason, I couldn't stop myself."

The warmth of her touch sent sparks racing through his body. It became more difficult for him to think. She moved even closer and slid her hands around the back of his neck. As if with a will of their own, his arms wrapped around her waist.

"This is definitely a terrible idea," he murmured to her.

"Completely," she agreed as she pulled his head down toward hers.

Their lips met. Soft at first, each subsequent kiss grew more urgent than the last. The two lovers grasped each other with a hunger born of desperation. Their unrestrained passion continued until they were both left breathless.

Still holding him, Korti gently pulled back. She rested her head on his chin as she struggled to catch her breath. "Such... a terrible... idea..."

"Really... bad..." Seishin agreed, his body and mind in direct conflict.

Abruptly she pushed him away. There was a fire in her eyes and the hint of a smile on her lips. "Lucky for you, it is not your brains that attracts me."

Before he could retort, she bolted for the stairs.

"Kortiama!" Seishin took off after her.

She led him on a wild chase, up the stairs, across the hallway, and up the tower staircase. She did not stop until they entered the guest room at the top of the tower.

Seishin caught up with her in front of the large four-poster bed. Korti wrapped herself around him and pulled him down onto it, showering him with another round of deep, passionate kisses.

Seishin lost himself in the moment. His will had all but crumbled, yet one last thing still gnawed at his mind. Nearly breathless, he managed to pull himself upright. "Why did you come all the way up here?"

Korti arched a single eyebrow at him. "Because this is my room."

Seishin let out an ironic laugh. "And it's the room I'm staying in."

Her puzzled expression abruptly faded, replaced with that familiar dazzling smile. "Leave it to your uncle. I swear, that man can read minds."

All Seishin's inhibitions melted away. His voice dropped to nearly a whisper. "I'm just glad he's not here now to read what's on mine."

Korti fixed him with a smoldering stare. "Oh, really? And just what might that be?"

Seishin leaned in again and ardently pressed his lips against hers. The two lovers went well into the night reveling in their blissful reunion.

Seishin shot upright. Near darkness surrounded him, tempered only by silvery moonlight that streamed in through two tall arched windows. He felt around the bed, but Korti no longer laid beside him. Instead, she stood in front of one of the windows.

"Korti?"

"Shhh." She put a finger to her lips.

Seishin frowned as he slipped out of bed and stole over next to her.

"It's about time you woke up," Korti admonished him in a soft voice. She nodded out the window. "We have company."

Seishin followed her gaze. The rain outside had stopped, the moon illuminating the courtyard far below. Seishin watched as a shadow slipped across the grounds. He scanned the rest of the yard, but could detect no further movement.

"How many are there?" He whispered back.

She held up three fingers. "That's all I've seen so far, but there may be others."

Seishin wondered who could be out there. Rikton's men?

"Any chance you were followed?" he whispered.

Korti shook her head. "I'd know. I use magic to watch my back. They'd have to be ghosts…" She stopped and cursed under her breath. "Dragon dung!"

"What?" Seishin grasped her by the shoulders. Even in the moonlight, he could see the pained expression on her face.

"I was so preoccupied earlier that I forgot to re-conjure the spell on the walls."

Seishin shrugged. "Too late to worry about that now." Years of training and experience led him to a quick decision. "Let's head downstairs. Up here we'd be backed into a corner with not much room to fight."

The two of them gathered their weapons and went downstairs to the second floor. Side by side, they checked each door along the way. They found nothing until they reached the open hall above the foyer. Below them, the front door hung wide open.

Silvery light slipped through the entryway, cutting a swath through the inky blackness. Yet there were still too many dark corners for Seishin's comfort. He slowed his breath and stilled his mind. There was definitely at least one other presence somewhere nearby.

Seishin signaled to Korti to watch their backs, then the two of them silently descended the stairs. They only made it about halfway down when a figure leapt at Seishin from out of the shadows.

A sharp blade went straight for his gut, but Seishin expertly parried the blow. He immediately retaliated with his free arm, slashing his attacker across the torso. The figure fell backwards and tumbled the rest of the way down the steps. A black-robed form lay at the base of the stairway, unmoving in the pale moonlight.

Seishin exchanged a brief glance with Korti, then the two of them edged the rest of the way down. When they reached the bottom, Seishin checked their attacker. Whoever it was, they were dead. The duo carefully stepped over the body, then crept out into the foyer back to back. They hadn't gone more than five steps when they were accosted again.

This time, the attack came from multiple directions. Seishin fended off two darting blades, while Korti expertly handled a third. The ambush lasted less than a minute. When it was over, three more dark-robed bodies lay at their feet. Still, neither of them had gone unscathed; both had their share of cuts from those razor-sharp swords.

Seishin silently hoped the blades weren't poisoned. He kept watch while Korti examined the bodies.

When she was done, she drew up next to him and whispered, "Well, they aren't Dasati, if that's what you're thinking."

It had been exactly what Seishin was thinking. Though Tharne orchestrated his escape, Rikton might think Korti was behind it. If so, he might have sent his men after her.

Korti pointed toward the front door. "The rest of the house, or outside first?"

Seishin stilled his mind once more, but could feel no other presence nearby. "I'm not sensing anyone else in here."

"Outside it is, then." Korti ushered him toward the doorway.

The night was still. A full moon illuminated most of the courtyard, with only a few shadows stretched across the grounds.

Seishin got the vague impression of another presence, but could not tell the direction or how close. He motioned to Korti. The two of them cautiously waded forward, circling each other as they went. They had gone perhaps two dozen steps when more figures separated themselves from the shadows.

Seishin counted six in all. Garbed in hooded robes like those inside, their features were hidden from the pale moonlight. The silent forms swiftly encircled them, forcing him and Korti to halt. They hovered there without a word, just out of striking distance.

Seishin silently berated himself. *How could I have missed so many of them?* Somehow, they had been able to mask their presence.

"Any idea who they are?" Seishin whispered to Korti.

"None," she responded, sounding equally confused.

After nearly a minute of silence, one of the figures spoke. "Draigo Kazari?"

Seishin's brow furrowed. The speaker was a man, though his voice was high-pitched with a crazed lilt. Whoever it was, they were obviously looking for his uncle.

"Who is this Draigo?" Korti asked before Seishin could reply.

The dark-robed man wagged a finger at her. "Tsk, tsk. Don't play games with us, dearie. We know who Eyro really is. No mere gardener can wield a blade like a Shin Tauri master."

"What is he talking about?" Seishin whispered over his shoulder.

Korti's reply was strained. "Draigo played the part of the villa gardener up until my choosing as Lord Captain. He revealed himself as a swordmaster during that battle."

"Exactly." The hooded man affirmed.

Seishin squinted at the dark-robed man. "What do you want with him?"

"Want? Want?" The crazed man's voice rose in pitch. "Why, we want him to die, of course."

An eerie chant rose from all the figures at once. "The time is nigh and all who wield the cursed blade must die…"

The strange chant sent chills up Seishin's spine. It carried a dark energy with it that seemed to increase their captor's power. He exchanged a brief glance with Korti, but she appeared as mystified as him.

She addressed the original speaker, her voice laced with irritation. "The cursed blade? What in the devil are you all babbling about?"

A high-pitched cackle erupted from beneath the dark hood. "Not devil, my dear. Demon,"—the man leaned forward, his voice dripping with malice—"and we will expunge any who might wield the cursed blade."

Something clicked in the back of Seishin's mind. He breathed the words before he could stop himself. "The Shin Tauri blade…"

"Yes, yes, the cursed blade," the crazed man agreed fervently. "The legacy of the House Kazari. None of that line who could take up the blade must be allowed to live."

"Seishin!" Korti breathed his name in a hoarse whisper.

Seishin glanced at her and saw the fear in her eyes. He realized in that moment that he would probably not walk away from this. Yet he couldn't bear the thought of Korti dying because of him. Seishin gave her a brief smile, then turned his eyes back forward.

With a deep breath, he stilled his mind in the way of the Shin Tauri. His breathing slowed as he reached inside and found his spirit. The energy surged out from his abdomen, into his arms, and across his blades. The air around them seemed to catch fire. Yellow flames danced up and down the shafts of both weapons.

"I am Seishin Kazari, of the line of Tibarn," he declared with conviction. He nodded his head toward Korti. "She has nothing to do with this. Let her go and we can settle this between us."

A hard elbow connected with Seishin's side. "Seishin! I'm not going any…"

The dark-robed man cackled again, cutting off Korti's rebuttal. "The whelp! We've found the whelp!" He rubbed his hands together with obvious glee. "The whelp and the uncle in one fell swoop! Fortune has indeed smiled on us this day, my brethren."

The whelp? His show of power had not quite elicited the reaction he anticipated. Still, there were more important things at stake here. "Perhaps you didn't you hear me? Let her go. This is between us."

"And perhaps you didn't hear me," Korti countered, her voice as hard as stone. "I'm not going anywhere."

The crazed man interrupted him before he could contradict her. "I'm afraid she's right. I'm sorry, my dear, but you're now a loose end we can't afford."

Korti drew herself up and threw her shoulders back. "Do you have any idea who you're dealing with? I am Kortiama Ozden, Lord Captain of the Dasati. Strike us down, and you'll have all the Clans of the Coast on your heels."

The man clucked his tongue again. "Tsk, tsk. It's you, dearie, who don't know who you're dealing with. We will tear this world apart. Your clans would sooner side with us than be ground to dust like every other non-believer in Arinthar."

Korti curled her lips in disgust. "If you think I'd believe that, you're crazier than I thought."

The dark-hooded man cackled again. "Perhaps, but I'd rather be mad and alive than the alternative."

He motioned toward Korti and Seishin. "Enough of this. Take care of them."

Seishin tensed as five dark figures rushed them from all sides. Korti was good with a blade, but he didn't know how many she could handle at once.

A dark form lunged at him with frightening speed, but Seishin had read its movements. He caught its blade with a flick of his wrist and deftly knocked it aside.

His assailant off balance, Seishin could easily have run it through, but that would still leave him with two more close at hand. In a split-second decision, he kicked the figure and sent it flying into its comrades. All three went down in a heap on the courtyard stones.

Throwing caution to the wind, Seishin spun around.

Korti faced off against two opponents. She expertly parried one blade, then immediately countered the other.

Her deft maneuver left an opening in her opponent's guard. Without thinking, Seishin lunged and ran her assailant clean through.

Korti screamed at him. "What are you doing? I've got this! Stay back to back."

Her words washed over him like a bucket of ice. She was right—his impulsive maneuver had left them both at risk.

Seishin spun around just in time to parry a blade aimed at his torso. His eyes went wide as two more blades lunged straight for his beloved's back.

Seishin had only one chance. His breathing slowed, and with it the world around him. This time the energy surged into his legs.

With seemingly impossible speed, Seishin placed himself between Korti and the two assailants. He swept the one blade out of the way, but the other skewered him straight through the abdomen.

Seishin grunted as pain lanced through his body. It felt as if his midriff were on fire. His breath left him and his knees gave out. He fell to the ground, the world spinning around him.

"Seishin!" He heard Korti scream.

Dark forms hovered over him, only to be driven back by a flash of something silver. "Get away from him, you motherless curs! I'll cut out your tongues and feed them to the sharks."

"Now, now, dearie, there's no need for name calling," the demented voice cackled. "Be a nice girl and die al…"

The dark-robed man halted mid-word, then abruptly crumpled to the ground. A familiar squat silhouette stood behind him, the moonlight glinting off a sharp curved blade.

"Uncle…" Seishin tried to speak, but then the world began to spin again and everything went black.

Seishin slowly opened his eyes. It was daytime. He lay in bed, bright sunlight streaming into the room from the two tall, arched windows. A gentle hand touched his face. He turned to see Korti leaning over him. "Well, it's about time, sleepy head. We thought you were going to be out all day."

Seishin smiled, then abruptly remembered they had been attacked. He bolted upright and glanced around the room, but everything appeared to be normal.

He felt a hand on his chest. "Easy, lover."

Seishin shifted his gaze back to Korti. "The assassins?"

"All dead. Draigo and I took care of the rest."

Seishin remembered his uncle had appeared out of nowhere and slew the crazed man.

"It's you we were worried about. You nearly died." Korti stared at him accusingly. "You're just lucky I had a potion of grand healing on me. Those things don't come cheap, you know."

A potion of grand healing? Seishin arched an eyebrow at her. "Do you always carry around such rare items on your person?"

Her mouth curved into a half-smile. "A girl can never be too careful—especially in my line of work."

Seishin lifted the sheet and peered at his abdomen. The wound had completely healed. Only the slightest scar remained.

He gazed back at Korti in wonder. She had just spent a small fortune saving his life. She really does care. Seishin reached over and took her hand. "Sorry to worry you."

Korti gave him a hard look. "You better be."

Her expression softened as she leaned in and kissed him. After a few moments, their lips parted. Korti laid down beside him and put her head on his shoulder.

Seishin allowed himself to enjoy this moment. Deep inside, he knew it couldn't last forever. She'd have to go back to her people and he would return to Isandor. All of sudden, he bolted upright. "Did you tell my uncle what that crazed man said?"

Korti peered up at him and sighed. "Of course, I did." She patted the bed next to her. "Now why don't you lay back down and relax."

Seishin was sorely tempted. "I'm sorry, I can't—not until my parents have been warned."

"No need for concern, young Kazari," a familiar voice sounded from the doorway. "They have been warned." Aldurin stood there with his uncle.

Seishin breathed a sigh of relief. "Thank you, Aldurin."

Draigo came into the room and looked over Seishin's wound.

"Nice to see you recovered so quickly. Maybe next time you won't be so foolish as to let your guard down."

Ouch. Seishin felt the sting of those words. Still, he had been stupid. He should have trusted Korti to handle herself. He cast a sidelong glance at her. She stared back at him with an I told you so expression.

The blood rushed to Seishin's cheeks. "Sorry." His short-lived embarrassment faded as his mind returned to their attackers. "Uncle, do you have any idea who those people were?"

"He doesn't, but I might," Aldurin answered for Draigo. "Get dressed first, then meet us downstairs. We have much to discuss."

Seishin opened his mouth to speak, but Aldurin held up a hand. "What I have to tell you will answer many of your questions, but I'm afraid it will also raise many more."

The two of them left so that Seishin could get dressed. As he pulled on his clothes, he wondered what Aldurin had to tell them. "Just once, I'd like a straight answer from that wizard."

Korti responded with a light, lyrical laugh. "Oh, my dear Seishin. You've got a lot to learn about magic users."

Seishin narrowed an eye at her. "And I suppose you know better?"

The corner of Korti's mouth lifted upward. "Trust me, my mother's a witch and she's the same. Asking her for a straight answer is like asking the waves not to crash against the shore."

Seishin responded with a close-mouthed laugh. "I think it's an older generation thing. Has my uncle ever imparted words of wisdom to you?"

Korti snorted. "All the time. Did you ever notice everything is like a river?"

Seishin grinned at the imitation of his uncle. The two of them continued to discuss the idiosyncrasies of their elders as they headed downstairs.

Love and Honor
Chapter 5

When they arrived downstairs, they found Aldurin and Draigo seated at the long table. An appetizing lunch lay spread out before them. Strangely, Seishin found himself not all that hungry. He picked at his plate as Aldurin spoke.

"The group that attacked you were members of a demonic cult. Apparently, their goal was to stop anyone who might wield the Shin Tauri blade."

Korti cocked her head to one side and eyed the elven wizard curiously. "They told us that last part. What exactly is this Shin Tauri blade?"

A look of exasperation crossed Aldurin's face. "We don't have the time for a history lesson…" He abruptly halted, and glanced over his shoulder. "I am not being pig-headed!" he declared vehemently.

Korti cast a confused glance at Seishin. He merely shrugged, not quite sure how to explain the elven wizard's "invisible" companion.

After a short one-sided conversation, Aldurin let out a deep sigh. "Yes, yes, you're quite right. She deserves an explanation."

An obviously bemused Korti sat back and folded her arms across her chest.

Aldurin paused as if to collect his thoughts before speaking, then took a deep breath. "The Shin Tauri blade is a great bane to all demons. Seishin's and Draigo's ancestor, Tibarn, used it to banish the mightiest of demons in the Thrall Lord's army."

Korti pointed from Draigo to Seishin. "You mean, you two are descended from the legendary hero, Tibarn?"

Seishin wore a wan smile while Draigo merely nodded. Korti seemed quite impressed. She gave them both an appreciative nod before shifting her gaze back to Aldurin. "So where is this great blade now?"

Aldurin briefly explained what happened to the blade after the Thrall Wars. He ended with, "…and as far as the rest of the world knows, the blade still resides at the Kazari family shrine."

Korti cast a glance at Seishin, the corner of her mouth rising ever so slightly. "And I thought my family had secrets."

Seishin's cheeks warmed with embarrassment. The subterfuge around the blade had been his greatest source of shame up until his father had been put in prison.

Korti leaned back in her chair and tapped her chin lightly with two fingers. "So, one has to be from the line of Kazari to wield this blade?"

Aldurin shook his head. "That is a fiction spun by the bard who chronicled our adventures during the Thrall Wars. The truth is, there is no magic tying the blade to any one specific bloodline."

Korti sat forward and narrowed her eyes at the elven wizard. "Alright, let's assume this cult believes the tales, like everyone else. Why come after Draigo now? They said they discovered his identity when I was chosen Lord Captain, but that was nearly three years ago."

Aldurin's expression turned grim. He leaned over the table, his voice dropping to just above a whisper. "There have been signs of late that the demons are staging another invasion into our world."

A deathly silence fell over the table. Seishin exchanged a worried glance with Korti and Draigo. There had been three previous full-scale demon invasions of Arinthar throughout history. Each one was extremely bloody, almost completely decimating the once-great races of dragons, giants, and fae in turn.

The human race had risen to power after the last war. They had been lucky to avoid another confrontation with the demons—that is, up until now.

A sudden chill had fallen over the room. Draigo suggested they adjourn to the fireplace while he got them more tea.

Seishin sat on the couch next to Korti, while Aldurin took a comfortable chair. The three of them watched the fire in silence. Aldurin steepled his hands together as he stared into the dancing flames; Korti slipped her hand into Seishin's and moved closer for warmth.

Draigo returned shortly with a steaming teapot and four empty cups. He filled them all, passed them out, then sat down himself. The ex-general took a long sip, then fixed Aldurin with a hard stare. "What kind of signs?"

Aldurin sat forward in his chair and met Draigo's gaze evenly. "These cults have suddenly grown bolder." He peered at Seishin and Korti. "Your encounter was but a single incident. There's been an increase in demonic-related killings and ritual sacrifice across the entire globe."

Korti and Seishin exchanged a glance. Her eyes mirrored the growing sense of dread he felt inside.

"There's also been unrest in the magical community," Aldurin continued. "Aside from the usual portents, mages have been disappearing all over Arinthar. My colleagues and I believe it's related to disturbances we've discovered on the astral plane."

Seishin's inner sense of foreboding intensified. If an invasion was imminent, as Aldurin suggested, no one would be safe—not Korti, his family, Isandor, not even the pirate clans. He suddenly felt very small in an increasingly dangerous world.

"If only we still had the Shin Tauri blade," he murmured to himself.

"The blade may not be completely lost to us," Aldurin responded unexpectedly.

Seishin nearly jumped out of his seat. "You have news of it?"

Aldurin gave him a curt nod. "That is why I left the other day." The elven wizard took a brief sip of tea before continuing. "I met with an old friend who carried a clandestine message from the Queen of Lanfor. It appears she has something that might help us find the blade."

Korti sat forward next to Seishin. "Do you have any idea what this 'something' is?"

Aldurin merely shrugged. "No, I do not. The Queen did not impart that information in her message, and I don't feel it prudent to contact her via magical means."

"Hmm," Draigo mused aloud. "I suppose this means we'll need go to Lanfor before heading to Isandor."

Aldurin shook his head. "I'm afraid not, my old friend. You must get to Isandor as quickly as possible. We will need her legions if we are to stand against entire hordes of demons." He waved a hand at Seishin. "The boy can follow up on the blade."

Aldurin's comment caught Seishin by surprise. He had carried the weight of Isandor on his shoulders, but now the fate of the world might be riding on them.

Korti must have sensed his trepidation. She stared at him now, her eyes filled with fear. "No," she said flatly. She stood up and cast a dark stare at Aldurin. "It's too much to ask. He's just a boy. Surely you can send someone else."

Aldurin returned her stare evenly. "There is no one else. We are short on time, and the boy is our best bet."

Korti sneered at the elven wizard, then turned her heated gaze upon Seishin. "Surely you're not going to go through with this fool's errand?"

Seishin stood up and gently grasped her by the arms. "I have to admit, I am not crazy about it, but I don't see as I have much choice."

Korti shook herself free of his grasp and glared at him. "Then you are a bigger fool than I thought."

She turned toward Draigo. "You of all people must realize how absurd this is. Can't you talk some sense into these buffoons?"

Draigo's expression remained stony. "I'm afraid I cannot. I trained Seishin as I trained you. He can handle this task."

Korti's cheeks turned flaming red. She swept her gaze between the three of them, her hands waving about wildly. "Then you're all idiots! We should be marshaling our forces, not running off in all directions after some phantom weapon that hasn't been seen in over a hundred years!"

Seishin felt torn. The world as they knew it could be coming to an end. The last thing he wanted was to be separated from those he cared about. Yet he had sworn to do the right thing despite his own desires.

Korti stood with her hands on her hips, staring at him expectantly.

"Please excuse us," Seishin said, not taking his eyes off Korti. He held his hand out to her. She stared at it for a moment, then begrudgingly took it.

Seishin led them into the foyer. He halted in front of the portrait of Korti's parents. "When you showed up last night, you said you wanted to make them both proud of you. Do you really expect me to do anything less?"

Korti pressed her lips together and shook her head at him. "That's not fair—using my own parents against me."

Seishin shrugged. "You didn't give me much choice."

The barest of smiles crossed her lips. Seishin wrapped his arms around her waist. She slid close to him and pulled his head down until their lips met. One long, passionate kiss ensued. Seishin reveled in it, knowing it might be the very last.

When their lips parted, Korti gently pulled back and rested her head on his chin. "Do what you need to do. I have my own people to worry about." She pushed away from him and went to the door.

Korti halted in the open doorway and turned to face him one last time. He could see the mixed emotions in her eyes. "If you manage to live, you know where to find me." With that, she closed the door behind her.

Seishin stood there alone in the foyer, feeling numb inside. He had placed honor above his own desires, yet with that choice came an incredible sense of loneliness. It took him a few moments to recover, but in the end he drew himself up. The young Shin Tauri went to rejoin the others and face the road that he had chosen.

Art of the Steal

Jeffrey L. Price

The Fagin
Chapter 1

The old bard wiped the chicken grease from his hands and downed the last of his wine, then stretched his hands out toward the crackling fire, skillfully ignoring all the eyes staring intently at him.

"Please," pleaded a young, golden-haired maiden with wide, bright green eyes. She was just coming of age and blossoming into her full womanhood. The Old Bard sighed inwardly, mourning the passing of his youth. Back in his adventuring days, he'd have thought nothing of sweet-talking his way into the lovely young lass' bed. But alas, those days were far, far behind him. Now he was more concerned with keeping his belly full, having a warm, comfortable place to sleep, and maintaining a steady stream of gold coming into his purse from the wealthy patrons he served. And his current patrons had indeed paid him well to keep them entertained on their long trek across the wilderness. The caravan route to and from Tarsmoor was a long, lonely, and often treacherous one, and he wasn't about to risk getting left all by his lonesome out here with nothing but the clothes on his back just for a night's pleasure with the girl, no matter how lovely she appeared.

The Old Bard sighed to himself again. Perhaps his old masters had been right after all. Age really *did* bring with it a small amount of wisdom.

"Please!" The girl pleaded again.

"Pretty please!" her younger sister piped in. She, too, had long, golden locks just like her older sibling, only hers were more tightly curled.

The Old Bard made a show of shaking his head no. "I've told you enough tales for one night. It's late; you should be in bed," he said, pretending to scold them.

"I'll be good! I promise!" the younger girl said with all the earnestness a six-year-old could muster. "Besides, I'm not tired yet!"

"Oh, please? Won't you tell us just one more?" the older girl asked. The pleading in her eyes was echoed in the rest of the faces around the campfire.

The Old Bard smiled to himself. He knew he had them.

"Oh, all right," he said, pretending to give in. "Perhaps I *could* be persuaded by a cup of your very fine sweet wine."

The young maiden got up and quickly filled his cup from her family's private cask of wine. The Old Bard took it gratefully from her hands and took a long, slow pull from the vessel. He let the deep, rich purple liquid linger on his tongue and the back of his palate. The wine was from one of the finest vineyards in Thac. He had once visited the place in his travels, but that was ages ago. Yet the taste of the wine brought back a flood of memories, and he could almost smell the sweet scent of the grapes on the summer breeze again…

But those were memories for another day, and he had a willing audience before him—and he made it a point to never disappoint a willing audience.

The Old Bard held his tongue for a moment longer, letting the anticipation build in the faces of those before him. Then, when he sensed they could stand it no longer, he finally spoke.

"I have already told you stories of the Heroes of Ravenford," he began. "About the bard-king Elladan, and his stalwart companions Aksel the Wise, the powerful wizard Glolindir the Grey, the stealthy rogue Seth, the quiet forest-archer, Xellos, and the battle prowess of the noble Lord Lloyd Stealle, and his friend, the dragon-slaying barbarian, Cyclone.

"But there is one member of their company I have yet to speak of…"

"Donatello!" the young maiden exclaimed.

"You know your history well, my dear," the Old Bard complemented her.

The young woman blushed. She wasn't often complemented on anything other than her looks.

"There are many tales about that dashing swordsman's adventures with the Heroes of Ravenford, and *some* of them are even true. But very little is known about him before that time."

"I heard he sprang from the womb of The Lady of Luck herself, because she was bored with the affairs of mortals and wanted to introduce a little more mischief to the world!" said the young maiden.

"No, no, NO!" her little sister countered. "He was a young elven prince, stolen by a band of gypsies and raised as one of them!"

"You're both wrong!" said a young boy of about twelve. He was a brash lad training to be a knight in his employer's household, and the Old Bard had already forgotten how he was related to his patrons. "I heard he was the bastard son of the Pirate Queen Rowena and some merchant she'd captured!"

"Alas, all those stories may be true, or none of them, for our friend Donatello seldom spoke much about his early life, and on those rare occasions he did, he never told the same story twice!"

"But *you* know, don't you, Sir Bard?" the little six-year-old girl asked him earnestly.

The Old Bard flashed her his best smile, winked and tapped her gently on the nose. "You bet I do, young one! I've discovered what even the great bards of Lukescros haven't been able to uncover. I've spent many a fortune and a good number of my years tracking down the secrets of Donatello's past, and it's not a story I tell just anyone."

"May I remind you, Sir Bard, that we are paying you well for your services," the girls' father, his patron, said haughtily.

"Indeed you do, M'lord," the Old Bard nodded deferentially at him. "But there are some tales… some tales that are so grand…

so enthralling… so captivating that they deserve something special, don't you agree?" he asked with a sweeping gesture that encompassed everyone seated around the fire.

"Indeed it does," his patron's wife said enthusiastically as her husband harrumphed, unconvinced. But at the urging of his lady-wife, he removed a small, jeweled golden band from his finger and dropped it in the bard's cup of wine.

"Your payment, bard," he said unhappily. "So this had *better* be a good story!"

Unfazed, the Old Bard took another draught of his wine. After he set the cup down, he raised his had to his mouth and gently removed the ring which he'd stuck his tongue through and momentarily examined it. It was worth at least a month of his wages.

"Oh, it will be, my lord," he said. "It will be."

"The true circumstances of Donatello's birth, I'm afraid, are lost to the mists of time, but the first time the world seems to have taken notice of him was when he was about four, still practically a newborn in elven terms.

"He was spotted wandering the streets of Kreel, stealing food from the carts of the merchants along the high street. He was well-dressed for an urchin, and so small and innocent-looking, he went mostly unnoticed. He could pluck a mouthful of bread or piece of fruit from a cart and disappear into the crowd, appearing no different from any of the other children accompanying their parents on a shopping trip. And on those occasions a merchant did catch him trying to pilfer his goods, he'd either wordlessly pretend to be the child of a distracted patron or just look up at the merchant with a pitiful expression in his big green eyes and the merchant would let him go.

"No one can remember how long Donatello survived like this, but it wasn't long until he came to the attention of The Fagin, a seemingly kindly, well-to-do merchant who had a soft-spot for the city's young waifs and strays. But in secret, he was the leader of the town's notorious thieves' guild, who used the orphans he collected to steal the people of the city blind.

"On the fateful day The Fagin first saw him, Donatello had stolen from one merchant once too often and this time the merchant decided to give chase instead of letting him go.

"The Fagin watched the chase with interest as the youngster nimbly maneuvered his way through the crowd. He showed great promise and just as the boy was about to make good his final escape through a small crack in a wall, The Fagin stepped in, blocking his path.

"Gotcha!" The Fagin exclaimed, grabbing hold of the surprised boy as the merchant finally caught up with them. "Now then, what's this commotion all about, eh?" he asked.

"That… that… urchin… stole a baguette from my stand!" the merchant huffed and puffed. "Been doin' it for a while now. Only just caught 'im!"

The Fagin looked down at the boy, pretending he was seeing him for the first time, when in fact he'd already sized up the lad. His fine clothes were now filthy and tattered, and he was so malnourished that if he turned sideways, he'd've practically disappeared.

"That true, boy?" he Fagin asked.

"Donatello looked up at him with his big, sad, green eyes and slowly nodded yes.

"What'sa matter boy?" the merchant taunted. "Cat got your tongue? Well I bet the cats the town guard wield will make you talk, alright!"

"Easy now, Mr. Burntkrust! Can't you see you're scaring the boy?" The Fagin admonished. "This boy is starving! He needs a good home and decent meals, not a whipping!"

"What about all the bread he stole from me?" the aggrieved baker asked. "What am I to do about that?"

"This boy can nary afford to give you a pound of flesh," The Fagin said, pinching Donatello's scrawny arms. "And taking it from his hide will not return your lost earnings to you. I will make you a deal, Mr. Burntkrust. Let me take him to my school for the wayward youth of our fine city, and I will pay you for what he took."

"Well as you can imagine, Mr. Burntkrust liked the sound of that, and he immediately began trying to coax The Fagin into paying him a greatly inflated price for all the bread Donatello filched. "Dunno, that boy looks small, but he can sure eat a lot,' the baker began. "And been stealin' from me for a while, understand. Musta cost me… twenty-five gold crowns by now."

The Fagin didn't flinch. He opened his purse and gave the man his price without haggling. He could afford to be generous—for now. He'd have his gang of orphans take the man for at least twice that by the turn of the new moon.

The matter settled, The Fagin brought Donatello to his 'orphan's school,' a small and slightly run-down manse situated on the bank of the river Greystrem, conveniently near the outlet for the city's sewer system. There he turned the boy over to a young, exotic-looking, mocha-colored beauty named Xira, who The Fagin introduced as his wife.

In reality, though, The Fagin had many such 'wives,' for his lust for gold was only equaled by his lust to possess beautiful girls.

But Xira was his current favorite. She not only satisfied his carnal desires, but she had the unusual knack of being able to reproduce any document she saw, and the The Fagin knew how to put that talent to good use. He had her reproduce royal writs, deeds, and titles of nobility, selling them to unwitting and overly anxious visitors who came to the city seeking to better their lot. He had her duplicate ancient illuminated manuscripts and passed them off to traveling monks and clerics as the originals. He even had her recreate a famous painting or two, so that when he had the original stolen, he could replace it with the forgery so the original owners would be none the wiser.

Now, having lived so long on the streets alone, Donatello was naturally mistrustful of anyone new. He'd followed The Fagin home because he'd had no choice in the matter. But Xira was a kind and gentle woman, and she took good care of the boy. She bathed him and found him new, clean clothes and fed him. She spoke to him in a soft, lyrical voice and gave him a comfortable place to sleep, even tucking him in at night. And despite his initial misgivings, Donatello found himself warming to her.

During those first few weeks with her, Donatello would sit on his small stool, munching on the food she'd given him to make him strong, and watch her work at the table. One day she noticed his intent stares, and lifted the boy onto her lap and began to show him what she was doing.

"You like to try, yes?" she asked him.

Donatello looked up at her and nodded. She took a scrap sheet from the side of her desk, moved it in front of him then gently took his small hand in hers, helped him to pick up her quill and began to teach him how to draw.

"Why you no speak?" she asked him as they practiced making shapes.

Donatello just shrugged and went back to drawing.

Xira looked at him sadly. "What happened to you that scared away your voice, my little one?" she asked. He didn't answer her. In fact, he never answered her when she'd ask him something. Since the day The Fagin had brought him to her, she'd never been able to coax a word from him—not even his name.

But while Donatello's voice was slow in coming, he proved himself a fast-learner, quickly picking up the drawing skills Xira was showing him. In the weeks that followed, they'd spend hours together at that table, Xira working on another assignment from the Fagin, and Donatello making pictures of trees and forests and houses and people Xira didn't recognize.

Those were perhaps the happiest days of the young elf's early life, but like so many things, those happy times don't last.

One day after Donatello had regained his strength and put on some much-needed weight, The Fagin made a rare daytime appearance in their room.

"Well, my young friend," he said in a friendly way that still somehow carried a tone of menace. "You're looking fit and fiddle! Looks like our Xira here has treated you well. Been feeding you well, eh?"

Donatello slowly nodded. He'd begun saying a word or two by now, but only for Xira.

"Getting enough to eat, have we?"

Again Donatello nodded.

"Glad to hear it!" he said in the same overly friendly voice that Donatello knew meant the exact opposite. "But all those victuals don't come cheap, my boy, and I think it's time you help earn your keep around here. Don't you agree?"

Donatello cast a quick glance at Xira. But she was staring at the floor, her expression blank. His eyes quickly returned to The Fagin's expectant face. He nodded in agreement, sensing he didn't have much of a choice.

"Good lad!' The Fagin said, patting him on the head patronizingly. "I knew you were a smart boy the moment I spotted you."

The Fagin then took Donatello's hand and led him to a large hall on the lower level of the manse to meet the other "students" at the "school." They ranged in age from about four to fifteen, and while most were human, he did spot the occasional small, tapered ear of a half-elf, and at least one dwarf.

And so it was among this collection of cast-offs, strays, and ragamuffins that our friend leant the art of the cutpurse, pickpocket and lock-pick.

At first it seemed like they were teaching him a secret game they played against the townsfolk and city watch. It was like tag-and-run or hide-and-seek. And Donatello especially enjoyed evading the lumbering men of the city guard. He thought them slow and bumbling oafs, and couldn't understand why they had such difficulties following him through the crowded streets, down narrow alleys, over high walls or between tight gaps in some walls.

Yet in truth, Donatello's slight stature, nimbleness and fleetness of foot made even the most experienced of his new brothers and sisters look clumsy by comparison, just as The Fagin had foreseen.

It soon became apparent that Donatello was becoming the most talented member of The Fagin's band of child-rogues and lavished the boy with attention, praise and gifts while punishing the others, demanding they be more like his star 'pupil.'

Now, you might think that this would have engendered lots of jealousy toward Donatello from the other children, but you'd be wrong! Donatello cared little for the rewards The Fagin gave him, and shared his good fortune with all his new found brothers and sisters—especially Xira. He'd save the prettiest trinkets for her, or sometimes use whatever fortune he'd acquired to buy brushes, pigments, inks, or scraps of canvas or parchment for her just so he could spend time drawing or painting with her at her table.

"What are you going to paint for me today, my little Artist Dodger?" she'd often ask him, and thus the boy with no name finally earned the first of the many aliases he'd become known by.

He proudly used this new moniker as he continued to refine his skills on the streets and in the back alleys of Kreel. But as the years passed, Dodger began to grow weary of all The Fagin's games. The thrill he got from stealing and evading pursuit began to wane, and he tired of losing his brothers and sisters to either the dungeons or gallows when they got caught, or watching them disappear when The Fagin 'graduated' them from his school.

The Fagin would assure Dodger that those fates wouldn't befall him, but as the weeks rolled into months and months into years, Dodger became less and less reassured by those promises, and by the time he'd turned into a teen, Dodger finally left The Fagin's employ.

No one knows for sure what finally prompted the young elf to leave the only home he'd ever known. Some say Dodger finally tired of the cruel way The Fagin treated the children who didn't meet his ever-more-demanding quotas. Others say it was The Fagin who kicked Dodger out, fearing the way his band of tiny thieves looked up to the boy, and the loyalty he'd earned by protecting those who couldn't meet the quota by making up for their shortfall with some of his own plundered loot.

There are darker stories still, that claim The Fagin slew Xira in a jealous rage after discovering her and Dodger together.

But whatever the reason he left, the parting was less than amicable, and Dodger found himself once again alone on the streets, trying to eke out a meager living whatever way he could.

"Now, thieving in a city without the backing and protection of a guild is a sure invitation to the gaol or grave, and many a rogue's story has ended this way," The Old Bard said as he leaned toward his audience and began speaking in a conspiratorial whisper. "But it seems The Fates had another lot in mind for our young hero."

Lord Flynn
Chapter 2

The Old Bard stared into each of the faces gathered around the campfire. He saw how the reflections of the flames in their eyes echoed the curiosity burning within them to hear the rest of his tale.

He smiled to himself as he held their stares, drawing out the moment a bit longer. He took another swallow of the sweet wine to lubricate his throat then continued his story.

Dodger soon realized that he needed to leave the city if he was going to survive. He knew little of the world outside the city walls, but knew it was sheer folly to try to traverse The Adventurer's Highway alone on foot. For just a few leagues beyond the farmsteads that supported the city was the Haunted Forest, a place said to be rife with marauding bands of goblins, gnolls and even an ogre or two. It was even rumored that common rodents which lived there grew to unusual and monstrous size.

Dodger had seen the condition of many a band of travelers who'd risked a journey through the woods. Even the more well-armed parties looked battered and bruised and their first stop once inside the city was to God's Way to visit one of the many temples there to heal up their wounded.

Dodger supposed he could take one of the other three roads leading to and from the city. The road to the south lead to a series of small hamlets and Dodger had no desire to become a farmer. He loved the energy and excitement of the city and didn't think he could stand the hard work, long hours and monotony of country life. He had met—and robbed—his fair share of people from those villages and found them all to be bores.

The road to the east lead into the mountains, and to the Dwarfish mines. Dodger had also run across a few of them, and with the exception of a group of seven miners and their human companion, he found the dwarfs to be a dour lot. Besides, he had no desire to spend the rest of his life underground, digging through the earth just to make someone else rich.

He supposed he could take the road to the west. He knew it eventually led to the coast, and he'd overheard men in the alehouse and taverns talking about a port city out that way, but didn't know much more than that. From the drunken talk, it sounded like the type of place he'd like, big and bustling, with ships bringing in new people and things every day. He could do well there, he thought, and if things got too rough, he could always stowaway on a ship and go somewhere else.

But what would happen if he got there and discovered the 'city' was no more than a glorified fishing village? He had no more desire to become a fisherman than a farmer.

That pretty much only left the Adventurer's Highway to the north. Countless times, he'd overhead the advice handed out by veteran adventurers to the city's youth who *oohed and ahhed* over their fine masterwork equipment and marveled at the way they freely spent their gold.

"Crave fine things, do you now?" they'd enviably ask. "Well then, boy," they'd say even if the 'boy' they were talking to turned out to be a girl, "You need to go west—follow the Adventurer's Highway. That's where you find your fame and fortune… that is if you survive!" Then they'd laugh and go back to their drinking.

Dodger had always like the sound of that, but he couldn't convince any of those veteran adventurers to take him with them. Even when he tried to sign on with newly forming parties, the reaction would always be the same. They'd take one look at him and exclaim, "We'll not be having any child in our group! Now go run back to your momma, boy! We gots important grownup stuff to discuss here!"

Well as you can imagine, Dodger would have been happy to run back to his mother, if he'd remembered who'd she was, or where he was from. But he didn't, and he knew that every day he remained in the city, the chance became greater that The Fagin would find a way to arrange his disappearance, the way he'd arranged the disappearance of so many of his foster brothers and sisters over the years.

So, since he couldn't hire himself out to one of the many parties leaving the city, Dodger decided that he'd just stowaway on one of the caravans that came and went from the city on a somewhat regular basis.

And this my friends, is where The Fates stepped in. For Dodger was no fool, and he chose the most well-protected caravan he could find—one guarded by twelve professional swordsman dressed in chainmail, and one cloaked holy man who bore the symbol of Arenor around his neck.

What Dodger didn't know was that he'd chosen the caravan belonging to Edward, Lord of Flynn, and Blademaster to the royals of Bardak and Palt. And while he *was* able to secret himself aboard one of their wagons, he *wasn't* able to keep his presence a secret for long. The third day into their journey, he was discovered trying to steal some food from the cook's wagon.

By now, they were well into the Haunted Forest and the lord's men were already on high alert. Unlike the clods and bullies who made up the city guard, these men were no lumbering oafs and knew how to work together as a unit. While he was still faster and more agile than they were, they soon had him surrounded. Any hopes of escaping them were dashed when the cloaked man stepped forward, held out his holy symbol, and began gesturing at him while chanting some strange prayer. In an instant, Dodger felt invisible bands of force ensnare him like half a dozen lassos suddenly pulled tight. He couldn't move his arms or hands from his sides, and his legs felt like they were glued together. He was totally immobilized and it was all he could do to remain standing.

"Well, what have we got here?" an older human asked as he approached the group. He was wearing a crimson and black tunic, black trousers, and a traveling cape made from the finest of leather. At his side was one of the finest swords Dodger had ever seen—a long, slender blade, with a cupped guard and a grip banded in black leather and braided gold.

"A thief, M'lord," one of the men said. "Caught him pilfering our supplies."

"That true?" Lord Flynn asked.

Dodger stared back at the man, making his eyes as big as saucers and putting on his most pitiful expression. "Please, sir, I only wanted some food," he whimpered, trying to sound as pathetic as possible. "I'm just a poor orphan…"

"Do you take me for a fool, boy?" Flynn growled angrily, not fooled for an instant by the Dodger's act. "You're a thief, plain and simple! No doubt sent to case out this caravan before your gang tries to raid it. Well," he said drawing the ornate sword from his side. "I know how to deal with your lot. I'll send you back to your masters with your hands in a box! Take him!"

The lord's men grabbed Dodger and led him over to a nearby tree stump. There they pushed him to his knees, tied his wrists together, and lashed them to the stump. Still caught up by the cleric's spell, Dodger was powerless to resist. The men stepped back as their master approached, with his sword held high above his head.

But before Flynn could bring it down and sever Dodger's hands from his wrists, a band of goblins riding worgs burst through the trees, gibbering and screaming their war chants as they fell upon the caravan.

In an instant, Dodger was all but forgotten, as the lord and his men turned to face the new and more pressing threat. The invisible bands of force that had immobilized him faded away a moment later, and once able to move again, Dodger worked furiously to free himself from the stump as a melee erupted around him.

In the confusion of the battle, Dodger managed to slip away into the tree line, and even with his wrists still partially bound, managed to climb to safety high up in the canopy of one of the trees. Hidden from sight from both his captors and the attacking goblins, he sat down on one of the branches and used his teeth to undo the last of the knots.

The lord and his men were more skilled than their attackers, but the goblins had numbers on their side. At first, Dodger was unsure who'd eventually win the fight, and wasn't going to stick around to find out. But then he watched as two of the raiders climbed aboard one of the wagons, killed its driver and made off with it.

Immediately the lord's men sounded a new alarm, and Flynn himself began running after the departing carriage—in the back was his golden-haired daughter. Spurred on by his toddler's terrified screams, the lord flew faster than Dodger had ever seen a human run, but he was nowhere near as fast as the two horses whipped into a frenzy by the goblins. Even the lord's priest was unable to stop it. By the time the holy man finished chanting his prayers, the fleeing wagon was too far out of range.

"Now at this point, any normal person would have taken the opportunity to make good his escape. But as we all know, our friend was no ordinary person. For instead of running away, Dodger immediately began giving chase to the fleeing wagon through the treetops.

"Without a moment's thought, he began running, leaping and sometimes even swinging himself from limb to limb following the cart. Unlike the goblins, he didn't have to stay to the forest path, and was soon able to get ahead of the stolen cart. He stopped when he came to a tree with a thick bough that crossed over the path. Then, using the rope that had once been used to bind him, he attached it to the branch and leapt off.

The goblins on the wagon looked up just in time to see Dodger swinging down directly at them. He knocked the driver clean off the cart, dropping into his seat in an almost casual way.

"Mind if I drive?" he asked the driver's surprised cohort. "I get wagon sick riding in the back."

The goblin just looked at him for a moment like he was insane, then bared its teeth, growled something in its guttural tongue, and reached for its short sword.

"I guess you do!" Dodger said, only now realizing he was unarmed. He quickly reached for anything he could use to defend himself, finding only the handle of a lever at his side. He grabbed it with both hands as the goblin swung at him. True to his name, Dodger managed to dodge the blow by diving over the side of the speeding cart, using his grip on the lever and his momentum to swing himself back up onto the wooden roof of the carriage. When he landed, a bit unsteadily, he found the lever had cracked off in his hands. He didn't have time to worry that he'd just broken the carriage's brake and there was now no way to stop it. He was just relieved to have a weapon as the goblin climbed up after him.

"Back off, or I'll beat you with my, um, fearsome, um, wooden stick!" he threatened as the goblin approached, undaunted.

"Okay, don't say I didn't warn you," Dodger said, clumsily swinging his makeshift club at his foe.

The goblin easily parried the blow, then launched its own attack. Dodger again managed to avoid the swing, but was forced to retreat almost all the way to the back end of the roof.

Up until this point, Dodger had never been in a real fight. In fact, the only weapon he'd ever used was a dagger, and then he'd only used that to cut purses or as an improvised lock pick. He hated fighting, because he did not like hurting other people. Of course, he didn't like getting hurt all that much himself, either. That's why running away always seemed like the best option whenever things turned ugly. Only now, he didn't have that choice.

"Look, why don't we settle this like two civilized…" Dodger began, but stopped as the goblin bared its teeth and snarled at him.

"Okay, so you're not civilized, I get that! I'll tell you what. I'll let you keep the wagon and all the loot, and I'll just take the kid in the back and be on my way. Believe me, human children are more trouble than they're worth! Sorta like chicken wings. They're a lot of work for just a little meat, and they taste awful! So whaddaya say? We have a deal?" he asked.

The goblin answered him in true goblin fashion, and took another swing at him.

This time, Dodger used his 'club' to block the attack instead of retreating. The sword bit deep into the wood, and for a moment became stuck in it. The goblin grinned, and pulled his weapon back, trying to use the opportunity to wrest the club out of Dodger's hands. But fear had made Dodger's grip strong, and as he struggled and twisted to keep hold of the weapon as the goblin pulled his sword free, he wound up striking the goblin in the face with one end of the stick of wood.

Green blood spewed from the goblin's broken nose as it howled in pain.

"I warned you not to mess with my fearsome wooden stick of goblin bane!" Dodger said, trying to sound threatening, but it came out more as an apology.

The enraged goblin was neither appeased by the apology nor cowed by the threat. It just hefted its sword above its head, and with both hands brought it down toward Dodger's head.

Dodger took hold of 'goblin bane' with both hands, thrusting it up and out over his head in an effort to deflect the downward swing. The goblin's blade crashed into it with a mighty crack, all but splitting it in twain.

While the attack had failed to cleave Dodger in two, Dodger's only means of attack and defense was now useless, and the goblin knew it. It bared its teeth again as it took a moment to steady its balance on the bouncing wagon before striking what was sure to be the final killing blow.

Dodger put that momentary pause to good use. He glanced behind the goblin while he steadied himself, then cast aside the fistful of splinters in his hands, so they'd be free for what was coming.

"I see nothing's going to stop you from getting your point across," he said, eyes locked on the goblin's blade. "But there is something you *really* ought to do before you kill me."

The chronicles are unclear on whether the goblin really understood what Dodger was saying, but it did pause, looking at him quizzically.

Dodger pointed behind the goblin, yelled "Duck!" then somersaulted backwards, catching the edge of the roof in his hands and using it to swing into the open doorway in the back of the carriage.

The goblin had barely enough time to turn around before a low-hanging tree limb swept him off the roof.

Dodger watched from the inside of the wagon as the goblin's body hit the ground with a loud thud.

"I guess a tree's bark is worse than that goblin's bite!" he quipped, smiling at the startled little girl at his side. She had stopped wailing and was looking at him with eyes as wide as a full moon.

"So, kid, whaddaya say we get outta here and look for your father?" he asked the little girl.

She nodded slowly, still unsure about him.

"Good girl!" he said encouragingly as he glanced around the inside of the wagon. "Say, your father wouldn't happen to have any rope in here, would he?"

The little girl nodded again and quickly found some for him. Dodger took it, then grabbed a large kite shield he found among the now scattered belongings bouncing around inside of the wagon, and set it on the floor, curved end down. He quickly stepped onto it, hooking his feet into the handholds and shifting his weight around to test its balance as the shield rocked side to side like a boat in the swells.

"Eh, I guess it'll do," he said to the toddler as he secured one end of the rope to a metal ring hanging from the ceiling. He grabbed a hold of the other end with his left hand, then beckoned her to come to him.

As you can well imagine, the little girl was hesitant at first, but with some more urging and another warm smile from Dodger, she finally came to him. He scooped her up with his right arm and hugged her to his chest.

"Hold on real tight, and don't let go!" he told her.

The little girl nodded that she understood, then buried her face in Dodger's shoulder.

"Okay, kid. Here we go!" he said, hopping backwards out of the wagon, the shield attached to his feet. They landed with a bounce and were immediately yanked forward, but Dodger's keen agility and sense of balance kept them upright as they surfed along the ground, being pulled by the cart.

Dodger slowly let out the rope he held in his left hand, until they were well behind the fleeing wagon. When he reached the end of the tether, he tossed it aside and used the hand to help him maintain his balance as they gradually lost speed. He brought them to a stop with a great sliding flourish, then hopped off the shield.

"Ride's over," he said to the little girl, who was clinging to him more stubbornly than a leech. She looked up at him with a mixture of fear and exhilaration in her face.

"Want to go again?" he asked, grinning.

The little girl looked at him for a minute, unsure if he was serious, then shook her head vigorously *no*.

Dodger just laughed. "Okay," he said. "Then what do you say we go find your father? I bet he's really worried about you."

This time, the girl nodded her head *yes,* and Dodger lifted her onto his shoulders and began walking back the way they had come, whistling a happy tune as if they didn't have a care in the world.

When Dodger and the girl found Lord Flynn and his men again, they had just finished mopping up the rest of the goblin horde. "We need to go after my daughter!" the distraught father said, trying to rally his men. "I've already lost my wife, I'll not lose her, too!"

"No need for that," Dodger said, strolling in among them. Flynn's little girl was still riding on his shoulders, her small hands gripping his large pointed ears like reins, and she was giggling happily.

"Here. I think you lost this," Dodger said walking up to the human. Immediately every sword in the party pointed at Dodger as Flynn snatched his daughter off the elf's shoulders.

"Ouch! The ears! The ears!" Dodger winced as the girl reluctantly let go of him.

"Seize him!" the nobleman commanded once his daughter was safely back in his arms.

Following their liege's orders, a dozen hands shot out and roughly grabbed and restrained Dodger. He wasn't really all that surprised by the rough treatment and had half expected it. But what did surprise him was the little girl's wails when her father's men began to bind him again.

"Miranda, honey! What's the matter?" Flynn asked.

"Don't hurt him, Daddy! Don't hurt him! He's my friend! He saved me from those ugly little green men!"

The lord glared at Dodger with a look he would see many, many more times in the future, from both suspicious fathers and spouses. Dodger just returned the look with a sheepish smile on his face.

"What foolishness have you filled my daughter's head with?" he demanded. "Did you think getting her to ask me to spare your hands would really work, thief? Now I think I'll have your head!" he said drawing his sword.

At those harsh-sounding words, Miranda began crying again. "Please, Daddy! Please don't hurt the little man!"

"Honestly sir, I'm *not* as clever by half as you'd give me credit, for it never even occurred to me to try that," Dodger answered honestly. He wasn't even sure what he had been thinking. His experiences back in Kreel had taught him it was extremely unlikely that anyone, not to mention a nobleman, would just let him go simply because he'd done them a favor.

"So why did you do it?" the lord pressed.

"Dodger shrugged. "'Cause she's a child and was in danger, and I don't like seeing anyone or anything threaten a child," he said after a long, contemplative pause.

Flynn still stared at him skeptically, but his priest looked more convinced. He gently placed a hand on his lord's shoulder.

"He *is* telling the truth, M'lord. Killing him would be unjust," the holy man said. "Yet, so would letting him go. He did, after all, steal from your household..."

"Hey, wait a second, priest! I told the truth! Doesn't that count for something?" Dodger protested. "How d'you expect me to learn any moral lessons when you keep confusing me this way?"

The priest ignored Dodger's outburst. "As I was saying, M'lord. He did steal from you. Perhaps a more fitting punishment for our young rogue here would be letting him work off his debt for his food and safe passage, by having him provide service to your household."

Lord Flynn looked just as happy about that prospect as Dodger did. Though crusty and gruff, the lord was a fair man at heart. "And just what service do you have in mind?" he asked, still skeptical.

"Well, it appears Miranda likes him, and he's already shown a willingness to protect her, and since you've just lost your page…"

The lord mulled it over in his mind for a moment, then reluctantly agreed. "Okay, I guess we can give it a try," he said, resheathing his sword. "If it doesn't work out, I guess I can always cut off his hands later."

As it turned out, Dodger did make an excellent page, and worked for the lord for years, well past the point of repaying his debt to the nobleman's household. Yet neither of them would admit they liked the arrangement.

Every night, after Dodger had finished tending to all of his master's needs, Flynn would excuse him, saying, "Good night, Dodger. Try to steal from me tonight, and I'll make good on my promise to cut your hands off in the morning."

As for Dodger, he would bitterly complain to anyone who would listen about all the things he'd have to do for his master. "A page, he calls me! More like a slave! I have to fetch him his meals, water for his bath, bring him his clothes, and help him dress! You'd think the man couldn't do anything for himself!" he'd grumble. "And then he has the nerve to use me as a live training dummy for his pupils!"

The last part was true, for the lord often did use Dodger to help train the young nobles he tutored in bladecraft. Luckily for Dodger, none of them seemed to be any good. Even weighted down by the heavy, padded surcoat and old, oversized steel helm Flynn had given him for protection, he could still easily avoid the young nobles' attacks. For not only were they slow of limb, but appeared to be slow of mind as well.

No matter how hard the lord tried, nor how much he berated them, few, if any, of his students could master the techniques he was trying to teach them. As you can image, this did nothing improve the blademaster's ill-tempered humor. He'd rail at class after class of noble youths that his lowly page could use a sword better than they could.

And he was right. Dodger had been forced to attend so many

of Flynn's training sessions that he knew all the attack and defensive moves by heart, and could execute them better than even some of the lord's own men.

At the time, Dodger didn't appreciate all the training Lord Flynn was inadvertently giving him. Given a choice, he would have spent most of his time tending to Miranda. She was growing into a spirited child with an easy laugh and sense of adventure. She loved the pictures he drew for her, and would make up the most wildest of stories about them. Dodger loved listening to the imaginative tales she'd tell.

"Draw me a dragon," she asked him once. "With bronze scales, green eyes, and huge wings! And make it a girl dragon, 'cause girl dragons are so much better than boy dragons! When I'm bigger, I'm going to visit the islands in the Dragon Sea and make friends with one. Then I'm going to fly on her across the water to the Great Forest, and visit with the elves who live there. And I'd take you there, too! Maybe they'll even be able to help you find your mommy and daddy."

Dodger smiled as he drew her picture. "I'd like that very much," he said.

This was perhaps the happiest time of our friend's life. We know this because he kept these memories mostly to himself, hoarding them as a dragon hoards its treasure. But as he'd learn over and over again in his life, good times don't last.

Again the Old Bard paused as if lost in a memory. Then he took another long draft of his wine. When the cup was empty, he held it out for more, and this time no one protested and the cup was refilled with sweet wine. The Old Bard took another long sip, then after wiping his mouth on one of his long sleeves, he continued with his story.

"As I'm sure M'lord and M'lady can attest, human children grow up fast," the Old Bard resumed. "And in a blink of Dodger's eye, Miranda had sprung up from a child to a lovely young maiden, with long blonde locks and eyes as green as newly budded leaves in spring. She had many suitors, but none caught her fancy, and she seemed to prefer spending time with her father's page than go courting with any of the sons of the nobles her father visited.

"I don't ever want to get married and settle down," she told Dodger one day after they'd come back from one of their rides across the countryside.

"I'm afraid your father might have something to say about that, M'lady," Dodger said, rather breathlessly, as he dismounted his pony and staggered over to help her off her filly. Miranda's idea of a relaxing ride usually included racing her horse at full speed across the countryside, jumping over hedgerows, fences, and streams, and it was all Dodger could do to hang onto his own mount to try to keep up with her. If her father ever found out he let her do this, he'd surely have boxed his ears. But Miranda was an accomplished rider and could not be persuaded to ride in a more demure, lady-like fashion.

"Well, it's his fault! We've been traveling from place to place all my life, and I don't think I could stand being tied down to one place. There are just too many places in this world I want to see!"

"Like the islands in the Dragon Sea, and the Great Forest?" Dodger teased.

Miranda stopped and looked at him and smiled, surprised that he remembered. "Yes," she said. "I still have those pictures, you know."

"I'm honored, M'lady."

"In fact, I have *all* the pictures you've ever drawn for me," she continued.

For perhaps the first time in his life, Dodger didn't know what to say. He felt flushed, and was sure his face was turning red all the way up to the very tips of his pointed ears. He'd never thought his pictures were all that good, and never believed anyone would ever treasure them.

"I'm sure one day you're going to be a famous artist, like the great master painter Doña Atello of Isandor."

"M'lady is too kind," Dodger finally said, not able to look at her.

Miranda took his chin in her hand and turned his head to face her. "Don't let my father's opinions dissuade you. You're a great artist! The only art he knows about is warcraft. I've seen some of the Doña's paintings at the castles we've visited, but I prefer your works. She might have a slightly better technique, but her pictures are full of muted colors and are dry and lifeless. Yours are bright, colorful, and full of joy! I think you will be just as famous as her one day..."

"And what will they call me? *Don* Atello of Nowhere?"

Miranda laughed, and it was like music to Dodger's ears. Suddenly he wasn't embarrassed anymore. "Don Atello! I like that. From now on I think I'll call you Donatello!"

And she did. From that day onward, whenever Miranda would address him, she'd call him by his new nickname, Donatello. A few of the lord's other servants overheard her doing it and began calling him that too, usually in a mocking manner. At first it bothered him, but the new name quickly grew on him, especially whenever Miranda used it.

That was perhaps the last of Dodger's happiest days with Lord Flynn and his daughter. For soon after, the blademaster's patrons began to dry up as the fighting style he taught fell out of fashion, in favor of the newer styles being taught by the Stealles in Penwick. As their days of wandering the continents dwindled, Lord Flynn retired to his ancestral home in Bardak.

Few folks came to visit them there, with one glaring exception—Lord Ocimum Wraithbone. After switching sides during the War of Ash, the former Parthian Lord relocated to the vacant halls of Versarni in Lanfor. Wraithbone liked to show off his wealth and power, often using it to buy things and people he found of interest. And while he had little use for an aging blademaster, he did have an eye for his daughter.

Lord Wraithbone met Miranda at her sixteenth birthday fete and immediately became enchanted by the young woman. But Miranda did not share his attraction. She found him ugly, and his merest touch raised goose pimples on her arms.

"Did you see the way that ugly old troll was staring at me?" Miranda asked Donatello after the soirée had ended.

"You'd have to be more specific, M'lady," he replied as he walked her back to her chambers. "I saw lots of old trolls ogling you tonight."

Miranda laughed. "You're so bad! You shouldn't be saying such things, Donatello."

Dodger returned her smile with an impish grin of his own. "Yes, M'lady. But then again, neither should you!"

Again Miranda laughed. "Well, I promise not to tell my father what you said, if you don't tell him what I said."

"Deal!" Dodger said, extending his hand and they shared the secret handshake he'd taught her as a child.

The next evening, he brought Miranda a small rolled up canvas, bound with a ribbon. Miranda took it from him excitedly.

"I wonder what it could be!" she asked, hastily undoing the ribbon and unrolling it. On the canvas was painted a picture of a troll, huddled under a bridge, gnawing on a bone. When Miranda saw it, she burst out laughing, immediately recognizing the face he'd drawn on the hideous creature.

It was Ocimum Wraithbone. In fact, if you've ever seen Donatello's painting of The Fall of Sir Kirk, you've seen the face of that troll. For from that day on, whenever Donatello drew a picture of a troll, it always had the face of Ocimum Wraithbone.

They were still laughing when Miranda's father walked in.

"I'm glad I've found you in such a good mood, my dear," he said as they entered.

Miranda quickly hid the small canvas behind her back as she turned to face her father. He was trying hard to look happy, but his face had never lent itself to smiling.

"I have some… wonderful… news for you," he said ignoring his daughter's rather obvious surreptitious behavior. "I have just made arrangements that will secure your future—a husband befitting one of your station."

Miranda looked crushed and confused.

"But father," she protested. "I don't want to marry! And I don't care about this drafty old castle. I want to stay with you! I love our travels together, and never knowing where we are going to end up each night!"

Donatello noted a strange twitch in Lord Flynn's eye as he walked over to his daughter and gently placed his hands on her shoulders.

"That was fine when you were a child—but you are a grown woman now. It's time to put away childish dreams and fulfill your obligations."

"I don't care one copper about my duty!" she said petulantly, stamping her foot for good measure. "I won't do it! I just won't!"

Flynn's face turned ashen as his hands fell away from his daughter. In the thirteen years Dodger had worked for him, he could never recall seeing his master look so devastated.

"Dodger, you are dismissed," he said turning to his servant. "I need to have a word with my daughter in private."

Now the last thing Dodger wanted to do was leave, but the haunted look in the Blademaster's eyes made him think twice about questioning his master. Reluctantly Dodger bowed, and as slowly as he could, he left the room. He felt his heart sink when he heard the door shut with an ominous thud behind him.

Dodger knew he shouldn't have loitered by the door trying to make out what was going on the other side of it, but he couldn't bring himself to leave. The door was thick, and the walls solid stone, and even his keen elven ears couldn't quite make out what was being said in the room. All he could hear were muffled voices and lots of crying.

After what seemed like an eternity, the voices stopped and all he could hear were Miranda's sobs.

At the first sign the door was about to open, Dodger dashed down the hall and disappeared into the shadows. A moment later, Lord Flynn stepped out of the room, pulled the door shut behind him and locked it from the outside. Even from down the hall, Dodger could see his face was still ashen, and his shoulders sagged as if he was carrying a heavy burden on his shoulders.

The Lord took a deep breath and stepped away from the door, then stopped and looked around.

"Dodger!" he called out into the emptiness. "I know you are lurking around here someplace. Show yourself!"

Dodger could have easily remained hidden in the shadows and made his way undetected back to his room, but something in his master's voice compelled him to step out into the flickering torchlight.

The old blademaster frowned. "I knew you wouldn't be far," he said walking over to the young elf. "You never are. You watch over my daughter like a dragon guarding its horde. And for that I've always been grateful. But so help me, you let her out of that room before she consents to this marriage, I swear I will cut off *both* your hands and throw the rest of your miserable hide in the dungeon for good!"

Dodger watched him walk slowly away, and when he was sure he was gone, he made his way quickly over to Miranda's door. He gave one quick last look over his shoulder before reaching into his belt and removing two extremely thin metal rods concealed in a slit he'd cut on the inside face of leather strap circling his slender waist. With practiced ease, he slipped the picks into the lock and within seconds heard it click open. He put his tools back into their hiding place, cracked the door open, and slipped inside the room.

Miranda was laying on her bed sobbing into her pillow.

"M'lady?" he called quietly.

The sound of his voice startled the remaining tears from her eyes and Miranda practically flew across the room into his arms.

"Donatello!" she sniffled. "How'd you get in here? Father locked me in until I agree to the marriage he arranged for me!"

Dodger gave her one of his sly smiles. "You should know by now that none of your father's locks have *ever* stopped me from going anywhere in this keep," he said. "And they never will."

Miranda laughed despite herself. But her mirth quickly morphed back into sobs.

"Oh, Donatello! He wants me to marry that horrible old troll Lord Wraithbone!" she said crying uncontrollably again.

Donatello took her head and gently pressed it against his shoulder and began to rock her slowly back and forth the way he'd done when she was a child.

"Hush, M'lady," he whispered stroking her long golden hair. "I'm sure he isn't really all that bad…"

Miranda looked up at him with her bloodshot green eyes.

"You didn't meet him, Donatello!" she protested. "He made my skin crawl when he touched me. He's a wicked old man! I just *know* he is!"

Dodger wanted to reassure her that all the rumors she'd heard about Lord Wraithbone were untrue. But he'd heard the stories about the nobleman's purported experiments in the dark arcane and unholy arts too many times himself to dismiss them as just gossip among servants.

"Donatello, talk to my father, please! Get him to reconsider! He'll listen to you!" Miranda begged.

Dodger doubted that. The only time her father recognized he existed was to bellow at him for doing something wrong.

Miranda seemed to read his expression and know what he was thinking. "Oh, Donatello, don't think that way!" she said immediately. "He's bellicose with everyone. If he didn't like you, why would he have kept you in his service all these years?"

"Because if he got rid of me, he'd actually have to *pay* someone to be his page," Dodger thought to himself. Thankfully he had other ways to supplement the handfuls of copper his lord grudging granted him each month.

"You will talk to him, won't you?" she begged.

Dodger sighed. He found it difficult to refuse her when she looked at him with her lovely green eyes.

"As you wish."

With those three words, Dodger found himself standing in the doorway of his lord's private chambers. Flynn was seated in his great chair, facing a fire blazing away in the fireplace, a tankard of untouched ale resting on one of the chair's massive arms.

"I don't recall summoning you," he said, startling Dodger. As was his habit, Dodger had slipped into his master's quarters so silently that he thought he'd gone totally unnoticed, even though he'd been standing there watching the old man for quite some time.

"You didn't," Dodger said, quickly recovering from his surprise. Lord Flynn had an uncanny ability to spot him lurking around when he wanted to, a feat which had forced Dodger to abort many a scheme to supplement his income.

The lord didn't immediately answer and Dodger thought he might have nodded off, so he slowly walked over to him.

"She sent you?" he asked, not bothering to favor him with even a glance. He didn't even seem angry or surprised that Dodger had disobeyed him yet again.

"Yes," Dodger answered, uncharacteristically short of words. His sudden lack of loquaciousness was brought on by the sight of his master's face.

Lord Flynn looked at least twice his fifty-some years. Every line chiseled into his broad, handsome face now looked like a fissure, and his cheeks, usually puffed out and red with perpetual anger, were now sunken and sallow as decades-old parchment. Even his eyes, usually full of fire, were now dull and lifeless. It was like Dodger was staring at a living corpse, like one of the ones Lord Wraithbone was rumored to have created.

Lord Flynn frowned and finally picked up his tankard and took a long draw on it. When he finally set it heavily back on the chair's arm and wiped his mouth with his sleeve, most of the liquid inside it was gone.

"Do you really think I want to give my daughter to that... that... old buzzard!" he spat.

Dodger couldn't tell whether the anger in his master's voice was directed at him or himself. "But it is the only way!" he continued, bringing his fist down hard on the chair's arm, spilling what little remained of his drink. "You've heard rumors of what Wraithbone can do? Well, I've seen it firsthand. If I refuse him Miranda, Bardak will pay a horrible price."

There was a short, awkward silence as Flynn stared into the fire, obviously remembering some event from his past. When he spoke again, his voice was barely above a whisper.

"You've no doubt heard about the Battle of Grevon?" he asked Dodger.

The young elf nodded silently. *Who hadn't?* He might not have had much in the way of a formal education, but everyone knew of that miraculous victory during the War of Ash.

"Well, I was there. We fought until the last man... Until *I* was the last man. The battle was lost—Lanfor was about to fall, as was I. That was, until Wraithbone intervened...

Again, there was another long silence as Flynn watched the flames in the fireplace leap and crackle.

"I made a terrible bargain then. But it was the only way! If Lanfor fell, the war would have been lost! *I had no choice!*"

Flynn finally turned to face Dodger, then grabbed him by the lapel and pulled him so close their noses were almost touching.

"Wraithbone turned all our dead into zombies! With them, we were able to clear the field and win the day. Afterwards, I had to destroy them all!"

Dodger stared at his master in disbelief.

Flynn saw the look on his page's face and released him, laughing a humorless laugh.

"I've done plenty of bad things, for good reasons," Dodger said, finally finding the courage to speak. "Miranda will forgive you for that."

"That she would," Flynn nodded, sorrowfully. "She's more than ever I deserved… I swore I'd protect her…"

Dodger felt his hopes rise. Perhaps he was going to be able to convince his master after all.

"Then *don't* give in to him. Don't give your daughter to that evil man. We can find some other way to save Bardak! She *is* your own flesh and blood, after all!"

"My own flesh and blood," Flynn repeated. *"My own flesh and blood?"*

Before Dodger could question why his master kept repeating that phrase, Lord Flynn let his hand fly and it struck Dodger hard across the mouth, dropping the elf to the floor.

"You forget your place, thief!" the old man scowled. "I'll not be lectured by some urchin I picked off the street! You will keep a civil tongue in your head, or by the gods I *will* clap you in irons and throw you in the dungeons for good!"

Dodger lay on the floor for a moment, stunned that the old man had actually hauled off and hit him. In all the years they'd been together, the worst the blademaster had ever done was yell and throw things at him, or make the occasional half-hearted attempt to swat him with the flat of blade whenever he'd stepped out of line.

Dodger wiped away a trickle of blood from his split lip with the back of his sleeve and slowly stood up to face his master.

"'Pologies, M'lord," he muttered. "Meant no disrespect. Just trying to look after your daughter's interests."

The anger in Lord Flynn's face faded almost as quickly as it had come over him. His hand, which was still raised, began to quiver and he let it drop back into his lap.

"You have always done so, haven't you?" he asked with a sigh, and Dodger thought he saw a twinge of regret form on his master's face. "But I'm afraid this is one thing you can't protect her from. Even we nobles must pay a price sometimes."

That didn't make sense to Dodger. The rich and the noble always seemed to be able to buy themselves out of any trouble. It was just the way things worked when you had lots of gold. And Dodger knew, from personal experience, that Flynn had plenty of it in his coffers. So why not use some of it now to make this problem go away?

What secret could be so terrible that even a dragon's horde of treasure couldn't buy off the creepy, troll-like Wraithbone? Flynn had spared no expense when it came to caring for his daughter, so why now was he jealously guarding his coppers like The Fagin?

And why had his master gotten so upset when he'd refered to Miranda as his own kin? He'd always treated her as such. He wondered if he'd ever understand the ways humans thought, and it made him wonder what other dark secrets this man, whom he'd grown to grudgingly respect, was keeping from him.

"Now go," Lord Flynn ordered before he could speak again. "Clean yourself up. I do not wish to be bothered anymore this night."

Miranda was upset when she saw Dodger's swollen lower lip when he returned to her chambers to break the bad news to her.

"Oh, Donatello!" she cried, rushing over to him. "Did my father do this to you?"

"It is nothing, M'lady," he said, as she dipped a small square kerchief in some wine and dabbed it on his lip. "I've had worse."

"I'm so sorry! I shouldn't have asked you to speak to him when he was in such a foul mood."

Dodger gently moved her hand away from his mouth, guided her back to the chair she'd been sitting in when he'd entered and placed her hands back in her lap. Her attempt to make his lip feel better was only making it feel worse.

"Think no more about it, M'lady. Your father is always in a foul mood," he said smiling at her.

Miranda laughed despite herself, and Dodger was glad to finally see her smiling again. He liked the way she smiled at him.

The mirth, however, didn't last long, and her face became somber again. "I take it my father didn't change his mind, did he?"

Dodger shook his head. "Perhaps it won't be so bad," he said, trying his best to sound positive. "I mean, that old troll *is* very rich, and with all that money, I bet you'll be able to travel anywhere you want and go all those places you always wanted to see. Who knows? He may turn out to be really nice…"

Miranda raised an eyebrow.

"Okay, probably not. But you probably won't have to spend *that* much time with him. And I'm sure if I asked your father nicely, he'd let me go with you as your servant, as part of your dowry."

"No!" Miranda said, getting up out of the chair and pacing the room. "Neither of us is going. I won't let him!"

"I don't see how you're going to stop him," Dodger said. "Your father has made up his mind and he won't be swayed."

Miranda paced back and forth, thinking. From long experience, Dodger knew she could be just as stubborn as her father, if not more so. So he said nothing and just watched her.

"Then we'll run away!" she said finally.

"Your father would just send his men after you," he said. "So would Wraithbone. You wouldn't get very far."

"But with *you* I would! You could teach me to hide like the way you used to back in Kreel. You said you were uncatchable!"

Dodger was sorry now that he'd ever told her any of stories about the way he'd spent his misguided youth as part of The Fagan's gang.

"It was not actually as fun as it sounded," he lied. "Besides, the city is the first place they'd look for us."

"Then we'll stick to the countryside or, better yet, the woodlands!" she said undaunted. "You're an elf, and everyone knows you can't find an elf in the woodlands if they don't want to be found."

Dodger didn't have the heart to tell her that was just a myth. Even if it wasn't, having grown up in a city, he had no more idea on how to "disappear" in woodlands than she did.

"Those are no places for a lady such as yourself. They are dangerous and full of all manner of wild animals and foul creatures. Remember the goblins in the Haunted Wood?"

"You protected me from them, and that was before Father taught you how to fight! He'd never admit it to you, but he told me that you were his best student and would make a fine swordsman!"

Given the loutish oafs he'd seen her father try to train, that wasn't saying much. Still, her confidence in his abilities touched him.

"Life on the run is hard, M'lady," he said, still trying to convince her of the folly of her plan. "They'll be no roaring fire to sit besides on cold nights, nor soft pillow to rest your head on. If you're lucky, the only heat you'll have to warm you will come from a smoky fire made from some hastily gathered twigs and leaves and the only place to rest your head will be a hard rock. We'll never be able to stay in one place too long, and the only money we'll ever be able to have is that that I can steal."

"You could always sell some of your paintings," she offered encouragingly.

Dodger smiled at her sadly. "I doubt they'd even bring in a copper," he said. "Even if they did bring in more, what kind of life would you have with an itinerant artist?"

Miranda walked over to him and knelt down in front of him. She took his hands in hers and looked into his big green eyes.

"I would rather spend a thousands lifetimes with you, enduring any hardship, than spend a minute as Lord Wraithbone's wife."

Dodger felt himself blushing all the way to the very tips of his pointed ears.

"Um… Thank you, M'la…" he began, suddenly short of words.

Miranda placed her right index finger against his lips. "Miranda," she told him. Then to his surprise, she kissed him.

Miranda
Chapter 3

T*he Old Bard paused to give his patron's daughters a chance to imagine themselves in the moment. He knew how much young girls delighted in the tales about true love, and despite herself, so, apparently, did his patron's wife.*

He wanted them to savor the moment, because he knew what was to happen next would make his story that much more heartbreaking...

"Unable to convince her of the folly of her plan, and perhaps a bit giddy that she requited the feelings he'd never allowed himself to admit, the two young lovers planned their escape from Flynn Keep.

They agreed that Miranda would pretend to agree to the betrothal so her father would free her from her rooms and allow her free run of their home. In the meantime, Dodger would use the time to gather the few items they'd need for their journey together.

Within a fortnight, they made good on their plan and escaped.

At first, the young lovers stayed true to their plan to stay away from any road or well-traveled path as they made their way cross-country though empty fields and wood. But after a while, Dodger could see the harsh conditions taking their toll on his young noblewoman, especially after the nights began to turn colder. So against his better judgment, he agreed to let Miranda rest one night in the relative comfort of the next inn they encountered on their journey.

The inn they finally found was on the edge of the wood, near a long-forgotten crossroad. It was made from a few roughly hewn large timbers, mud and thatch, and looked like it hadn't been occupied in decades. But there was a yellow-orange glow leaking out of the shuttered windows and smoke slowly curling up out of the stone chimney.

"Looks like someone is at home," Miranda said brightly.

"Yeah, that's what I'm afraid of," Dodger replied glumly, once again wondering why he'd let Miranda talk him into this.

"You worry too much!" she scolded him playfully. "We're leagues from home and haven't seen any sign of pursuit now for weeks! I doubt anyone way out here would know who I am, let alone recognize me!" she said, taking his hand and pulling him toward the front door.

Dodger stood his ground, stopping her. He pulled her back toward him, reached over her shoulders, and pulled the hood of her now soiled and worn traveling cloak over her head until her face was obscured in shadow.

"Just in case," he said, then he let her lead him to the door.

The inn was more crowded than they'd expected. There were at least a dozen patrons gathered in the common room, not including the innkeeper behind the bar, his wife, and a young serving girl rushing between tables carrying tankards of frothy liquid.

Dodger hurried Miranda away from the door and made her comfortable by the fire before he headed over to the bar to get them something warm to eat. It took a while to get the innkeeper's attention, and even longer for his wife to bring him back two steaming bowls of whatever passed for stew in these parts. By the time he carried the food back to Miranda, he could see she'd already drawn some unwanted attention from a brutish man with a thick bushy black beard and his two clean-shaven pals.

Miranda was doing her best to ignore them, but they persisted. And when the bearded man grabbed her roughly by the shoulder,

Dodger immediately set the bowls down on the nearest table and rushed over to her side.

"Unhand her!" he demanded, pushing his way between them.

The big bearded man released Miranda, then turned to look down on him with his dull brown eyes and broad, flat nose.

"And what ya gonna do if I don't, little man?" he asked contemptuously, shoving Dodger away.

"Then you will find your hand on the floor," he said, throwing open his cloak, revealing the hilt of a finely crafted small sword he'd nicked from Lord Flynn's armory. "Next to your head!"

The big bearded man made a show of raising his hands in front of him as he took a step back. "Ooooh, you're scarin' me, little man," he mocked. His friends laughed and simultaneously tried to grab him from either side.

Dodger had anticipated the move and was already drawing his sword when they attacked. He slammed the heavy pommel of his weapon into the face of the man on his right, breaking his nose and sending him to sprawling to the floor, howling in pain. He used the momentum of the swing to carry him around to face his second attacker, and as the man shot by him, Dodger slashed at his unshielded back.

The weapon's keen blade easily cut through the man's heavy leather jerkin and opened a long, deep gash along his back. He, too, dropped to the floor yelling in pain. With two of his opponents now disabled, Dodger turned his attention to the ringleader. Unlike his two friends, the bearded man was armed with a crude, broad blade, and in the time it had taken Dodger to dispatch his cohorts, the bearded man had managed to draw it.

"You'll pay for that, you pointy-eared bastard!" he spat, lunging at Dodger.

In the years he'd spent as Lord Flynn's practice dummy, Dodger had seen plenty of men fight like the bearded man, and he'd come to quickly realize that they depended more on their brute strength than any skill with a blade to get them through a fight. They posed little danger as long as he could avoid getting bull-rushed and wait for the inevitable over-powered and over-reaching swing to open up a vulnerable area to attack.

Dodger didn't have to wait long for that to happen. He easily parried the bearded man's very first strike with a sharp beat against his blade and before he could even react, Dodger sliced at his now exposed wrist, making good his threat to sever the man's hand from his wrist.

The big man dropped to his knees, grabbing his bloody stump.

"You cut my bloody 'and off!" he howled.

Dodger pointed the tip of his blade at the man's Adam apple. "I warned you!" he said angrily. "Try anything else and your head will join it!"

"I think you need to leave, stranger," came a voice from the bar.

Dodger looked up from his opponent and saw the innkeeper standing behind the bar nervously pointing a loaded crossbow at him. Every eye in the place was staring at him and Miranda.

Dodger didn't think it was fair that they were being kicked out when they didn't start the fight. He would have argued the point despite the loaded weapon aimed at them, but Miranda's soft touch on his arm made him reconsider.

He lowered his sword, and with a flick of his wrist cut the bearded man's coin purse from his belt and batted it over toward the innkeeper with the flat of the blade.

"Sorry 'bout the mess," he said, slowly began backing himself and Miranda toward the door. "We'll just take our meal and go," he added, grabbing a few loaves of hard bread from a nearby table as they passed and handing them to Miranda.

No one made any attempt to stop them, and once they'd made it outside, Dodger resheathed his sword and grabbed Miranda's hand, and together they ran back into the woods.

"I'm sorry you didn't get to spend the night at that inn. I know how much you were looking forward to it," Dodger apologized once they'd made camp far away from the road and inn.

Miranda tried to hide the disappointment on her face behind a smile. "It's not your fault, Donatello. You were right. We shouldn't have gone in there. But at least you managed to get us something decent to eat!" she said, nibbling on one of the loaves he'd stolen on their way out. "Besides, you've done my father's sword proud, the way you fought for my honor back there. I know you'll always keep me safe."

It was those few words which would haunt our friend the rest of his life. For while he did manage to keep Miranda safe for perhaps a month longer, word of their exploits at the inn finally made their way to the agents of Lord Wraithbone, and his men finally caught up with the pair as they tried to board a ship to Thac.

By all accounts, Dodger fought well—preventing any of the wicked lord's dozen or so men from men from grabbing Miranda. But Lord Wraithbone wasn't a patient man, and when it became clear his men couldn't quickly subdue the elusive elf, he decided to take matters into his own hands.

"You have proven yourself to be quite a nuisance, little thief, and have stolen something very valuable from me! Something which someone like you has absolutely no right to possess!" he began.

"Miranda is not some prize you can win, nor a jewel you can steal and place under glass to admire in some secret vault! She is a person who has a right to choose her own destiny!"

"How little you know of her true worth and destiny!" Lord Wraithbone replied, beginning to form symbols in the air with his hands.

Dodger recognized the motion. Lord Flynn's priest used to make the same pattern every time he wanted to immobilize him, something he seemed to have cause to do quite often. That priest always seemed to know when Dodger was up to some scheme and he'd inevitably appear at the last minute, putting an end to his plot with that blasted immobilization spell.

Well, this time Dodger wasn't going to get caught by it. Quick as a flash, he drew his dagger and hurled it at the dark lord before he could complete summoning the blue bands of magical force which would wrap around him tighter than any rope.

Any other man would never have been able to deflect such a lethal projectile. But Lord Wraithbone was no ordinary man. Some say he consorted with demons, while others claimed he was part demon himself, but whatever the case, the evil man was protected by charms that easily turned aside such missiles.

Lord Wraithbone stopped mid-gesture and cast his evil gaze upon Dodger. "I was going to let you live," he began icily. "But after such impudence, I think you shall have to *die*," he said emphasizing the last word and pointing a crooked finger at him.

Unseen by anyone else, four great tentacles suddenly rose up from the ground and grabbed each of Dodger's limbs and began trying to tear him apart, while another set of four rose up and began viciously slashing at him with razor-sharp barbs on their ends.

Dodger immediately fell to the ground, crying out in pain as he struggled with his unseen assailant. Miranda immediately knelt down beside him, unsure of what sudden terror had overtaken her hero.

"It's okay, Donatello! Nothing's there! It's not real!" she said, half trying to comfort him and half trying to shake some sense back into him. Her words however, were no match for the dark vision Dodger imagined was killing him, and before she could try again to break the spell he was under, Lord Wraithbone's men-at-arms grabbed her and began hauling her back to their master.

"See what becomes of your latest 'protector,' My Lady, and how easily he succumbs to phantasms of his own making. You should have chosen a better hero. Neither your father and his sword nor this fool can keep you from me!"

Miranda looked at Lord Wraithbone in horror. "You killed my father?" she sobbed.

"He went back on his word, then tried to prevent me from going after you," he began. "There are consequences for crossing me. Your father needed to learn that the hard way, just as this thief is learning now."

Miranda looked back at Dodger writhing on the ground. He didn't look like he'd last much longer. She'd already lost her father and couldn't bear to lose another person she loved.

"Stop it!" she pleaded. "Stop it, and I will go with you and be your bride."

Lord Wraithbone looked at her dispassionately. "It appears, My Lady, that you'll be coming with me regardless."

"Spare him, and I promise I will never try to run away from you again and I'll willingly do whatever you ask of me!" she pleaded again. "Just promise me you won't kill him!"

Lord Wraithbone raised an eyebrow and gazed at his soon-to-be bride with renewed interested. "Do you swear it?" he asked. "On your family's honor?"

"Don't!" Dodger managed to cry out through his agony. "I'm… not… worth… it!"

"He's right, you know," Lord Wraithbone agreed. "He's not worth it. This lowly thief, who deems himself a noble knight, isn't fit to be in your company, and doesn't have even a tenth of your potential, my dear!"

Miranda took a last look at Dodger writhing on the ground. The sight of her love in pain made her decision easy. She steeled herself and looked up at the evil man in front of her.

"I don't care!" she said defiantly. "I'd rather have a hundred lowly thieves with noble hearts like him, than even one of you! But if you promise to spare him, I'll swear to anything you want!"

"Noooooooooooo!" Dodger cried.

Whether it was Dodger's despair or Miranda's acquiescence that made Lord Wraithbone pull his lips back in a gleeful smile, we will never know. All that's certain is that he accepted the bargain.

"Done!" he said, snapping his fingers, and the imaginary tentacles choking the life from Dodger vanished, his struggles ceased, and he went limp on the ground.

"Donatello!" Miranda exclaimed, trying to break free from the grasp of the men-at-arms who were restraining her and run over to her lover. But the guards held her tight.

It took a moment, but Dodger finally began to stir. He looked over at Miranda and weakly reached out his hand to her. "I'll find you!" he promised. "I'll… never stop looking… for you! I will… *free you!*"

"Oh, I very much doubt that!" Lord Wraithbone said, making another sign in the air with his hands.

Instantly, Dodger's hands were drawn tight to his sides and he stiffened out straight as a board.

"You promised not to kill him!" Miranda cried, looking at him with hatred in her eyes.

"Fear not, my dear," he said, stroking her cheek with his boney fingers. "He is *not* dead. Only unconscious and immobile. The effect is only temporary, I assure you. But he soon may wish he was dead."

Miranda looked up at her new husband-to-be, eyes wide in fear. "What do you mean by that?" she asked.

"Well, I did promise you I'd keep him alive, and unlike your father, I don't go back on my word. But your pet seems to be bound and determined to follow us and ruin our 'wedding,' and we can't have that, can we? So I'm taking you where *no one* from Lanfor is ever going to find us—the Isle of Deimos. And just to make sure we never see his filthy elven face again, I'm having him sent to the pirate coast, where he's bound to spend the rest of his days chained to an oar as a galley slave!"

The Black Pearl
Chapter 4

irates!"

Everyone around the campfire suddenly turned to look at the brash twelve-year-old boy who'd suddenly jumped up from his seat. He was holding his hand up in the air in victory.

"Yeesss! I knew it! I told you Donatello came from pirates! Didn't I? Didn't I?"

"Yes, my young Sir, you were correct," the Old Bard said crustily. "Very clever of you indeed! Perhaps you would like to tell this part of the story yourself? I know the others are anxious to hear its conclusion, as am I."

"Um... Ah," the boy stammered as he looked around at all the faces staring at him in annoyance for interrupting the story. He slowly sat back down on log and nodded at the Old Bard.

"Uh, you've been doing—uh—an adequate job so far. Why don't you um, continue, Sir Bard," he said sheepishly but still trying to retain some dignity.

The Old Bard smiled to himself and nodded his head deferentially at the boy. "As you wish, young master," he said, then returned his attention back to the rest of his audience.

Dodger didn't know how long he'd been unconscious, nor did

he remember being taken to the Pirate Coast, but when he finally did come to, he found himself shackled hand and foot in the hold of a large wooden ship. He was surrounded by at least five handful of men, all dressed in rags and similarly shackled. One of them was standing over at him, trying to pluck the last copper button off his jerkin.

"Oiy! Dis one's alive after all!" the man said when Dodger suddenly sprang into an upright, sitting position and instinctively swatted away the hand plucking at his buttons.

One of the other prisoners turned a disinterested eye toward the elf. After a second or two, he shrugged and turned away. "Won't be for long," the other said. "All skin, bone, and ears, that one. Bet ya your ration he won't last a week."

Dodger didn't like the sound of that.

"Surprised they threw one of their own kind down 'ere with us," a third piped up.

"Naw, he ain't one of dem," replied the man who'd tried to steal his buttons.

"He ain't got no webs between his fingers like dey do," Buttons continued, holding up one of Dodger's hands so everyone could see it.

Dodger immediately pulled his hand back and stood up and began brushing himself off.

"Look gentlemen, I hate to disappoint you, but I don't intend to die. At least not here, and not anytime soon."

Dodger's pronouncement was met with a chorus of laughs.

"No one ever *intends* to die here," a new voice said. It belonged to a tall, young human with a raggedy, newly grown black beard. He was dressed in the remains of once-fine clothing and spoke proper common. From the way he moved and spoke, Dodger guessed he could have once been a well-to-do merchant or a lesser noble. "Nevertheless, they do. You're a prisoner of Black Pearl, and her heart's just as black as her lovely raven-colored locks…"

"Who?" Dodger interrupted.

"You ain't heard o' da Black Pearl?" Buttons asked in disbelief.

"I don't get around much," Dodger said.

"She's just one of the most notorious cap'ns in the Sphyrena pirate clan, ain't she? She and that devil-taking brother of 'ers'll sooner slit your throat than give you a second look."

"Well then," Dodger said pulling a loose nail from a nearby wall. "I'd better be going."

"No one escapes from the Black Pearl," the young merchant said.

"You only say that because no one has," Dodger said pausing for effect, then pulled his hands free of the shackles he'd picked while they were speaking. "Yet!"

The young merchant looked unimpressed. "Nice trick, but I think you'll find escaping a ship at sea a bit more difficult than picking your way out of a pair of rusty manacles."

"Just watch me!" Dodger said with bravado while freeing himself from the shackles around his legs. "And for your information, these shackles *aren't* rusty. They're just patinaed from the salt air," he said, tossing them at the young man. "I hear some people pay more for things with a nice patina!"

Speechlessly, the young man watched as Dodger made his way over to the door, pressed his ear against it, then jiggered the lock for a second or two. Then with a quick smile back at his companions, he cracked opened the door and slipped out of the cell.

Now the hallways in a pirate ship are cramped and dimly lit, but that didn't bother Dodger one bit. He was used to "skulking around in the dark" as his former master, Lord Flynn, used to say. In fact, the shadows cast by the few flickering lanterns that lit the lower decks actually worked to his advantage, letting Dodger fade away into the inky blackness whenever one of Black Pearl's men came wandering by.

But as he made his way up toward the top of the ship, it became harder and harder for him to avoid detection. At one point, he was even forced to duck into a random room off a hallway when he spotted a trio of ship's officers headed his way. Luckily for him, the lock on the door proved no harder to open than the one on the hold's door, and he was able to slip inside the cabin, unseen by the men.

The cabin's sole occupant however, did notice his abrupt entrance and let out a startled yelp.

"Who are you?" she asked, reflexively trying to cover herself with her arms.

Equally surprised, Dodger whirled around at the sound of her voice and saw a short woman with a curvaceous figure and long black hair standing before him. She was dressed in a long, sheer white chemise and had a silver comb in her hand that she'd been using to brush her lovely obsidian locks.

"Who are you?" she asked again, this time sounding less startled and a bit more haughty.

"I… ah… I… um," he stuttered. He couldn't ever recall seeing anyone as lovely before in his life. Even his true love, Miranda wasn't as pretty as the woman who stood before him now. He was speechless and didn't know how to answer her.

Up until now, the only person who'd ever really called him 'Donatello' was Miranda, and introducing himself that way seemed wrong, especially after he'd failed to save her from Lord Wraithbone.

Nor did introducing himself as "Dodger" seem right either. He'd been given that name as part of The Fagin's gang of youthful cutpurses, and he no longer considered himself a lowly thief. He was an elf on a mission now. An elf out for revenge against the evil caster who had stolen away his true love, and the name 'Dodger' didn't fit that persona. Neither did any of the other names Lord Flynn used to call him—even the ones he could repeat in polite company.

The woman deserved an answer, and Dodger recognized the unmistakable tone of a high-born unaccustomed to waiting for a reply. So he just said the first thing that came to mind.

"I'm… um… I'm here to rescue you, M'lady!" he said, extending his free hand to her. "I'll get you away from these murderous pirates and see you safely back to your father's household."

The woman raised a delicately arched eyebrow and smiled at him. When she did, Dodger could have sworn her teeth sparkled.

"So you're to be my hero, then?" she asked, setting down the comb and slowly walking over to him. "Aren't you a bit short to be my knight in shining armor?" she added running a finger slowly down his chest.

Even this early in his life, Dodger was no stranger to the womanly wiles, yet the lovely young creature who stood before him now made him feel all flustered and he had a difficult time thinking straight.

"Um… I've been… um… told that… um… good things come in small packages," he began.

The black-haired beauty standing uncomfortably close to him smiled again, and this time Dodger was sure her teeth *did* sparkle when she did it.

"Well, I look forward to unwrapping you and seeing how big your package really is…" she said, fingering the clasp of his belt.

"My lady!" Dodger said practically slapping her hands away. He was shocked by her forwardness. He'd have expected such a thing from tavern wench, not a woman of courtly values, but the surprise helped clear his head and return his thoughts to that of escape. "This is hardly the time! We must be gone before anyone realizes we're missing!"

"And just how do you propose we do that? We're at sea, you know."

Dodger nodded. "I saw the bottom of a small boat hanging off the side of the ship on my way up here. If the Lady of Luck is still smiling on me, we might be able to slip into it, cut it loose, and drift away before anyone notices that it—and we—are gone."

"That's your plan?" the woman asked, unimpressed. "Rely on luck, and hope for the best?"

Dodger shrugged and gave her an impish smile, "It's always worked before."

"It's a wonder, then, you've lived as long as you have," she replied, and Dodger couldn't tell if she sounded surprised or disgusted. "Besides, even if the Lady of Luck does show us her benevolent face, why should I get in a boat with you? How do I know *you* won't try to ransom me, or worse?"

Dodger looked hurt that someone should think him capable of doing such a thing. He'd never do what Lord Flynn had tried to make his daughter do, nor do to anyone else what Lord Wraithbone had done to him.

"Because I won't!" he swore vehemently. "No one should be held against their will or forced to live a life against their choosing! Now I may be no knight, but you have my sworn word I'd never do that!"

The dark-haired woman raised an eyebrow again as she noticed the change in his body language.

"Never?" she asked.

"Never!" he replied.

"You wouldn't even ask for a reward?"

Dodger shook his head. "Well, a 'thank you' would be nice," he said, turning back toward the door. "And maybe some new clothes," he added, sniffing at his jerkin and shirt, before pressing his ear against the door. "I think these are getting a bit ripe."

"A 'thank you' and some new clothes is *all* you'd want for saving me?" she asked incredulously as he listened at the door for any sounds of activity in the hallway. "You'd want nothing else?"

"Well, if your father could spare a horse, that'd be great, too. But only if he could spare one."

The woman slowly walked toward him again, letting the top of the chemise fall off one of her shoulders.

"Nothing else?" she cooed, sidling up next to him and pressing her body against his.

Dodger was so engrossed in listening at the door, he barely noticed her presence beside him.

"No," he whispered back to her distractedly as he strained his ears, trying to pick out every last sound from behind the door. "Now hush, M'lady, or we might miss our only chance to escape!"

The dark-haired woman exhaled sharply, momentarily annoyed that Dodger hadn't noticed her obvious charms. She frowned and began to walk away from him when he suddenly grabbed her by the hand.

"Finally!" he whispered excitedly to her. "The coast is clear!"

He cracked the door opened and began to pull her through it with him.

"Wait!" she whispered back, stopping him.

Dodger turned and looked back at her, half in annoyance and half in alarm.

"You might need this," she said, offering him a small, thin blade with a swept hilt and ringed guard. "You did say you were skilled in its use, did you not?"

Dodger took the weapon gratefully, never bothering to ask from where she'd suddenly procured it, nor why her captors had locked her in a room with such a fine weapon. Truth be told, the questions never occurred to him, and it was something which he'd soon rue not asking about. For now, he was just happy to be armed and have the favor of the Goddess of Luck.

For it did seem that the Lady of Luck was indeed smiling on them. Every time they should have been discovered by one of the crew, the dark-haired woman managed to find some obscure nook or cranny for them to hide in until the danger had passed. In short order, the duo found themselves peering out from behind a louvered door onto the main deck.

"What do you see?" the dark-haired woman whispered in Dodger's ear.

The main deck was abuzz with activity. There were sailors everywhere, hauling on ropes or swabbing the deck or doing the dozens of other chores required of a ship at sea.

At the rails to either side of the main mast, Dodger could see the pulleys that held the dinghies he'd spotted from below deck. They were only a few yards away. If they could just make it over to one of them without being seen, he was sure they could slither over the side, drop into the boat, and hide under a tarp until nightfall. Then they could slowly lower the craft into the water and make good their escape.

The trick, of course, was making it across the deck unnoticed.

"How we supposed to do that?" whispered the dark-haired woman.

Dodger watched the crew work for a moment longer before answering. As incredulous as it may seem, he told her that it was quite possible to hide in plain sight. He had done so countless times in the city, blending into a crowd to avoid detection from the town guard or the mark he'd just robbed. The trick was to appear just like everyone else and *not* to draw attention to yourself.

The dark-haired woman seemed doubtful of this, but Dodger managed to convince her and they soon found themselves slowly walking across the open deck carrying some random boxes they'd come across.

They had just about made it all the way to the mainmast when the dark-haired women dropped the box she'd been carrying. It crashed to the deck with thunderous sound, and suddenly all eyes turned their direction.

"Uh oh," she said.

Immediately Dodger tossed aside his box, drew his sword from his belt and pushed the woman protectively behind him.

"Don't worry, M'lady!" he said as the pirates drew their own weapons and began encircling them. "I've had experience fighting ruffians of their kind. Now which one of you wants to be the first to die?" he yelled, summoning as much bravado as he could, while keeping his point dancing between them.

To his great surprise, the pirates didn't attack. They just slowly continued closing ranks on them until their backs were practically up against the mast. Even then, the pirates didn't attack.

At first, Dodger was relieved. While Lord Flynn had trained him how to fight a group of attackers, he'd never gone up against more than four opponents at once. They were surrounded now by at least twenty. It could have been more, but Dodger had stopped counting at twelve. Yet even though the pirates had them vastly outnumbered, they still held their attack.

"Odd," Dodger said more to himself than to his companion. "I wonder why they don't attack?"

"Perhaps, my little hero," the woman said, "They have heard tales of your prowess with a blade and are afraid of you."

Dodger thought about that for a second or two, completely missing the mocking tone of her voice.

"Naw," he said, shaking his head. "That inn was too remote for word of that fight to make it all the way down here. Besides, that would mean they'd have to know who I was already. Gotta be something else."

"Perhaps they are just awaiting word of their captain," she suggested.

Dodger shot a glance back at her and nodded.

"Of course! That's got to be it! Do you see her anywhere?" he asked.

The woman casually brushed back the hair on either side of her head, revealing two large pointed ears.

"Yes," she replied.

Immediately Dodger's eyes began scanning the crowd, looking for the infamous pirate captain.

"Where is she?" he asked.

The woman just cleared her throat.

Dodger cast another quick look back at her.

"What?" he asked sounding annoyed. "I'm trying to find the captain!"

Again his companion cleared her throat, and this time Dodger turned and gave her a long look. It took almost a full minute before comprehension slowly dawned on his face.

"*You're* the Black Pearl?" he asked, flabbergasted.

"Actually, I'd prefer Mor'Findl," she said, grinning at him. "It is my given name, after all."

Dodger looked at her, even more confused now. "Wait, your name is Black-Hair?" he asked. "So why does everyone call you Black Pearl, then?"

"Humans," she sighed. "They have no ear for our language. Now take him, boys!" she commanded, stepping away from Dodger and back toward her men.

Immediately, her sailors started to converge on the confused elf.

Backed against the mizzen mast, Dodger reached back and wrapped his free hand around one of the ropes attached to it. He then raised his sword and smiled back at Mor'Findl.

"Sorry to disappoint you, Captain, but I don't have time to play this game. Gotta fly!"

With that, Dodger slashed the rope free from its tie-down. An instant later, he was yanked up into the rigging as one of the mast's spars came swinging down, forcing the Black Pearl and her men to jump backwards to avoid being hit by it.

The crew of the *Spirit of the Sea* recovered quickly and began swarming up the rigging after Dodger.

Mor'Findl watched from the deck as Dodger led her crew on a merry chase along the yardarm, sails, and ropes as he tried to avoid capture.

"Slippery eel, that one," her first mate said to her as he stood beside her, watching the goings-on above.

Mor'Findl nodded appreciatively. "That one has potential, don't you think?" she asked him. "Get my sword."

The first mate rolled his eyes. He knew what she was planning on doing. "All due respect, Capt'n," he said, "the crew will get 'im soon enough."

She silenced him with a look and he soon returned, carrying a black great coat adorned with silver trim and a short curved sword that had a cupped guard shaped like a skull and crossbones. She slipped on her coat, grabbed a hold of another line, took the sword, and with the flick of her wrist, shot herself up to the rigging. Soon she was standing on one side of the main mast's highest yardarm, facing Dodger, who was balanced on the other side.

"Well done, my little hero!" she called over to him. "But it's time to bring this little game to an end, don't you think?"

"I can keep playing forever, Captain," he called back.

"Oh, I doubt that. My men will eventually catch you, and I'd hate for them to have to kill you. So why don't we end this in a civilized way?" she suggested. "A duel. Just you and me. You win, and I give you my word I'll take you to the nearest port and let you go free. I win, and you're mine."

Dodger looked down into the rigging below him and across to the other masts and saw all the angry faces glaring at him, wanting his blood. The Black Pearl was right. It *was* only going to be a matter of time before they got him. This duel was his only chance at survival.

"You're a pirate! How do I know you'll keep your word?" he asked.

Mor'Findl smiled. "You don't. But the way I see it, you really don't have much of a choice, do you?"

Dodger considered that for a moment. She was right. So he just shrugged, then raised his sword in a salute the way Lord Flynn had taught him.

The Black Pearl smiled back at him, returning the salute with an elaborate sweep of her cutlass. Then like a dancer on her tiptoes, she gracefully closed the distance between them with a series of short leaps.

Once in striking distance of each other, they traded a series of faints and test cuts, probing each other for weaknesses.

"I ought to warn you, Captain, that I've been trained by the best blademaster in all the realms," Dodger said as he continued to press his attack.

"Is that so?" she asked nonchalantly as she parried each thrust and cut. "Which one? Stealle?"

"No."

"Kazari?" she asked, making a feint to his head, then at the last second turning it into a slashing attack to his flank.

Dodger turned aside her attack, then riposted with a cut of his own to her head. "Not even close."

"Surely not Kirk of Blackwood?" she asked, easily evading his cut before thrusting at him again. "He's a bit of a Troll, don't ya think?"

"Never heard of him!" Dodger replied, stepping back so her point fell just shy of him. He beat the blade away, then made a cut for her wrist, which had become momentarily exposed. "I was trained by Lord Edward of Flynn!" he said triumphantly.

"Ah! Then that explains it!" she continued, sounding disappointed as she parried his blade at the last second, then went back on the offensive.

"And just what's that supposed to mean?" Dodger asked, twisting his torso to avoid her attack before whirling back around with a low-line sweep in an attempt to take her legs out from under her.

Yet again the Black Pearl avoided his blade, following it up with a series of quick advancing thrusts aimed at driving him back off the yardarm they were on.

"You fight like such a man! Thrust, thrust, thrust! All you want to do is stick your point in! There's no style, no finesse," she said, taking his blade in a series of circular motions and forcing him to retreat. "A woman likes a little foreplay, you know!"

"And your *point* is?" Dodger asked, disentangling his blade from hers and made a renewed series of attacks, attempting to push her back and put more space between himself and the end of the yard-arm he was now perilously close to being pushed over. "Or you think a little insult like that will take me off my guard?"

"I see witty *ripostes* aren't your *forte*," she added, ceding ground in an almost casual manner. "In fact, they are kind of *lamé*."

"No offense, captain, but so was that one!" he said as they exchanged blows again.

"Oh, I don't know, I've been told my repartée is usually a *cut* above the rest!" Mor'Findl said, beating hard on his blade, driving his point way off target, and brought the tip of her own weapon up under Dodger's chin.

Dodger gulped and glanced down at the curved blade threatening his neck.

Well, I have to admit, your humor does seem to have an *edge* to it," he shrugged. Then quick as a flash, he beat away the Black Pearl's blade and went back on the offense.

"Yes, it does," she agreed, "But you know what else you'll learn about me?"

Dodger shook his head *no* as he attempted another series of moves to drive her back toward her end of the yardarm.

The Black Pearl flashed him one of her thousand-candle-smiles. "You'll find that I can be very disarming!"

With that, the lovely pirate captain quickly stepped in, grabbed the back of his head with her left hand, pulled his face toward her and gave him a passionate kiss.

By the time Dodger had recovered from the surprise—not to mention his breath—Mor'Findl was holding both his sword and her own in a V about his neck.

"Wha… that's… that's… That's cheating!" he sputtered.

The Black Pearl gave him another one of her sultry smiles and all his anger at her quickly evaporated.

"Pirate!" she giggled, then nodded to some of her crew, who'd been watching the fight from the surrounding rigging.

"Take 'im, boys," she commanded, and they did.

If Dodger had been expecting them to clap him back in irons and lock him in the bilge, then he couldn't have been more surprised to find himself taken to the Black Pearl's cabin and tied to a comfortable chair.

"You going to torture me?" he asked her when she finally entered her cabin. "Because I won't tell you anything! Nor will I give you the pleasure of hearing me scream!"

Mor'Findl unbuckled her sword belt and placed it on a nearby table. Then she slowly removed her great coat and hung it on a peg jutting out from the wall.

"Oh?" she said raising a delicately arched eyebrow as she sauntered over to him. "We'll just see about that. I have ways of loosening men's tongues," she added, sitting down in his lap. "As for making you scream… I think I can manage that, too." Then she kissed him.

Dodger felt like his head was spinning, and he wasn't sure how long her mouth had been pressed against his. It could have been seconds, minutes, or even hours. He didn't care. He liked it, even though he knew he shouldn't have, and it took him a couple of seconds to realize that she'd stopped kissing him.

"Well?" she asked, looking at him with that same sultry smile that was filled with smoldering desire. "Ready to talk yet?"

It took all of Dodger's concentration to even form a coherent thought, let alone speak, but somehow he managed it.

"It's… um… going… to um… take a lot more that that to… um… get me to… um speak," he said trying to sound brave. "Do your worst!"

The Black Pearl's smile grew wider. Dodger's head began to swim again and he felt like he was being submerged in a warm bath and drowned by the power of her spell, but he didn't care.

"As you wish," she said obligingly, then ripped his shirt open and slowly began massaging his chest while kissing him again.

Dodger could never recall how he'd gotten out of that chair and into the Black Pearl's bed. Nor would he ever say exactly what happened when they got there, other than to quip that it was a life-changing experience and something he'd never forget.

Mor'Findl was quite the experienced courtesan and lover, and there is little doubt that Donatello owed much of his legendary prowess with the fairer sex to his experiences with her.

"See, I told you I would make you scream," the Black Pearl told him when they'd finally sated their desire. She was lying on top of him, her fingers tracing a random pattern on his smooth, hairless chest.

Dodger was on his back, still trying to catch his breath from their extended bout of lovemaking, his hand running up and down the small of her back and below. Part of him knew it was wrong to have done what he'd done with this woman, when his true love was in the clutches of some evil priest-magi, but the spell the Black Pearl cast on him made it hard to care.

"Several times, in fact," he said, unable to resist returning her smile.

Her grin grew wider. "Eight times, I believe," she said. "But who's counting?"

Dodger blushed, and the pirate captain's giggle sounded like water rushing over some pebbles in a stream.

"So, my Little Hero, why so anxious to escape? And why did you not ask for more than some new clothes and a horse as reward for 'rescuing' me?"

"Because it's not money that I desire," he said, "it's revenge."

Mor'Findl propped herself up on her elbow so she could get a better look at him, her interest clearly piqued.

"And just who, pray tell, is this walking dead man?"

Dodger's eyes narrowed to slits at the sound of her mocking tone, and quick as a flash, he rolled over on top of her and pinned her to the bed. "Do not mock me, sea wench!" he threatened. "You both may have gotten the better of me once, but by the gods, he'll taste my steel, as will anyone who gets in my way!"

The pirate princess looked up at him and smiled as if she didn't have a care in the world.

"That so?" she asked brightly, and in an instant, Dodger found their positions reversed. Now it was he who was pinned to the bed, only this time he was face down, with his head pulled back and the Black Pearl's dagger at his neck.

"Lesson one, my foolish little hero," she said, leaning down to whisper malevolently into his ear, "*Never* threaten anyone unless you are *absolutely sure* you can carry out your threat. Savvy?"

Dodger gulped audibly. "Yes."

Mor'Findl sat back up, withdrawing her dagger from his neck. "Good, because I really like these sheets and would hate to ruin them with your blood. Now tell me who it is that has earned all your enmity."

Dodger rolled right side up and looked over at her. She was all sweetness again, but just beneath the surface, he could sense how cold, hard, and dangerous she was, and in that moment, he was reminded of Lord Flynn's finely forged razor-sharp blade and the beautifully ornate scabbard he carried it in.

He sighed and let out a deep breath. There was little point now in keeping any secrets from her, and he found himself telling her all about Miranda, her father, Lord Wraithbone, and what the evil man had done to each of them.

The Black Pearl listened without comment until Dodger had finished his tale.

"So you've vowed to kill Lord Wraithbone, a man even the Parthian emperor fears, for kidnapping your love?"

Dodger nodded *yes*.

Mor'Findl laughed a humorless laugh, got up from the bed, and moved to retrieve her dressing gown.

Despite himself, Dodger found himself momentarily distracted by the swing of her hips and rhythmic way the cheeks of her bottom moved as she walked across the room.

"I should call you 'Little Fool,'" she began, pulling the gown over her head and covering her naked form. "Because anyone who thinks he can take on a man like Lord Wraithbone, alone, without an army at his back is either delusional or insane. Even the pirate clans with all our amassed power won't dare cross him. It's said his powers are second only to that of the Thrall Lords themselves! So you might as well resign yourself to the fact that this love of yours is lost, and stay with me as part of my crew. I can always use a cabin boy to warm my bed. And if you're half as good with a blade as you think you are, then, you'll definitely stand a better chance of survival with me than chasing after a necro-magi like Wraithbone all by your lonesome."

"And if I choose not to?" Dodger asked.

Mor'Findl looked back at him and smiled predatorily. "You're assuming you have a choice. You don't. You can either stay with me, here, above decks, seeing to my needs, or serve me below decks, bound by enchanted shackles to an oar for the rest of your existence. The choice is yours."

Dodger didn't relish the idea of going back to being a galley slave, and the thought of spending more time in Mor'Findl's bed had its definite appeal, yet he knew he couldn't stay, even if he wanted to.

"Either is a death sentence for me," he told her after the briefest of considerations. "I *have* to go. I think I'll die if I don't… I gave her my word."

"The word of a cut-purse?"

"A cut-purse, perhaps, but I do love her," he said forlornly. "I think I finally understand what her father meant when he used to constantly tell me that your word is the only precious thing nobody can take from you."

The Black Pearl scoffed at that remark. "Then you *are* a Little Fool," she said. "Look where all his honor and his word got him! Food for maggots! Do you want to end up like that?"

Dodger shook his head no.

Mor'Findl slowly walked back over and sat down on the bed next to him. "Look, my Little Fool," she said gently, placing a hand on his chest. "Ne'er I've seen someone with such promise to become a great pirate. Under my tutelage, you could go far with the Sphyrenas. Perhaps even someday commanding your own ship, standing tall and proud alongside my brother and all the other captains who fly the silver barracuda on an azure flag."

Dodger took her hand from his chest and held it in his hand. "I appreciate the offer, I really do," he said looking at her with big, sorrowful green eyes. "But I can't."

Mor'Findl let out an exasperated sigh and withdrew her hand from his. "Let me make this easy for you, Little Fool. Your love is gone, and so is the object of your revenge…"

"What do you mean?" Dodger asked, confused.

"Your mortal enemy was trading with us to retrieve an artifact that was supposed to lead him to Mad Emperor Narodon's missing seventh tower. To activate it, he needed the soul of an innocent, which I presume is why he wanted your lover…"

"Then I have to go! NOW!" Dodger exclaimed, practically leaping off the bed.

"It's too late," the Black Pearl said, stopping him before he could take another step. "We saw him begin to use it as we sailed away. His ship and his minions have all vanished and no one has seen him since."

"But… but…" he sputtered. "I promised…"

"And so you did," she agreed. "But you failed…"

"I can't have!" Dodger protested. "He might not have killed her! He could have just trapped her soul! It's possible she's still alive!"

"*Might* have, *could* have, *possible?*" she asked him, her voice taking on a hard, cold edge. "Stop trying to delude yourself," she scolded. "She's gone. You failed her, and it's time you come to terms with it!"

Dodger didn't want to believe it. He *couldn't* have failed her. He couldn't let go of that tiny spark of hope in his heart, that somehow, some way, Miranda was still alive and awaiting his rescue.

"How?" he asked bitterly. "Just how exactly am I supposed to do that?"

"By forgetting her."

"Forgetting her?" he asked incredulously. Forgetting her! I'm not like you, I just can't do that!"

"Then it's high time you become just like me!" she spat back. "Look, Little Fool, life is cruel and often short—you of all people should understand that by now. You need to learn to roll with the wind and the waves, or else be capsized and pulled to a watery grave. You need to learn to take pleasure whenever and with whomever you can, because there's no guarantee you'll be around tomorrow!"

Dodger slowly sat back down on the edge of her bed. "I don't think I can do that," he muttered dejectedly.

The Black Pearl smiled inwardly, seeing the wind disappear from his sails. He was alone now, floundering and adrift like a ship with no rudder in a gale. She was adept at commandeering such vessels and giving them direction again.

"Then stay with me," she whispered into his ear as she wrapped her arms gently around his sagging shoulders. "Become part of my crew, and I will teach you."

Dodger looked at her with a blank stare and nodded. "Then teach me," he said. "Teach me to do what you do. Teach me to forget."

Epilogue

He can't have forgotten!" the younger sister cried, hands balled into fists and shaking her head back and forth, making her long, tightly curled, golden locks dance about her small head. "He just can't have!"

"Oh, don't be such a ninny!" the brash twelve-year-old admonished his younger compatriot. "Everyone knows he didn't."

"I would not be so sure, my young lord," the Old Bard interrupted, trying to reset the mood so his listeners could once again become lost in his story. "For such was the Black Pearl's allure that many a man was convinced to take up arms against his own kith and kin by a single glance from her.

"You see, our friend Donatello *did* forget, at least for a while. He accepted Mor'Findl's offer, binding himself to her service by taking hold of a barracuda tooth she wore around her neck—for this was no ordinary tooth. It was enchanted, and symbolized her right to command one of her clan's ships of the line. Anyone touching that tooth and willingly agreeing to join that pirate band was branded with a silhouette of a barracuda over their heart."

"But Donatello didn't have a tattoo like that over his heart," protested the older sister.

The Old Bard nodded in agreement. "You are correct, M'lady, he did not. But when he was the Black Pearl's cabin boy and known to the crew of *The Spirit of the Sea* as 'Little Fool,' he did."

"Then what happened to it?" the youngest child asked. "How'd he get rid of it?"

"Why, by saving the life of Mor'Findl herself," The Old Bard said, gently tapping the child on the tip of her nose. "But that, my dear, is another story.

Fortune Tellers

K.J. Fogelman

Fortune Tellers

HERE I WAS…
Standing on the edge of a steep precipice, staring down at the twinkling torch lights of a carnival some distance below me. It was one hour past midnight, a perfect time for jumping and ending it all.

What I meant was, ending the chase of the guard who was charging up behind me on horseback.

"Hold it right there, thief!" his voice bellowed from the darkness.

I glanced back at the guard, smiled, and gave him a special one-finger salute before gracefully falling backward over the edge of the cliff.

Okay, okay—it wasn't that dramatic. My foot slipped on a stone, I tripped over my own feet, fell, and *then* gave him the salute. But that doesn't sound as dramatic, does it?

As I tumbled through the air, I rubbed a ring on my finger. Suddenly I became light as a feather and began to float. Righting myself as best as I could, I spied a plump haystack and angled my body toward it. Only, about a hundred feet away from it, I realized it wasn't a haystack, but a giant pile of straw mixed with something smelly I most certainly did not want to land in.

Let's just say that, in my desperation, I did some flailing, kicking, maybe a little cursing, and sailed right into the top of a tent. Thankfully, most carnival tents are very sturdy and made to hold back a lot of weight and weather. Unfortunately, this tent was not one of those, and with a loud *rrrrip* I fell right through.

I landed in the middle of a meeting between three people. There may have been some groaning on my part. When I opened my eyes, they were all hovering over me, providing me with a good opportunity to look them over—one was obviously the ringmaster, the other a fortune teller, and the last a fire-eater.

The fortune teller was the most interesting, and held my gaze with her violet eyes, golden hair, perfect lips, just the right amount of cleavage—eye-candy all the way around, if you're into blondes. Her strange violet eyes unnerved me, but I had played lots of staring games before, and I refused to be the first to blink. After holding my gaze for a good long moment, the fortune teller gave me the strangest smile.

"Looking for a job, sweetie?" she asked, her eyes sparkling as if with a hidden secret.

I glanced at the other two, both men. I hopped up to my feet, squared my shoulders, and…

Okay, okay—I stood slowly, with lots of groaning, aching, and popping of joints. I brushed my tattered skirts off and straightened my shoulders with much grimacing.

The ringmaster stroked his black mustache, trying not to laugh as he looked me up and down. "Sorry, girl, but I already have someone for the magic act. However, if you would like to audition for the clown act…"

During this time, an idea had been forming in my head. I needed to get out of town for special reasons, as alluded to earlier. What better way to do that than to run away and join the circus?

Thankfully, I had used a bit of magic to change my appearance before my less-than-graceful landing. I stroked my now frizzy, strawberry-blonde hair, trying to make it lay flat, rather than spread to the four corners of the earth. "I'm awful sorry, sir. I was told you'd have a job for me." I lied like a trained professional. "I'll take any job you have. I'm a hard worker."

An amused smile flashed across the ringmaster's face. "Sorry, but I don't believe good help just falls out of the sky." His levity quickly died away as the fortune teller stepped up and began to circle me.

A moment of silence slipped by, then she grabbed my hand, looked at my palm, and traced the lines on it.

The ringmaster shifted on his feet. "What do you see, Elistra?"

The fortune teller peered at me and winked, then faced him. "I must take her as my assistant."

"Aw, but I wanted her as *my* assistant!" The fire-eater hurried forward, grabbing a strand of my hair. "Do you realize what kind of fire tricks I could do with this haystack?"

I jerked away from him and slapped his hand. "Hey! Who do ya think you are?"

"I'm Qualar, and I think your hair is fabulous." His green eyes were fixated on the frizzy blonde mass atop my head.

"Not for burnin', it ain't." I scooted closer to Elistra.

Qualar waved his hands in the air dramatically. "Not burning— Fire tricks! There's a difference."

I turned to Elistra. "Please save me from the fire maniac."

The ringmaster cleared his throat loudly. "I don't pay for stray puppies."

Elistra raised an eyebrow. "You don't pay any of us, actually."

He shrugged. "I make sure you have enough to eat. I don't see a reason to feed her, too."

"I'll take care of her needs."

The ringmaster motioned Elistra to join him at another corner of the tent. The two stepped to the side and lowered their voices. I could tell he took the fortune teller seriously, but wanted a legitimate reason to keep me around. Couldn't say I blamed him.

"When you aren't busy assisting Elistra with her mind readin', future tellin' ways, you wanna come do some fire tricks with me?" Qualar edged closer, leaned on his fire stick, and smiled.

"Um," I frowned as I looked him over. "Pass."

His smile fell. "Why not? Fire tricks are fun!"

I waved my finger in a circle, motioning at his face. "You've got crazy written all over your mug, and it makes my hair cringe in fear."

Qualar squinted one eye and raised the opposite eyebrow. "Are you putting me in the crazy box just 'cause I play with fire?"

I nodded.

He waved a finger at me. "Now listen here miss… miss… I didn't catch your name."

"I didn't throw it."

He huffed. "What do you want me to call you?"

I glanced at Elistra and the Ringmaster, noting that both were looking in my direction. "You can call me Frances."

Qualar nodded. "Alright, Fran dear, let me educate you on the finer points of why playing with fire doesn't automatically make you crazy."

Elistra appeared next to my side, laughing lightly. "Perhaps you can educate my new assistant over supper, Qualar?"

The fire-eater nodded. "Cake. I'll talk over cake. You can have the supper stuff." He opened the tent flap for both of us ladies.

I glanced around the tent to find the ringmaster gone. "So, it's official? I'm your assistant?" I eyed the fortune teller carefully.

She nodded, that mysterious smile coming to her face again. "I think you're going to have a lot of fun with us, *Fran dear.*"

<hr>

I WAS ALL ALONE…

There, in Elistra's tent, I laid out a set of clothes she'd given me to try on. A quick peep out the tent opening told me that it was early morning. All the circus members were busy finishing their morning tasks and wrangling up some food for themselves. Elistra had gone to fetch us some food as well. I thought as *her* assistant, that would be my job, but I got the feeling that she wanted to do more than get breakfast. I didn't argue. A few minutes to myself would be all I needed to straighten out my other affairs.

Assured that I was alone, I stepped back to my new set of clothes and stared at them. I didn't like them. It wasn't that they were shiny and drew a lot of attention; I just didn't care for clothes in general. Yet, they were a necessary evil if I were to be a functioning part of human society. Besides, Elistra would notice if I didn't wear them.

Even land-kissin' druids wear clothes, hon.

While mentally psyching myself up for the outfit, I turned my attention to the prize that I had won last night. I carefully unwrapped a blue silk cloth from around a wooden cylindrical object about as large as my forearm. It was made out of the finest red wood and surrounded with rings that twisted and clicked, all engraved with unfamiliar text. As far as I could tell, it was some sort of puzzle box. I was dying to know what was inside of it, but what had prompted me to, um, liberate it from its previous owner was the fact that it was riddled with gemstones.

I bet there's a couple of plat worth of gems on this thingamajig.

"Elistra! I gotta talk to you about…"

I froze as the tent flap flew open. Thankfully, I had my back toward the opening. I slapped the silk back around my treasure, only slightly worried that I was naked as a jaybird. I looked back at the opening to find Qualar standing there frozen, staring, mouth open.

"Get out, fire-brain!" I shrieked, grabbing for a blanket off the bed.

Qualar shook himself. "I plum forgot you were staying here! Where's Elistra?"

I pulled at the blanket, trying to cover myself with it, but it snagged on something and resisted coming off the bed.

"She went to get breakfast! Now get ou…" A final tug made the blanket pop loose and fly into me unexpectedly.

Normally, I am as nimble as a goat. A newborn baby goat. With palsy. So, it was no surprise when I fell backward, hitting the center tent pole hard enough to tilt it sideways and bring half the tent down—right on top of Qualar. It also knocked the lamp off the pole, lighting a rug on fire.

I coughed as smoke filled the room.

"THAT. DOES IT." An angry, muffled voice sounded from where Qualar had once stood. "We're getting you a gypsy wagon!" He slowly crawled out from under the folds of tent, reaching out toward the fire. "No more tents for you, Fran dear." The fire swirled into the air and flew toward Qualar, forming into a ball in his hand. He stared at it for a moment, mesmerized, then popped the flaming sphere into his mouth and swallowed it, plunging the lopsided room into darkness.

I gasped in surprise, then coughed as smoke coated my throat. I quickly wrapped the blanket around myself, using one corner of it as a fan, in hopes of clearing the air of smoke.

"What's going on in there?" Elistra's voice called from outside.

"It wasn't me!" Qualar called back, his voice moving closer to me.

"It was all his fault!" I shouted between coughing fits.

"She knocked it down!" Qualar's voice was directly next to me now.

I huffed. "I wouldn't have if y…" Hands wrapped behind my neck, fingers entwining with my hair, pulling me into a warm, smoky kiss. I punched my free hand into Qualar's chest, trying to shove him away without dropping my prize or my blanket. Unfortunately, at the same time, I found my lips—without my permission, mind you—kissing him in return.

One of his hands strayed down my neck, then wrapped around the silk-covered cylinder pressed against my chest. "Mmm… What's this?" he asked against my lips.

All fuzzy feelings gone, I pushed away from him and stepped back, clinging to my prize. I lost grip of my blanket, stepped on it and stumbled backward. The calves of my legs ran into a trunk, and I tripped and fell against the other side of the tent.

As you can see, with this amount of luck, this is why I don't play games with dice. I only roll low numbers and still get accused of cheating.

With a creaking, the support pole came tumbling down, flattening the tent on top of us.

"What's going on? Are you okay?" Elistra cried from outside.

Qualar let loose an exaggerated moan, "Oooouch. I'm hurting!"

I growled. "That's what you get for handlin' my goods, fire maniac!"

Outside, Elistra huffed loud enough for me to hear, "Kids these days."

THERE I WAS…

If someone had taken a dull spoon and used it to slowly remove each one of my toes, I would have welcomed the torture with open arms. As it was, I had to stand with Qualar outside a small tavern in broad daylight. It was the worst.

"Was it a bottle?"

I rolled my eyes. "No, fire brain. It weren't."

"A weird-shaped diary?"

"No! You've guessed that already!"

Eight days and two towns had passed since the tent incident, and Qualar was dying to know what it was that I had been hiding in the tent. Thankfully, he didn't see it and had no idea what it was, but that had only added to his curiosity.

Qualar stepped in front of me, searching my eyes while narrowing his. "Was it… a jug?"

I rolled my eyes again, looking down the busy town street at a woman cradling a tiny baby close. "If it were, I'd be drinking you out of sight and out of mind right now."

Qualar snorted. "Not likely! Say, how long is Elistra gonna be in there?"

Elistra had been approached by a Deepwood tracker and a woman wearing holy vestments. They said they needed to talk alone with her and offered to buy her a drink, an offer which was not extended to Qualar and me.

I shrugged in answer to Qualar's question, continuing to watch the woman with her baby until she disappeared around a corner.

"I'm hungry. Let's go find something to eat."

I gave Qualar a long, tired look. "Do you have any money, Maniac?"

Before he could answer, a muffled cry made us both pause. Qualar made eye contact with me, raising a questioning eyebrow. I shrugged, but froze when I heard an infant's wail come from the same direction I had seen the woman and baby.

"Help, some–!" A woman's cry was cut short, though the baby's cry continued.

In an instant, Qualar and I were dashing down the street. We rounded the corner just in time to see a half-orc, a man, and a halfling struggling with the young woman. The half-orc had his hand firmly placed over the young woman's mouth and nose, his other hand holding a sharp blade to her throat. The young woman's face was red for a lack of air, and tears streamed from her eyes, running down the hand clamped around her face.

The man pried at her arms, trying to take her wailing baby from her.

The halfling tapped his foot impatiently. "Come on, missy, stop makin' this so hard."

I ducked into a shadowy doorway and Qualar came to a halt. "Hey!"

All three of the woman's assailants turned toward him.

Qualar put his fists on his hips. Only, I could tell his fingers were digging into the pouches on his belt.

"How many men does it take to assault a helpless girl?" he asked.

The halfling sneered, drawing a knife. "Two and a half?"

Qualar paused, surprise registering on his face. "Wow. You beat me to the punch."

"The jokes of tall folk are predictable." The halfling nodded at Qualar, glancing at the half-orc. "Get him." He jumped up on a rain barrel and jerked the woman by the hair, poking his knife tip against the underside of her jaw. The half-orc turned her loose, letting her catch her breath, and drew a second knife. The human man, looking strangely relieved, pulled a hammer from his side, glowering at Qualar.

Qualar took a solid step back, raising his hands, his fingers curled around something small. "Now, easy boys. We don't want this to get messy."

The half-orc and the man rushed forward. Qualar took in a sharp breath. He threw a wad of dust on the ground between him and the thugs, then bent forward and breathed out. Fire exploded from his mouth, touching the dust just as the two unfortunate henchmen stepped on it. The dust exploded, fire and dirt spraying in all directions, lighting the two on fire.

While the dust was still thick and the two scrambled to put themselves out, I slipped from my hiding place and dashed across the ally toward the halfling. I came to a skidding halt when the halfling whisked his cloak with a whispered word and disappeared. The young lady stumbled forward, then glanced back at the empty space where the halfling had been, her expression perplexed.

"Where did…" she started, but I interrupted her.

"Get, girl! Run while you can." The words had barely left my mouth when I felt a pressure on my leg. A previously invisible barrier surrounding me popped like a bubble and shrank back into my necklace.

Dragon dung. My shield.

The halfling reappeared at my side, a startled look on his face. "Mage armor?"

I scowled and sliced my knife down toward his shoulder, a blow he easily deflected before dancing to the side and drawing another knife.

I crouched low, readying my dagger in my hand. "You aren't the only one with fancy nick-knacks to help him play unfair."

The halfling smirked. "Good. I will enjoy plundering yours when we're done here."

I took a step back as he advanced, steadying myself and watching his movement. I totally had it under control and knew I was going to disarm him of his two knives with my one dagger, but Qualar ruined all my fun.

A thin sheet of dust blew between the halfling and me.

"Sorry, but can I cut in on this dance of death?" Qualar's words were the only warning I had before a wall of crackling fire and sparks sprang up in front of my face. I closed my eyes and fell backward, but not before my eyebrows and bangs died a painful death. I heard the halfling cry out, then all went silent.

I opened my eyes to find the halfling was nowhere to be seen.

"Let's get out of here!" a voice cried from down the alley.

"Yeah, I wasn't paid for this dragon dung," a second gruff voice agreed.

I turned to watch the scorched man and half-orc dash out of the alley, ducking around a corner and out of sight.

I whipped my head from side to side. "Where'd the little guy go?"

Qualar reached down and took my hand, helping me to my feet. "Dunno. He did something fancy with his cape and disappeared. I thought it was a neat trick! Where did the girl and her baby go?"

One more quick glance around told me that the young lady had taken my advice and disappeared. I shrugged in answer to Qualar's question, reaching up and rubbing my singed eyebrows.

"Those will heal in no time at all." Qualar said.

"Coming from the guy who didn't singe his eyebrows off," I grumbled under my breath.

"Let's get back to the wagon and see if Elistra has something that will help. Maybe she has a magical potion of eyebrow growing!"

Goofy as he was, Qualar was alert for trouble as we walked back to Elistra's wagon. He held my hand as we walked, indicating that he didn't completely trust that I was steady on my feet. I tried to reassure him that my eyebrows had nothing to do with my sense of balance, but he ignored every word of it.

"Once we're inside the wagon, maybe I should check to make sure you don't have any other burns?" Qualar asked as we came up to Elistra's gypsy wagon.

I knit my brows, knowing they weren't there, a bit of a smirk turning up the corner of my mouth. "Check where, exactly?"

Qualar shrugged as he grabbed the door latch. "Oh, I don't know. I figured a head-to-toe search would be the way to start, ya know?"

As he opened the door, I saw a quick movement in the shadows of the dark wagon.

I set my hand on Qualar's shoulder and drew my knife. Qualar took a quick step back, inhaling sharply.

"Shhhhh!" a voice hissed from inside the wagon. "Please! I really need your help!"

I stared for a long moment until my eyes adjusted to the darkness. Though hidden under one of Elistra's blankets, I recognized the face staring back at me as the young woman with the baby. My eyes drifted to her arms, concealed by the blanket.

"Where's your baby?" I whispered.

She hesitated, then pushed the blanket aside, revealing the tiniest baby I'd ever seen sound asleep in her arms. "Please, help us. We're in serious trouble. My family wants to kill my baby."

I AIN'T NO SOFTY…

I like to think of myself as calloused and cold-hearted as a standard criminal comes.

Note: I said *standard* criminal. There is a line I do not cross in the cold-hearted world, and that is when it comes to the murder of innocents. Not-so-innocents? Eh, they're fair game. But innocent little babies are as innocent as they come. Especially when they have bright red ringlets of hair… and big green eyes… and coo like a dove.

I sat next to the campfire blazing brightly in the darkness. The tiny baby nestled in my arms sucked at her fist before holding it out and cooing at me. I smiled and cooed back. (No judging! What's a hardened thief like myself supposed to do when a baby coos at them? COO BACK. Okay? It's an unwritten rule.)

"How old is she, Rashel?" Elistra asked.

"About f-four months, I think? Yes. Four months." The mother answered from inside Elistra's wagon, where she was changing.

"What's her name?" I asked.

"Raina."

I smiled at Raina, stroking her tiny soft face with my finger. "Hi, Raina."

Okay, I'll just admit it: I'd fallen in love. It wasn't hard to do. She was so sweet and adorable.

Qualar moved up behind me, peering down at the baby as he popped some seeds into his mouth. "She's so itty bitty!" He exclaimed for the umpteenth time. "Why is she so small?"

I looked up at the fire-eater and scowled. "What kind of a question is that, burn-brain?"

"No, i-it's okay." Rashel said as she stepped from the wagon wearing a set of Elistra's clothes, "Her father was… well… he wasn't human. He was a bit on the smallish side."

Elistra walked around Rashel, checking to make sure the clothes fit. "Not a human? Is that why your family wants to kill the child?"

Rashel nodded, her eyes glued to the baby in my arms. "He was the nicest person I'd ever met, but they never understood that. When he died suddenly, my parents said I needed to wipe my slate clean and pretend it never happened. They wanted me to marry into a well-to-do family in Dunwynn."

I wrinkled my nose. "Dunnies—bunch of manure-shoveling xenophobes."

Rashel nodded. "Of course any proper Dunwynn family would shun my family if they knew I had a... *half-breed* child. So, when my family said that they wanted me to wipe the slate clean..."

"They meant wipe it clean with blood." Qualar finished somberly for the girl.

Rashel nodded, looking down at her feet. "For the greater good of the family name."

"How did her father die?" Elistra stepped behind Rashel and began to braid her long brown hair.

The young woman twisted a toe in the dirt. "Wolf attack."

Elistra narrowed her eyes. "Did you see it?"

Rashel shook her head, and the violet eyes standing behind her narrowed further, filled with suspicion.

"Where did you live?" Qualar asked, finishing off another handful of seeds.

Rashel looked up, eyes focusing back on Raina. "I grew up in a little town east of Bardon's Gap."

For a brief moment, my mind flitted to a mansion in Bardon's Gap that I had, um, *familiarized* myself with some time ago. It was the same very same mansion where I had acquired my mysterious cylindrical object.

Qualar poked a stick into the fire. "And where are you on your way to?"

"Bendenwood, I presume?" Elistra finished Rashel's braid off, laying it over her shoulder.

Rashel nodded, looking back at the seeress with concern. "How did you know?"

"I'm a fortune teller, dear," she said, as if that explained everything.

Rashel knit her brows and nodded slowly in belied understanding.

I wrinkled my nose again. "Why Bendenwood? It's just a bunch of tree huggers and basket weavers. Only thing that could possibly make it any worse is if a bunch of elves lived there too."

"My family won't argue with druids. It was the safest place I could think of for us to stay." Rashel smiled, looking at me. "Basket weaving is an old hobby of mine."

I frowned with a sigh and looked down at Raina. "Your future looks full of tree hugging, flower picking, and basket weaving, little one. I'm sorry."

The baby slobbered on her fist, staring at me intently.

IT WAS PITCH BLACK…

Under my blanket. Almost.

The moon was out and full. The embers of the fire were dying, but still aglow.

Crickets chirped, the wind whistled softly through the trees, and Qualar's snoring was loud and sounded like a choking banshee.

I had slipped under my blanket to block out the evening light and give myself some privacy, but unfortunately, there was no hiding from the sound of Qualar getting the restful sleep I wished I was getting.

The thought occurred to me that my blanket *could* stifle his snoring. Permanently. But then Elistra would be sad to find that her fire-eater had unfortunately suffocated sometime during the night, and I couldn't very well do that to the poor girl.

With a soft sigh, I silently reached into a small purse on my side. My hand sank further and further into it, until I was almost elbow-deep in the tiny bag. I thought about my jewel-encrusted cylinder, and suddenly felt something slip into my hand.

I pulled it out and held it in front of my face. My eyes were very sharp in the dark, and even under my blanket, I could make out the individual symbols surrounding the cylinder. I twisted the symbols around and listened to a soft clicking inside the cylinder.

Puzzles like this are child's play. If only I could understand what language these symbols were in...

I studied them carefully, trying to make out some sort of pattern. "Spiders! Giant spiders!"

The campfire roared to life.

I sprang to my feet at Qualar's outcry. I spun around breathlessly, looking for any sign of enormous arachnids. Heart slowing, I angled my eyes down to the still-sleeping man. Qualar whimpered again, then rolled over, his breathing even and slow.

I growled under my breath. "You and that stupid spider dream."

My gaze was drawn to the wagon when I heard the baby cry. It was only a small cry, soon put to rest as her mother began to softly console her. Soon, everything was quiet again, except for the crackling fire that was now bright and alive.

I shifted my gaze to Elistra on the other side of the fire and found the fortune teller sitting up, shaking her head softly as she stared at Qualar. She made eye contact with me, then softly patted the ground next to her.

I scooped up my bedroll, carefully tucking my cylinder inside my blanket, out of sight. I spread everything out next to her, wadded my blanket up and flopped down on the ground with it in my lap.

"One of these days, I'm gonna make a fake giant spider and hang it above his head while he's asleep, and maybe, if I'm very lucky, he'll die of fright." I whispered.

Elistra cleared her throat softly. "More likely than not, he would just start the wildfire of the century trying to kill it."

I sighed and nodded, staring at the slowly dying fire.

"What were you holding in your hand a moment ago?"

I internally froze at the seeress' question. "Um... blankets?"

Elistra softly giggled. "No. It's hiding inside the blanket now."

I mentally cursed myself for being so hasty to respond to the boy who cried spider. As I tried to think my way out of showing it to Elistra, the fortune teller leaned close, her violet eyes catching mine.

"If you want help with the puzzle, you'll have to trust me with the secret."

I squinted at her, knowing better than to ask how she knew it was a puzzle. After a moment of thought, I shrugged and unwrapped the blanket from around my prize. I held it out to Elistra, keeping a vice-like grip on it.

She did not try to take it from me. She leaned forward, her brow furrowing and her face growing very serious. For a moment, I saw a flicker of recognition in her face. Something about this cylinder was familiar to her.

I held my breath until she pointed at the symbols. "There are at least four different languages on each wheel. Draconic, Dwarvish, Elvish, and one other I don't know."

I frowned. "But, I know Elvish. I don't recognize any of these symbols."

Elistra nodded. "The Elvish and Dwarvish symbols on this are from very old dialects. They aren't used anymore."

My hand quivered slightly as I spiked a suspicious eyebrow.

The fortune teller glanced at me, a hint of a smile turning up one corner of her ruby lips. "I used to have a book about the old languages. It was one of my favorites."

"Do you still have it?" I asked. When she shook her head, I twisted my lips sideways in disappointment. It sounded like it would have been a very expensive book. Not that I would've taken it and sold it, mind you. Not from Elistra. At least, not right away.

Elistra twisted a couple of the little wheels on the cylinder. "All the symbols on the top mean Light. The next one below that is Dark. The next one is Freedom, and the next is Slavery… no! Chains. My mistake. Followed by Angel, and Demon after that, and Life and Death after that."

I looked at the symbols carefully, realizing just how complicated this puzzle got. "If each wheel is filled with symbols that all mean the same thing, how are we supposed to line them up with one another?"

Elistra shrugged and twisted the top two symbols around, letting them rest in a couple of different positions. "You may have to try lining each language up. Or, it may be oldest to newest. Either way, I don't think it will unlock until the entire puzzle is solved." She pulled her hands away and yawned, stretching. "Have fun with that. I'm going to get some sleep before the next spider apocalypse."

I tore my eyes away from the cylinder and glared at Qualar's back. "How disappointed would you be if he was dead in the morning?"

"Wait till we're on sanctified ground, that way you can be sure he doesn't come back to haunt you." Elistra laid on her side and pulled her blanket over her head as she spoke.

I shrugged, an evil grin crossing my face. "Like I wouldn't enjoy killing him twice."

THERE I WAS, SLEEPING IN THE RAIN...

Was, being the key word. As soon as my face started getting wet, I woke with a start.

Thunder rolled in the distance. The rain hissed as it lightly fell on the smoldering campfire.

Elistra and Qualar were both sound asleep.

The door was open on the wagon, and a raccoon sat just inside, gnawing too happily on a cheese wheel.

"Hey! Get out of there, you nasty varmint!" I lunged to my feet as the coon did, and chased it away from the wagon, flapping my hands like a graceful swan... or a dying crane, one or the other.

I frowned at the discarded cheese wheel, then poked my head inside the wagon. The bed at the back was empty. Rashel and her baby were not there.

I quickly looked around the outside of the wagon where the draft horse was supposed to be tied. It was gone.

A string of curses in multiple languages spewed from my mouth.

Qualar stirred. "So... much... cursing... why am I wet?" He scrambled to his feet, sputtering a few curses of his own.

Elistra sat bolt upright. "Is Rashel gone?"

I nodded, watching as the seeress rubbed the sleep from her eyes. "How'd you know?"

"I'm a fortune teller, dear."

I snorted. *That's right. Stick to your cover story.* But I knew better by now—a faker can always recognize another faker. It was probably one of the reasons she had taken me in.

Elistra stood and moved to the wagon, slipping past me and

ducking inside, out of the rain. She assumed a cross-legged position on the floor and closed her eyes.

Qualar moved to my side.

"What are you doing?" the two of us asked as we stared at the fortune teller.

"I suspected Rashel instantly," Elistra said. "The clothes that I gave her have an amulet sewn into them that I can track with my mind."

Qualar crossed his arms. "Why track her?"

Elistra kept her eyes closed, her face stone. "Because she stole from Fran."

My heart stopped. I spun on my heel and rushed across to my blankets. I jerked them up from the ground, shaking the raindrops from them. My treasure was gone.

Just for good measure, I checked Qualar's blankets, then Elistra's. The emptiness of both made my hands shake, and my heart pounded hard in my chest.

I went back to the wagon and clutched the doorpost, staring at the seeress impatiently.

"Well? Anything?"

Elistra frowned, eyes still closed. "She is halfway to Bendenwood. Off the road. Waiting. Waiting for something. She has the cylinder with her. And the baby."

I grabbed a dry cloak off the floor of the wagon and threw it around my shoulders, marching in the direction of Bendenwood.

"Fran!" Qualar hurried to my side.

"Shove off, fire-eater!" I snarled. "I don't need your help to strangle the little wench."

"You wanna ride me?"

I scowled at him. "Excuse me?"

He sighed, "Not like that! I mean you can actually ride me and get there faster!"

I turned to yell at him, but all my words were forgotten as I watched his body twist and elongate. His arms raised and his hands turned to hooves. Antlers grew from his head, and his brown hair raced across his body, covering it in fur.

Next thing I knew, a beautiful elk stood in front of me. He snorted in my face, then turned sideways and scratched his back with the tip of one antler.

I smacked him in the shoulder, making him groan and prance to the side. "Are you a druid? Are you a stinking druid, you little coal-cruncher!? You're supposed to be weaving baskets, not spewing fire to attract girls!"

"Fran! Focus!"

I turned to find Elistra watching me with her hands on her hips. "You don't have much time! Whoever Rashel is waiting for won't take long to get there. You must hurry and make sure they don't get the cylinder. It's more important than you realize."

She said the words with such conviction that I pushed aside the numerous questions running through my mind.

After gracefully flipping onto Qualar's back… and my rear hitting the ground on the other side of him… he finally knelt and let me slip on before galloping away with me into the trees.

THERE I WAS…

Lying on the ground, staring at my reflection in a silver sword. The icy sting of a sharp blade slid across my throat, followed by the warmth of my own blood coating my skin. Somewhere nearby, baby Raina wailed and cried. Terror gripped me as I started to choke, knowing that I was going to die very soon.

Oh, wait…

I'm getting ahead of myself.

Let me back up a few minutes or so.

I stared at Rashel from the cover of the forest. She sat cross-legged in a small clearing, the baby sleeping next to her in a basket. The draft horse was tied to a tree. And Rashel was fiddling with MY prize.

She squinted at the runes surrounding the cylinder, turning each wheel in a different direction.

I had been watching her for a solid five minutes… okay, maybe less… perhaps two minutes… I wasn't keeping track of time, alright? I was fuming. She had MY prize and was trying to solve MY puzzle.

All the same, I was no fool and knew better than to rush in. Qualar was checking the perimeter for Rashel's expected guests. I just needed to wait and come up with a plan.

As a plan was forming in my mind, there was a loud click from the cylinder that startled Rashel. She dropped my prize on the ground and stared as it began to glow with a purple light.

A breathless moment of silence passed.

All logical plans in my mind melted in the inferno of my rage.

She had solved MY puzzle.

Before I knew what I was doing, I summoned the magic deep in me. My skin tingled as I changed my appearance, just before stepping out into the clearing.

"What have you done?" My voice sounded like the halfling that had attacked Rashel in the alley.

Rashel jumped to her feet, spinning toward me. She frowned.

"Oh. Garth." She glanced down at the cylinder. "Well, I didn't mean to open it. Besides, what does it matter? My father will be happy. Anyway, aren't you supposed to be hiding and waiting for them to get here?"

My heart stopped in my chest.

"I am hiding." The halfling's voice rang out just before he appeared right behind Rashel, smirking at me.

Rashel looked between the two of us, then nervously stepped behind the halfling.

I had meant to intimidate Rashel with this disguise. I had no idea that she actually knew the filthy little halfling.

I narrowed my eyes at him. "Garth, eh? I never would've guessed."

He snapped his fingers at me. "Got ya, shapeshifter."

I sensed it coming and rolled out of the way just before the net dropped on top of me.

My heart raced. Every impulse in my body said to run into the woods, but my eyes locked onto the cylinder which still glowed with that purple light.

Elistra's words rang in my mind. *It's more important than you realize.*

Without thinking, I rushed Rashel and the halfling.

The halfling crossed his arms and looked over his shoulder. "Trym! Do your thing!"

Without warning, a beam of silvery light slammed down on me. At first, it looked like sparkling moonlight, but then the pain hit me. I stopped dead in my tracks as ghostly flames lit across my skin. My muscles twitched and spasmed as shooting pain raced under my skin.

I fell to my knees, gasping. I clawed at the ground, moving an inch at a time closer to my cylinder. A scream escaped my throat finally as the pain became too much, but then my scream turned into an unearthly wail.

The baby woke and cried out.

Rashel's face contorted into one of horror.

Garth smirked and moved toward me.

Another halfling, a female in plate armor, stepped from the woods, her face a picture of concentration, her eyes glowing faintly with magic. She held a giant silver sword in her hands that grabbed my attention. I could see my reflection perfectly in its polished blade.

I watched with horror as my shape changed in my reflection. I grew long and frighteningly thin. My clothes melted into my body. My fingers elongated and grew knobby with claws. My hair shrank into my head, and my skin turned inky black. My eyes grew large and white, without pupils.

Finally, the halfling woman stopped in front of me. She stabbed her sword in front of my face so I could get a good look at my true reflection.

"We have ye now, doppelganger," she hissed in a thick accent.

The magical moonlight disappeared, and I gasped for air as the agony it brought left my body.

Two more halflings, both wearing black clothes and hoods, dropped from the trees and grabbed the net off the ground, moving closer to me.

Garth, arms still crossed, circled me. "We've been watching you a long time, doppelganger. My cousin here, Trym, was one of your unfortunate victims."

Trym squatted in front of me, grabbing me roughly by the jaw and staring me in the eyes. "I had a *really* neat javelin that shot lightning. Remember it?"

I snorted. "Wanna buy it? I'll give it to you half price."

The halfling drew her fist back and punched me in the nose.

Garth went on. "I have admired your work, beast. I can particularly respect the time you stole the crescent scepter out from under Eboneye's nose last year. That was beautiful."

"Thank... you..." I gasped, reaching a shaking claw up to touch my bleeding nose.

"As dangerous as it was to steal directly from Eboneye himself, though, I'm afraid you met your match when you stole from the baron. You see, this thing," he nudged the cylinder with his boot, making the purple light shine brighter, "cost him a lot of time, blood, and money. He was going to give it to the duke of Dunwynn."

"To save the family name from shame." Rashel added softly, stooping and picking up her crying baby.

Trym eyed me with disdain. "He offered us a *lot* 'o money ta find ye. I woulda done it fer free, though."

I snorted blood from my nose. "And that is why... you will always be poor, short stack."

Trym kicked me over onto my back, placing her giant sword across my throat.

Rashel shrank back a few steps, her face going pale as she knew what was coming.

Garth leaned over and smirked at me once again. "It's been a fun game, beast."

Trym tensed and drew her arm back.

And now we get to the part with the icy sting of the blade, and throat slicing, and blood and crying baby and all that good stuff.

As I choked on my own blood, a desperate, angry roar filled the air.

"BEAR!" Rashel's voice shrieked in terror.

Before I could blink, a giant, brown ball of fur barreled into the group of halflings. It knocked them all away, then planted itself over the top of me. Belying its size, a huge paw lashed out, punching Trym across the clearing where she smacked hard into a tree. The creature then snapped at Garth, but somehow missed the slippery little halfling.

As my eyesight began to fade, all I could think about was my precious treasure. I turned to the side just enough to see the glowing purple cylinder. I reached out with a bloodied hand and touched it.

As my fingers closed around it, a trickle of blood seeped into the crevices. Then a strange thing happened. The cylinder began to hiss and pop, and the purple light flashed even brighter.

Suddenly, everything around me disappeared. I saw myself lifted high above the landscape, looking down on the world as if I were a star.

My eye was drawn to seven ancient towers that somehow seemed to stand out over everything else. One was in the mountains, another in a marsh far to the south, four across the seas, and the last hidden beneath the waters between.

As I stared at the towers, a massive storm formed before me. The clouds bubbled and brewed until they made a face that looked similar to Elistra's, but the eyes were hollow, cold, and dead.

Lightning crackled throughout the massive cloud as a voice filled my head: *You don't belong here, little abomination.*

Although I'd been called worse before, the words stung. I opened my mouth to shoot an incredibly witty insult back to the cloud, but it must've known that my superior insult would've burst it. With a wave of a cloudy hand, and a brilliant flash of lightning, the world shifted around me. The cloud and the towers all bobbed and weaved like reflections in a puddle, and then changed to a marble floating against a background of black silk.

As everything grew still around me and I could see things clearly again, I realized that it was not a marble at all.

I was far above my world, among the stars. The entirety of Arinthar was laid before me in a beautiful, silent globe. I could see the great mainland of Laurentia and the chain of isles that ran west of it. I could even see my home isle of Thac, though it was very small in comparison.

After a long moment of staring, mesmerized, at my beautiful world, a light at the corner of my eye caught my attention. I turned to see the sun, blazing in all its golden glory, surrounded by the far whiter light of the celestial realms beyond. There are no words to describe the beauty that I saw there. It rendered me speechless, which, as you may know by now, is no mean feat.

I'm not sure how long I floated there in the ether, transfixed by that vision. Yet eventually my mind wandered back to thoughts of home.

As I turned my gaze back to Arinthar, I noticed something I hadn't seen before. Five ghostly, nearly invisible chains were anchored to different spots around the globe. I admittedly didn't pay a lot of attention in school, but I couldn't recall anything being taught about chains attached to our world.

My eyes followed the ethereal chains down to another world I had not previously noticed. It was almost as black as the space around it, but rivers of lava and fire rippled across its cracked, arid surface.

As I looked closer, I saw countless millions of beings roaming in packs across the surface. Some were very large, others very small, some white, some black, and some red, but all of them were hideous in appearance.

All except the succubi and incubi, of course. Some people I knew wouldn't care if they were burning in hell, as long as they could be with that army of deliciously good-looking...

I stopped myself as I realized what I was staring at.

Demons!

As if it had heard my thoughts, one of the creatures, the largest of them all, stood and fixed its gaze upon me. His reptilian skin was red and black. His long, muscular arms did not end in hands, but in hideous hooked claws. A long, powerful tail swept behind him, filled with rows of deadly spikes. His skin was stretched tight across his face and rib cage, making him appear almost skeletal. Four giant spikes rose from his back, and four thick horns formed a crown around his head. Blazing eyes full of malice locked onto mine and froze me in terror.

Visions began to pour into my head. I saw Arinthar burst into flames. Every being on my beloved world—everything from men to dwarfs, and even dragons—were caught in the inferno. Yet, they did not die. No, somehow, they were forced to live as the flames ate away at them.

I could not look away as they writhed in agony. Their screams and pleas filled my ears. Beyond it all, I could still see the giant demon's face, and hear the rumble of his laughter in the background.

I don't know how long the visions continued. It seemed like centuries. I not only lost track of time, but I forgot who I was, or that I had even ever been. All I knew was torture. All I could feel was pain. I wanted my existence to end. I begged for death.

Yet the giant demon would not let me go. It reveled in my anguish, feeding off my pain. I think it would have kept me there for all eternity, but for the sudden flash of light that tore me away from the visions. To this day I'm not sure what it was, but it was far brighter than the sun and hurt my eyes. I threw my arms in front of my face, trying to hide from its blinding rays.

I suddenly felt myself falling, spinning out of control. I careened through the emptiness for what seemed like forever. I lost all track of time, all sense of direction. And then, just as suddenly, I was lying on the ground.

I tried to cry out in pain, but could not. Hands grabbed me by the throat. I grasped them by the wrists and struggled to pull them away.

"Dangit, Fran, let me heal you!" Qualar shrieked. "Just stop and let me heal you, please!"

It was then I realized the hands were caressing my throat gently. A soothing warmth vibrated from them, making my pain disappear.

My grip on his wrists loosened.

I opened my eyes for a brief second, but saw only blurry light and shadows.

I suddenly gasped, my throat working to move air into my lungs again.

Nearby, Raina was still crying frantically, her tiny voice making my heart bleed.

After a moment, Qualar sighed. He moved his hands, his fingers probing my neck for a moment before gently cradling my head. He pressed his face next to mine, sighing with relief again. I could feel warm tears on his cheeks.

"Is she okay?" I heard Elistra ask.

A sudden tiredness came over me. I was vaguely aware of Elistra, Qualar, and another man's voice speaking together over me as I fell asleep.

MY NOSE TICKLED…

And, like any normal person, I gently swatted my face to shoo the fly that was undoubtedly bothering me.

Only, it wasn't a fly.

It was a feather.

And my hand was filled with whipped cream.

"Yesssss!" I heard Qualar hiss.

I sat bolt upright, flailing my arms to try and catch him.

"You little fire maniac! I'll get you for that! Just you wait!"

I grabbed the sheets covering me and quickly wiped the cream from my face, gagging at the warm milk smell it was leaving behind. When I finally felt clean enough, I opened my eyes. I blinked several times. Everything was so blurry, I couldn't make up my mind which way was up, and which was down.

I wiped my eyes again, to be sure I had everything out of them, but it did no good.

My heart started to race inside my chest.

"I… I'm… I can't…"

I heard a tent flap open, and Elistra's soft voice was right next to me in an instant. "There, there now, Frances. Just breathe. I know. You can't see very well, can you?"

I shook my head, holding my hands up, but unable to find them amidst the mass of blurs.

Elistra rubbed her hand over my shoulders comfortingly. "Your cylinder burst into magical flames and burned your eyes. The druids will do what they can to help you."

I wiped my hand across my nose and sniffled, trying to hold back tears.

Elistra pressed the palm of her hand up against the side of my head. Although my eyes were open and I could see nothing, a vision formed in my head.

I was sitting on a cot covered in furs, covered by a wool blanket that now smelled of souring milk.

Across from me there was a vanity with a mirror. I was shocked to see Elistra—beautiful, young Elistra—sitting next to a bone-thin, inky black monster.

I raised a long finger and touched my face. "Have the druids seen me like this?"

The seeress shook her head.

I focused on my image in the mirror. I felt the familiar tingling under my skin and watched as I took on my previous form: kinky, wild strawberry-blonde hair, brilliant blue eyes, and pale white skin speckled with freckles.

I stared at my new reflection for a moment, then sighed. "The druids won't help a beast like me."

The fortune teller met my eyes in the mirror. "Honey, the druids spend their entire lives trying to *become* beasts."

I shook my head. "No. They spend their lives trying to become the cute, fluffy, man-eating beasts. Not the monster that mothers tell their children about to make them behave, that cause men to fear their closest friends, that the paladins are trained to hunt and kill."

The tent flap opened again, and a man walked in who I recognized as the ringmaster I'd seen with Elistra the first time I met her. Only now, he was not dressed as a ringmaster. He was in tracking leathers and had a longbow slung over his shoulder.

"Frances, this is Eldon Rahn. He helped Qualar with your attackers."

I crossed my arms. "Nothing like coming in last minute when my throat is already slit."

He snorted. "What can I say? I like *cutting* it close."

Elistra and I both sucked in a breath. "Cute. Don't quit your day job."

He chuckled, and sat down on the floor. "I take it you don't think too highly of druids."

I shrugged.

"Well, once you're done with them, I have a place near Deepwood Fort you can live."

I spiked an eyebrow. "What makes you think I'm interested in settling down?"

He grinned, glancing at Elistra. "Just a hunch."

The tent flap opened again, and Qualar walked in, followed by a tall elf woman. She had very fluffy, curly, bright red hair and sharp green eyes that locked onto me. She raised her chin, looking me over.

"So this is the doppelganger?" Her question was directed at Qualar, her voice tinged with disdain.

"She's *my* friend," Elistra answered, before anyone else could respond.

The elf woman raised an eyebrow at the seeress, her expression belying little emotion. "I see." Her gaze fixated back on me for a moment in study before speaking again. "I am the High Druid, Lysandra. And you are?"

Perhaps it was the circumstances. Perhaps it was because she was a snooty elf. And druid. But I definitely took an immediate dislike to this woman. "Not interested in whatever you're peddling."

Lysandra squinted, then turned her gaze toward Elistra. "Is my job finished here, or not?"

Elistra let out a deep sigh. "Please give us a minute."

"Very well," Lysandra answered, doing little to hide her irritation. She motioned to the others and then left the tent. Eldon followed close behind, but Qualar hesitated a moment. He leaned in close and gave me a strained smile. "I'll be right outside if ya need me."

I knew he was just trying to be nice, but I was in no mood for it. I waved him away. "Whatever."

Qualar grimaced at the rebuff, then shuffled out of the tent to join the others.

As soon as they were all gone, Elistra grasped me by the shoulders. She was surprisingly strong for such a slim woman. "Alright now. Enough with the pity party. You played with forces beyond your control, and you paid the price for it. Now it's time to move forward."

I peered at her incredulously, shrugging her hands off my shoulders. "Move forward? After what I saw? And without my sight? And how do you suppose I'm going to do that?"

A knowing smile spread across the seeress' lips. "There are more ways to see than with your eyes."

I opened my mouth to retort, but realized that I was seeing her in my head. The images she had put there had not faded. In fact, they had grown clearer. What's more was I could even see the part of the tent *behind* my head. My brow knit into a single long line. I moved my hands above and behind my head, waving them all around, able to see them from all directions. "What in Thac did you do to me?"

Elistra laughed. It was a light sound, like bells ringing from inside a steeple. "Oh, my dear Fran. I merely awakened an innate talent. You actually have far more of them than you know."

"Oh yeah? Like what?"

The seeress took me by the hands, her expression growing deathly serious. "Like those that will be crucial to our survival in the coming years, my dear friend."

I narrowed a single eye at her. "Survival? Do you know what I saw when I touched the cylinder?"

Elistra nodded thoughtfully. "I have an idea."

She then told me things that truly opened my deadened eyes. Elistra explained that there is no destiny, or fate, but a myriad of possibilities all casting their shadows based on the impact of each individual event. Thus, the visions I had seen were of but one possible future—one of a tangled flow of constantly shifting threads that she is always trying to trace. Seeing all potential futures is impossible, but some possibilities create a tangled knot of such tremendous size that anyone with a little of 'the sight' can't miss them. And one such knot just happened to be the imminent demon invasion that would fall upon this world.

The threads beyond that were in constant flux, but many of them ended similarly to the visions I had seen—most, in fact, according to the seeress. In only a very few did Arinthar survive.

When Elistra was done, I found myself shaking; my entire body was drenched in cold sweat. It took me a while to find my voice, and when I did it was shaky. "And… you really think… I can make a difference?"

I saw the fear in her violet eyes as clear as if I was staring into them with my own. "Oh, hon. I'm not sure if any of us can. But if we don't try, then we are all lost, and everything we hold dear with it."

I felt her hands tremble in mine. Or perhaps it was my hands trembling in hers. Either way, we both sat there staring at each other with tears in our eyes. I took a deep breath. "Okay. If you think I can make a difference, I'll try… but do I really have to work with these tree-huggers?"

Elistra abruptly laughed, the sound breaking the pallor that hung over us. She smiled at me, her parted lips lighting up the entire tent. "Yes, I'm afraid so, my dear Fran."

That smile of hers was so infectious that I couldn't help grinning back. "Alright, but that elf woman is insufferable. She's got a stick up her butt, and I aim to remove it."

Elistra laughed again. "That's more than fine. I've yet to meet an elf without that snooty attitude."

Smile growing, I crossed my arms. "Watch yourself. The day you meet one without that attitude, you'll find yourself head-over-heels and off to marry 'im before ya know it."

We both laughed at that point.

As our giggles faded, the tent flap popped open. Qualar stuck his head in, a tentative expression on his face. "Everything alright in here?"

Elistra turned to him and nodded. "Everything's fine now."

Qualar's expression made me nearly laugh again. I smiled and waved him forward. "Come in. I haven't thanked you properly for saving my life."

A grin broke across his face. He cast a quick glance behind him. "A kiss or two or three will do in thanks! And, what about the others?"

I wrinkled my nose. "Well, I ain't thanking them with a kiss."

Qualar rolled his eyes. "The high druid still has questions."

I sighed and peered at Elistra. She gave me a short nod.

"Alright, fine," I told Qualar. "Bring them in."

TIME FLIES…

Especially when you're having fun. Less so when High Druid Lysandra is sitting in your house, slightly inebriated from drinking too much of your home made "water keifer."

The actual name of my "keifer" will remain nameless. What the High Druid don't know won't kill her.

"You know, Fran," Lysandra leaned forward, resting her elbows on my table. "When Elistra convinced me to help you six years ago, I didn't like you very much. And now, even with your crazy Deepwood accent and the locals loving you, not much has changed. I still don't like you. I don't know why I allowed you to be a part of the druidic council… well… yes, I do know. But I can't believe I let Elistra talk me into it."

I grinned, kneading some bread dough in a bowl.

I used my senses to look outside at two little girls playing with dolls in the garden. One was Raina. Her mother had died that fateful night six years ago, stabbed by a poison dagger. I had taken the baby in and adopted her.

The other little girl was Eldon Rahn's granddaughter, Kalyn. She was turning into Raina's best friend. There was something special about her, besides the fact that she'd gotten a hold of my heartstrings, too.

Lysandra drained the rest of her keifer out of a chipped teacup, then poured more from the teapot. "Why did you choose to look like an old lady?"

I chuckled and dumped the bread dough into a loaf pan. "Well, lemme tell ya, Sandy girl: Fer one, it makes me look older 'n wiser'n you… even if you is an elf. Fer another, nobody 'spects an old blind woman o' doin' anything suspicious, it keeps the leader of the fire maniacs from hangin' 'round too much, and I can judge folk out loud, 'n they just blame it on my age. And *lastly*, it annoys ya to know I could be prettier'n you."

Lysandra scowled at the back of my head. She raised her teacup and saluted me. "Dream on, you old witch."

Rescue at Redune

F.P. Spirit

Rescue at Redune

It was nearly dusk as the *Avenger* rounded the horn at Sentilla Point. Daylight slowly receded toward the horizon, stars twinkling into existence as night blanketed the fading sky. Sentilla Light flared to life on the nearby shore, the brilliant beams of the mystical tower arcing across the twilight backdrop. Evening winds whipped through the hole-ridden spire, creating a beautiful, haunting melody that echoed across the waters.

Lieutenant Commander Pallas Stealle stood tall at the prow of the *Avenger*. The lithe young man cast a dark eye at the ancient lighthouse as they drifted past. *You'd think after all this time someone would've figured how to stop that incessant racket.*

Second in command of the mighty warship, Pallas had no time to enjoy such frivolities as music. At just twenty-six years old, Pallas had worked his way up through the ranks to attain the prestigious position. Yet because of his youth and noble background, there were those who cried favoritism at his improbable achievement.

The corner of Pallas' mouth upturned ever so slightly. *They'll see. I'll prove them all wrong.*

A cry from above interrupted his silent brooding. "Smoke on the horizon!"

The young man glanced upward, barely discerning a shadow in the crow's nest high above. The figure pointed up the coast, in the direction they were headed.

Pallas swept his gaze northward—there was a darker patch of sky off in the distance. He leaned over the rail for a better look when a tingling sensation brushed his brow. Pallas felt a familiar presence somewhere close by.

As if on cue, a voice called out from behind him. "That must be Redune!"

Pallas glanced over his shoulder to see a uniformed figure approaching the prow. A tall, muscular man with chiseled features and dark hair speckled white at the temples drew up next to him. *Captain Lagrange Hightower.*

Pallas had sensed his captain's aura. It was a gift that ran in his family—the Stealles were *spiritblades,* masters of the soul and sword.

Captain Hightower pulled out a spyglass, raised it to his eye and peered up the coast. "It is indeed Redune, and there appears to be a large ship in the harbor."

A large ship? Pallas' breath caught as he stared into the encroaching darkness, but Redune was still too far away to see with the naked eye. A horrific vision flashed through his mind in its stead.

Thick, choking smoke hung like a grey veil in the air. Scarlet flames leapt from windows and danced across rooftops. Black husks of crumbled, burnt-out buildings still smoked in all directions.

"I can almost make out her colors."

Corpses were strewn all about, some piled in great, decaying mounds. Cries and shouts were heard around every corner, mixed with the ring of steel on steel. Dark shadows fled down the street, accompanied by desperate cries for help.

Hightower lowered the glass, his voice grim. "It's as I feared—pirates."

Pallas' heart began to race.

Dozens of ships out in the harbor, their black hulls sitting there as if watching the carnage with delight. Flags flying atop their dark sails that all Penwick had come to dread—the Clans of the Pirate Coast.

"Alert the crew, Lieutenant Commander."

Pallas forced the gut-wrenching images from his mind. "Yes, Sir!"

With a quick salute, the young man spun on his heel, focusing his will as he marched across the forecastle. His body swiftly calmed in response as he bellowed out orders.

"All hands on deck!"

This is no time for hysterics. This is what I've trained for.

"Prepare for battle!"

Why I've driven myself so hard all these years.

"Dim the lanterns!"

So that I can protect others.

"Ready the weapons!"

So that no one else will suffer the fate of the thousands who died in the raids on Penwick.

The crew responded with equal speed and precision. In no time, the great warship was prepped for the impending conflict. A grim smile spread across Pallas' lips. *They're a crack outfit.* All had lived through the carnage of the raids and were more than eager to protect their homeland.

The *Avenger* itself was specifically built for hunting pirates. From its reinforced, fireproofed hull to the large complement of cannon, and the specialized weapons it carried, the ship was a veritable floating fortress.

The *Avenger* was battle-ready in record time. Pallas strode briskly back to inform the captain, his mind racing as he went. *Small time marauders wouldn't have a large ship. Still, it's been five years since our last run in with the pirate clans. So why now—and why Redune?*

The captain peered through his spyglass as Pallas drew up beside him. He didn't need to see Hightower's expression—he could feel the tension exuding from the man in waves.

"Ship's ready for battle, Sir!"

"Very good, Lieutenant Commander, because we're in for one hell of a fight."

Pallas stiffened. "It's the clans, isn't it?"

Hightower held the glass out to him. "See for yourself."

Pallas grabbed the miniature telescope and held it to his eye. A quick adjustment brought the harbor into focus. Redune stood more than a mile away, but Pallas could clearly see a large vessel moored at the long docks. A low-riding galleon, numerous hatches lined its hull, all obviously rigged for cannon.

Pallas swept his gaze to the top of the mast, his shoulders tensing as he saw the colors flapping there in the evening wind—a squid with tentacles snaking upward as if to snatch its prey.

"Archite." The word passed his lips as if it were a curse.

The Archites were indeed one of the thirteen clans of the pirate coast. This would be a deadly encounter. The best chance for Redune and the *Avenger* was to strike fast and decisively.

Hightower mirrored his thoughts. "Have the helmsman bring her about. We'll move in and hit them with everything we've got."

"Aye, S—"

Pallas started to lower the glass when a sharp movement caught his eye. Three figures hustled across the deck of the galleon, the middle one struggling against the other two.

"What it is, Pallas?" Hightower breathed impatiently.

"I think… they have a hostage…" He adjusted the lens for a closer look.

The outer pair were most definitely pirates, but the third was not. The figure appeared to be that of a woman—a lady of finery, in fact. Garbed in a fancy green dress, long tresses of bright copper hair swept down below her shoulders. Though there was a vast distance between them, Pallas felt a familiar tingling brush his brow.

"Hostage or not, our course is clear," the captain interrupted.

Pallas lowered the eyepiece and stared at Hightower. He stood stiffly, his knuckles white from gripping the rail. Pallas could literally feel the waves of anger radiating from him—anger laced with more than a tinge of fear.

"We need to blow these pirates out of the water and show the clans they're not welcome on our shores." Hightower emphasized the statement by slamming his fist into his other hand.

Pallas knew he was right, but there was something all too familiar about the red-haired woman. His brow tingled again, followed by a sudden flash of intuition. "Begging your pardon, Sir, but I don't think we're seeing the whole picture."

Hightower fixed him with a stern gaze—he was well aware of his second-in-command's gifts. "Do you feel this is some sort of trap?"

Pallas shook his head. "I'm not sure, Sir, but I'm sensing there's more going on here than meets the eye." He hefted the spyglass in his hand. "With your permission, I'd like to take one more look around."

Hightower considered it for a moment, then nodded. "A *brief* look, Lieutenant Commander. We can't afford to lose the element of surprise."

"Agreed." Pallas nodded as he lifted the glass to his eye.

He swiftly scanned the docks again, this time looking beyond the pirate vessel. Sure enough, behind the galleon sat another ship. Completely dark, it had been easy to miss in the fading light.

Pallas' jaw tightened as he focused in on it. *Is Hightower right? Is this some sort of elaborate ruse to draw us in?*

He swept his gaze across the darkened deck, but saw no sign of life. From what he could tell, it was a smaller ship than the galleon—not typically one that would be used by the pirate clans. On a hunch, Pallas focused on the top of the main mast. As luck would have it, the last rays of the setting sun caught the edge of the standard flying there.

A crimson crescent on a dark background? That's the flag of the House Dunamal—Alys Dunamal. It has to be.

Pallas spun to face the captain. "The hostage—it's the daughter of Alburg Dunamal, Sir."

Hightower sputtered as he struggled with this new development. "D-Dunamal? The baron's Master of Coin? The richest merchant in Penwick? Are you sure, lad?"

Pallas described to him the dark ship and the flag that flew above it. "Plus, I'd recognize that red mane anywhere. Alys and my sister, Thea, were inseparable when they were young."

"Dragon dung!" Hightower cursed, running his hands through his slowly greying hair. "There's no way we can blow them out of the water with Dunamal's daughter on board."

Hightower wasn't wrong. Alys was Dunamal's only daughter. They'd be lucky to be merely stripped of their commissions if anything were to happen to her. Not to mention, Thea would never forgive him. *I'm not sure I'd forgive myself.*

The strained silence that had fallen over them was suddenly interrupted by a cry from overhead. "Ship astern!"

Pallas exchanged a worried glance with Hightower. If another pirate vessel was coming up the coast, they'd be in for the fight of their lives. The two of them took off at a run toward the rear of the ship.

As Pallas reached the stern, his eyes fell on the new vessel. It had just rounded the point, its deck well lit and running lights burning bright. Hightower caught up with him moments later, the older man huffing from exertion.

Pallas nodded toward the approaching ship. "They're not exactly trying to hide from us, Sir."

Hightower gave him a grim nod as he caught his breath. "Well… let's see what… we've got here…." He then pointed his spyglass at the new ship. A few seconds went by, then he let out a long sigh, his tall frame visibly relaxing. "Thank the gods. She's no pirate, just a merchant ship."

Another merchant? As Pallas gazed at the approaching vessel, something clicked in the back of his mind. It would be risky, but if the merchant captain were willing, it just might work. "Begging your pardon, Sir, but I think I might know a way we can rescue Mistress Dunamal *and* still save Redune."

Hightower arched an eyebrow at him. "Speak your mind, Lieutenant Commander."

Pallas swiftly detailed his plan. It would require a two-pronged assault of spiritblades like himself. Thankfully there was a full complement on board, all rigorously trained by his father.

Pallas would board the merchant vessel with a small team. Their objective would be to get as close as possible and rescue the hostage.

The second team would infiltrate Redune and drive out the loot-ers and cutthroats. The remaining crew would sail the *Avenger* into port and blast the pirate ship to smithereens once Pallas' team was clear.

Hightower listened carefully to his proposal, all the while gingerly rubbing his chin. Pallas could feel the older man's tension slowly ebb. When he was done, the captain nodded. "I see. Very good, Lieutenant Commander—make it so."

"Yes, Sir!" Pallas responded with a crisp salute. The young officer spun on his heel and rushed back across the sterncastle, barking out orders as he went.

"Draw in the sails!"

"Bring us to a stop!"

"And flag down that merchant ship!"

Night had fallen like a thick blanket over the nearby coast. The only lights visible were from Redune itself, and the deck of the large pirate ship moored in its harbor.

Pallas and his small team huddled behind a stack of crates on the deck of the *Endurance*. The merchant vessel had just cleared Sentilla Point when they flagged it down. The ship's captain, one Edward Rochino, had little love for pirates and quickly agreed to their plan.

Pallas swept his gaze toward the mouth of the harbor. There was no sign of the *Avenger*—with her lights out and sails drawn, the warship was nearly invisible in the encroaching darkness. His eyes shifted back to the approaching pirate vessel when he was hit with an awful feeling of déjà vu. Vivid images flashed through his mind from five years ago.

The Avenger just off-shore, its hull smoking and charred. Waters swirling around the masts of a sunken pirate vessel. Bodies and wreckage spewing out across the surface.

Pallas blinked and the scene changed.

Four youths lying still on the rocky ground before him. A slim figure with long black hair. Vacant blue eyes staring up at him from an all-too-familiar face. Thea…

Pallas' heart hammered in his chest. It was all he could do to stop from shaking.

Eyes stinging as he laid out the last body. Gangly arms. Coppery tresses. A freckled face bereft of that dazzling smile. Alys…

Pallas nearly choked on his own hubris. He had failed them. They died. His vow to watch over them, all his years of training, and they died nonetheless. Only by the grace of the gods, and one very stubborn bronze dragon, had they been brought back.

Pallas took a deep breath and willed his racing heart to slow down. *Never again.* He had failed them once, he would not do so again. *On my family's honor, Alys Dunamal will not die again this day.*

That oath brought Pallas back to the here and now. The pirates had let the merchant vessel sail into port unchallenged. It was as he surmised—to them, it was just another opportunity to plunder.

Redune had two long docks. Captain Rochino expertly maneuvered his ship to the far side of the second pier, putting the darkened merchant vessel between them and the pirates.

A number of shadowy figures moved around on the quay. "Throw us your lines!" a voice called out of the blackness.

The heavy-set, dark-bearded Captain Rochino strode up to the ship's rail. "Much obliged. What's with all the smoke?"

Rude laughter wafted its way up from the docks. It was quickly hushed, replaced by a placating voice. "Nothin' ta worry about. A kitchen fire got outta hand at the inn. It's under control now."

"Good to hear," Rochino responded affably.

Pallas was duly impressed with his performance. Whether by the luck of the gods, or some other force, they had been fortunate to run into such an able-minded merchant.

Once the *Endurance* was moored, six ragged-looking men swaggered up the gangplank. They spread out onto the main deck, brandishing short, thick swords. The lead ruffian declared in a gruff voice, "Everythin' on board now belongs ta us."

A few of the cutthroats held brown bottles in their off-hands. Some swayed where they stood. They all appeared inebriated to one degree or another, but Pallas wasn't taking any chances.

Rochino played along, leading the pirates to the cargo crates where Pallas and his men were hidden. On Pallas' signal, the spiritblades poured forth, dispatching the pirates swiftly and mercilessly.

When it was over, a lone sailor scurried down from the rigging and joined them on deck. "Captain Rochino, Sir. It's just as we thought. Nothing but a skeleton crew aboard the pirate ship—the rest of the vultures must be in town looting and pillaging."

Rochino's eyes narrowed sharply. "Any reaction to our little shindig over here?"

The thin sailor shook his head. "They didn't seem to pay us no mind, Captain."

Rochino nodded at the sailor, then sent him back up to the crow's nest.

Pallas' lips pressed into a thin smile. "Thanks for the ride, Captain. We'll take it from here."

Rochino let out a soft chuckle. "'Twas my pleasure, lad."

The docks were deserted as they disembarked the *Endurance*. Dark clouds still hung over Redune—distant shouts and gruff laughter echoed across the quay. By Pallas' calculations, the main contingent of spiritblades should be reaching the town soon. He and his men needed to board the pirate ship before any of the remaining crew were alerted.

The group crossed to the edge of the dock, where they slipped silently into the dark waters. They swam below the surface, only stopping briefly to refill their lungs along the way. A few minutes later, they passed beneath the wide hull of the pirate ship, resurfacing on the side facing away from the docks.

Pallas led the climb up the side of the vessel, signaling for a halt just below the rail. The night around them remained still, except for the gentle lapping of the sea against the ship's hull. Even the sounds from town had died down. He knew that wouldn't last much longer, but stealth was their best bet in this situation.

The pirates were most likely holding Alys for ransom. That meant no harm would come to her until they got their payment—unless, of course, their hand was forced.

Despite his mounting tension, Pallas focused his will and waited.

His patience was finally rewarded with the sound of footsteps on the deck above.

Pallas motioned for the others to wait, then took a deep breath and stilled his mind. He felt himself melting inward, deep into the very core of his being. Pallas continued his inward dive, probing the innermost reaches of his essence until he encountered an area coursing with brilliant blue light. He had found his spirit, the inner spark that fueled the gifts of the spiritblade.

The young 'blade tapped into that power, warmth flooding outward through his torso and into his limbs. His body tingled with energy as he envisioned himself fading into the shadows. In mere moments, Pallas had all but disappeared to the outside eye.

Just another shadow along the side of the ship, Pallas slowly lifted his head 'til he could see onto the deck. A solitary figure stood directly above him, staring out over the waters of the harbor.

Pallas froze in place, watching silently as the pirate lifted a tankard to his lips. The lone ruffian gulped the contents down in one swig, wiped his mouth on his sleeve, then turned and walked back across the deck.

The shadowy 'blade hoisted himself up and swept his eyes around the ship. Two more pirates stood on deck, one near the gangplank and the other by a door beneath the sterncastle. *Most likely where they're holding Alys.*

Neither of the other two cutthroats seemed very alert. The third pirate had plopped himself down, with his back to the main mast, and poured himself another tankard from a nearby barrel.

Three here, and who knows how many others onboard. They had to do this as quietly as possible.

Pallas lowered himself back down and whispered a quick plan to his team. Moments later, he and two other 'blades were up and over the rail, slipping like wraiths through the shadows across the main deck.

Things appeared to be going smoothly, but unfortunately their time had run out. Pallas drew within a few yards of his quarry when shouts erupted from the direction of town. The rescue of Redune had begun in earnest.

The pirate in front of him abruptly started. He glanced around, his hand going to his sword hilt.

"Dragon dung," Pallas cursed under his breath. Throwing caution to the wind, he lunged the last few yards, slamming into the man before he could draw his weapon.

Moments later, the pirate was dead at his feet. Pallas swiftly scanned the deck, but the two other cutthroats had been similarly dispatched. Thankfully, none had made much of a racket.

The 'blades all regrouped just below the sterncastle. There were two doors here. Pallas chose the one that had been guarded. It opened to a steep stairwell that disappeared into the shadows below.

"Why the grim face, Pallas?"

Pallas turned away from the practice dummy he'd been hacking at so intently. A gangly young redhead stood there watching him with keen interest. "I'm trying to concentrate, Alys. I need to be the best 'blade I can be."

Alys tilted her head, her freckle-ridden face lit with the most dazzling smile. "But why? Why do you always push yourself so hard?"

It was difficult to stay annoyed at that infectious smile. "Father's not getting any younger, and someone needs to protect this town."

Alys' green eyes sparkled as she twirled the parasol in her hands. "Well, if I ever need protecting, I'll know who to turn to."

A determined expression crossed Pallas' face as he led the way down to the decks below.

A dim light shone at the bottom of the steep staircase. Pallas halted just above the ceiling line, then crouched down and peeked ahead. Before him lay a short corridor, maybe a dozen yards long at most. Midway down its length, two lanterns hung directly opposite each other. The lamps gave off barely enough light to illuminate the hall, leaving deep shadows clinging to either end.

Pallas spied three doors on each side of the corridor, but what caught his attention was a large figure standing in the shadows at the other end. Thankfully, Pallas' eyes were accustomed to the dark.

The figure was a huge pirate—a massive man with bulging arms folded across a barrel-like chest. Behind him, Pallas could barely make out the frame of a wooden door. *That has to be where they're keeping Alys.*

The situation did not look good. He couldn't quite make out the cutthroat's face, but noted his alert posture. *This one will not be so easy to sneak up on.*

Pallas considered the possibility of rushing the man, but immediately dismissed the idea. He didn't want to take the chance of the cutthroat slipping through the doorway and harming Alys before they could reach him.

Even if they did reach him in time, they'd be in for a tough fight. The hallway was not very wide. In these close quarters, it would be difficult for more than one person at a time to confront the large pirate.

Pallas was still weighing his options when a loud banging echoed down the hall. It was accompanied by muffled cries.

"Let me out!"

The guard did not seem amused. "Quit yer whinin'. Ye ain't goin' nowheres."

There was a moment of silence before the prisoner responded in an irate tone. "Do you know who I am?"

The guard glanced over his shoulder, a wicked laugh spilling from his lips. "Aye, indeed… we knows who ye are."

Pallas saw his chance and took it. With a quick signal to the rest of his team, he leaped down and blended into the shadows at the base of the stairs.

"Let me go and you will be richly rewarded!"

The guard glanced backward once more. "Aye. That's the truth o' it. Yer father will pay a pretty penny if he ever wants ta see that pretty little head o' yers again!"

Good girl, Alys. Keep him talking, Pallas thought as he stole forward through the waning shadows.

"Oh, he'll pay, no doubt," the young lady continued, "but I hope this ship of yours is fast. Once you've collected your bounty, you might not find it so easy to get away from my father."

That last statement really got the guard's attention. He nearly turned around completely as he barked back at her. "Don't ye worry none, lassie. No one messes with the Arch…"

Pallas rushed forward the last few yards, sword poised for a fatal blow. Yet the bulky pirate was quicker than he anticipated. A huge hand shot out and clamped like a vice around his neck, effectively cutting off his breath. Abruptly he was lifted into the air, his feet dangling off the ground.

"Wadda we got here? Looks like ya got a would-be rescuer," the huge pirate scoffed.

"Rescuer?" Alys cried through the door. "Who would come to rescue me? No one even knows I'm here!"

The rush of multiple footsteps sounded in the corridor behind Pallas. "Let him go, pirate!"

The rest of the 'blades had come to his rescue. Unfortunately, the huge cutthroat didn't seem the slightest bit intimidated.

"Drop yer weapons or I'll snap 'is neck."

The pirate wasn't kidding. Pallas felt the huge hand tighten around his throat. He would pass out soon if his neck didn't actually snap first.

Pallas had one chance. He reached inward again, desperately seeking his inner spirit. He found it almost immediately, as if it sensed the urgency of his need.

Pallas called forth the energy, sending it coursing through his limbs. Yet this time he sent it out beyond. Shadows abruptly sprang from his fingertips. They wound around the pirate's arm, swirling in tight circles, causing the grip on Pallas' neck to loosen.

The huge man barked at him, his voice suddenly laced with fear. "Hey! Wadda ya doin'? Cut it out!"

Pallas paid him no mind, continuing to weave the shadowy tendrils toward the pirate's thick neck.

"Cut it out!" the man cried, his voice now wild with fear. He dropped Pallas and backed away against the door.

Yet Pallas did not relent. He continued sending forth the shadows, wrapping them around the pirate's neck.

The huge man slumped to the ground, no longer able to cry out as the tendrils squeezed his throat closed. In seconds, his life faded away and he went still.

"What's going on out there?" Alys' voice sounded through the door.

Pallas gingerly rubbed his throat as he answered. "Fear not… we'll have you out… in a moment…"

There was a short silence as two of the 'bladesmen moved the heavy body away from the door.

"Who is that?" Alys asked in a hushed tone.

One of the other 'blades handed Pallas a key ring from the fallen guard's belt. Pallas let his senses pick the right key.

"An old friend," he answered as he inserted the key into the lock and twisted. His answer was punctuated with a loud click. Pallas pushed the door open to reveal a well-lit cabin beyond.

A solitary figure stood in the doorway. Copper tresses framed a fair-skinned face, which was dotted with faint freckles. The deep green dress that clung to the figure attested to the fact that this was no longer a gangly girl. Alys had grown into a rather shapely young woman.

Emerald green eyes danced with a light of their own as they fixed on him. The corners of her mouth upturned slightly, then suddenly spread into a dazzling smile. "I should have known my rescuer would be none other than Pallas Stealle."

Pallas suddenly realized he had been staring. He abruptly broke off his gaze, cleared his throat, and bowed. "Lieutenant Commander Pallas Stealle of the Royal Penwick Navy, at your service."

Alys looked him up and down, her tone playful despite the circumstances. "Lieutenant Commander? All things considered, I guess I shouldn't be surprised."

Pallas felt the heat rise to his cheeks. "Yes, well, we can catch up later. Right now, we need to get you out of here."

Pallas offered the young woman his hand. She entwined hers with his, with an unexpected result. Pallas felt a gentle warmth shoot up his arm and through his body. It was not unlike when he connected with his own spirit.

His cheeks felt hot again and he noted a slight blush in Alys' face. Pallas gave her the briefest of smiles, then led her out into the corridor. The pair moved ahead of the others, whispering back and forth as they went.

"Was anyone else taken prisoner?"

Alys' voice caught. "No… I'm afraid not. Most of the crew were killed—those that didn't escape to Redune."

"The crew of your father's ship?"

Alys sighed. "Yes. After five years, I was finally sailing home again."

Pallas gave her a sympathetic nod. Alburg had sent Alys away after she was resurrected. None of her friends had seen her since.

"We had just reached Sentilla Light when the pirates appeared. We couldn't outrun them, so the captain made for Redune. The crew tried to make a stand on the docks, but the pirates were brutal." Alys ended with a shudder.

Pallas could feel the anguish coming off of her in waves. This Alys was a far cry from the spoiled little girl he used to know. "I'm truly sorry, Alys."

Alys wiped the tears from her eyes and nodded. "I'm sorry, too."

Pallas gave her a warm smile as they reached the top of the stairs. "Alright, we need to be extra cautious from here on. No telling what's waiting for us out there."

The deck of the pirate vessel appeared deserted. Pallas had hoped to escape into the cover of night, but the moon had risen. The docks were now bathed in a silvery sheen. Loud cries and the ring of steel echoed across the harbor as the small band hurried down the gangplank.

"What's going on?" Alys whispered anxiously.

"Our crewmates are routing the pirates from Redune. We best hurry in case any try and make for their ship."

No sooner had the words left his mouth than Pallas' fear came to fruition. A half-dozen figures appeared at the end of the quay, hastening away from the town. The 'blades fanned out to meet them, weapons readied. The small group pulled up short and stared warily at the line of armed swordsmen. They started to grumble amongst themselves.

"It's more o' dem Penwickers!"

"How'd they get in front o' us?"

One of them noticed Alys.

"Hey! Whadda ye doin' with our prize?"

Pallas placed his arm in front of her. "Stand back. This won't take long."

"Actually, allow me." Before he could stop her, Alys pushed his arm out of the way and sauntered out in front of the 'blades.

Caught by surprise, Pallas hesitated. Yet as he reached for her, a high-pitched wail erupted across the docks. Pallas stumbled, his balance thrown off by the sound. Everyone else, pirate and 'blade alike, seemed affected—everyone except for Alys.

His eyes went wide as the truth dawned on him. *That noise is coming from her!*

Alys' wail rose swiftly in power. Thankfully, the brunt of it was directed at the pirates. One by one they fell to their knees until they were all laid out cold. With a dramatic wave of her hand, Alys ended her high-pitched assault. The young lady wore a satisfied expression as she sauntered back past Pallas. "They're all yours."

Pallas eyed her quizzically as the rest of the 'blades finished off the pirates. "What in Thac was that?"

Alys dipped her head toward the ground, a demure smile on her lips. "I'm a bard, silly—a diva, in fact. It's one of my talents."

One of Pallas' eyebrows arched. "I remember you singing all the time, but now you've learned to weave magic into your songs?" The corner of his mouth upturned slightly. "Heh, guess *I* should've known."

Alys gazed up at him, her eyes sparkling with delight.

With the pirates out of the way, the 'blades proceeded down the dock. Yet Pallas still felt he had missed something—something important. His whispered to Alys. "Tell me, with that voice of yours, how did the pirates catch you?"

A pained expression crossed Alys' face. Yet before she could reply, the sound of heavy footfalls echoed down the docks. Another group of figures had appeared at the end of the quay, effectively blocking their path. This new group moved slowly down the pier, not stopping until they were about a dozen yards away.

As the 'blades spread out to meet this new threat, a tall, dark-bearded man stepped out in front of the rest. Twin sword hilts jutted from underneath his long coat. The pirate's hands rested on them comfortably as he addressed his comrades. "More Penwickers? The place is practically crawlin' with 'em."

Dark laughter erupted from the new group of pirates. There were seven in all, each standing there almost too casually. Yet Pallas could not spy an obvious opening in any of their postures. He felt a tug at his arm.

"That's the captain and his handpicked men," Alys whispered into his ear.

Pallas gave her the briefest of nods as he warned the others. "Careful, men."

The well-trained 'bladesmen reacted immediately, adjusting themselves into guarded stances. Pallas felt the surge of spirit energy as some called forth flames to encircle their blades.

Despite the display, the pirate captain did not appear impressed. "Watch it, boys. These be more of 'em fancy blade folk like the ones we met in town." A smug grin split his lips. "Too bad it didn't do 'em no good."

Wicked laughter echoed across the pier. Once it died down, the captain drew his blades and motioned his men forward. "Well then, let's be makin' this quick."

"Steady, men," Pallas said as he moved to the front of the line. He drew his blade with an air of confidence, but inside he wasn't quite so sure of himself. If these pirates actually fought through the other wave of spiritblades, then this would not be an easy fight.

The pirates hadn't covered half the distance between them when a shrill cry rang out from behind the 'blades. "*No!* Not again. You won't get away with it this time!"

Pallas glanced over his shoulder to see Alys marching forward.

He immediately moved to block her path, but she opened her mouth and let out a high-pitched shriek. Pallas reeled as if he had been struck with a physical blow. It was far worse than when he had been standing behind her.

Alys cast him an apologetic glance as she brushed past him. Once again, she moved to the forefront of the line, her high-pitched wail growing in power.

Across the dock, the pirates had begun to crumble. Weapons dropped to the planks below as they desperately tried to cover their ears. A few had already dropped to one knee.

All of the cutthroats appeared affected except for the captain. Somehow, the tall pirate managed to stand his ground. He fixed Alys with a baleful stare, the corner of his lip twitching into a sneer.

All of a sudden, Pallas felt a surge of spiritual energy wash over him. It was powerful, but dark like a blackened soul. A moment later, the pirate captain took a step forward—then another.

Pallas watched the uncanny spectacle with disbelief. *Could this pirate be some sort of spiritblade?* He'd heard talk of dark 'blades. The pirate lord, Eboneye, who led the raids on Penwick, was rumored to have been one.

Alys redoubled her efforts, her cry growing further in power. The rest of the pirates crumbled to the ground.

The captain halted a moment, then Pallas felt another surge of spiritual energy, this one stronger than the first. Once again, the captain plodded forward.

Pallas had to do something. He didn't relish putting himself in the path of that cry, but if he didn't, Alys would be skewered for sure. Steeling his will, he reached inside and drew on his spirit. He wrapped the energy around himself like a cocoon, then stepped out in front of her.

The pressure on his ears was immediately unbearable. It was all Pallas could do to stand. Amazingly, the captain continued his advance. *How in Thac is he even moving?*

All of a sudden, Alys went silent. The pirate captain lurched forward, barely catching himself before he fell. He righted himself, then stood his ground, a wicked grin on his lips.

Pallas chanced a glance back at Alys. Her eyes were wide with fear. She grabbed her throat and tried to speak, but no sound came out of her mouth.

She's been silenced!

Pallas grabbed the frantic young lady, his mind racing as he drew her behind the line. The pirates must have a dark mage—someone who could cast a silent spell. It was no wonder they caught her. He swept his eyes around the docks, but saw no sign of a mage.

Meanwhile, the pirates began to recover behind their waiting captain. Pallas could feel the tension in the air as the 'blades held their ground.

"Orders, Sir?" one of them asked Pallas.

Pallas was torn. The 'blades were good. He had no doubt they could stand against this group, but the captain was another story. From the power he felt from the man, he could probably take them all—and if he didn't, that mage just might. Still, it was better to go down fighting.

"Attack!" Pallas cried against his better judgement. He cast a quick glance at Alys. "Stay here…"

The young woman wasn't looking at him. Instead she was pointing frantically back at the pirate vessel. Pallas followed her gaze. A dark-hooded shadow stood behind the ship's rail. It was weaving its hands in a circular motion.

A shiver ran up Pallas's spine. His mother being a wizard, he had seen that type of gesture many times before. *It's casting a spell.* He watched in horror as a tiny red sphere ignited between the robed figure's hands. *A ball of fire!*

In the split second before it was launched, Pallas's mind whirled. The 'blades could survive the attack, but Alys would not. He shouted out a quick warning, then forced all other thoughts from his mind. The young 'blade drew from his spirit just as the red ball shot from the mage's hands. He threw his arms around Alys and envisioned himself someplace else.

The deadly spell was on them in less than a second. A huge explosion erupted from the ball and a wall of flame came rushing toward them. The intense heat nearly overtook them, but then the world shifted. One moment they stood on the docks, the next they were on the deck of the pirate ship.

The docks lit up like some huge torch as the flaming wall expanded outward. It completely engulfed everything in its path—both pirates and 'blades.

Pallas inwardly winced. He had deserted his men in favor of Alys' survival. He prayed that he had made the right decision.

The dark-hooded figure now stood before them, outlined by the light of the explosion. Pallas felt an unabiding anger well up inside him—anger at the pirates, anger at the mage, but mostly anger at himself for not being able to protect everyone.

Pallas let go of Alys and lunged at the dark figure. Yet somehow it must have sensed his presence.

A blue light coalesced in the air before it. In one swift motion, the mage leapt over the rail and disappeared into the expanding oval.

It made a portal!

An unrelenting rage boiled inside of Pallas. "Oh, no you don't!"

He lunged after the mage, just catching it by the robe before it disappeared. As Pallas fell into the light after it, something grabbed him from behind.

Moments later, they reemerged on the pier. Pallas twisted his head around to see Alys clinging to him, a wan smile on her lips. He mentally chided himself—in his rash attempt to catch the mage, he'd nearly left her behind.

"Sorry..." Pallas began, but halted when the robe in his hand went slack. A dark-haired woman sprinted agilely away from him, garbed only in a black chemise.

A gruff laugh echoed across the pier. "Ha, they almost got ye there, lassie."

Pallas turned to see the pirate captain standing a few yards down the dock. There was not a mark on him—he was completely unscathed by the fiery blast. His men, on the other hand, had not fared so well. Most had been laid out by the explosion, their bodies badly burnt. Only a couple still stood, but they looked quite singed.

Beyond them, Pallas spied the 'bladesmen. Two had been downed and one looked somewhat charred, but the more seasoned ones had minor burns at best. Pallas felt a twinge of guilt as he called out to his comrades. "Hang on, men. We'll get you help soon."

The pirate captain laughed once more, his tone laced with contempt. "Har, har, har. Laddie, I'm afraid it's ye who'll be needin' help."

Pallas glared at the man, then suddenly remembered the mage. He glanced over his shoulder, but she was nowhere to be seen.

Way to go, Pallas.

What should have been a quiet rescue had turned into a disaster. His men were hurt, he'd lost track of the mage, and this dangerous cutthroat stood in his way.

One of the still standing 'blades called back to him. "Do you need help over there, Commander?"

Pallas shook his head. He'd already put them in enough danger. "Belay that. Stand your ground and protect your shipmates, sailor."

"Yes, Sir!" The standing 'blades took up defensive positions against the remaining pirates.

The captain, however, crowed over the exchange. "Commander, be it? One 'o Penwick's finest, then? Well, it's me lucky day. I've been wantin' ta cross swords with one 'o ye."

The dark-bearded pirate fell into a fighting stance, his tone mocking. "Whene'er ye be ready, *Commander.*"

Pallas let out a deep sigh. There was no way around this. He'd have to face the captain and watch for the mage as well. His lip curled up to one side. *Not exactly a tactical advantage.*

Alys still held onto him. He gently removed her arms and gazed at her. Though she could not speak, he could see the anguish in her eyes.

Keen sympathy welled up inside him for the ordinarily carefree young woman. He grasped her hands and did his best to smile. "Don't worry. This will be over quickly. Just promise me you'll stay put."

Alys put on a brave face and gave him a firm nod. Pallas held onto her for a moment longer, then turned to face the waiting captain.

A wicked smile split the pirate's dark beard. "Very touchin' speech there, laddie. Yer right 'bout one thing, though. This'll be over real quick-like."

Pallas declined to answer, his jaw firmly set as he approached his dangerous opponent. He drew within a few feet, then fell into a well-practiced stance.

The duo eyed each other for a few moments, then Pallas felt that same surge of dark spiritual energy. He watched with keen interest as a glow enveloped the captain's blades. The energy crackled and spit just like black flames.

So, he is a dark 'blade. Well, two can play at that game. Once again, Pallas reached inward, drawing on his spirit. It was a bit harder this time—each use of spirit energy drained the body and mind. Pallas refocused his will, coaxing the energy forth nonetheless. The warmth traveled from his lower abdomen and up through his arms, encircling his blade with sizzling red and yellow flames.

"Oh ho, laddie," the captain bellowed. "It seems ye know a trick or two yerself. That should make this all the more fun."

Without warning, the pirate launched himself at Pallas. He slashed and spun, his blades darker than the surrounding night.

Gods, he's fast!

Pallas' brother favored two swords, but it was nothing like this. It was all he could do to keep up with the pirate. He barely managed to parry a slash when another came at him from a different angle.

The swift and merciless flurry continued, black and red flames dancing around each other as they intertwined with each strike. Blow after blow rained down on Pallas. He was put totally on the defensive, slowly but inexorably being pushed back along the dock.

Incredibly, the pirate's pace picked up. Pallas found it nearly impossible to follow. A split-second off on his parries, the tip of the captain's blades swiped across his arms. Deep gashes appeared in his leather armor and traces of blood seeped through.

Pallas could feel himself losing. All his years of training, all those promises to protect his loved ones, and none of it was enough. He was going to die here, at the hands of a pirate of the clans.

The thought made Pallas go cold inside. *No. Not like this. Not to one of them.*

His father's voice suddenly echoed through his mind. *"There will always be someone better than you, but no one is perfect. Everyone has a weakness. The key is to find it and exploit it."*

Those words lit a fire inside Pallas. Energy flooded up from the core of his being. He found himself moving faster—anticipating the pirate's moves. *There.* He parried a slash. *And there.* He countered a thrust.

A strange sense of calm came over him, the rest of the world fading away. All that was left was their fiery blades dancing in the darkness.

At the same time, the pirate's frustration grew. His attacks became bolder, wilder, in an attempt to break Pallas' defenses. Finally, the pirate made a mistake, overextending himself on a particularly vicious lunge.

Pallas knocked the man's blade aside, then twisted his grip and followed through with a quick slice across the torso.

The captain swiftly backpedaled away. He halted a few yards back and glanced down at his chest. His puffy white shirt had a gash in it with a short red line of blood seeping through. The pirate peered up at Pallas with a slight twitch in his eye. "Look at what ye did there now. Ye went and damaged me fine shirt."

A feeling of elation washed over Pallas, but he swiftly pushed it back down. This was far from over. Another buildup of dark energy proved his restraint to be justified. Pallas concentrated his will, trying to sense what his opponent was planning, when the feeling abruptly faded. At the same moment, the flames on his blade went out.

Numbness spread over Pallas' body. He could not sense any energy from the captain. He tried to draw on his spirit, but could not feel it. It was as if he was suddenly blind.

The captain jeered at him. "Hah. It looks as if ye lost yer edge there, laddie."

Pallas sluggishly glanced around 'til his eyes fell on a familiar figure. The dark-haired woman had reappeared across the dock, her pale hands clasped together to form a strange symbol. Cold fear gripped him as he realized the truth.

That's witchcraft! The mage wasn't a mage after all. She was a witch and she had cursed his spirit sight, the same way she had cursed Alys' voice.

Pallas gulped. Without his gifts, he had no chance against the pirate captain. Still frozen with fear, he nearly jumped when a red-headed blur flew across the dock. *That's Alys!*

The young lady had doffed her dress and now dashed across the pier, directly at the witch. The witch tried to weave another curse, but Alys proved faster. Like an acrobat, the fiery redhead caught the witch in the stomach with her heel. The dark-haired woman went flying backward, her concentration completely broken.

The witch righted herself, a knife appearing in her hand. Before she could use it, though, Alys leapt into the air. Her foot whipped around and collided with the witch's arm, knocking the dagger out of her hand. Alys landed in front of the witch, poised for another leap.

A deep chortle resounded behind Pallas. "Looks like ye got yer own battle there, lassie."

The witch responded with a hiss. "No thanks to you. Are you just going to stand there all night?"

The captain grimaced back at her. "Stop yer bellyaching. This'll be over in no time. I'd worry more 'bout that fiery little redhead if I was ye."

Amazing as Alys had proven to be, Pallas was also worried about her. Still, if she could keep the witch off balance, the witch wouldn't be able to cast more curses. Not to mention, Pallas had his own fight to deal with.

The pirate captain had gone still. Pallas could no longer sense spiritual energy, but he knew an attack was imminent. A moment later, the pirate disappeared.

Pallas' training was the only thing that saved him. He spun around as the captain reappeared behind him, a single sword thrust at his torso in a deadly lunge.

Pallas caught it on his own blade, but it still slid past him, slicing across his abdomen. Sharp pain lanced through his body.

Pallas glanced down. His leathers and the skin underneath had been slashed wide open. Red blood poured from the gaping wound. He felt suddenly lightheaded. His knees gave out and he dropped to the deck.

The sword fell from Pallas' hand, the blade clattering onto the wooden planks. He desperately clamped down on the wound, marginally slowing the bleeding.

A dark laugh caught his attention. The pirate captain stood over him, a wide grin on his grizzled features. "Like I told ye before, laddie, it's ye who'll be needin' the help."

Pallas watched helplessly as the captain poised his blade for a final strike. Tears welled in his eyes. He had given it his all, but it wasn't enough. He had failed miserably.

Pallas wanted to scream with frustration, but he'd be damned if he gave this cutthroat the satisfaction. He met the pirate's gaze, his voice coming out in short ragged breaths. "If you're expecting… me to beg… you're sadly mistaken."

The captain hesitated, his eyes narrowing. "Ye got guts, lad, I'll give ye that."

Those words struck a chord deep inside Pallas. A stark image abruptly flashed through his mind.

It was no longer the pirate captain holding a sword over him. Instead it was his father, Kratos Stealle—the most renowned blade in Penwick history. "So Pallas, what are you going to do now?"

Pallas lay on the ground, his own sword just out of reach. "What do you mean? There's nothing to do. I've lost."

Kratos gave him a stern look. "Where are your guts, lad? If I'd given up so easily, your mother would be dead and Penwick would be a pirate port."

Kratos lowered his blade and extended a hand to his son. "Remember Pallas, where there's life, there's hope."

At that instant, Pallas felt a strange tingling in the center of his brow. Something burst inside him—spiritual energy flooded through his being and filled his entire body.

The world around him had come alive once more. Pallas could sense the dark spirit of the man standing over him. Farther down the dock, he perceived the life-force of the 'bladesmen and the rest of the pirates. On the other side of the quay, a single spirit burned, the other one winking out.

Alys!

Pallas felt a sinking feeling in the pit of his stomach. Biting back the pain, he leaned over and peered past the captain. He was met with an amazing sight. Alys stood over the body of the witch, a knife hilt sticking out of the dark-haired woman's chest. Alys had killed her, breaking the curse over both of them.

"Pallas!" Alys cried as their eyes met. Her voice had returned, just like his spirit sight. Unfortunately, her cry had also garnered the captain's attention.

The tall pirate halted his killing blow, his eyes now fixed on the fiery redhead. "Now what did ye have to go 'n do that for? I'm gonna catch hell from her family for this."

Alys placed her hands on her hips and glared at the pirate. "You can go to hell with her for all I care."

The captain sneered at Alys. "Ye know, lassie, yer becoming more trouble than yer worth."

Alys responded with another high-pitched wail. Pallas braced himself, but somehow she managed to direct it solely at the maddened pirate.

The captain grimaced. Pallas felt another surge of dark energy as the man began a slow, inexorable march against Alys' sonic assault.

Pallas went cold inside. The captain was an expert swordsman— nearly as good as his father. Alys didn't stand a chance.

My father? A sudden flash of inspiration struck the young man. Kratos had been badly injured during the pirate invasion twenty years ago. Yet he had used his talents to stave the wound and finally beat Eboneye.

Holding his abdomen with one hand, Pallas picked up his fallen sword. The young 'blade then steeled his will and sent energy out through his fingertips. Yet this time he directed it into the sword, not around it.

The blade glowed a dull red at first, but quickly grew red hot. Pallas clenched his teeth and placed the flat of the bright glowing sword against his wound. There was a sizzling sound and the acrid smell of burning flesh.

The pain was excruciating. It was all Pallas could do to hold back his screams. Still, he did not falter. He held the blade against his skin until the bleeding stopped.

When it was finally done, Pallas almost passed out. It took all his remaining will to stay conscious. *Just… one more thing…*

Alys continued to shriek at the captain, but the incensed pirate was nearly on top of her. In another few seconds, she would be dead.

One last time, Pallas reached down into the well of his spirit. Unfortunately, it had run dry. Tears of frustration welled in the young man's eyes as he strained to find even the tiniest bit of energy.

Across the quay, the pirate captain drew back his sword. In another second, he would run Alys through.

At that moment, something broke inside Pallas. He didn't care what happened to himself. His life was over—spent. The only thing that mattered now was the feisty little redhead he had vowed to protect. *Gods, please grant me this one last boon. Please allow me to save her.*

As if in answer to his prayer, a rush of energy burst forth from deeper inside than he'd ever gone before. His will suddenly took hold, and in the blink of an eye, he flashed across the docks.

Pallas reacted by pure instinct. He jabbed forward with all his remaining strength, skewering the dark pirate with his blade. At the same moment, he felt a burning sensation in his chest. Gazing down, he noted almost nonchalantly that the pirate's sword had pierced him as well.

Both men fell to the ground, their eyes locked upon each other. A wicked grin spread across the pirate's lips as the life drained from his eyes. "Nicely played… there… laddie…"

A wave of lightheadedness passed over Pallas, causing the world around him to spin. Cool hands touched his head and a familiar face stared down at him. "Pallas! Pallas! Stay with me!"

The voice sounded worried, but Pallas couldn't fathom why. A whistling noise caught his attention. It was quickly followed by an explosion. *Cannon fire…*

The voice spoke to him once more. "It's the *Avenger*. Just hang on, Pallas… they're almost here."

Pallas tried to smile at the voice just as everything went black.

Pallas slowly opened his eyes, but everything around him was foggy. He blinked several times until his vision finally cleared. A familiar visage stared down at him—a heart-shaped face with freckled skin and deep blue eyes, framed in a thick mass of long reddish-brown hair.

"It's about time you woke up."

The figure was garbed in the white robes of a temple priestess. Her voice was filled with mirth, but there was a slight undertone of relief in it.

"Thea?" Pallas asked groggily. "What are you doing here?" All at once, his memory came flooding back. "Where's Alys?"

Pallas shot up, sweeping his eyes wildly about. The docks were gone. Instead he sat in his cabin aboard the *Avenger*.

A pair of strong hands grasped his shoulders. "Easy, tiger. She's fine. As for you—you're all healed, but your body still needs rest."

Pallas glanced at Thea uncertainly, then examined his arms. His wounds were gone. He threw off his covers and lifted his shirt. The gash in his stomach had completely disappeared—not even a scar remained.

Pallas peered at his sister. "Your handiwork?"

Thea nodded, the side of her mouth upturning slightly. "The ship's cleric closed the wound, but I cleaned up the rest of it."

She took a step back and looked him over, her head shaking with mild disapproval. "You really did a good job on yourself this time. What were you thinking?"

Pallas let out a short laugh, but immediately regretted it. His body still ached all over. An embarrassed grin crossed his lips, his hand going to the back of his neck. "I guess I kind of rushed in to save the day. I must have been channeling our kid brother."

Thea laughed gaily at his jest. "Did you just make a joke?" She placed a hand on his forehead. "You must be sicker than I thought."

The side of his mouth curled upwards. "I'm not perfect, you know—despite the nickname you gave me."

Thea's cheeks reddened slightly. "Oh… you know about that?"

"Uh huh." Pallas nodded as he swung his feet over the edge of the bed. His strive for perfection had garnered him the nickname of *perfectly Pallas* from his siblings.

Thea dropped her voice to a conspiratorial tone. "Just don't tell Lloyd when you see him. He'd kill me if he knew you knew."

Pallas narrowed an eye at his sister. "Our kid brother is here, too? Come to think of it, what are you doing here?" He swept his eyes around the cabin. "And where's Alys? You said she's ok."

Pallas stood up, immediately regretting it. His body felt heavy, as if he were wearing a full suit of armor.

Thea grasped him by the arm, helping to steady him. "Easy, I told you. You have to give yourself a chance to recover."

Pallas took a deep breath and gave her a wan smile. "Maybe I am turning into Lloyd. So, are you ever going to answer my questions?"

Thea let out an exasperated sigh. "The whole family's here. When the message reached us about what happened, Mom teleported the lot of us. You and Alys were already on board by the time we got here."

Pallas eyed her sharply. "So where is she now?"

A soft chuckle escaped Thea's lips. "Is that more than just a passing concern I sense?"

Pallas felt the blood rise to his cheeks. "Well, I… I mean… she was nearly… we were nearly…"

A wide smile graced Thea's lips as she placed a gentle hand on his shoulder. "It's okay, Pallas. I was just teasing you… though she has grown into a lovely young woman."

Pallas' cheeks continued to burn as he shook his head. "It's not like that, Thea."

Thea arched an eyebrow at him. "Really? Because she hadn't left your side in the last twenty-four hours, not until we rendezvoused with her father's ship, that is."

Pallas felt a warmth in his chest as he thought about Alys watching over him. His voice cracked as he responded. "She hadn't?" He cleared his throat. "I mean… Alburg Dunamal is here?"

Thea gave him a knowing smile. "Yes. It appears the crusty old coot really does care about his daughter. When he arrived, she had to go meet him. Still, she wouldn't leave your side unless I promised to watch over you."

Pallas tried to mask the swirling feelings inside his chest with a short laugh. "Huh, guess that's what we Stealles do best—watch over each other."

Thea laughed in turn, then gently rapped his shoulder with her fist. "Well, I owed you one, anyway."

"Hey, that's what overprotective brothers are for." Pallas exchanged grins with his "not so little" sister. She had grown into a fine woman, just like Alys.

Alys. Warmth swirled in his chest at the thought of the lovely young redhead. Again, Pallas tried to hide his feelings, this time with a smirk. "Anyway, give me a hand. You said Alburg Dunamal is here. This I've got to see."

The smell of salt air invigorated Pallas as he stepped on deck. Thea gently held his arm, steadying him only when absolutely necessary.

Over by the rail, Pallas spied Captain Hightower in deep conversation with an austere-looking gentleman. Between the pair stood a familiar copper-haired young lady. *Alys.*

Pallas' heart skipped a beat at the sight of her. Still embarrassed, he covered his reaction with a smart remark. "Looks like the captain is getting his ear chewed off."

Thea responded with a soft laugh. "I daresay Alburg could keep him there for the next day or so."

Pallas considered joining the trio when a familiar voice rang across the deck. "Hey! Look who finally woke up!"

Pallas turned to see his younger brother, Lloyd, striding toward them. He was accompanied by their parents, Kratos and Lara. As they joined them, Kratos looked him over with a critical eye. "Well, I certainly hope the other guy looks worse."

Lara gently elbowed Kratos in the side, then stepped forward and kissed Pallas on the cheek. "Despite what some folks say, that was very brave of you, Pallas." She stepped back and tapped her chin with a single finger. "Still, you had us worried there for a while."

"Nothing Thea couldn't fix!" Lloyd exclaimed enthusiastically.

Their reunion was interrupted when someone grabbed Pallas

from behind. He turned to see Alys standing there, her comely brow furrowed with deep concern. "Thank the gods you're okay. We've been worried sick over you."

Pallas flushed at her close proximity. He tried to speak, but suddenly found himself tongue-tied.

What in Thac is the matter with me? It's just Alys—the same gangly little redhead who used to annoy me all the time. Yet no matter how much he tried to deny it, this was not that same girl. This Alys was very much a woman.

It was Lloyd, of all people, who came to his rescue. "Nah, he's fine. We Stealles are made of stronger stuff than iron."

Pallas groaned to mask his flustered state. He never thought he'd be happy to hear one of Lloyd's infamous family-name puns.

Alys seemed to enjoy his brother's dry sense of humor. She giggled and grinned at him before turning to Kratos and Lara. "Anyway, if you don't mind, may I borrow your son?"

Lara arched an eyebrow as she exchanged glances with Kratos. Pallas had hit marrying age quite a few years back. His parents had been trying to set him up with eligible young women ever since.

Kratos now wore a knowing look that would normally have made Pallas groan. Yet for some reason it didn't bother him this time.

Lara gave Alys a sweet smile. "But of course, dear."

Before Pallas knew it, he had been whisked away toward the ongoing conversation between Alys' father and Captain Hightower. Pallas felt just a bit nervous about joining them. Alburg had not exactly been a fan of the Stealles since that deadly incident five years ago. In fact, he had made it quite plain that he thought it was all their fault. Yet his nerves were replaced with curiosity as they approached the duo.

The pair were gazing intently at an unrolled parchment Alburg held in his hands. When Dunamal saw them, however, he swiftly rolled up the paper and handed it to Hightower. The entire thing made Pallas all the more suspicious. *What is Dunamal up to now?*

Alys still held onto his arm as she drew up in front of the pair. "Father, you remember Pallas Stealle—the young man who rescued me *yet again.*"

Pallas nearly choked. Alys was taking great liberties with that introduction, especially when she knew how her father felt.

The elder Dunamal regarded Pallas silently, his expression unreadable. Thus, he caught Pallas completely by surprise when he extended his hand out to him. "Thank you for saving my daughter, young man. If it were not for you, I might have never seen her again."

Pallas' eyes widened at the unexpected reaction. Thea's words from before ran through his mind. *It appears the crusty old coot really does care about his daughter.*

Pallas was hard pressed to keep a straight face as he tentatively shook hands with Alburg. Yet for the first time since he had met him, Pallas noted genuine warmth in the old man's expression. Even so, Pallas felt somewhat embarrassed for being singled out. "It was really the efforts of the entire crew, sir."

Captain Hightower admonished him. "Pallas, no need for modesty. It was your idea that ensured the young Lady Dunamal's safety."

Pallas was not sure how to react. He was far more used to hearing subtle innuendos about his lineage than receiving praise for his accomplishments. In the end, he responded with a smart salute. "Thank you, Sir."

Hightower crisply saluted him back, a smile spreading across his chiseled features. "That is why it gives me great pleasure to present you with this."

He held out the same parchment Dunamal had handed him just a few moments ago. Pallas raised a single eyebrow as he stared at the rolled-up paper.

Hightower thrust it toward him. "Take it, lad. You've earned it."

Pallas, now thoroughly mystified, accepted the parchment from his captain. He slowly unrolled it, his eyes going wide when he saw what was written there. *No way. No bloody way.*

Alys practically bubbled with delight as she stared over his shoulder. She ran a finger along the parchment, pointing out the signature at the bottom. "It's a commission from the Baron of Penwick himself, assigning you captaincy of the *Avenger.*"

Pallas felt numb as he stared at the paper. Captaining the *Avenger* was something he had dreamed of ever since he was a youth. The very first time he had seen the great man-of-war, he promised himself that someday she would be his.

Alys, still hanging onto his arm, gave him a gentle tug. "Well, say something, Pallas."

As the shock wore off, Pallas began to smile. However, just as suddenly, his smile faded. Guilt-ridden, he gazed at Hightower. "But… what about you, Sir?"

Hightower eyed him for a moment, then smiled warmly. He shifted his gaze to Alys and her father. "Would you two excuse us for a moment?"

Alburg responded with a prudent nod. "Why of course. Alys and I have some family matters to discuss anyway."

Alys seemed less than enthusiast about leaving them, but her father firmly escorted her a few paces down the rail. When they were out of earshot, Hightower addressed Pallas in a soft voice. "Don't worry about me, lad. I was going to retire in a year or two anyway."

He turned to face the rail, motioning for Pallas to join him. "However, it would seem that Master Dunamal is willing to make my waning years quite comfortable." He placed a hand beside his mouth and lowered his voice to a conspiratorial whisper. "He just made me a nice, tidy offer to run his fleet of merchant ships."

Pallas eyed Hightower with disbelief, then cast a suspicious eye at Dunamal. *What are you up to, old man?*

Alburg, however, was deep in conversation with his daughter. When Alys saw him looking over, she waved to him enthusiastically.

Pallas couldn't help but smile back, his suspicions all but forgotten. He turned to Hightower and replied in a low voice. "Are you sure about this?"

Hightower surprised him with an uncharacteristic wink. "I'm certain." He then stood up straight and snapped to attention, giving Pallas a sharp salute. "Welcome aboard the *Avenger*, Captain Stealle."

Pallas' eyes shot wide open. Not to be rude, he snapped to attention and saluted back. "Thank you, Sir!"

Before he could say another word, he felt a small hand slip into his. Alys stared up at him with a brilliant smile.

"Congratulations, Captain."

Without warning, the ardent young lady stood on her toes and gently kissed him. Pallas' head swam, the smell of her skin and warmth of her lips having an intoxicating effect on him. It only lasted for a few moments, then Alys pulled away and whispered softly in his ear. "That was for saving my life."

She let go and stepped back, a mischievous twinkle in her eyes. Pallas felt the blood rush to his face, quite certain that he must be as red as a beet. He nearly jumped out of his skin when Alburg addressed him.

"Ahem. Yes, congratulations indeed. I am sure you will want to celebrate first with your *family*, but do come by afterwards to visit our home."

Pallas raised an eyebrow at the unexpected invitation. *A Stealle at the Dunamal house? Next thing you'll be telling me is that Lloyd is the next Duke of Dunwynn.*

Still, Alburg seemed quite sincere. Perhaps Pallas should have felt more wary, but Alys' attention had him feeling rather agreeable. He cleared his throat and gave the austere gentleman a curt bow. "Certainly, Master Dunamal. It would be my pleasure."

Alburg responded with a curt nod, then extended his arm to Alys. "Very good. Now we must be off."

Pallas peered past Alburg and noted one of his merchant ships anchored a short distance from the *Avenger*.

As the Dunamals strode away, Alys glanced back over her shoulder. Her eyes danced as she mouthed a silent message to Pallas. *See you soon.*

Pallas felt the blood rush to his cheeks again. There was no denying the strange affect she had on him. A firm clasp on his shoulder shook him out of his reverie.

Pallas turned to see Thea staring at him with her arms folded across her chest. The rest of his family stood behind her. "Well, you may be the new captain of this ship, but until you're better, you still answer to me. Now back to bed. Priestess' orders!"

Pallas let out a short laugh, then gave her a mock salute. "Yes, Sir!"

Thea grasped him by one arm, while Lara grabbed the other. The two ladies led him away, with his father and brother in tow.

Yet Pallas could not help glancing once last time at the receding Dunamals. He noted with covert pleasure the winsome young redhead casting a glance back at him.

The Battle of Fish Eye Cove

Cove

Timothy P. Doran

Fisheye Cove
Chapter 1

The newborn sun was already starting to burn off the morning's misty chill from the small cove. Soon the white crescent of beach would be sparkling in the sun, and the only way to escape the blazing heat would be to plunge into the cool ocean waters. Usually she looked forward to such a treasured early summer's day, but Meriwynn Fichgotz knew the holiday was a sham.

The baron was dead, and a dread pallor was falling across her entire village.

Ma suggested the trip in a cheerful, off-handed way, the smile never quite reaching her eyes. It took only one meaningful look from her to convince Pa, and she packed the family off with honey rolls and greenberry jam usually reserved for holidays.

Even her Uncle Vic had agreed to go along. He hadn't done a serious day's fishing in the half-year since he had returned to Ravenford, but he was the one who suggested Fisheye Cove as the perfect place for a day trip.

At the last minute, Ma declared that they needed her at the keep, and the family was to go without her. There was no arguing with Mama Fichgotz.

So, they sailed their small fishing boat down the coast before the sun was fully up, and arrived at the cove at first light. Fisheye Cove was perfectly round, and almost completely surrounded by a rock wall. The wall of unevenly squared and fitted rocks rose a tall man's height over the waves and was twice again as wide. It was rough and carelessly strewn, like the work of giant children.

The cove was mostly shallow, one or two fathoms at most, except for the very center, where the bottom fell away in a circular well, the depth of which her father had been unable to measure with his longest line.

Their small fishing boat was anchored at the north end of the cove, and Merry's father and uncle were already preparing the nets in the gentle waves near the inlet. There they patiently waited for the yellow-jumpers that were the Baroness' favorites. The jumpers would be harder to catch this time of year, and smaller, but like all good fishermen, they were patient and determined.

Merry's younger brother, Gulhawk, had found a wealth of driftwood and was busy making implements of war for his games. Before he could try to rope her into his escapades, or her father found some net that needed mending, Merry made her way down the beach and carefully out along the south breakwater to a particularly large boulder that marked the end. There she brought out her journal and settled down.

She turned her back to the rising bluffs that rose toward the rounded peak of Stone Hill in the distance. At the shore end of the curved breakwater, she and her brother had found evidence of some ancient stone structures, now overgrown by trees and shrubs, and an old, mostly buried road that headed, she imagined, to the old ruined keep on the hill. Someday when she was older, she would follow that trace of road to see where it truly went.

To her left, the coastline ran almost due north to the mouth of the Raven River, and her hometown of Ravenford. It then curved back east and somewhat south, so that she could faintly see the rocky heights of Gelcliff across the water. And she thought that she could almost make out the lighthouse at the tip of Cape Marlin. The lighthouse had recently been burned to a stony husk in a magical conflagration by some evil conjurer yet to be caught.

To Merry's right, the coast curved south out of sight behind a large ridge, and then appeared again traveling eastward, out to Colossus Point. Once, several years ago, her family had sailed out past the rocky prominence at the foot of the colossal statue. In her wild dreaming, the towering stone figure was the earthly incarnation of some forgotten goddess, so lifelike that it might come alive at any moment and recognize her as the long-lost heir of a fabled kingdom far from here.

Some of her imaginings were too wild to share, even with her story journal. She held onto the precious book like one of the lost treasures she wrote about. Merry knew she didn't really have to worry about her family finding its secrets; she was the only one among them who could read.

Her brother had been invited to the classes that the Lady Gracelynn taught for all the village children, but he rarely attended and could barely recognize letters. "There's little reason for a fisherman to read," her father would say in his gruff way, but she knew he was terribly proud of her, and after a few drinks would go on at the tavern to anyone who would listen about how gifted his girl was.

Merry carefully untied the ribbon from around her book. Knots were one thing the Fichgotz family members were uniformly experts at. Her brother would never fall for a thief knot, so she used a grief knot instead, relying on the flat of the ribbon and an extra tuck to keep it from slipping.

She began humming a little tune as she produced a small quill and ink bottle from her pouch. It was a glorious half-hour before she was interrupted.

"There you are, Princess! Never fear, I am here to rescue you!" the voice of Gulhawk cried dramatically behind her. Merry didn't need to turn around to know he was striking some improbable pose.

"Get out of here, vermin!" she snapped over her shoulder.

"Gods!" he complained, "You don't need to bite my head off."

Merry looked back in disgust. Gully was dressed only in short trousers. His skinny arms were brandishing a piece of whitened driftwood that looked like an enormous, flattened and bent chicken bone with a bad case of gout.

"What's that?" she asked resignedly.

"It's my axe!" he exclaimed.

"You're the one who's going to need rescuing if you don't march back around the cove and leave me alone," she warned in a tone she hoped conveyed the proper amount of menace.

That was exactly the kind of challenge that 'Sir Gulhawk' was looking for. "Ho, it isn't a princess; it's a sea-hag in disguise! Good thing I brought my trusty axe."

"Oh no," she bemoaned, "poor Sir Gulhawk is greatly mistaken." Merry rose and turned on her brother. "It isn't a lowly sea-hag he faces, but something far more dangerous!" She paused for dramatic effect; then her eyes went wide as she looked over his head.

"A dragon!"

Gully still thought it was part of the game until the powerful form of a true dragon flew less than thirty feet over his head. The great beast's scales glistened like metal in the early morning sun; the wind of its passing stirred their hair with the tang of a pre-storm breeze. Merry staggered as she felt pure primal fear buckle her knees and turn her guts to jelly as it passed.

The dragon banked as it glided beyond the cove, then when over deeper water, it suddenly dropped beneath the surface with barely a ripple.

"That was…" Gully began to shout, but Merry's hand cut him off and pulled him down as the second dragon skimmed over the treetops and into the air over the cove. This one was smaller, its body no bigger than their fishing boat. And with the morning sun on its bright scales, it seemed almost radiant. The second dragon also didn't invoke the same fear in her as the first dragon, perhaps because it was farther away, or maybe because it seemed slightly confused.

It looked first at the ocean where the larger dragon had vanished, then at the fishing boat and the people with nets in the waves, and then back the way it had come.

Merry was certain that it was yelling to her father and uncle as it flew over their heads. It was too far to be sure, but she thought the dragon was telling them to swim for deep water.

Not likely, she thought. Dry land and the woods would be safer, with the ocean full of storm dragons. She looked at the over hundred feet of broken and slippery rocks along the breakwater to shore. She would have to chance it as quickly as she could with Gully in tow.

She didn't make it a step before the next wave of dragons appeared over the bluffs, diving for the cove.

Even as the certainty of their imminent death became clear to her, Merry thought how odd and beautiful it was to see the multicolored flight of dragons descend out of the morning sky.

Theria was tired, annoyed, and hungry. She had been flying all night trying to catch those cursed storm dragons, their bronze-scaled tails always in view, but frustratingly out of reach. *May the five-headed Lady consume their souls*, she fumed to herself.

The larger of her quarry, Vestiralanna, couldn't be in good shape, not after her days of exposure to the shard. And Theria didn't know how she had managed to hold on the last few hours and stay ahead of them. The smaller storm dragon, she didn't know, but Theria assumed she was a relative, and probably the one who had rescued Ves.

Truly they should have caught them hours ago, but their luck was poor and their coordination worse. It didn't help that she was grouped with the biggest flock of young idiots ever to hatch from dragon eggs.

And now the chase was over; their quarry had reached the sea. There was no catching them unless the Dragon Master returned. Even with the power of the shard, the princess certainly couldn't catch dragons as powerful as these in their own element.

Theria spotted an opportunity to grab a quick meal before heading back. But as she alighted on the rocky spur, her luck proved no better than it had all night. The girl dropped into the crevice between two of the rough blocks, and she was left holding a scrawny stick of a boy, hardly more than a toothpick.

Theria was considering how to best pluck the human girl out without getting too much foul-tasting seawater on the little snack when Berikarth exploded a fishing boat on the other side of the cove. His azure-scaled form certainly looked impressive while wing-ing over the shallows and searching for another target to take his frustrations out on.

A desert dragon's primary element was earth; Berikarth was almost as far out of his element here as Theria. Worse, his spirit manifestation was lightning, same as the storm dragons. Since his spirit breath was totally ineffective against his current foes, turning the sad little dinghy into kindling was the most amusing, if not actually the most useful thing she'd seen him do today.

She did have one water-spirit dragon supposedly on her team. Yiglelot, the ebony-scaled swamp dragon, flew high and wide around the cove where the storm dragons had taken to the sea. In his annoyingly whining way, he had made sure to tell Theria that he did not like salt water. His obvious fear of storm dragons colored his words.

She sat on the sun-warmed rock to watch what other foolish antics her unfortunate companions would do next.

Sad, stupid Irovnia was creating an iceberg at the mouth of the cove. Every fire dragon knew that ice dragons were notoriously not very smart, but Irovnia took stupidity to a new level. If the Dragon Master hadn't forbidden it, Theria would have put the foolish cold-wyrm out of her misery long ago, if only to save the honor of all dragonkind from the embarrassment of her existence.

Theria certainly was tired; she almost bit the head off of the little twit in her claw without thinking and munched it raw. *Eww, uncooked human spawn is the worst—who knows where the little vermin has been?* She supposed she should barbecue it now, and the one in the crevasse, too. But you have to be careful; it was always hard not to overcook such small portions.

Just then, Berikarth launched another lightning bolt at a pair of men in the water. What really caught her attention was the way the bolt arched away from them. Standing in the surf, a short distance from the men, was a young girl holding a small glowing sword aloft. The lightning seemed caught on the blade for a brief instant, then it shot outward at a tangent and caught Yiglelot's ebony form as he was flying over.

The redirected bolt from the sword was followed up immediately with a second, obviously more powerful bolt from the girl's finger that also targeted the ebon-scaled swamp dragon.

Yiglelot spat acid at the girl and flapped rapidly for shore. The idiot was running instead of concentrating his attacks with Berikarth. Although, that second bolt had looked especially powerful and nasty and it left a jagged after-image in her eyes.

The swamp dragon's acid spit seemed to roll harmlessly off the girl. She obviously had some kind of protection charm up. And to her credit, she seemed only mildly disgusted by being covered in dragon bile.

The girl gave Yiglelot and Berikarth a middle-finger salute, which Theria was sure, from her brief interactions with humans, was considered rude. She then dove into the surf, swimming strongly toward deep water, but angling away from the fishermen.

Interesting, she thought, *the little one exposed herself to try and save the miserable humans.* She had also concentrated her attacks on the one other water-dragon there, in an obvious attempt to secure their escape to the sea.

Reassessing the squirming morsel in her hand, Theria decided it might be more useful alive for a while. Her grumbling stomach disagreed, but she ignored it. It helped that the bony creature was so unappetizing, and she suspected he had just peed himself.

Theria carefully put the boy on the stone and lightly pinned him with one rear claw. These creatures were so fragile, she was afraid she would crush it before it was time. She cast a protective glamour against lightning on herself and began working on tactics.

The girl in the water continued to swim on the surface like a regular human. Did she actually think that they were stupid enough to believe that? Berikarth obviously didn't; not bothering with another lighting attack, he swung around to cut the dragon-girl off from deep water.

That would be a good tactic, but he was forgetting one very important thing in his over anxiousness for a fight. There was a larger storm dragon out there, and Berikarth was over deep water himself.

"Pull up!" she yelled to warn him, but it was too late.

The bronze-scaled form breached the water at incredible speed, arching into the air directly in front of Berikarth. Theria had to admit it was nice form; the insufferable storm dragons certainly had grace.

There was no way Berikarth could avoid her. It was a simple grapple, and they both plunged into the cool ocean depths. Normally it would be a bloody and near-even battle; Berikarth was almost as large and vicious a fighter as Theria. But this would be no contest; an earth-dragon had just been pulled beneath the waves by a water-dragon.

She suddenly realized that she had rather liked Berikarth; he was the least annoying of the flight. As the thrashing and bubbling waters grew still, Theria assessed the situation. Irovnia was looking around nervously from atop her crude ice fortress; not much help from that quarter. Yiglelot was sitting on the beach, licking his wounds and avoiding Theria's gaze. *By the five-headed lady, he was also a water dragon, and the craven idiot was afraid to go near the ocean!*

In the sudden quiet, Theria noticed the human. The girl had climbed back up the rock and was using an oddly bent stick to beat on the hind claw that still held the other little tidbit. Theria hadn't even felt it.

She almost laughed at the pathetic creature until she saw her eyes. The tears had dried, and in their place was a grim determination, beyond fear and desperation. The little human girl hadn't run when she had the chance. She was here; knowing she would surely die, but willing to give it all for the slim chance of helping her pathetic sibling.

But most interesting to Theria was that there was hatred in the girl's eyes. Certainly, there was hatred for the fire-dragon that was going to kill her brother, but more importantly, there was the spark of hatred of her own weakness for being unable to stop it.

Theria knew that hatred, it burned brightly inside her like the volcanic fires of her home. She had learned to hate her own weakness when she first encountered Garrikon, that cruel and vicious old fire wyrm. He had brutally shown her the true meaning of power when he'd had his way with her and left her near dead.

At first, it had been her hatred that had spurred her to hatch the egg he had given her. But later she had learned to care for her little Scorch, until their secret lair was discovered and Garrikon came to crush the life out of both of them.

She had felt the same spark of hatred when Garrikon had little

Scorch beneath his mighty claw, the same way the little one now squirmed and bled beneath her own claw. Theria had learned the lesson of dragon mercy that day, and now she would teach it to these creatures.

She carefully raised her leg from the little vermin and noticed he stuck for a second, like some offal she had stepped in. The human had inadvertently been impaled by her claw while she watched the sea battle. It didn't look like he would immediately die from it, but these things were so soft and weak that it was hard to say. The heat from her claws had mostly cauterized the wound, but enough blood was flowing to enhance his bait value, at least for the short-term.

As the human girl cradled the dying boy, Theria drew back a little, reared in her best dramatic fashion, and inhaled noisily. It was a glorious, overacted sham, she wasn't sure if the storm dragons would believe it. But they had little choice; if they truly wanted to save these tiny morsels, as improbable as that seemed to Theria, they would act now. Otherwise, she would just eat and leave.

By the Third Head, the bronze-scaled little one was fast! If Theria had not been tensed and ready for exactly this, she would have missed her. As it was, she just barely caught her tail as she pounced, but that was enough.

The young storm dragon didn't roll on her back, claws and jaws up in typical dragon fighting fashion, but exposed her back, her forelegs forming a protective circle for the humans beneath her. The fool was still trying to protect them!

She was just thinking this was going to be too easy when the lightning blast arced along the bronze tail and hit her full-on. How the little storm dragon managed to channel her element outside her breath attack was almost as big a shock as the bolt.

Shattering her protection charm, the coursing energy flowed through Theria, seeming to sear every nerve in her body. It was a strange sensation for a dragon who had never felt burning before. A lesser dragon would have let go, but the damage only fueled Theria's rage. Even so, her little bronze-scaled adversary might have made it to the water in the brief second Theria was stunned, if not for the two fragile liabilities still encumbering her claws.

This had gone on long enough; Theria wanted the pleasure of a real fight.

The conflagration Theria released made the rock glow red. There was no chance of her prey evading it while held. But instead of trying to protect herself, the fool used her precious wings to deflect the fire from the humans. The stark raving idiot wouldn't be flying anytime soon, and just to shield some worthless sub-creatures!

With a great thud, an azure carcass landed on the near end of the rocky breaker, and in an instant, the large storm dragon, Vestiralanna, reared astride it. The winds seemed to have picked up, the few clouds in the sky drawing closer and darker.

Theria had never heard the roar of a storm dragon before.

It was impressive enough to give lesser dragons pause. The atmospherics were a nice effect, but this one was not yet in her prime, and no true tempest came. Theria imagined she heard a slight gasp from the beach where the idiotic swamp dragon Yiglelot was watching nervously.

This is more like it! She thought.

At first glance, the two dragons may have appeared close to the same size. They were approximately the same length and wingspan, but Theria was a fire dragon. Her powerfully muscled body massed half again as much as the smooth, streamlined bronze form of a storm dragon.

Theria had already carefully planned for this encounter; there was no way of keeping it to these rocks. She would have to grapple and pull her adversary to shore. The cove side was the best option; the water was shallow, barely to her shoulder. And Irovnia had serendipitously blocked most of the cove mouth with solid ice.

She would prefer to fight completely on dry land but didn't think a sea dragon was stupid enough to give that advantage. The only thing that brought her true rival this far out of the water was the threat to the little one.

Theria noted that her opponent looked barely scratched in her encounter with Berikarth, and her spirit breath was certainly unused against the azure earth dragon, so it would be fully charged.

Also, Theria knew the little one was far from out of the picture.

She was effectively neutralized only in her insane notion to protect the humans. Theria didn't want a second enemy at her back, even a small one. And that one had an impressive electrical charge. She would be an annoyance while Theria concentrated on her larger foe. She was certain that bolt had to be the little one's maximum power, so it would be a while before she recovered her spirit energy for another lightning attack.

Theria wasn't really worried, but it was best to slant the odds even more in her favor. "Yiglelot. Irovnia. To the sky!" she called.

"I am Vestiralanna, daughter of Yatharia, daughter of Bilantilis, daughter of the great wyrm under the sea, Leviantianus. If you have quarrel here, I claim it is with me." The pronouncement rumbled across the cove, like warnings of a storm to come.

The black and white dragons circled high and wide around the cove. Apparently, they were unsure of who to be more afraid of—the storm dragons or Theria. It was time they were reminded.

"I am Theriaxus, daughter of Helstragia, daughter of Perviltaxus, daughter of the great wyrm at the fiery core, Ignitanus. This one has tried to steal my justly caught prey—if she does not relinquish them, she will die with them!"

It wasn't a bad presentation, but it lacked something. She really needed to light something on fire to get in the mood, but there was nothing here to burn! She wished Berikarth had not sunk that boat. She was a fire dragon—being surrounded by this much water was really starting to irritate her.

"Speaking of justly caught prey," Vestiralanna said. "I haven't quite finished with mine." With a sudden and savage strike to the blue's chest, a rather impressive quantity of water was expelled from his mouth. There was a cough and a ragged intake of breath.

Berikarth was alive! Her luck was just going from bad to worse this day, but for some unfathomable reason, she felt glad.

"I grow weary of this one," Vestiralanna continued, as she shifted her weight on the unconscious dragon's blue-scaled throat. His breathing became noticeably more erratic. "Perhaps a trade?"

A storm dragon was playing her! Theria laughed with a puff of smoke. There were two ways to handle this—the reasonable way that her annoyingly calm bronze-scaled foe probably expected, and the fire dragon way. She, of course, chose the latter.

In an instant, Theria, the savage, proud and mighty fire dragon, pounced on her adversary.

———

To Merry, it felt like the world was ending. The very air seemed to explode with fire and lighting, and they were suddenly off the rocks and falling toward the water.

"Take a breath!" she heard a girl's voice call out to them. The dragon that held them rolled onto its back as they hit the surface and they were spared the worst of the impact, but they were pulled under the cool water in a grip of bronze.

They sped just under the surface for a brief moment, and then descended rapidly. Looking up, Merry saw the bright sky shrinking in a dwindling round disk. She felt her heart clench as a dark dragon shape appeared, silhouetted in the disk of sky.

There was no more than a slight tingling in the water as a lightning bolt blasted up and into the dragon above. The silhouette vanished.

"Ha! Eat that!"

She heard the voice again. It sounded almost childlike, and it was perfectly clear underwater. Merry felt she must be going mad, or the sudden water pressure was getting to her.

In the brief flash from the lightning, Merry had seen they were in a round shaft of worked stone. The dragon made a sharp turn into a side passage and they were in total darkness. She could only feel the unbreakable clawed grip and the water rushing against her. They were moving fast, but it seemed an eternity, and her lungs were ready to burst.

They shot from the water still in total darkness, then she was placed roughly on a cool, hard, wet floor. The slight sloshing of water echoing off stone walls gave the impression of a large chamber. The bulky presence of the dragon was there for a second, and then it was gone without a splash.

"Poor little guy is hurt pretty bad." Merry heard the voice again; then a soft chanting incantation and a faint blue glow appeared briefly. The glow dimly silhouetted a humanoid shape bending over the pale, unmoving form of her brother.

Standing in the returned darkness, it was all too much for Merry. The dragon had left them here, probably to eat later. Her left arm throbbed with pain from burns she had barely noticed before, and now some ghoul had come forth from the darkness to devour her poor dead brother before it attacked her. She felt something hard in her right hand and realized that she had somehow held onto Gully's stupid stick.

She staggered forward, raising the club weakly.

"Good idea," the voice said, and then chanted a single word. In an instant, the room was ablaze with light shining from the end of Gully's club. It was just a young girl who was leaning over her brother; she was touching the end of the now-glowing stick Merry held.

The girl turned back to Gully, and Merry froze at what she saw. Horrible blackened burns covered the girl's back; her garments were a tattered and fused mess in that area. Was her first fear correct? Was this some undead ghoul child? No one could survive burns like that, let alone be doing… doing what to her brother? Merry looked, and in the light, she could see Gully's wound closing, his burns fading. She was healing him with magic! His breathing came in shallow gasps, but he was alive.

The realization flooded through her, as her shocked mind finally began to right itself. When the second dragon suddenly grabbed them, she had struggled against it, thinking they were just scraps of food being fought over by great beasts.

The vision of the flames dancing hungrily over the rocks and washing around them came to her. Just the air from it burned their exposed skin. Yet they'd survived because the other dragon held them and took the brunt of the inferno. At that time, she imagined she heard another girl's cry of pain. That same voice had spoken to them while they were carried to this chamber—this girl's voice. This must be that dragon, and she had saved them! Merry sat heavily on the floor.

"You look pretty out of it." The dragon-girl was kneeling in front of Merry now. "You better rest a bit."

She took Merry left arm in her cool fingers while chanting a quiet incantation. Soon the throbbing pain subsided and the red burns began lightening.

"My name is Rukastanna Greymantle. Please call me Ruka," the dragon-girl introduced herself when she finished the spell.

"I'm Meriwynn Fichgotz." Merry went to rise, but Ruka's hand on her shoulder stopped her. She wasn't sure how one should introduce oneself to a dragon-turned-girl; she was going for a curtsy.

"Merry fish guts?" Ruka pondered off-handedly. "Cool name."

"Shouldn't you be healing yourself?" Merry asked. She didn't correct the girl; her hated childhood nickname wasn't important now.

"I'm fine. I've had worse." But the grimace of pain that crossed Ruka's face as she stood up gave lie to that statement. "Light cures would just be a drop in the ocean anyway."

The dragon-girl wandered around, gingerly stretching her burned back.

"This room is safe enough," Ruka commented with one hand on a damp wall. There were two tightly shut doors and a large square opening of water in the floor. The room seemed formed of solid stone blocks of a uniform dark grey color.

"Uh-huh," Merry was dubious, but her mind was still reeling and everything seemed unreal. She was trying to figure out if this normal-seeming young girl could really be a dragon.

"You swing a mean club." Ruka went on rubbing her shoulder. "You should be able to handle yourself." It was a pretty obvious lie to Merry.

"But, just in case…" Ruka drew a strange-looking sword from a sheath at her belt. The handle was carved like a dragon's neck, the hilt was made to resemble gaping jaws, and the blade was its tongue or its breath. The whole sword was formed of a hammered bronze that seemed to glow with an inner light and blue sparks traveled continuously up and down the blade. "This is Inazuma, the lightning blade. He'll protect you." The last was said sternly, and as if to the sword itself.

Ruka spoke several strange words, again to the sword. It sounded similar to the language that the great dragons above had used to roar their challenge to each other. An odd-sounding male voice responded in the same language. The dragon girl's eyes seemed to glow amber for a second as she slammed the sword several inches into a crack in the stone floor with one mighty strike.

"Where are you going?" Merry started, but she already knew the answer. "You can't! The huge dragons are battling!"

Ruka grinned at Merry, but there was a deadly intensity to her eyes.

"Precious members of both our families are out there. And I'll do whatever it takes to save them all."

Dragon Fight!
Chapter 2

Theria grappled the storm dragon with both foreclaws, and let loose with her fire. Her opponent responded with a lightning strike. The weight difference was better than Theria had guessed; the slender bronze might be half her mass. She easily pulled her opponent off the curved breakwater and toward shore. Through the cove, it was half the distance than it would be to go around the rocks, but immediately Theria began to regret it. The storm dragon didn't resist initially but pulled Berikarth in after them with her rear claws.

By the fifth head, this upstart sea dragon angered her! Didn't she realize that Theria could care less about that useless, blue-scaled idiot? If he wasn't totally underwater, she'd fry him herself! She gave a savage heave toward shore, which forced Vestiralanna to release Berikarth and dig her own claws into the sandy bottom.

Theria loosened her bite on the bronze throat and called out, "Irovnia, get Berikarth out of here! Yiglelot, after the little one!"

The small storm dragon had struck earlier from the ocean side of the rocks and had little choice but to continue on to the cove side when Theria had released her, so she should be somewhere in the cove with the humans. Perhaps she was drowning them, just to ruin Theria's snack. She would deal with that one later—first she needed to put an end to the one she had in her grip.

The sleek, streamlined form and smooth scales of bronze offered little purchase for her claws, but Theria's powerful muscles constricted like iron bands around the slender body, and she pulled inexorably toward shore.

Theria's main handicap was ensuring she kept her head above water—there was so much of it, her scales couldn't boil it off. And grappled as they were, neither could effectively do more than bite. But even so, the storm dragon's bite was trivial to the damage that Theria's massive jaws were doing. At this rate, she might not need to get her foe all the way to shore.

A lightning bolt blasted up out of the water a short distance away, catching foolish Yiglelot full-on.

"There's a huge hole in the center!" the black dragon yelled, as he flapped once again toward shore. Theria noticed his flight was ragged and he barely stayed aloft. The weakling was almost taken out by a few lightning strikes. Theria was sure he wasn't coming back until the fight was over.

The darker shadow in the center of the cove could be anything to a fire dragon's eyes, but it was large enough to swallow her. One little slip was all it would take to put her underwater and shift the balance in a water dragon's favor.

She had almost been tricked right down that hole; her adversary was dangerously clever! Theria pulled savagely away from the hole but found little good footing. The ocean surged in a sudden powerful wave that was clearly tinged with dragon magic.

Vestiralanna was no longer weak and ineffective. In the rising rush of surf, her body slammed into Theria's, pushing her inexorably toward the now-swirling black opening. It was a struggle just to keep her jaws above water.

A sudden panic struck. *There is no path to the Fiery Halls through water!* She bit and clawed savagely at her foe, more in terror now than fury. And then cold exploded around her.

Theria had thought the waters of the cove were cold before, but that was nothing. She felt dangerously chilled as her back claws finally found purchase against a mass of solid ice.

Irovnia had completely blocked the eye of the cove with ice and nearly froze them all solid in the process. To be tricked by a vile storm dragon and then saved by an idiot cold-wyrm was too much. Her fires exploded with her anger!

She used the flames to immolate herself and boil as much of the surrounding water as possible, burning and scalding her grappled foe in the process.

Vestiralanna's head came up, looking obviously exhausted and desperate, then her eyes began glowing like green orbs.

Another foolish lightning bolt would be nothing to the strength of a Dragon of the Flames, Theria thought. *Time to show this wretched sea creature the true power and might of dragon spirit!* She gathered her breath. With her anger building, her fires would be fully back in another moment.

The bronze jaws breathed out a white fog, like steam from her fires. But it was not pleasantly scalding like steam; it was uncomfortably cool. Theria was caught inhaling and felt she was drowning in the ocean depth, the taste of salt and smell of seafoam overpowering her. She couldn't get her breath! She felt herself going under, the warmth and light fading as she sank deeper. She had to get out of it!

When Theria looked around, she was flying high over an old, ruined keep on a hill. Her breath was coming in ragged gasps. The warm sun was burning the last of the chilly grip of the ocean from her mind.

May the five-headed lady have mercy on me, she prayed but knew she didn't deserve it. She had forgotten that storm dragons had another form of spirit breath, the fog of despair.

As Theria descended to the cove a second time, she quickly cast a glamour against both lightning and enchantments on herself. She didn't expect to find her bronze-scaled adversaries there, but when next she met them, she would be ready.

Yiglelot, that cowardly swamp dragon, was nowhere to be seen, probably hiding in some stream or pond inland. Irovnia had pulled Berikarth onto the beach using an ice float. Theria wondered briefly if the stupid ice dragon had frozen him to death in the process, but she saw Berikarth beginning to stir.

The cove looked quiet; Irovnia's icy bolder still covered the center hole but was looking smaller and beginning to float. And her original ice mound that had blocked the inlet was floating down the coast, almost out of sight. And there was no sign of fishermen or children.

All in all, it was an utter failure.

Theria landed by the breakwater, grabbing the largest boulder she could move. She hauled it to the center of the cove and placed it on the ice. It held the icy plug down, firmly covering the hole again. And when the ice melted, the boulder would plunge down, crushing anything below. Then she settled on the scorched slab of rock, where she had so recently fought.

There at the end of the breakwater, with water almost all around, steeled herself in the vain hope for a rematch. But nothing stirred in the waters and it was time to report in.

Closing her eyes to focus, Theria reached back along the psychic leash that tethered her to the dragon shard. The shard was farther than she would have thought; if the airship had followed the pursuit at full speed, it should have only been a few dozen minutes behind her. Also, the link was weaker, more tenuous than she ever felt it before. *What are they up to?*

Our quarry has escaped to the sea, she projected through the shard to the princess. The link seemed to waver and flicker as she listened for a response, and it took so long she began to think the message hadn't been heard. Theria was just about to try and send more forcefully when she heard the faint reply.

Wait there—the strained voice sounded like the faded remnants of a shout echoing up from a distant cavern—*we are coming.*

The princess was losing control!

Theria had no idea what could have caused this, but this was her chance. The spirit link that tethered her to the shard was frayed and weak. Slipping those bonds would be trivial now, even for little Scorch. She just had to grab him from the ship, and they would both be free.

She would play this game just a little longer.

As she settled in to wait, Theria couldn't help blowing puffs of eager smoke through her wicked, fanged grin. Finally, her luck was turning.

Wexel Hookwright was practically numb with fear—or it could have been cold. Even in the bright sun and summer sea, the water near the huge boulder of ice was frigid. He looked over toward his brother-in-law, Hevik Fichgotz. Ever since the sea dragon had whispered to him that his children were safe, he seemed drained. Wex had to physically restrain him in the cove when they saw that crimson fire dragon with Merry and Gully. He was certain he had saved Hevik's life, and he was equally certain he had a black eye as thanks for it.

Most of the ice was well under the water, and beneath that, their mysterious dragon ally was carefully pushing the frozen boulder further down the coast. He must be getting used to dragons, for this smaller beast beneath the waves evoked no fear in him now.

When the dragons flew over the cove, he was in awe—it was like a wonderful dream come to life. He recognized the first dragons from his grandfather's stories, the great bronze-scaled storm dragons. Old sailors' tales were full of them. They were sometimes punishers of the foolish or wicked, but usually, they were depicted as protectors of the good, and saviors of sailors in trouble.

The second dragon actually spoke to them; he thought it was inviting them to swim out to sea with them before it dived into the ocean. A foolish notion, but he was tempted.

Then the dream suddenly turned to nightmare.

A huge, crimson fire dragon swooped down and landed on the south breakwater opposite them. A white ice dragon descended like an arctic wind and began freezing the ocean right outside the cove. And then with a thunderous clap, a large blue-scaled dragon shattered the Foam Lady's keel with a blast of lightning.

In just a few moments, the pleasant cove was transformed into a death trap.

"Gully!" Hevik screamed when they saw what looked like a ragdoll in the huge crimson claws. They dropped their nets and began to swim that way. What they would have done, Wex had no clue. But all strength seemed to leave them as they saw the blue dragon come around directly toward them for another pass. Its great mouth opened and a clap of thunder echoed across the cove.

Not only did the bolt miss them, but it seemed to arc and ricochet off the waves to hit a black-scaled dragon that had just entered the cove. The gods themselves must be protecting them! As he tried to blink the spots from his eyes, not quite believing the miracle, he thought he saw a girl in the water making a very unladylike gesture at the dragons. He blinked again, and the image was gone.

From down in the water, he couldn't see where the blue dragon had flown off to, but he heard a great roar and splashing from the seaward side of the breakers. Then all became silent for a few moments as each of the dragons stared out to sea, their horrid visages unreadable.

In that brief silence, a faint but familiar sound came from across the cove, one that both men had heard a thousand times—Merry was yelling Gully's name. Both men strained to see and were dumbfounded by the vision of little Merry swinging an ax at the dragon. And then a second miracle happened—the huge crimson-scaled dragon released Gully and backed away from Merry's onslaught.

In a flash, the children were gone from sight, a bronze-scaled form in their place. Multiple bright lines of electricity, like from storm clouds over the ocean, arced up from the bronze body into the crimson dragon that had pounced on it.

And then they witnessed the fire.

"No!" Hevik had yelled, but his voice was lost in the infernal roar. Unlike the quick lighting strikes, the fire seemed to go on for an excruciating eternity, although it could only have been seconds. Wex grabbed his brother-in-law as he tried to swim by. They flailed at each other briefly and went under.

When they surfaced, their struggles ceased, and their eyes went wide at what they saw. Two elemental beasts of legend faced each other. The terrifying fire dragon, its eyes aglow and smoke still streaming from its mouth, faced a new adversary. Its bronze scales glistening with sea spray, the waves crashing with unnatural vigor at its back, a mighty storm dragon had come to challenge the interloper in its domain.

The two dragons roared at each other in some ancient language of a forgotten time. The challenge seemed to echo with the crash of wild ocean storms, and the response burned with the fires of the deepest pits.

The heavens themselves resounded with the clash as the two dragons collided; the air alternately sparkled and burned. A great wave hit them as the beasts had driven themselves off the rocks and began writhing in the surf of the cove. As they righted themselves, Wex saw a lightning blast erupt from the waves of the cove to strike the black dragon that tried to return to the fray.

The surf of the cove surged and they were briefly caught in the flow. The errant current moved them away from the center, where the dragons fought, and deposited them against the ice blocking the cove mouth. And then the waters receded, leaving the two of them knee-deep in an area that would normally be well over their heads.

The icy dam behind them creaked with the weight of the ocean behind it, and angry surf splashed over the top. The ocean itself was coming to battle at the storm dragon's call! It was like Gran's old stories.

Hevik grabbed Wex and hauled him forcefully to the side as the giant boulder of ice shifted inward to where they were just standing with a resounding crack. A torrent poured in around the bolder and over their heads, and they found themselves again upended at the mercy of raging surf.

A small mountain of water raged away from them, rising toward the center and driving the combatant beasts toward the cove eye. Even the massive fire dragon could not stand against that watery onslaught and was slowly being forced along. It was only a matter of moments before both beasts were over the plunge.

An arctic blast from the white dragon struck at the rising surf of the cove. The waters over the center eye quickly froze solid, blocking the hole. The ice spread outward, stopping the motion of the two grappling dragons and coating them with a thin veneer of frost. Then the small ice dragon flew raggedly back to shore, landed with a thump, and lay there panting from its effort.

A roar of rage and a pillar of fire burst from the fire dragon. It melted the ice around it into hissing steam and left the two dragons in an almost dry crater with icy walls. The surf of the cove went still, and the bowed neck of the storm dragon showed its exhaustion. The bid to drown the fires of its enemy had failed.

The smoke from the fire dragon's maw started to flow inward as it prepared another blast of its infernal breath, but its fires were slow in coming after that last blast. The storm dragon's head also came up, exhaling only misty vapor.

A glistening white fog seemed to envelop the thrashing beasts, obscuring them briefly. When it cleared, the fire dragon was flying west over the hills, rapidly dwindling from sight. The sea dragon leaped over their heads in a graceful flying dive, only broken slightly by its rear claw striking the original ice boulder behind them. Then the bronze scaled form vanished into the waves of the open ocean.

The ice struck by the dragon's passing creaked backwards, then settled a little more seaward, no longer blocking the inlet completely. Another quiet seemed to settle over the cove as the two men tiredly tread the now calm but cold water, unsure where to go. There was no sign of Merry and Gully, and little chance that they could have survived that battle.

As he scanned the shore, Wex wondered what had happened to Hevik's younger brother Perovich. He had supposedly gone into the woods to look for sweet roots, which usually meant he would dig up a few and nap. The thought that the loafer had slept through the greatest disaster in Hookwright or Fichgotz history was almost amusing if it wasn't for the fact that Merry and Gully were now gone. And they were liable to follow soon; there was still an ice dragon on shore and a black-scaled one somewhere nearby.

Oddly, a small seal was making its way out from under the new center ice isle. Wex watched it bemusedly, thinking it was odd for it to be in these waters in the summer. He was remembering some of the other stories his gran had told, about seals and selkies.

It swam right up to them and stopped. Floating in the waves next to them, it seemed to survey the shore the same way they were. The poor thing must have been caught in the dragon fight; the fine fur on its back was blackened and singed off in some spots.

The seal waved to them like it wanted their attention, then put a flipper to its mouth in the same manner a person would indicate silence. It made a series of odd gestures with its head and swam a short distance around the icy boulder in the mouth of the cove. When it popped back up again, it was obviously waving for them to follow.

"What is that thing doing?" Hevik wondered, his voice distant and unfocused.

"Quiet, we're getting out of here," Wex smacked him upside the head to try and snap Hevik out of his dazed shock.

"We can't leave yet, where are the kids?" Hevik at least whispered this time.

"They're fine, the seal told me," Wex lied.

When they reached the far side of the ice, the creature had vanished underwater. There was a faint cracking sound, and at that moment the little iceberg broke completely free and began drifting away from the cove.

Wex nearly screamed as a dragon's head emerged from the water just inches from Hevik and him. It was the 'smaller' storm dragon, but its head was as large as a man's torso; a frill of horned projections framed its beak-like mouth on either side. Its most striking feature was its eyes—large, luminous green with faint amber flecks that seemed to swirl as they regarded the two men. At this range, he could feel its breath upon his face, carrying the salty scents of the sea.

"Do you think it can talk?" Wex whispered.

"Yes," the dragon responded, "and with a better mastery of pronouns than some." The voice formed from the monstrous throat must have been some kind of magic. It was clear, surprisingly gentle, resonant, but soft, probably so as not to attract attention from shore. The voice was also young and decidedly female-sounding.

Wex's mind raced, wondering what a pronoun was, and whether he had in some way insulted the dragon. "Ah m'lady dragon, I'm sorr…" Wex swallowed quite a bit of seawater as the dragon pulled him under.

He was too tired to even struggle at that point. The irony of surviving the huge dragon battle, only to be drowned because he inadvertently insulted a lady dragon, seemed somehow an appropriate end to his life. As he was pulled deeper into the cold depths under the ice, he took one last look toward the surface, thinking of how all his life he loved the sea. He always knew he would die in its embrace.

Through the rippling waves, he could see a white-winged form circle the iceberg twice, and then fly off.

"Next time you hide underwater, try not flailing around and blowing bubbles so much." The dragon whispered after hauling him back to the surface. "By the Eternal, you'd think I was trying to drown you or something." Wex definitely thought he detected amusement in her tone.

"M'lady dragon, have you seen my son and daughter?" Hevik asked hesitantly. He seemed none the worse for the dunking, and it was not fear of the dragon that made his voice quaver; it was fear of her answer.

"The valiant Meriwynn and her brave brother are safe." The dragon's voice trailed off, and she looked at the ice as if she could see through it back to the cove.

Wex wondered where the kids were, how they could be safe, and how long they would remain that way.

Time had little meaning to the sword Inazuma; the ancient blade had spent a millennium in battle, and perhaps another sundered and broken at the bottom of the sea or in a slumbering twilight dragon's hoard. Patience, he had learned.

Darkness also meant nothing to him—it was just another flavor to the world around him. It in no way limited the clarity of the magic senses he used. So, when the minor magic on the stick finally faded and went out, he could see the girl's face clearly.

The ancient sword had taken a thousand lives at the end of his blade, and seen the extinguishing of ten thousand more. Great dragons full of elemental power, proud elven masters of arcane lore, and noble human wielders of divine might—all had fallen within his witness. What was one peasant girl's silent tears to all of that?

The girl, Meriwynn, had her unconscious brother's head in her lap, stroking his hair with one hand. And she was still clutching the driftwood stick with the other, even after the final light had faded from it.

"Don't worry, everything will be alright." The girl's quiet voice spoke into the darkness.

Inazuma wasn't sure whether the lie was for her brother or herself, but the sword felt that it was high time he made some truth of it. He renewed the sparks along his blade to shed some dim light. Usually a purely visual warning for intimidating foes, like a rattlesnake, his strike was just as deadly without the show. Since lightning was a natural aspect of his core enchantment and required no spirit energy, the sparks were easier to maintain than creating magical light.

"Meriwynn, child of fish guts, we have dallied here long enough."

Inazuma had not projected the language of man aloud for unremembered years. It sounded strange, even to him, and the dim and inconsistent light from his blade could not hide the girl's shocked expression from his sight. He felt it was probably better if he did not speak directly to her mind at this point.

The girl jumped back, looking around for the speaker and holding the stick as a weapon. Hadn't she heard him speak earlier? It was a good thing her brother looked like he had a hard head.

Inazuma pondered for a bit; it was best when dealing with common people to project an illusion of life. Using his illusion power would drain precious amounts of his spiritual charge, but it would be worth it.

Now, what image would children such as these respond to? He supposed the kindly old man route was best, but which to use? He had spent several decades in the company of the wizard Hergelmist, who pulled off the ruse of a bumbling senile very well; the children of that time seemed quite taken with him. But he surmised that considering the circumstances, these youngsters would want someone stronger-appearing, but not threatening.

Inazuma summoned part of his magical energies and formed an illusion of old Marious in his simple blue robes and a wide-brimmed hat, with the peak half-collapsed on itself, perched upon his head. He remembered clearly the liveliness and power of the eyes set in the wrinkled old face, framed by the barely tamed beard and hair of grey, and he recreated it in detail.

It was Marious who had first reached out to Inazuma's spirit as more than an implement of war. Born from a forged spark of dragon spirit and the fervent prayers of man for victory, back in those days, he was wildly bloodthirsty and solely focused on battle. It was Marious who taught him that power without higher purpose was a blaze that would eventually consume itself in the fires of madness. More so than any of the legendary heroes who had wielded him, that great but gentle wizard was his spiritual father—and he was the greatest teacher of magic Inazuma had ever known.

He formed one of Marious' favorite staves and set a bright flame upon it. Such was the power of Inazuma's illusions that the flames felt like they gave off heat, although they could not actually burn or harm anything. Although very draining to produce, the brightness and perceived warmth of those flames might go a long way to assuage the dread and despair of children trapped in this cold, damp, and dark chamber.

"My apologies for startling you, dear child," he began, forming the sounds from the illusionary mouth of the old man. "I am Inazuma, the sword, and the spirit in the sword."

The girl curtsied very nicely, with just the perfect bow of the head to an unknown lord. She obviously had at least some small training outside of fishing boats.

"I am Meriwynn *Fichgotz* of Ravenford."

The girl emphasized the pronunciation of her last name; she seemed to have regained some of her spunk. He had seen her beating on a fire dragon with no more than a stick—there was some strong metal in this fisherman's daughter.

Inazuma smiled at her and bowed in return. A dramatic, theatrical gesture such as Marious would give to the old kings and queens in an age gone by. It was so much more effective to communicate through the illusion. With a dozen visual clues, he let her know she had nothing to fear from him, and he considered her an equal in this endeavor.

"Well, Miss *Fichgotz*, let's see how your brother is doing." He certainly didn't need to bend over the boy to see him clearly, but that action would make the girl feel better.

"Will he be alright?"

"He will be awakening soon, and we must prepare."

"How?"

"First, you must take the sword." Inazuma thought it best to refer to himself in the third person, to avoid confusion and enhance the illusion of humanity he was establishing. He ceased the sparks along his blade, and motioned an illusionary hand for the girl to pick him up.

Meriwynn leaped back from the shock that jumped from his hilt to her hand before they had even touched. Since his re-forging, he had only been wielded by Rukastanna—not just a storm dragon, but an electro-master of profound ability who encouraged the free flow of power in both directions. Together, they could create lightning far more powerful than either alone.

It had been several centuries since the hands of man had held his hilt. How had they found the balance, he tried to recall? He made an effort to focus all his elemental power down-blade, but it would require an equilibrium of charge he was not sure they could find between them, or that perhaps the children of man no longer possessed.

The brave girl queued up her determination, gritted her teeth, and firmly grasped the hilt. The strands of hair that had fallen out of her braids rose like living things; she began to shake slightly, her eyes rolling.

"Let go!" Inazuma shouted directly into the girl's mind. The illusion of old Marious vanished. It took all of his concentration to suppress the current long enough for her to release his hilt.

Meriwynn dropped to her knees clutching her right hand; she was flexing her fingers, getting the feeling back in them.

"Burned by dragon fire on my one hand," she said, holding up her left hand, "shocked by an enchanted dragon-blade on the other. It's my day of extremes." The girl looked over to Inazuma as she spoke. He was once again forming weak sparks on his blade to give the room some dim illumination.

"I'm afraid you'll have to carry yourself," she said softly.

Inazuma's re-formed image smiled sadly at Meriwynn as he made his illusionary hand pass several times through his own hilt. He omitted the staff and flame illusions to conserve power, and released the arcing sparks along his blade again for some dim light.

If she had been able to, Ruka would have been back already. Inazuma was beginning to think he might spend the next century stuck in this room. He didn't want it to be with the corpses of children if he could help it.

"If you are to travel out of this room without me, the first thing you will need is light." Inazuma's conjured image squatted down in front of the girl to better hold her attention. Dear old Marious was a truly great teacher; the sword tried to remember how he had done it.

"All people have the spirit of magic within them, but only the clever ones can figure out how to use it. And I know you are very clever," he began.

The symbol for light was not one of those permanently engraved in his metals. But among the many magical symbols of his being, Inazuma had the runic pattern for major illusion. And light was the most basic building block of all illusions. Therefore, he could recognize it when he saw it.

All dragons have a phenomenal amount of spirit power, and Ruka, in particular, had an excess of youthful energy, with little finesse or restraint. So, when she casually placed the symbol of light on the stick, the afterimage of it remained for quite a while. With his spirit sight, Inazuma could clearly see it, even after the actual light faded. He stopped the sparks on his blade to plunge them into darkness, then he traced that image with lines of illusionary light and began the slow process of instructing Meriwynn to study the runic symbol and try to image it onto the wood herself.

Inazuma was truly amazed—he thought he was humoring both the girl and himself, and expected them to be there for hours with no progress. But she definitely had the spark of sorcery and was fast on the uptake. He only had to show her the rune for light a half-dozen times and she began to envision and impose it on the stick herself.

And a mere handful of minutes after that, she was pouring her spirit through the symbol and had the end of her stick glowing and illuminating the whole room. Granted, it was the most basic of cantrips, but she cast it spontaneously, with no memorization or formulas. She didn't even need a mnemonic word like Ruka used to pull the symbol to mind.

"Wow! That is so cool!" The girl's younger brother had awoken while she was practicing her magic.

"Yeah! Isn't this neat?" Meriwynn turned to show him the now-glowing stick.

"No. This!!"

While Inazuma had been concentrating on teaching the girl and guiding her spiritual energy, the full force of his power flowed through his blade and hilt. He wasn't prepared; he hadn't suppressed any portion of his elemental charge.

The boy, standing barefoot in a small pool of seawater, had firmly grasped his hilt with both hands. He couldn't stop the surge. Inazuma didn't want this small life added to the karmic debt he already owed, but there was nothing he could do—the circuit was complete; the power needed to flow.

The earth tried to take some of his power, but it couldn't contain it. Even wedged tightly between two stone blocks, the grip of rock could not hold him; his bronze blade slipped from its grasp. Inazuma was wrenched from the stone and thrust skyward, firmly held by small hands and skinny arms he would have thought too weak for such forceful action.

With a great crack, Inazuma released a bolt at the ceiling. The tiny pieces of stone raining down did nothing to flatten the boy's hair—every strand of which was standing straight up—or to diminish his huge grin as he held the Lightning Blade Inazuma aloft.

"I am Gulhawk the Mighty! You can keep my axe; I want this sword!"

Dragon Halls
Chapter 3

Perovich Fichgotz painstakingly pried brick after brick out of the old archway. This section had not been accessible until a recent tree-fall smashed part of the old wall and revealed the bricked-up archway.

He wiped some grime-streaked sweat from his forehead before it could run into his eyes, then looked for better leverage for a stubborn brick. This was it—the adventurous delve into the forgotten temple he had imagined all those years ago, only he hadn't imagined it would be this much work.

He remembered coming to these ruins as a kid, following his older brother Hevik around. They would roam the overgrown courtyards and skip stones across the murky pools, pretending they were princes in a palace. He idolized Hevik back then, his bravery and sense of adventure. Someday, they said, they'd follow that old road and see where it went.

Father would shout at them to get out of there and be careful. Brave young Hevik would sneer at such concerns, making up stories for Perovich about the vast riches buried beneath the temple and how they'd find it and both become lords.

That was before Hevik met that girl from Gelcliff. He ruefully remembered what a wretched brat he was to her back then. But, as Irweena pointed out to him numerous times since, if he hadn't been such a scamp, they wouldn't have survived the desolation of the dark dragon that took the rest of the family.

When his constant pranks and tricks failed to drive the girl away from his obviously addle-headed brother, he decided to steal his brother's wave-skipper and run away. They'd be sorry when he was gone, and he'd show them when he was a fabulously wealthy adventurer and shared none of it with them.

Of course, Hevik knew exactly where he had gone, and found him in these very ruins before the sunset. Hevik had borrowed the Dreller's small boat and packed food and a tent, and brought the dreaded girl with him. They stayed up all night and Irweena joined in their daring games among the ruins and told adventure stories of her own. She was good at stories, really good. And by morning, he was almost as addle-headed about her as Hevik was.

That was the last of the golden glory days, at least for his brother. Returning home after that trip to the Desolation broke something in him. Hevik grew up overnight and retreated into the practicalities of work and risk avoidance. He would not approve of Perovich's little exploration, and wouldn't recognize an adventure if it fell out of the sky in front of him.

With no warning, the remaining half of the bricks blocking the arch fell outward toward Perovich. He just barely avoided being brained by a large section. But that did it! He now had an opening big enough to get through. He stumbled upon the entrance several weeks ago without tools or gear to explore with, and he had planned to come back this very week.

It was great fortune that Irweena had suggested the family fishing trip today. Not only would he have the big boat to haul his loot back with, he'd be able to gloat the whole trip home about his new-found wealth. Those fools out fishing were missing all the adventure.

He crept carefully down the stone steps and into the depths of the temple ruins, using his stout oaken staff in one hand to test the steps ahead. The wicker-and-pitch torch sputtered brightly in his other hand; there were five more in the satchel at his side. He had prepared for this excursion carefully this time, carefully and secretly.

The stairs curved left and ended in an arched entrance to a large vaulted chamber. The high, half-circle shape of the chamber brought the ceiling low at the sides where he entered. A row of pillars ran the length of the room on either side, a double arm's length from either wall. In the center, a channel, twenty feet across, was cut from end to end and filled with still, dark water with neither wave nor ripple.

As he cast his gaze down the long chamber to his right, his heart skipped a beat. The far eastern end of the chamber was bathed in an unnatural blue-green light that waved as if underwater. Standing there, in the center of the light, its scales dully glinting, watching him with its great emerald eyes, was a huge bronze dragon.

Merry was worried about Gully. He was four-times touched by dragon power this day, stabbed by dragon claws, burned by dragon fire, healed by dragon magic, and now charged with dragon lightning, and he held a dragon-forged blade of terrible power. It was like one of her stories come to life, but it shouldn't be happening to him. He was too young; it was too dangerous!

Merry jumped at a sudden static shock. Gully had stealthily reached over to touch the small of her back. He was now doubled over with laughter. She knew Gully; he would never grow tired of that prank. He was *too annoying* to have that kind of power!

"Can't you do anything about him?" she asked the sword. She wished it would become the old man again; she didn't like talking to the thin air.

"It would be imprudent for me to take control at this point." The sword spoke directly in her head. "I am still not entirely sure how he is able to wield me at all."

She didn't like the implications of the sword taking control, but she also didn't like the way Gully's hair was standing up and waving slightly like it was alive with a life of its own. Or the extra nervous energy—even more than normal—that he seemed to have as he paced around the room swinging the sword.

She dodged another of his shock touches as he came back over to her. Gully stepped in uncomfortably close and looked up at her with a huge, maniacal grin.

"What's with the worried face? Never fear, I can protect you now."

She couldn't really blame the sword for the mania—that was pure, undiluted Gully. The only difference was now his wild game was all too real.

"Young masters," the sword spoke out loud. "We should get going; there is no telling how much longer this room will be safe."

"What do you mean?" Merry asked.

"I cannot be certain what has transpired in the cove above, or which dragon is likely to come through that opening next," the sword explained. "It would be best to expand our exit options."

"I think he means we should go explore," Gully explained eagerly.

***

Ratnosk made his way carefully out of the safe, dark tunnel and into the sea cavern. The bright, horrid sunlight was streaming in the cavern opening and reflecting off the ocean waters, casting light to the deepest recesses of this cave.

Reaching into his belt pouch with one clawed hand, he pulled out his goggles of shadow and carefully placed them over his eyes. Protected from the harsh glare of day, he made his way across the narrow ledge and around the bend into the main cavern, where he immediately stopped at what he saw.

Two savage-looking Fokari sat on the rocky ledge above the water, no more than twenty feet in front of him. And floating in the water in the center of the cave was a large boulder of ice. In the heat of summer, that could only mean one thing. These were sorcerers and this was an attack on the tribe!

The invaders seemed as shocked to see him as he was them. This was his chance to escape, warn his people, and become a hero accepted back in the nesting circles. He turned on his tail to run back along the narrow ledge to the tunnels and ran headlong into the claw of a dragon.

There are few higher honors than to be slain by one of the Great Ones, true incarnations of divinity on earth, except perhaps to be chosen to serve. He threw himself prone and hoped for a quick death—it was the most a second-rate trap-jack like him could wish for when in the presence of a god incarnate.

"What are you doing here, little one?"

The Great One spoke to him in the true tongue! He shuddered in excitement. Her voice was like the dulcet tones of the dragon harp in the Hall of Choosing. The Great One was allowing him to live, at least for now, and she had actually spoken to him! He gathered his resolve and responded in the ritual formula that each of the people were taught from hatching, but never dared hope to actually use.

"Oh, glorious and powerful master of spirit and elements, I have no greater wish, and there is no greater fulfillment, than to serve you in both my life and my death. Take of me what you will and I will give you my all."

Even to his ears, his voice was high and unworthy, his pronunciation coarse, his tempo horrible.

Huge eyes of deep green regarded him for a moment. The undulating light reflected off the waves at the cave entrance highlighted the spectacular glow of the Great One's shimmering bronze scales. Ratnosk held his breath awaiting the answer that could define his existence.

"Just great!" the dragon sighed, one powerful claw going to her head, "Kobolds!"

Merry mourned the loss of her book as they walked down the corridor of stone; she would have liked to map these corridors as she went. She had started out counting paces, but gave that up to keep up with Gully; he didn't even seem to care that she had the light. The feel of the magic sword he grasped tightly in his hands was good enough for him as he forged ahead.

She held up her glowing club to cast its light as far as possible as they stopped at the top of a stairway. There was no sign of a bottom, but there was the faint slosh of water.

"No," she whispered as Gully started down. "We want up."

She didn't want to mention to Gully that she already felt they were under sea level. It was odd that the room they came from had a water level just below the floor, yet these stairs went down quite some ways. When they opened the chamber door, she had felt her ears pop, and there was constant moisture dripping from the walls and ceiling of these corridors.

She couldn't help feeling that this place was filled with air, like the old tin cup she used to play within the bath. One casual tilt and the precious air would bubble out.

They backtracked to a four-way intersection, Gully pushing past with a static shock to get back in front. All four corridors faded into darkness at the far reaches of her light. To the left was the way they had originally come down.

"Go right again," she mouthed to him, motioning with the club.

This passage went perhaps a hundred paces and ended at a door. They had a difficult time getting that first door open between the two of them, and this one looked even more solidly wedged shut. She motioned him back from the door.

"We kick it in and I charge?" Gully asked in an excited whisper.

"No. We go back and see where the other passage goes."

"What? Are we just going to wander back and forth, afraid of going anywhere?"

"A smart warrior knows the lay of the land. And keep your voice down."

"Why?"

"I don't know, maybe because it's smart! Just do it."

She thought for a minute and then whispered, "Inazuma, can you see what's behind that door?"

"I'm afraid not," the sword responded. "My magic does not allow me to see through objects as solid as metal, wood, or stone."

"Then we go back and keep looking," Merry said definitively.

***

Perovich whistled appreciatively as he approached the towering statue of bronze. *By the blessed gods, the eyes look like real emeralds!* He wished Merry was here to see this before he plucked them out.

Faintly rippling streams of shimmering light were coming from one of the deeper pools above; a vast sheet of transparent material formed the floor of the pool and held the water in place. The light cast from the sun was still to the front of the statue, but by midday, it would shine directly down.

The other end of the chamber was cloaked in shadows, but Perovich could make out a statue of a huge bearded man with a greatsword. The eyes appeared to be sapphire but were smaller than those in the dragon statue. Also, it was in darkness and was a more vertical climb.

So, humming happily and grinning like a kid, he took out the length of rope he had with him and assayed how best to manage the two-story climb up the smooth bronze neck to the top.

By the time he finally reached the great horns that rimmed the creature's head, his grin had changed to a grimace of determination. It had been slicker and harder than it looked, with two close calls that set his blood racing. If he fell and was hurt here, no one would know where he was.

It was funny how he didn't think of that until he was hanging upside-down by his knees twenty feet in the air.

His torch, left below, had long since sputtered out. So, he sat resting for a moment on the dragonhead with only the dim, wavering light filtering through the pool above. He was enjoying his conquest and assessing the safest way to remove the large green gems when the shadow fell upon him. He looked up into the water suspended directly over his head and almost fell off the statue.

He found himself only scant feet from the maw of a dragon of the darkest sort! The creature's pale-yellow eyes glared at him from its ebony skull-like face. Its head was framed on either side by a pair of large, slightly curved horns, and its vicious-looking teeth jutted from its mouth even while closed. It was pure black, looked utterly evil, and he was sure it was looking at him with malicious glee.

It raised its claw and struck at him. The invisible floor of the pool didn't so much as vibrate. The creature now appeared to be roaring at him, if such was possible underwater, but he could not hear it. Perovich couldn't help but wince as the dragon spat a huge quantity of nasty-looking green bile at the magical barrier directly over his head. Other than clouding the water a little, there was no effect.

Slowly regaining his courage, Perovich reached up and touched the barrier just above his head. There was no feeling, neither warm nor cool to the touch; his hand was simply stopped on a perfectly smooth barrier of magic.

He then did what was arguably the stupidest act of his short life, one that was already filled with a grand parade of spectacular fool- ishness. He taunted a dragon.

Ratnosk couldn't help but feel the new mistress was somehow displeased with him. And the more he bowed and scraped, the less happy she seemed. Here he was, the first representative of his tribe to be in the presence of a dragon for a dozen generations, and he was failing miserably to please her. Worse, he was failing his whole tribe, and at this rate, she would fly off, and it was all his fault.

He wasn't displaying his sincerity enough. He needed to try hard- er, perhaps with the dance and chant of servility.

"Just stop! Stand still, be quiet, and let me think."

He froze in place, holding as still as he could. It was an awkward position, and he had to shift his tail slightly to keep from falling over. Even in the smallest things, he could not serve properly. He waited for her to smite him for that transgression, but the killing blow did not come.

"What's your name?"

Her question startled him; it sounded like she was asking for his name. For an instant, he entertained the fantasy that he was to be a chosen one, a direct servant of a dragon. But then he came to his senses—she must be asking for his tribe name.

"We are the humble Bendtail clan, oh Magnificent One," he re- plied, his voice squeaking in his nervousness.

"How many are in your tribe and how far from here do you nest?" the dragon asked, moving lower in the water so she no longer towered over him. Her eyes were now level with his, although they were each almost as large as his entire head. Her jaws could snap him up in one bite and swallow him still squirming like he would with a small tunnel-runner.

He was taking too long to answer, Ratnosk thought with panic, but he didn't dare get it wrong. Holding still, he missed the use of his claws to help the count in his head.

"One hundred and forty-four, including the latest hatchlings, if it pleases you," he said, thinking how pathetically small and depleted his tribe had become. "And our current tunnels are but a fifteen-minute walk from here, oh Glorious One."

He carefully kept his pose and barely dared breathe as the dragon regarded him for a few moments.

"Relax," she commanded. He found that hard to do, but tried to comply.

"What's *your* name, little one?"

He could barely contain his joy; she was asking for his personal name. He was chosen! He wanted to dance, but opted for a first-degree bow as he said, "Ratnosk il Nurhoth, trap-jack, third-class of the Bendtail clan."

"Very well, Ratnosk, I am Rukastanna of the Greymantle clan," the dragon said.

He couldn't believe his great fortune. "Yes, oh Rukastanna the Radiant and Benevolent, it shall be as you command."

Then the dragon seemed to grow in size. Bringing her jaws frighteningly close, she said, "These humans and their family are under my personal protection. If any harm comes to them from your clan, then I shall declare vendetta on the Bendtail and expunge them from existence."

As she looked at him, her eyes seemed to shift from green to amber, the pupils narrowing to mere slits. The dragon opened her mouth wide, and from this short distance, he could clearly see sparks of lightning arcing across the rows of wicked-looking serrated teeth within her great jaws. He could smell the imminent storm bolt on the air. And even through his shadow goggles, the glare building deep within the dragon's maw hurt his terror-widened eyes.

"Are we clear?" she snapped her jaws shut with a rumble of swallowed thunder.

It was the first he saw her truly look draconic, and it sent shivers of both fear and joy down his spine.

"Yes, oh Mistress of a Thousand Glorious Virtues," Ratnosk cried as he prostrated himself again before her. "Shall we bring tribute, oh Incarnation of Supreme Generosity?"

"Yes. Yes, I think tribute would be nice," the dragon said thoughtfully, her eyes returning to their deep green glow, and her entire aspect brightening.

"Oh, and you wouldn't happen to have a boat, would you?"

Storm God's Revenge
Chapter 4

Perovich had no idea where this terrible creature had come from, whether it had been living here for days, or had just arrived. But here it was, and all his dreams were going to be snatched away, along with his loved ones.

He recognized the horrible visage of the dark dragon instantly; it matched the tapestries in both the temple's Hall of Memories and Ravenford Keep's great hall. It was also unmistakably the same jagged shape—although much smaller—as the great black skull in the dragon crypt of Ravenford.

Once a year, to mark the solemn remembrance of all those lost in the Desolation, the townsfolk of Ravenford walked by candlelight past the nearly five hundred markers of those who were lost. He and Hevik always paused to light seven candles for the parents and siblings he barely remembered now. And then they went down into the dragon crypt to stare quietly at the great bones and horrid skull.

They stopped that practice and closed down the dragon crypt years ago, and he had nearly forgotten the skull that had stalked the nightmares of his youth. But here it was again, a much smaller but no less horrible image of the Bringer of Desolation.

What overcame him then, even he couldn't explain—perhaps a manic reaction instilled by the cruel twist of fate, bringing his darkest childhood fears to his moment of triumph. Even if the barrier above held, the creature was out there with what little family he had left, and Perovich prayed that the creature hadn't noticed the fishing boat yet. And at that moment, he decided that he was going to do everything in his power to make sure that it wouldn't.

A strange courage instilled by fatalistic abandon overcame him. He was going to keep this creature from his family, and while he was at it, he would have his treasure too, if only for brief moments. He gestured his contempt at cruel fate to the dragon above and shouted.

"Listen, you ugly wyrm, this treasure is mine! It's not for moronic lizards that can't even break a little glass!"

The dragon might not be able to hear him, so he added several more gestures to make sure his point was clear. Then he proceeded to pry out the eyes of the statue with his dagger. And he held up the huge gems, bigger around than his fist, to further mock the dragon. But it was already gone.

There was no telling how long it would take the thing to find the entrance, or whether it could even fit, so he tossed the gems in his satchel and went down the rope the fast way, burning his hands in the process. Just as he reached the bottom, he heard a crashing as the fallen tree by the hole he had entered was violently thrown aside. *Gods*, he thought, *that was quick.*

He left the rope, staff, and his sandals where they were. Grabbing his torch stub, he ran for the side of the room opposite from where he entered. In the dim light, he could just make out a dark arch between two pillars there. Running, he fanned sparks from the stub, snagged another torch from his bag, and lit it. As he passed the open arch, he threw the sputtering torch in as far as he could.

On his toes and as quietly as possible, he sprinted down to the dark end of the hall and the other statue. He heard the crashing from the stairs as something large was forcing its way through. As he approached, he realized the statue was of Alaric, the Lord of Storms, one of the gods that no sailor wanted to anger. The statue's right hand rested upon the pommel of a greatsword, point down, in front of it. Its left hand held aloft a lightning bolt that glinted in the dim light. A cloak flowed down its back as if frozen in a storm breeze. The flared cloak provided just enough angle for him to pull himself upon it. Crouching in the stone folds behind the figure like some small child playing piggyback, he was off the ground and effectively out of sight of most of the room.

From here, he could see that there was a circular opening over this statue, too. But instead of looking up into a pool, it was a gold dome of some sort, with a rod and a sphere suspended from the middle of it. Both the sphere and the bolt held by the statue looked to be wrought of solid gold.

He forgot about golden treasure as he heard the dark dragon push its way into the room, and he began praying silently and reverently to the Lord of Storms for forgiveness for his wayward actions and thoughts.

Slowly, quietly, carefully, he pulled himself up and peered over the statue's shoulder. Across the hall, he saw the creature heading toward the tunnel the torch had been thrown into.

The dragon that appeared so huge in the pool above him was dwarfed by the gargantuan statue of bronze. It was small for a dragon, but it still looked large enough to consume a family of fishermen in one meal—and savage enough, too.

The creature walked with a slight limp and held one wing a little stiffly as if it pained him. Was it injured in a fight? What creature could hurt a dragon like that, he didn't know, but if it couldn't fly well at the moment, the gods had given them all a chance. If only he could slip by the beast, perhaps block the entrance somehow to slow it down. With the Foam Lady turned with the wind and him at the tiller, the creature would never catch them.

As he screwed his courage to leap down and make a quiet break for the exit, his gaze traveled up to the top of the great bronze idol across the hall, and he saw soulless black holes where beautiful green orbs had once appeared to gaze down. It made the statue seem somehow sinister and angry, instead of its previous awe-inspiring beauty.

At that moment, a low *clink* sound echoed across the hall, as if someone were toasting with crystal goblets. It wasn't loud, but it didn't need to be in that deathly still chamber. It took him a moment to register what it was. Somehow, while shifting his weight only slightly, the two large gems carelessly thrown in his satchel had clinked together.

The dragon turned and looked directly at him across the chamber. Even in the dim light, he could swear he saw an evil smile cross its crocodilian face, and then it spat.

The farther they went through the tunnels, the surer Inazuma was that he had been here before. It was a faint memory, and the place would be much changed in a thousand years, but perhaps.

He had been to the sea-pool chamber once in the last decade with Ruka; one of her stashes was hidden behind a secret door there. If she came out of this alive, they'd be moving that one again. He wasn't sure how much of the complex she had originally explored or cleared, but it had to have been over five years ago. He knew that these places rapidly filled with vermin and the occasional serious threat, so he kept his senses sharp and on the lookout for danger.

This last corridor did indeed lead to a stairway up, and Inazuma could almost feel Meriwynn's relief. Through his link with Gulhawk, he could sense even that fearless boy's spirits rise as they ascended. The first landing had closed doors on either side.

"Keep going."

The girl motioned her brother up the stairs with her dimming light stick when he paused to consider the doors. He felt the pull of the boy's desire to explore—it was infectious. He began wondering himself what was behind those ancient doors.

They made it only a half-dozen steps further up before the magic illumination on the stick gave out again. He sparked as much as he could to give them some light. Inazuma watched the look of concentration on the girl's face with interest; she was recalling the mystic formula for light. That she had the spirit energies to actually invoke the light magic again proved the girl had a natural knack for sorcery.

She held up the glowing stick and grinned at her brother. The boy swung Inazuma up in a grand salute and grinned even wider at his sister. As Gully turned back up the stairs, only Inazuma saw the girl's expression change—her worry for her family, and Gully in particular, was written clearly on her brow.

When they climbed to the next landing, they stopped and stared. A torch lay on the floor, still glowing red and smoking on the damp stone.

As Meriwynn turned a perplexed look to her brother, they heard a faint yell from up the next flight.

"Now you've done it, foul beast! The Lord of Storms will strike you down for that!"

"Uncle Vic?" Meriwynn said querulously.

The girl was stopped in indecision for a moment, trying to figure out what was going on. Not so her brother; in a flash, he was sprinting up the steps with Inazuma in hand. They burst up the final few steps and through an arch at a headlong run. The chamber was a grand half-cylinder, arched overhead, with decorative pillars down each side and a long pool down the center. The boy barely stopped himself from sliding across the slick marble floor into the pool.

In a moment, Inazuma had assessed the situation; what dim light there was in the chamber came from the ceiling of the eastern end. But he didn't need that to see the whole chamber clearly. A small swamp dragon was stalking a man who had climbed a statue at the western end and was jumping around on it like a monkey.

It was bad but not as bad as it could have been. The dragon was barely a young adult, and it had already been seriously injured by several lighting blasts from him and Ruka. If only Inazuma had a full charge, he felt they could win this fight with one more solid strike.

The truth was that although he could generate an endless supply of minor shocks or even bursts on a good hit, he couldn't generate his own lightning. He could only attract and capture other lightning sources, to expel when necessary. Ruka kept him constantly charged to full, but he had used almost all the stored lightning charge he had at the cove. As it was, he had no more left in him than a shocker-lizard.

There was little to do but force the boy to run. Just as he was about to do that, the far statue caught his attention. He had seen the figure depicted there before.

On the plains of Malgar, when the demon princes stepped upon the field in third-stage aspects, and even the elder dragons were flung about like toys, all seemed lost. Then the armies of Man stepped forward. They were individually weak and frail, and although they numbered in legions, it would still be as nothing to the demon lords. Even their allies would have laughed as the demons did if their plight had not been so dire. And then mankind revealed its true power. Faith.

In each of the ages, one of the greater dragon families had brought into the world allies to help champion the endless battle with the demons. The golden Sun Dragons chose the Titans, hugely powerful lords of elemental forces, but they were too chaotic, and the inevitable Dragon-Titan War shook the world to its foundation, ending the Age of Titans. The silver Cloud Dragons chose the Elves, masters of arcane lore who created great seals of magic to bind the demons, but eventually, they were corrupted and the seals were shattered, ending the Age of Fey. The bronze Storm Dragons chose Man, and a new type of magic was brought into the world—the power of divine faith.

From the ranks of mankind, great heroes stepped forth, wielding the full power of the faith of their comrades and kin. Toward the end of the battles, Inazuma met this one, Alaric, already named the Lord of Storms. At that time, Inazuma was wielded by General Bykarvo, commander of the fifth brigade of the Storm Legion. Alaric, wielding his greatsword, Blitzkrieg, had already risen to command the entire legion.

A millennium later, he had first seen that statue in this hall. Alaric had long since ascended through whatever mysterious power of faith Man uses to create their hero-gods. Even at that time, mankind had already forgotten why there was a dragon bowing to Lord Alaric at the other end of the hall.

One important thing struck him from that faint memory—both ends of the hall were lit then. The east was lit during the day with water-filtered sunlight, but the west was lit at all times back then by constant electrical storms generated in the dome above the statue of Lord Alaric. Reaching out, he could still feel the faint magic of that dome.

Inazuma had a plan or at least a faint hope.

"Charge!" he called to the boy's mind.

"Wait!" Meriwynn cried from behind them, but it was too late.

He searched for the inevitable fear that all must feel when facing a dragon, and was ready to push the boy if necessary. But there was no need, for there was not a trace of fear in the lad, only a wild joy as he surged forward. This was truly one of the descendants of the race of Man that had produced Alaric. And inspired, Inazuma summoned an illusion. He would only be able to hold the image for a few seconds, then he had to put all his remaining energy into an igniting spark.

As the dark dragon turned, he saw not a skinny lad improbably waving a short sword at him, but Lord Alaric himself in his full glory, shouting his battle cry and brandishing the mighty two-handed Blitzkrieg.

Inazuma had always admired that sword.

Perovich rocked back and forth on the statue as hard as he could, while carefully avoiding the areas the acid had splattered. It always worked in stories—the idol of the angry god would fall on the evil beast. And the dragon had just covered Alaric's beard and chest with caustic acid, marring the beautiful marble finish, which was justification for divine retribution if he had ever seen it. But the statue didn't so much as vibrate with his antics.

He was out of ideas. The best he could hope for was to stay high out of easy reach and be a difficult target for the dragon's acidic spray. As he jumped about, he heard the clinking of the jeweled eyes in his bag. He looked again at the angry-seeming dragon statue across the hall, and then at the grinning evil wyrm stalking him from below.

"Lord Alaric, if you help me to save my family from this," he prayed fervently, "I swear, I'll fix your dragon statue."

He didn't really expect an answer, and almost fell off the statue when he saw the mighty Lord of Storms himself charging down the hall.

"*Vile creature of darkness and evil, prepare to feel my mighty storm of righteousness!*" The voice boomed down the hallway, accompanied by a roll of thunder.

Oddly, Perovich thought he heard Merry yelling, "Gully, no!" faintly in the background.

As the Lord of Storms charged up, the dragon cowered down with its tail between its legs and sidled into the pool with a panicked splash.

Then the awe-inspiring Storm God raised his mighty sword, and out came… not the huge blast of lightning Perovich expected, but a small arc no thicker than his finger. The pathetic little bolt did not strike the dragon but instead went high and wide, toward the ceiling directly above the statue. And most astonishing and absurd of all, the image vanished and standing there was not the Lord of Storms, but little Gully holding a bronze short sword aloft.

Gully grinned up at Perovich and said, "Tricked you!"

"Gully, you fool! Get out of there!" he yelled.

"We just need a minute," Gully responded cryptically while sprinting toward Uncle Vic and the statue.

Perovich had no idea what crazy game the lad was playing now, and he could only watch in horror as the terrible head of the black dragon slowly rose from the water. The anger and hatred of the beast was almost palpable.

"Foolish human, I will melt you slowly from the feet up for that!" The dragon spoke with a voice like crushed gravel.

Gully ducked behind the legs of the statue and put his back to it. He held that strange short sword in both hands. The lad was looking up intently, not at him, but instead, he was focused on the ceiling above the statue.

The humming and crackling of energy building also drew Perovich's attention upward. Directly above him, he saw the dome was coming alive with sparks from the center sphere, and his hairs stood on end as small bolts started jumping between the rod and the dome walls. Perovich was beginning to get the idea that divine retribution was coming, but it would be too late.

"Run now, beast," Gully's voice called out, his voice echoing around the stone chamber, "for your doom is nigh."

He could just hear Irweena's voice saying, as she always did when Gully did something particularly foolish, *'It's Vic's fault; he's a bad influence on the boy.'* Although taunting a dragon like that was ten times as foolish as anything he ever did. Okay, maybe only twice as foolish, and it was time to rectify that.

The dragon didn't even acknowledge the boy's taunts. It pulled itself sinuously out of the pool and prowled with silent menace toward the statue. Its head was low, and its nostrils were flaring like it was sniffing him out.

The gemstone made a satisfying clink as it struck the top of its scaly head. The dragon looked up at him, its long neck bringing it shockingly close, and Perovich flung the second gem with all of his might. It was either ironic luck or poetic justice that he hit the dragon right in the eye with a dragon-eye gem.

"Right here, you stinking…" Perovich's taunt was interrupted by a blast of acid from the maw of the dragon.

He had been standing astride the great statue, his bare feet planted on the Storm God's shoulders and his skin crawling with the charge building above him. Even though he was ready for it, he was very nearly not fast enough. Thankfully gravity was on his side and he avoided the worst of it. Small splatters of the caustic bile sizzled through his clothes and burned his skin.

Dropping behind the statue, Perovich desperately caught himself on the cloak and hung on, out of sight. The dragon circled around the left side of the statue, its claws clicking on the stone floor in an angry scramble. Perovich swung to his right, trying to keep the statue between him and the dragon.

Gully bolted out, running hard and keeping the statue between him and the dragon's head and claws. Just barely ducking under a wild claw swipe from the other side of the statue, he ran straight into the tail that was suddenly swung around the opposite way. Gully went down hard, with the wind knocked out of him. He was dazed, and could only sit up and raise his sword weakly as the dragon circled back around to the front.

"Leave him alone!" Merry's yell echoed across the chamber, as a glowing axe came flying across the room at the dragon.

The beast jumped back, but what clattered to the floor was just a piece of bleached-white driftwood glowing with some eerie light.

The dragon stared at the stick for only a moment, but it was long enough for Perovich. Swinging all the way around the side of the statue, he ran down its sword arm, then leaped off the giant stone pommel and onto the dragon's head.

Perovich might just as well have tried to jam his dagger into a boulder as get it through a dragon's scales. And his one wild swing at its eye just hit the armored ridge. It had instinctively closed its eyes tight when he landed on it.

It is, after all, just a normal dagger, he thought as the vicious claws scraped him savagely, pulling him from the beast's head and flinging him across the room.

He rolled and mostly caught himself before hitting a pillar, his left side slit open in large gashes. The pain slowed him as he tried to dive desperately to one side, but he couldn't fully evade the next acid blast.

The pain of the slash across his ribs was nothing. He was wracked with excruciating burning as the dragon's foul magic bile started to consume him slowly. Perovich fell to the floor with a sick thud.

Rolling to his side with a sizzling whimper, he saw one of the dragon-eye gems he thought to claim lying on the ground between him and the beast. That dragon would now be the bringer of retribution for his greedy defilement, and also the bringer of his terrible demise.

I'm sorry, he thought, looking up to the statues, *I didn't realize this was a temple. Take me for my foolishness, but at least spare my family.*

A huge flash blinded him, and a booming crack echoed through the hall. Through the jagged after-images of that first bolt, Perovich could see serious lightning now jumping from the gilded dome above to the statue of Alaric's raised bolt.

The dragon had hunkered down at that blast, slithering slightly backwards to the pool, its entire attitude cowed. Perovich realized, somewhat ironically, that this terrible beast that was going to be the death of them, was just a cowardly little bully. But if it wasn't, they would already be dead.

It looked up into the growing storm above for a moment, then turned back toward its prey. The dragon drew back its head slightly with a gurgling rasp as it gathered more of its deadly acid.

Gully had staggered to his feet, but he didn't run. He thrust that strange sword he carried above his head in a dramatic posture. In the now-bright glow from the lightning dome above, it looked impressive, but this was the worst time for his theatrical imagination. Or maybe it was best to go out this way. Perovich gritted his teeth in pain, desperately trying to stand up and face their impending doom with bravado like his brave nephew.

"Too late, foul beast," Gully called.

The next bolt from the dome missed the statue entirely and struck Gully's sword. Perovich gasped, but the boy was unharmed; a joyfully wicked grin spread across his face as his wild hair stood fully on end.

With a forceful chop, Gully slashed the now-glowing sword down toward the dragon, leaving a bright crescent afterimage. And amazingly, a bolt of pure unbridled lightning blasted directly into the shocked maw of their dark adversary.

The dragon made a desperate dive into the water, and in a great wave, swam down the long pool, trying to escape. Bolt after bolt of powerful energy was drawn to Gully's sword, blasting after the beast until the roiling waters were still and a black carcass came floating to the surface. Then he blasted it three more times, just to be sure.

"I think that might be enough," Merry said. She stood next to, but not *too* close to Gully, whose sword still glowed and crackled with ready power.

"Indeed," a strange voice agreed. In his pain-soaked awareness, Perovich wondered if it was the Lord of Storms himself, or if anyone else could hear it.

"Hi kids," he said weakly, rolling flat on the floor and staring up at the lightning still playing across the dome and striking the statue's upraised bolt every so often. It was very beautiful, he thought.

Merry's concerned face leaned over him. She was holding a short, glowing staff, and he wondered distantly when she had become a wizard. For that matter, when had Gully become a lightning-hurling disciple of the Lord of Storms? Not that it mattered; what was bothering him now was that she was blocking his view of the pretty storm above.

He closed his eyes, hoping one of those bolts of lightning would hit him; it was starting to feel cold.

The caustic bile that coated Uncle Vic's left arm and side still sizzled, and Merry detected an acrid smell. She grabbed his right shoulder and hauled him toward the water.

"Gully, give me a hand."

Gully stood staring up at the statue and the lightning playing in the dome above it.

"Gully!" Merry shouted at him.

He blinked twice and looked at her, almost as if he didn't recognize her for a moment.

"Gully, put down the sword, come here, *and help me!*" Merry tried her sternest you're-going-to-be-in-trouble voice.

Gully clutched the sword closer and looked at her very strangely.

"Inazuma, let him go!"

"I am not holding him." There was a puzzled tone to the sword's voice. Then forcefully, Inazuma said, "Boy! Place me on the ground, NOW!"

Slowly, with a jerking action, almost like one of old man Heriponzo's marionettes, Gully placed the sword on the ground. He stared at it for a minute like he wanted to pick it back up.

"Gully, Uncle Vic could die!" Merry felt hysteria creeping into her voice. "Please, Gully…" She gave another heave and moved the limp form of her uncle several inches closer to the pool.

When she looked up, Gully had Uncle Vic's feet. He looked at her with that sheepish grin he always got when caught with his hands in one of Mum's pies.

"Sorry Merry, I was… distracted," he said softly. "Please don't cry."

"I'm not crying!" she snapped at him, wiping something from her cheek. "Now on three—one, two, three!"

Between the two of them, they partly carried and partly dragged their unconscious uncle to the edge of the pool.

"Keep his feet elevated while I clean the remains of this dragon spit off him." Merry was trying to remember what the Lady Gracelynn had said in her healing class. Mum had been in that one, along with a lot of the women from the village; the Lady called it 'first aid,' and said it was very important if someone was hurt badly.

"Shouldn't you raise his head instead?" Gully asked.

"No, that's not what you do for someone in shock."

"I didn't shock him, I swear!"

"That's not what I meant," Merry said, a little harsher than she intended.

She turned and asked, "Inazuma, is there anything you can do?"

The sword's voice seemed truly sad when it responded. "I'm afraid I know nothing of healing. My function and fate have always been to do the opposite. But I believe you are wise and correct in your actions."

Merry undid the buckle on Uncle Vic's satchel strap, then she began tearing strips from his shirt, most of which was ruined anyway. She soaked the fabric in the pool water and cleaned his wounds as best she could.

"Check his bag," she instructed Gully. "See if there's anything to keep him warm."

"Yeah, there's a cloak rolled up in here. And flint, tinderbox, three sacks, two tin flasks in a box, a bunch of travel cakes… great, I was getting hungry… oh, and a compass!"

While Gully was inventorying the satchel, Merry continued working on gently cleaning around the burns. As she was wiping his face, Uncle Vic began to stir.

He groaned slightly and opened his eyes.

"I always knew angels were pretty," Uncle Vic's whisper was raw, but he still had that familiar, infuriating, lopsided grin. She wanted to hug him, but thought better of it and only punched his good shoulder lightly.

"What are you doing here?" Merry asked.

"Oh, the usual," he quipped weakly, "fighting dragons." Then Uncle Vic's grin turned to a grimace of pain as he gasped, "Argh, I feel mostly dead."

"You are. Now lie still."

"I am sorry, but we cannot stay here," Inazuma said. "There are more dragons, and they will come looking for this one eventually. They could be here at any moment."

"You hear that too, right?" Uncle Vic was looking at the statue.

"It's the sword," Merry said tiredly, "and he's right. Other, bigger, worse dragons…" She shuddered slightly, remembering that horrible crimson beast.

"Huh? Oh, of course, the sword…" Uncle Vic said dubiously.

He shifted his head slightly and looked querulously at the blade on the ground a few feet away. Inazuma wasn't even sparking at the moment. Then Uncle Vic tried to sit up but fell back with a muffled cry.

"Oh shite, that's bad!" Merry gasped, looking at the raw meat of Uncle Vic's side that began hissing and smoking again after he moved. Despite her best efforts, the draconic acid was still eating into him, and now an alarming rasp had crept into his breathing.

"Flask… in… my bag," he gasped with his eyes closed.

Merry felt moisture on her face again as she dug into his satchel. Uncle Vic would most likely die here, and there was nothing she could do other than get him a drink to help ease the pain.

"Here."

She very carefully tilted his head while pulling out the cork with her teeth, and dribbled some of the drink down his throat.

"All… it," Uncle Vic faintly whispered between chokes as he swallowed.

Very gently, Merry helped him drink the rest of the flask. Only a few stray drops ended up down his chin. It was a very strange liquor—if that's what it was—with a thickness like syrup and a light blue color. Sniffing the now-empty bottle, the scent was like spring lilacs instead of alcohol. As Uncle Vic's breathing steadied, and his face unknotted, Merry realized it was magic.

In moments, his eyes opened, and Merry helped him struggle into a sitting position.

"One of Old Meg's healing potions!" Merry exclaimed, examining the symbol carved on both the flask and stopper, "she asks a terrible price for these!"

Years of servitude, an unborn child, or a piece of your soul were not uncommon in stories of dealings with the ancient Witch of Gelcliff.

"That's just to scare off the village simpletons from bothering her," Uncle Vic replied, "she likes actual gold as much as any old woman."

"You're drinking the second one," Merry declared. She had never seen a gold piece, but she had never seen a wound as bad as that one before, either.

"No way! The cost of one of those is almost as painful as dragon spit," Uncle Vic exclaimed. Then with a twinge of pain, he added another, whispered, "almost."

"Fine," Merry said firmly. "If you're strong enough to keep me from pouring it down your throat, then you don't need it."

She emphasized her point with a poke to his raw side, which made him grit his teeth and gasp, "Alright!"

Merry kept her glare on him as he grudgingly took the second small flask and downed its contents.

"You're almost as bad as your mother," Uncle Vic grumbled, but his grin had returned, and his side looked noticeably better.

"I'll take that as a compliment," Merry said, a relieved smile of her own finally breaking through. "Someone has to keep *both* of you numbskull boys in line."

She gestured toward Gully, who had the crumbs of a travel cake on his face.

"I knew he'd be fine," Gully stated with confidence.

He just shrugged in response to her raised-eyebrow look, then reached beside him for something.

"Hey, check this out!" Gully held up a huge green gem in front of his face; it was almost as big as his head, and it took both his hands to hold it. "We're rich!"

Merry just stared, astonished.

Uncle Vic sighed. "Sorry, Gully, we can't keep that."

The chamber seemed to sway slightly as Perovich stood up. He waved Merry away, but she grabbed his good arm and steadied him anyway. It was a good thing since the floor seemed less firm at the moment than the deck of a sloop in a gale.

He carefully turned and faced the statue of Alaric. The acid had run down the front, leaving small marks that seemed to be fading as he watched.

"I'm a man of my word," he said quietly.

Merry looked askance, but he just flashed his best grin at her. "It'll be alright, have faith."

"Uncle Vic, are you sure you didn't hit your head when that dragon tossed you?" she asked dubiously.

A splash brought them both about in alarm; Perovich immediately regretted the sudden movement as pain shot through his side. There were only faint, dark ripples in the pool near where Gully had just been standing a moment before.

Cold fear gripped their hearts as they both stood in shock for a few quietly strained moments before Gully's grinning head popped back out of the water. He was triumphantly holding the second emerald eye.

"I knew you threw two!" he crowed. Then he set the second giant green gem on the edge of the pool next to the first, and nimbly pulled himself out of the water.

"Gully! Don't do that!" Merry scolded.

"What?" Gully asked, sincerely perplexed.

The skinny lad stood there in the lightning-spawned illumination beneath the statue, the flickering shadow of the upraised heavenly bolt falling directly on him. Perovich almost didn't recognize his nephew for a moment again. *It must be weakness from the wounds,* he thought. He had to blink twice to bring the boy back into focus.

It was just little Gully, but he could see indomitable spirit and a love of adventure reflected in Gully's blue-gray eyes. He remembered that feeling; he was only a few years older than Gully was now when he stowed away aboard a southbound freighter to join the Penwick navy.

As Gully stepped forward, Perovich also noticed a large, puckered scar running from the boy's right shoulder halfway across his chest. It looked nasty, but several weeks healed, and Perovich knew the lad didn't have that injury only a few hours ago. He had seen a ship's priests call upon spirit energy to heal wounds like that in a matter of seconds.

"What happened to you?"

"Dragon," Gully said, tracing the scar with a grin. "Not a little one like your black, but a great big fiery red one!" He stretched out the words and spread his arms wide, emphasizing the size.

Ah, the boy has the knack, Perovich thought. The only thing sailors liked better than showing off their scars was exaggerating the size of their encounters.

"I suppose that one got away?" he refrained from chuckling; it would hurt his wounded side too much.

"Dunno, I suppose it's still out there…" Gully looked up at the domed ceiling at this end of the chamber as if he could see through it. His voice had gotten quieter at the thought.

The morning sun beamed down on the land in waves of glorious heat that lesser creatures may have found discomforting. Indeed, Theria found herself the sole creature on the sparkling white sands of the beach. She suspected the others were just too cowardly to stay near the ocean.

With the oppressive miasma of the dragon shard just a flickering whisper of its former power, Theria felt a great weight lifted from her spirit. And the burning fires of anticipation lightened the normal aggravation caused by incompetent companions—or at least they were far enough away to be tolerable.

A distinct fresh mound of earth in the hill just northwest of the cove marked the spot where Berikarth had burrowed. He claimed to heal faster underground, but Theria suspected the earth-dragon just wanted to escape the blazing sun.

Just beyond the hill, if she stretched to her full height, Theria could see the odd shape of the ice dome that Irovnia had built. The frost-dragon had dammed a small stream with ice and used the water to construct an elaborate dome structure with a small core, that— Theria was sure—was hellishly-cold.

The swamp dragon, Yiglelot, hid in a pool of stagnant water in the ruined old temple just inland that he was happily fouling even more. Most of the temple roof was intact, and the interior was shadowed and cool, a fit place for a lesser dragon of Yiglelot's sort. Theria was sorely tempted to set the vine-covered walls and most of the forest beyond ablaze, just to discomfort the black-scaled coward who had been so useless in the morning encounter.

But the Dragon Master had forbade drawing excess attention from the locals, and for some reason had specifically mentioned her tendency to burn large swathes of countryside. Theria would obey for now; she was not ready to incinerate that bridge yet.

So instead of being able to properly relax in a roaring conflagration, she was stuck just soaking up as much heat as she could on this sandy strip. But even that didn't bother her too much at the moment.

So, she stood and stretched her wings lazily up and down the beach, which was too narrow to fit her full wingspan width-wise. Earlier, she had flown low, but not too low, out over the deep water near the cove. Then she had sat upon the rock at the end of the cove, hoping to tempt the bronzes back, or perhaps to prove to herself she could conquer at least that small part of the water element. But the rock was too small for comfort, with annoyingly cool water all around, and no opponents came from the sea to challenge her.

By mid-morning, she had taken to sifting through the wreckage and flotsam from the fishing boat that had gathered in an undulating mass, tide-driven against the south breakwater.

Theria found assorted junk among the debris—pieces of boat, a left sandal, a large floppy straw hat, various net-floats ridiculously carved to look like fish, and a large basket floating in the middle of it. She had a brief image of an old story about a human hero set upon the ocean in a basket as a child because of godly jealousy, who later grows up to be a great dragon slayer.

Of course, there wasn't any such tasty morsel as a human baby in this basket. Her nose told her that long before she hooked one side open with as dainty a claw movement as she could manage. The basket was still nearly rent in half. She carefully set it between two rocks on the dry end of the breakwater. Theria knew what she had to do to examine it properly, and she would save that for later.

With a rush of air and swirling sand, she took to the sky and circled the area. Some of the debris had made it out of the cove, pulled south by the current to wash on the rocky beaches nearby. She had a sudden thought and scanned the ocean down the coastline.

The ice over the cove's center hole was significantly smaller, and the icy boulder from the cove's mouth was gone. Either it had totally melted or floated away. She had no experience with ice, how long it took to melt, or how or why stupid ice dragons made the horrible cold stuff. She could ask Irovnia, but a conversation with her would likely result in nothing more than a headache.

As she flew back to the cove, Theria noticed how out of place it seemed. From the air, it was pretty clear when one looked. The cove was the only spot of pure white sand; the rest of the rock-strewn beaches in the area were darker and tan-colored. The boulders of the two near-perfect semicircular breakwaters were a light gray, and although rough-hewn, the blocks were all of a square or rectangular shape. The native rocks on the rest of the beaches were much darker, almost black in shade.

She had known it was man-made, but why haul in the special materials for an ocean breakwater? The overgrown buildings near the cove appeared to be an ancient temple complex. Theria wondered if there might be more than meets the eye underground, or even underwater. Like all dragons, the thought of treasure intrigued her. *What better way to spend the time waiting for the airship?*

She had just decided to roust Berikarth to dig around the ruins site when she noticed a dark stain on the end of the south breakwater. It was darker than even the blackened burn marks she had left.

When she approached to examine the stain, she saw a broken ink bottle atop the rock. The ink stain trailed off into a crevasse between the boulders, the line of ink ending a short way down. It seemed to point, like a dark claw, to a small book caught just above the waterline.

Theria stared at it for a moment. It was no good; any shift of these boulders would send it into the water. And it was small, even for a human tome; her dragon claws could not handle such a thing without harming it, even if she could reach into that small space.

She sighed, looked around to make sure none of the others were nearby, and closed her eyes to concentrate. Finding the proper pattern stored in her mind, she drew it out and filled it with her spirit. It was difficult with such a small container, but she persevered and felt her form shift.

She didn't know many shapes of the lesser races; in fact, this was the only one she bothered with. She had already decided that she would never take the form of one of the hated humans. An elf form may be more suitable for riding in an airship, but not as practical as a flying dragon.

Usually, it was a good thing that the clothes and gear one was last wearing in humanoid form were stored with the spirit form, and reappeared when returning to that shape. Theria had learned that it was rarely acceptable to be unclothed in humanoid societies.

On the airship, they had given up telling her how a red ball gown was not practical clothing when she pointed out how impractical the whole small, thin-skinned, humanoid form was, and how it would be better if she just remained a dragon.

Secretly, she thought that if she had to give up the most beautiful form in the world for a while, she should at least look good in the new shape.

So, she stood on the end of the breakwater as a pale, soft biped, in a beautifully red, flowing gown with black silk roses, multiple buckles, and devious catches in nearly impossible-to-reach places. Her long red hair blew in the sea breeze with her gown, and as she pushed it out of her face, she thought again how impractical it all was.

Less than a quarter-hour later, she walked across the breakwater, back to shore, victorious. The gown was shed and cast off on the rocks behind her. She wore only the thin satin underdress.

The book was now in her hand, and she was a little wiser about the limitations of the humanoid form. But if the cursed metallic dragons could handle the forms of lesser races, then by the five-headed lady, so could she!

She did wonder how the human girl had seemed to fit so easily into the crevice; was she that much slimmer than this form? Theria supposed the main problems in that narrow space were these large mammal things in the front—did humanoid young really require such quantities of milk? Also, the extra padding in the tail area didn't help, either. She wondered if she just hadn't gotten the form right, but the princess had assured her it was perfect.

As she passed the beach-end of the breakwater, she snagged the basket with one hand, the straw hat with the other, and then settled on the warm sandy beach. It was time to try the contents of both the basket and the book.

"We better get going," Uncle Vic declared. He was moving a little better, but his face still twinged with occasional pain.

"Grab my bag and those gems, then help me fix the dragon statue."

Merry thought for a brief second that Gully was going to carry Uncle Vic's bag for them; she should have known better. He snagged another travel cake, threw the gems into the bag, and then tossed the satchel to her with a grin as if he was helping.

"Gee, thanks," she muttered.

Uncle Vic had bent with a painful grimace to pick up Inazuma.

"Don't!" Merry warned.

He gave her a confused look as his hand tried to grasp the hilt. With a twitching jerk, he released it, sat down hard on his rear, and scooted a little away from the sword.

"What the…"

Gully swooped in and grabbed Inazuma before Uncle Vic could even fully raise his hand to protest. Then, in one smooth motion, he bowed to them with an exaggerated sword-flourish like they had seen Knights of the Rose do on tourney day.

"Only the chosen may grasp the Draconic Sword of Destiny!" Gully intoned in a boyish attempt at deep, dramatic tones. He then shifted into one of his improbable mock battle-stances, only this time, instead of a pretend stick-sword, he held a true blade of power.

Merry just sighed.

"Don't ask me," Inazuma said resignedly, "I don't understand him either."

"Well, huh!" was all Uncle Vic said while struggling back to his feet with a grimace.

Merry quickly grabbed his good arm again and helped him up. They then all turned and faced the statue of Alaric.

"Thank you, oh Lord of Storms, for protecting my family," Uncle Vic said solemnly, "and I humbly beseech you to continue your protection until they are safely home again."

They stood in silence a moment until a crack of lightning jumped to Inazuma's naked blade.

"Sorry," the voice of Inazuma sounded almost sheepish, "I hate to interrupt whatever rituals you humans use to channel divine spirits. I thought it best to make sure I have a full charge. And we really should go."

"Yes!" Gully exclaimed, "let's go slay that fire-dragon with my lightning sword and rescue Pa and Uncle Wex!"

"I fear you overestimate my power, dear boy," Inazuma stated. "Before the might of a dragon like Theriaxus, my best bolt would be but an annoying scratch, and you all would be charred crisps in an instant. Even if Ruka was here, it is unlikely we could face a dragon of that power."

"I wonder where she..." Merry began but was interrupted.

"Wait! Ruka! Rukastanna Greymantle?" Uncle Vic cried, grabbing Merry's shoulder with his good hand and shaking her.

"Err, yeah," she stammered out. Merry was pretty sure that was what the dragon-girl said her name was.

"Goes around as a little girl," he held his hand up a little shorter than Merry, then spread his arms wide, "but with a *huge* attitude?".

Now that she thought about it, Merry realized that Ruka, in girl-form, was shorter than her. Although her presence made her seem bigger when she was in the room.

"Where is she?"

"I don't know. She was heading back to the cove to rescue Pa and Uncle Wex," Merry said tentatively.

"Then they'll be fine," Uncle Vic declared with confidence. "We better fix that statue and hike back to town. Knowing Ruka, they'll all be waiting long before us."

"How..." Merry's thoughts stumbled a little bit, "how do you know a dragon?"

"Maybe I'll tell you later," Uncle Vic replied, "but right now I can tell you that everything will be fine."

"You better tell me!" Merry declared, "and you better be right, too!"

"Trust me," Uncle Vic just smiled and led them over to fix the dragon statue.

Princess of Misfortune
Chapter 5

The old road was rough and overgrown, but it would have been better than trekking straight through the woods like they were. Uncle Vic had insisted that they stay under tree cover, which made perfect sense with the possibility of dragons hunting in the sky. So, they traveled cautiously through the woods, keeping the old road to one side as a guide.

He seemed to be moving well, if a little gingerly, using his staff more than usual. Uncle Vic was the kind who would bemoan every little cut or sniffle but never admit to feeling pain if he was truly hurt. And that's what worried Merry.

He had crept off to scout the cove as soon as they emerged from the ruins. It was a quietly heated argument, but he convinced Merry by demonstrating that even injured, he could move with far more stealth than they could match. So, she promised to sit on Gully if necessary, to keep him in their hiding spot a good distance from the dragon hall.

He put up a good front, skulking off and vanishing silently into the brush. But the pallor of his face on returning was as much from the exertion to his injured side as from what he saw.

There were still dragons about the cove area, and no sign, one way or the other, of Pa or Uncle Wex. Remembering the lengths that the dragon-girl Ruka had gone through to save them, and Uncle Vic's strange confidence, Merry held out some small hope that they were alright, too.

Then they saw the airship.

It was a thing out of Merry's favorite stories. A huge, wooden vessel of graceful curves and fanciful superstructure, floating in the air. The ship's rigging was composed of lines of coppery metal cables with silver and black sails set more to catch sunlight than breeze. Immense bands of glowing energy coursed laterally from the ship like great ring-shaped wings, a beautiful and most obvious part of the powerful magic that allowed it to soar the skies.

Gully wanted to run into the open and signal the ship, grabbing her hand eagerly; but Uncle Vic held them both back.

"What are *they* doing here?" he hissed, pulling the two of them back under the tree line as urgently as he could with his injured shoulder.

"Who?" Gully asked.

"See that gilded dragon on the flag? That's the symbol of the royal house of Lanfor, and the dragon is rampant. That could only mean that the princess is on board."

Merry had read a great deal about Lanfor. *Tales of the Magical Kingdom* was such a heavy tome that when she was younger, old Yoseff, the lorekeeper for the Baroness' Library, had to lug it over to a reading table for her.

Village children could not take books from the hall, of course, so she spent whatever spare moments she could find amidst her many chores in that dusty hall of beloved tomes. And that book on Lanfor was one of her favorites. Most of the stories were about the royal family; they all seemed to live such glorious, exciting, or tragic lives. Usually all three.

Since the death of King Flandril Farbican the First, over three hundred years ago, there has always been a queen of Lanfor—the same queen—Queen Amerelis. She was often called the Eternal Queen, or the Usurper Queen, depending on whether you were a loyalist or a freedom fighter.

The treachery of Flandril's first wife, Mariva the Apostate, and oldest son, Welbarvik, during the War of Embers, led to Flandril's eventual death. On his deathbed, he had his most loyal and powerful lords, his second wife, Amerelis, and his war companion and mount, the golden sun dragon, Lirasanna, take sacred vows.

Flandril's dying wish was that his evil son not take the throne and that Amerelis rule as queen until one of his line who was worthy could be found. He entrusted Lirasanna to weigh the worth of the potential heir. They all took sacred oaths to uphold his wish.

The book of tales was a collection of stories on the trials, battles, and travails of Flandril's decedents, written by those both loyal to the queen and those not. And although the depiction of the queen was starkly different depending on the author, it was clear to Merry that the royal family was at best terribly conflicted, and at worst a bunch of backstabbing scoundrels.

If this was a royal airship, then it could only belong to Princess Anyabarithia, the only known survivor of the purge called the War of the Eternal Queen. It was a brutal conflict of familial genocide where the revolutionaries believed that if they could just kill off *all* the descendants of Flandril, the queen and her dragon would have to give up their vows and abdicate.

The book was too old to have stories of this latest princess, but it had several about the adventures of her mother, Shandillis. Shandi was depicted as a good person, and in the stories, one of her dearest friends, Ves, turned out to be a storm dragon. Merry now had firsthand experience that that particular story might be true. Storm dragons could both be friendly, and disguise themselves as people.

"I bet they're hunting dragons," Gully declared. "We could help them."

"I don't know," Vic replied, but his tone indicated that he did know and would brook no argument. "I've heard stories about that one."

"Stories that you would be well-advised to believe." Inazuma's voice sounded muffled from within the tight bundle of Vic's heavy cloak that Gully was carrying. "My Lady Ruka and I were summoned to help rescue her sister from princess Anya's diabolical clutches.

Sadly, it was a classic case of a beautiful dragon kidnapped by an evil princess, just like in the old tales."

Merry didn't know what stories the ancient sword was talking about; most of the tales she had read were the opposite. She supposed that maybe dragon stories had a different perspective. And she made a mental note to ask Inazuma to recite some when they had a break in which he could be unbound from the cloak.

It took the sword himself to convince Gully to keep him wrapped. They had no sheath with them, and the slightest glint of sunlight off the polished bronze of his blade could give away their location to airborne dragons.

Merry had suggested that she could carry the unwieldy bundle of the sword for him once it was bundled, and she offered Gully his club back. He declined, uncharacteristically solemn, saying the sword was his burden to carry, and the 'magic stick' was hers. She laughed at that, assuring him it was just a piece of driftwood. Yet she still carried it around with her.

"What kind of stories?" Gully asked the sword.

"Not now," Uncle Vic stated, "and regardless, it's best if we don't get noticed by ones of such lofty station. It never ends well."

Merry supposed he was right. She was used to the gentle and nurturing care that the Lady Gracelynn displayed to all her subjects—or even the late Baron Gryswold—whose stern, ironclad rules applied to himself and his officers as equally as his subjects.

But she knew from her reading that was not the norm for nobility, let alone royalty. And this was royalty from another country. Her family would be less than nothing to the likes of them. The best they could hope for was to be ignored, and the worst was not worth thinking about. Some of the stories of the royal family implied things better off not imagined.

The ship passed close overhead, and although they couldn't see it through the leaves at that angle, they could hear the hum of the energy bands, and Merry was suddenly certain she could feel it, too. Not a vibration per se, but she could feel the energy of the great ship somehow, and it wasn't right. She envisioned it as a huge beast that she knew had become ill.

"I think they're in some kind of trouble," Merry said quietly to herself.

"One of their emitter crystals is missing, and some of the others are a half-turn out of alignment," a woman's voice spoke from the shadows of a tree limb above them, where she casually sat.

All three of them gaped and stared at the young woman. They had not seen her when they crept from the sun into the dense shade of these branches.

"This is a good tree to hide under if you don't want to be seen from above," the woman stated while climbing nimbly down from one of the wide branches. "I guess we are fellow travelers who wish to avoid any 'royal' pains."

Upon reaching the ground, the woman faced the three of them with a smile. She wore a knee-length dress of red and black with pale, faintly shimmering, yellow stars. Her ample bosom was wrapped in black, but her midriff was bare. The scandalous outfit looked like something a Rover might wear. During the recent birthday extravaganza for the Baron's daughter, a large group of those travelling entertainers had visited their village. They had set up a small street of wagons, tents, and stands. And this woman looked familiar to Merry like she had seen her at one of those tents.

"The fortune-teller!" Merry gasped.

"Misfortune teller is more like it," Uncle Vic groaned.

There was the whisk of steel death through the air, followed by a clash and groan of old metal as the blade stopped inches from Wexel's throat and hung there unmoving. Worn and pitted by age and spotted with what looked like dried blood, it would have taken his head clean off if it had struck. Off-balance and shocked, he fell back on his rear, looking up at near-death.

The small lizard-creature that Ruka called Ratnosk held a short metal rod jammed into some mechanism in the floor. The creature strained against it for a few moments more, then released it. The blade continued its arc into the wall with a snick that sounded sinister to Wexel.

Ratnosk threw himself prone in front of Ruka, his high-pitched jabbering language shriller and more panicked than normal. He went on for a painful half-minute before Ruka's raised hand and sharp word silenced him. The strange creature stopped immediately and just lay there like a limp rag doll.

She turned to Wexel and simply said, "He says he's sorry."

Even after seeing the transformation, it was still hard to believe this skinny young girl was a storm dragon. That was until you saw her eyes. It could have been his imagination, but Wexel definitely felt there was the hint of a distant tempest there.

"He also says that is the last of them," Ruka looked accusingly at Ratnosk as she said it, then barked a few words in the guttural language of dragons. The creature supplicated itself even more vigorously, squeaking assent.

"Better be," he heard her mutter to herself.

"Wait here," she instructed Wexel and Hevik, "We'll do this the dragon way." Then she turned and stomped down the rest of the deadly corridor, alternating one side then the other, and slapping the walls with her palms.

Ratnosk watched in obvious terror from where he crouched on the floor. And Wexel couldn't help also cringing in anticipation of another of those cruel blades snapping forth to split her slender young form in twain.

But he knew better, he knew those burns on her back were from a conflagration that would have fried a normal person to ash. If this form of hers shared her wounds, then maybe it also shared her draconic durability regardless of her appearance. At least she seemed to believe that.

Hevik only watched numbly from a few steps behind, holding the glowing piece of driftwood that Ruka had given them for light. He still seemed to be in shock from the day's events. *Do you think we died at that cove and are just doomed to wander in purgatory?* Hevik had asked. He had nodded to Wexel's denial of that possibility but hadn't seemed convinced.

If this was purgatory, they certainly had a strange guide. And it had been an interminably long trip here through tight, dark, and winding tunnels. It was enough to sap the spirit of any man.

Ruka reached the end of the corridor without any more blades springing forth. She turned, nodding with a slight smile at Ratnosk.

"I guess he was right," she said brightly, "there were no more tr— Ahh!"

And with that, the floor opened up and the dragon girl plummeted from sight.

When the grand airship of the princess of Lanfor finally appeared on the horizon, Theria waited on the beach, once again herself—beautiful, powerful, and crimson-scaled.

She could hardly wait to see Scorch. There were so many new stories to tell him—of battles with devious and dangerous storm dragons, antics of stupid ice dragons, and the power of a heart of fire that can prevail against anything. But there were also other stories she now had to tell.

The basket was left on the beach, most of the honey rolls and jam still packed carefully in water-resistant cloth. Theria decided she really didn't like sweets. All the fish cakes were gone; they were surprisingly good.

The book was back at the end of the breakwater, still hidden in the little crevice, but higher, easier to reach, and safer from the danger of the tide.

She secretly placed her magical mark upon the book. It was an old fire dragon spell, used to track especially prized items from ones' hoard, and the bane of many a would-be thief. With it, Theria was sure she could locate that book again, and perhaps, if she still lived, the girl who owned it. Her name, 'Meriwynn Fichgotz,' was boldly written on the first page. And the scent on the book clearly marked her as the same girl with the desperate bravery and fervent eyes.

There had been at least four humans in this cove who had simply vanished; the storm dragons had obviously taken them. And she doubted it was to eat them—they were notoriously fond of the invasive pests. After all, they were the dragonkin who had unfortunately invited the scourge of mankind in to plague this world.

She told herself the marked book was all part of a clever ruse to capture the storm dragons or their allies on land. But maybe, just maybe, some secret part of her wanted more stories.

Long before the shadow of the airship fell across the cove, Theria could feel the difference was more than just a weakening of the dragon shard. At this range, she could see the slight flickering of the elemental bands of energy that wrapped the flying ship. Something had happened—not just to the shard—but to the whole ship. The spirit of the ship itself was wrong, she could feel it in her spines.

As the airship slowed to a less-than-graceful descent over the cove, both Irovnia and Berikarth alighted on the deck at the princess' first call. Perhaps they were fearful of punishment for failure. Such trivial things as the pain of punishment were nothing to a true heart of fire—and fear was nonexistent.

The ship settled into the water outside the cove. Landing like that was not something they did often, and certainly not something they would do when in pursuit of prey. The ship, and therefore the princess, was in some discomfort, a fact that Theria felt like savoring for a brief time.

So even without the weakening of the crystal-fueled miasma, Theria would have waited until the last moment she could to answer the summons. She always did; she always tested the limits of that feeble magic. She always knew she could break it, and as always, it was little Scorch she stayed for.

When she finally and casually made her way to the ship, Theria purposely landed on the edge of the deck in her true form, settling in a pleasant little burn-mark a disgruntled wizard had left there the previous night. It was a tribute to the size and power of the ship that it only tilted slightly at her weight.

The fact that her presence was barely acknowledged surprised her and Theria gazed at the frantic confusion on the ship in growing irritation. Not only didn't Princess Anya accost her for a tardy return, but she actually wore one of her false smiles when she finally strode up. And the princess was not wearing one of her usual skin-revealing outfits, but a baggy gold robe and a high-peaked amber hat.

"I'm glad you're okay," Anya breathlessly exclaimed, as if they hadn't seen her lounging on the beach for the last ten minutes.

The princess' outward appearance, as always, was perfect—all happy smiles and sincerity. But Theria could smell the anxiety and near-panic under the surface. And it was clear as day in her pet wizard, Sigfus, ever close and protective next to his princess.

More than that, she could sense at least three powerful enchantments held around the wizard; he was prepared and trigger-ready to go off. She discreetly scanned the deck, noting the archer Oripeah leaning on the forecastle rail. She had one of her black slayer arrows out as if they would hurt a dragon of Theria's power. Delandria, the spiritblade warrior, stood near on the other side of Theria, her hands on the hilts of her insignificant swords.

She almost laughed; they were finally taking her seriously. A good laugh would have nicely fried the deck of this ship more effectively than some sad little burst of wizard-fire. Instead, she just grinned; she knew humans were unnerved by that. Seeing dragon-teeth exposed rightfully made them aware of their puny stature.

They knew she could now easily break the fragile hold the baleful shard had placed upon her. What was funny was that they didn't realize she could have all along. Once the true Dragon Master had left her here, there was only one thing that kept her playing this farce.

"Where is Scorch?" Theria asked with forced calmness.

The mind of her precious little one was firmly snared by the foul magic of the dragon shard. But maybe now she could break it free.

"Out scouting," the princess waved dismissively. Theria nearly snapped the fool's hand off right there for that attitude, but it was too early to be sure she could free Scorch.

"We have bigger problems," Anya went on. "Not all of our guests jumped off the ship last night. One stayed behind and has sabotaged…" She paused for only a fraction of a second before plunging ahead with, "some minor ship components."

Did she hope that Theria didn't yet know of the shard's weakening? Maybe the others, so accepting of being the princess' slaves, but not her. She knew the strength of every inch of her magical prison and probed it constantly.

Berikarth was still too weak from his recent near-drowning, Irovnia was an idiot, and Yiglelot, the sniveling coward, had serendipitously picked the right time to run off. The rest were too young and inexperienced, barely more than wyrmlings. All except Mallona.

Where was Mallona? The foolish traitor to the Way of Fire was always heeling at her mistress' side, the perfect pampered pet. She claimed to be Anya's friend—as if such a thing could ever be between a true heir of flame and a mere human.

Mallona even claimed that the princess did not subject her to regular exposure to the fell shard. At first, Theria thought her clever for that—a brilliant fire-dragon ruse—the trusting princess would be easy prey. But Mallona stayed devoted after repeated opportunities. Sadly, she was just as insane as her human mistress.

But why wasn't she here now? Had she finally come to her senses? No, if that were possible, then Anya would be dead.

"Where is Mallona?" Theria asked suspiciously, suspecting the answer.

"I sent her on an errand," Anya replied, her eyes shifting in that subtle way that spoke volumes.

Theria's spines began to tingle, and suddenly it all made sense. The shard was damaged, and the princess and her pet were inseparable in their petty evils. Anya would never send Mallona away. Not unless… *he* was coming!

She attempted to launch herself from the deck in that instant, but every inch of her powerful frame just quivered in the attempt and failed. The sudden spirit force that held her down was steeped in all-too-familiar dread and despair.

The Dragon Thrall Lord was here.

"I'm Elistra," the fortune-teller introduced herself, her smile widening. "What luck, finding a brave group of heroes out here. I am in sore need of assistance."

"Of course, milady," Gully sprang forward, beaming at her eagerly.

"Nothing you do is *luck*," Uncle Vic stated, eyeing the woman suspiciously. "And we are *not* heroes, and have no desire to be."

"The small heroics of helping each other in need is often the most valuable," Elistra replied, smiling at Merry and Gully. Then looking at Uncle Vic, she added, "I am glad to see you are well, Perovich."

Uncle Vic looked sardonically down at his injured side and burnt shoulder, then looked pointedly back at Elistra.

"Well, considering the circumstances," Elistra amended.

"Well enough," Uncle Vic agreed, and then added, "Are you going to tell me another fate of death and dark treasures?"

The smile faded from Elistra's face, and her strange eyes took on a vague, unfocused look. Those eyes were of a deep, violet shade, and looking closely, there seemed to be light flecks, like the first stars of an evening sky when the sun's faint, ruddy glow has not yet fully vanished.

"Death lies at the end of every man's path if you look far enough," she intoned calmly, "and it lurks around each corner for the bold like you. But your path may bring you face to face soon. If you look upon the beautiful face of death, know that you cannot cheat it. To win out, you must truly court it with your whole heart."

Merry saw a rare serious expression cross Uncle Vic's normally lighthearted face. It was a look she had not seen too often. She remembered him in her earliest memories more as an irreverent older brother, as he was closer in age to her than to Pa. Indeed, Ma and Pa had raised him after the rest of the family had died in the Desolation of Ravenford before she was born. Shortly after Gully was born, Uncle Vic left home to earn his fortune. It was many years later, but he made good.

According to Uncle Vic, what he brought back to Ravenford was barely a sliver of the fortune he briefly had. Of course, he normally exaggerated like a true sailor. But his reluctance to actually tell the tale made Merry think it must be true. All she could get out of him was that he lost a vast fortune due to a woman that he only referred to as 'The Jinx.' From the way he moped after speaking of it, she felt he also may have lost a piece of his heart with the gold.

But the wealth he did bring back, as much as he trivialized it, might as well have been a fortune to the Fichgotz. It allowed the family to purchase their own boat and to work for themselves, instead of toiling for others. And Merry knew that he was singly responsible for her having the luxury to spend so much time studying and learning like a well-to-do merchant's daughter, instead of a poor, working fishmonger girl.

The yarns that Uncle Vic would tell with a grin about the finding of his fortune were wild and usually littered with bad jokes leading to a worse punchline. But the few times when Merry felt he waxed almost serious; the tale always started with a portend of 'dark treasures' given by a fortune teller. But this couldn't be that seer; Elistra looked too young, barely older than Uncle Vic himself.

The silence after the fortune teller's cryptic declaration stretched on just a beat too long. Then Uncle Vic's grinning mask slipped back across his face when he saw Merry watching him closely.

"Wow! Even for you, that was one huge pile of stinking cow dung," he scoffed at Elistra.

"Yes," Elistra replied, her smile also returning, "it sounded just like the usual tired platitude to 'choose love over hate.' A professional hazard, I'm afraid."

"Well, since you've probably already foreseen that we will say yes," Uncle Vic's smile gleamed almost genuine at this point, "what is this favor that you need from us?"

"At the top of that ridge," Elistra pointed up the steep wooded slope south of the road, "is a cliff overlooking the sea."

She took out a light blue crystal, about fist-sized and cut with a dozen pentagon-shaped sides. Complex runic symbols were engraved within a pentagram on each side. The symbols seemed to be within the crystal, rather than on the surface. And looking at them, she also imagined invisible parts of them projecting above the crystal face.

"I want you to throw this into the ocean," Elistra said.

"My throwing arm is not good at the moment, I'm afraid," Uncle Vic gingerly rotated his burnt shoulder with a grimace.

"It shouldn't be a problem."

Elistra tossed the crystal upward, causing it to glow brightly, hang in the air for a moment, and then float slowly back down to her hand.

Merry felt mesmerized by the crystal. As it floated down, she envisioned lines of energy emanating from it. One straight down to the earth, one as a circular halo spinning at the top, and two more formed wing-like arcs at the sides. Her imagination must have been running away with her. She also fancied she heard faint singing words in her head as if the crystal itself were chanting some of those unknown runes.

She knew she hadn't seen those lines with her eyes, or heard the words with her ears, but she was certain they had been there nonetheless. Merry also felt sure that the crystal only fell back down because no one told it otherwise.

"Oh, let me throw it!" Gully called while grabbing for the crystal.

Without even realizing she was doing it, Merry found herself snatching the crystal out of Elistra's open palm before Gully could. Then when he rounded on her, thinking it was a game, she fended him off with her stick. For effect, she caused the bulbous end of the driftwood club to flare with light.

She was surprised how easy it was to light with just a flicker of thought now. The pattern was there already, just waiting for her to ignite it. The runic symbols for light had been almost seared into the wood's spirit by casual dragon magic—spirit magic of a power that echoed through the soul of the wood, even this long after that first light faded.

It had taken tremendous concentration to find that pattern at first. Searching desperately in that dark cavern for the runic patterns of light on the wood that Inazuma showed her, she had found a way to focus differently. It helped then that her regular sight was blinded, that absolute dark helped her imagine the symbols.

But that 'imagined' light symbol worked. It wasn't any more her imagination than the lines of force from the crystal. Merry realized now that she had been half-blind before. Seeing that crystal confirmed it. She had found a different kind of sight. And now she couldn't turn it off if she tried.

Gully took up the challenge for possession of the crystal with his normal competitive glee. His smile widening with more joyful anticipation than wickedness, he began to unwrap Inazuma. At first touch of the sword's hilt beneath the wrappings, his wild hair began to stir with static energy.

Uncle Vic was quick to step between them.

"Put out the glow-stick, Merry," he said, looking at her a little puzzled. He caught her eye briefly with a dozen unasked questions, then he turned to Gully.

"You can throw it," he said firmly, "*when* we get there."

"He's got the best arm," Uncle Vic pointed out to Merry, "the broken windows facing the riverside of old Higgs warehouse prove it."

"That wasn't me!" Gully said automatically.

"Of course not, but you have to admit that *all* the way across the river was a wicked throw."

"Yeah, it was," Gully smiled sheepishly, with his hand to the back of his head in mock embarrassment.

"But Merry gets to carry it up there, and no zapping your sister until we get there."

"What do you mean 'until we get there'?" Merry asked, worried by the conspiratorial grins shared by her impish brother and irresponsible uncle.

"Heh, heh," Gully chuckled, eyeing her evilly. "When you least expect it!"

She looked desperately at Elistra, as the one other possibly responsible adult with her. It was a long shot.

Ignoring the two perpetually childish boys, Elistra stepped up to Merry.

"There is too much here, and not enough time," she said, indicating the patterns in the crystal. "Many men have spent years trying to follow just one of the greater patterns, only to fail."

Merry already knew the crystal was beyond her understanding. But for some reason, it still hurt to hear it said.

Elistra only smiled at her and gently turned the crystal in her hand.

"This is the one to focus on," she pointed to one of the simplest patterns, with only a few dozen twists. "Ignore the rest."

"I don't have my book," Merry said sadly. She so wanted to try and copy that symbol. Although how she could do it with just two-dimensional paper anyway was lost on her.

"Books are crutches for wizards—*you* don't need them. So, don't try to analyze or memorize it, just follow it and feel its magic and purpose," Elistra said, looking at her meaningfully. "It will come in useful; I guarantee it."

"What does it do?"

"Don't be distracted by desires for effect, they'll misdirect you. Focus on just the pattern. When you learn it, you'll know."

"Don't get us caught up in your mystic mumbo," Vic declared. "The Fichgotz are just simple fisherfolk."

He looked accusingly at Merry when he said it.

"It might help," Elistra said, ignoring Vic and smiling at Merry, "if you *asked* the crystal to fly higher and longer. The further out to sea it goes, the better."

"Why throw it away at all?" Uncle Vic asked, stepping up between Elistra and Merry like he was trying to protect her. "Why don't we just sell it?"

Or keep it! Merry thought eagerly.

"Once they realize it's missing, they'll be able to track it using its mates. We want it far out to sea, to draw the airship and dragons away from the coast and your family."

"Whoa! The deal's off!" Uncle Vic cut her off vehemently. "I knew you were setting us up! We want nothing to do with you or your cursed crystal. Throw the damnable thing in the sea yourself."

"That would be a path of inevitable doom," Elistra said. "My presence is a far greater and more imminent draw of danger than the crystal."

"I would have just dropped it in a pond a while back, but I thought I might bump into you here, and this is the best chance I saw to save you." She gestured to all of them when she said it.

"So, you foresaw us being here?" Uncle Vic asked suspiciously, "What are you hiding now? What do we need saving from, if not your plots? What else do you know of our fate?"

"There is no fate." She said that firmly like an axiom. "I see far too many threads to follow them all—everything is constantly changing, and I see nothing for certain. For every possibility that brought you here, there were six more where you ended up in the belly of a dragon. But I believe you are most likely safe now if you *don't* dally, you take the crystal to the cliff, and you throw it *far.*"

"For me, on the other hand," Elistra seemed to look inward for a second, and shuddered, "the possibilities of my doom multiply by the minute and threaten to spill over to you. I must go very soon!"

"We'll take the crystal," Merry said, clutching it to her chest.

"We already gave our word," Gully declared, "and heroes don't go back on their word!" He looked at Uncle Vic, daring him to disagree.

"Not heroes," he muttered grudgingly. Then he shook his head and slapped his grin back on. "Okay, we throw it, but we don't have the magic to make it fly."

"Of course, all you really need is a good arm." Elistra grinned at Gully, "A simple task for a hero of Sir Gulhawk's mettle."

It occurred to Merry that they hadn't told her their names. Elistra obviously knew Uncle Vic, but how did she know Gully? And did this fortune teller see anything about her?

As if sensing her thoughts, Elistra turned once more to Merry and addressed her by name.

"Meriwynn, you have been touched by dragon magic today. And it has awoken your own sorcery. The only way to master it is to trust yourself," she paused, staring into Merry's eyes searchingly for a moment. "It's a leap of faith. I hope you take it."

Elistra started away from them, but then turned back for a second and called to all of them, "When you reach the top, follow the lover's gaze. If luck is with you, you will spy that which your heart desires."

Elistra began to run, her hands held strangely apart in front of her, and Merry imagined a silvery glob of energy growing between them. A moment later, the globular mass silently exploded outward into a giant glittery, translucent hummingbird that she leaped upon, and rode quickly away.

"What a beautiful bird," Merry whispered.

"What bird?" Gully asked, perplexed.

Uncle Vic said, "All I saw was the crazy seeress-witch flying away."

"Oh, just my *imagination* I guess," Merry said, smiling to herself.

Dragon Masters
Chapter 6

Wexel nervously sidled his way along the narrow stone ledge between the wall and the pit edge. He couldn't see the bottom, but he did clearly see the deep scrapes in the stone that marked where an enraged storm dragon had just clawed her way out. He then climbed over the broken rocks that were the remnants of a heavy stone slab that had blocked the end of the corridor moments before.

Ruka stood just inside the room, in girl form again, with her arms crossed, vainly trying to conceal her impatience as she watched Wexel and Hevik make their way to her. She was smiling at them in a way that Hevik could only assume was supposed to be friendly and reassuring. Even if he hadn't just seen her as a lightning-enveloped creature of rage incarnate shattering stone, he didn't think she could pull that off. She certainly seemed to be trying to assuage their fears, but even as a girl, there was just too much of the predator in her gaze and stance. The small lizardman supplicating at her feet didn't help her benign image much.

"It turns out," Ruka attempted to maintain her reassuring smile as she spoke, which only turned it into a creepy grimace, "that there was an easier way in."

She pointed to a small opening near the top of the far wall that let in daylight. That wall seemed made of jumbled, loose stones, held up by two great beams of wood stretching up nearly fifty feet high to the ceiling of the towering chamber. The narrow sliver of afternoon light streaming in made the room bright compared to their shadowy trek here.

"I think," Ruka said, an edge of ire creeping back into her voice as she looked down at the cowering Ratnosk, "that he didn't want to take us around outside; he claims this way was safer than the cliffs. I believe he just dislikes daylight that much."

"But he did deliver," Ruka admitted, waving expansively at the small ship that dominated most of the room.

The ship had a pair of small lanteen masts, with old sails still furled around them. The sight of the boat and the faint sound of waves outside brightened his spirit a little—until he noticed the chamber's other contents and purpose.

"It's a tomb!" Wexel gasped.

"Of course, what'd you think? People just hole their boats up for later generations?"

Ruka looked around speculatively, then went on. "You'd be surprised what crazy stuff kings and nobles want to be buried with."

"You raid tombs?" Wexel couldn't keep the accusatory tone from his voice.

"Sure," Ruka just shrugged, unoffended, "but I think someone has already beat us to this one."

Broken chests, shattered pottery, and what looked like a partial wardrobe flung unto the mast arm, hinted at a thorough looting. But the most damning evidence was the remains of a shattered sarcophagus mixed with scattered bones. The sarcophagus had apparently been pushed off a platform on the center deck of the boat.

The boat itself sat raised on a pair of beams as heavy as tree trunks. The boat-support beams were of a kind with the outer wall supports and ran right up to them. A pair of heavy chains hung from the shadows of the ceiling and lay in a loose pile on the floor with the ends attached to the aft side of the boat-support. *Probably how they got the craft into this tomb,* Wexel mused.

Ruka turned over the top half of the broken sarcophagus lid, and carved there in stunning detail were the head and flowing hair of a woman. But the nose had shattered when it hit the stone floor, giving a skull-like cast to what would otherwise have been a beatific visage.

"Hmm? Anyone you know?" Ruka asked, effortlessly holding the heavy stone carving up for them to inspect.

Both Hevik and Wexel shook their heads in silent negation.

Ruka propped the half-lid up against a wall, bowed briefly to the relief.

"I humbly request the use of your boat to assist these poor fishermen in their hour of need. If you grant us this, then they shall forever honor the name of… err…"

Ruka glanced around at the shattered remains of the sarcophagus for a moment until finding what she was looking for, then finished brightly, "Lady Magdeena."

They all stood quietly for a few moments, looking at each other.

"Well then, I guess we are good here," Ruka said, with a faint and somewhat condescending smile at Wexel.

Her smile vanished when the deep rumbling began. Wexel hunkered down near the edge of the boat as the chamber began to shake.

"Earthquake!" he shouted.

Hevik didn't react, he stood calmly in the open as dust and pebbles began to rain down. He was staring at the carved image of the Lady Magdeena with a bemused look. Wexel hadn't noticed before, but in the dim light, it looked like the stone face was smiling. And with the shaking, it appeared to be barely suppressing a laugh.

Miraculously, no large stones fell from the ceiling to strike the boat, Wexel, Hevik, or their strange allies. In fact, the entire room remained mostly undamaged by the brief but violent shaking, with the exception of the back wall.

The loose stones shifted, first with a deep rumble of warning, then seemed to explode outward from the room in a tumbling avalanche. The two great beams were set in a huge, solid block of stone at the top. Suddenly, without any other support, the heavy stone fell outward like a great two-hafted stone hammer. The beam bottoms were caught, and the whole thing swung as if hinged.

Heavy chains attached to the sides of the wide stone did not slow the fall. The chains were being pulled noisily through some mechanism in the ceiling. The other ends, attached to the aft side of the boat-supports, were rapidly pulling up the piled slack.

Wexel looked at Ruka, who looked back, realization hitting them both at the same time.

"In the boat!" Ruka yelled, one-handedly lobbing the squealing Ratnosk through the air to land on the deck.

Wexel was already scrambling over the taffrail. Hevik followed with a much gentler push from behind by Ruka; he still cleared the railing by a foot and landed on top of Wexel.

Ruka had only one hand on the rail when the chains ran out of slack and yanked the backends of the boat support beams toward the ceiling. The boat and its yelling occupants shot upward.

The front of the boat-supports were hinged like the wall beams, and apparently had a locking point where they stopped. That happened a split second after the great splashing thud outside signaled the huge block striking through water to bedrock.

Boat and passengers did not stop their ascent as quickly. The boat flew up another half-foot and its passengers soared upward twice that, seeming to float for a brief instant before the spirit of earth once more asserted its pull.

Somehow Ruka used that brief moment to vault over the rail and land nimbly on the deck, almost casually keeping the two men from striking their heads, as they all came down with a crash.

The boat hit the now steep-angled beams with a bone-jarring crack that loosened the furled sails. And the boat began sliding downward, gathering speed.

Wexel was sure he heard a girl laughing. He looked with alarm at the stone relief of Lady Magdeena as they sped from the tomb. Then he realized the laughing was from Ruka.

The dragon-girl whooped as the boat accelerated down the wood beams and hit the water with a tremendous splash that covered them all with spray.

"Alright! *That* was amazing!" Ruka declared. Smiling brightly, she seemed more like a young girl than she had since assuming that form.

"It's a shame we can't do it again," she waved back at the plunge of doom.

Wexel just groaned a little as he pulled himself upright. The 'meep' sound from Ratnosk indicated that he felt the same way the men did about it.

Ruka practically danced across the deck, loosening a sheet line and trying to get the old sail-cloth into position. It was the first he saw her struggle with anything. Wexel came over and tentatively tried to demonstrate, but Ruka just grinned wider and handed him the rope.

As he and Hevik set the sails with the wordless precision of a near-lifetime working together on boats, the two men finally began to feel the world right itself somewhat. With ship and wave under them and rope in hand, they felt just a tiny speck of control return to their lives.

Ruka made her way to the aft rail, staring at the open tomb mouth.

"Lady Magdeena, our most heartfelt thanks for your generous gift!" she called out in a voice unnaturally loud for her small form. "If there is anything that we can do to honor your name, send us a sign and I vow it to be done."

A sudden wind came up, and the one remaining garment that had been caught in the rigging blew free and wrapped itself around Ruka's shoulders.

She held up a pretty white sundress with frills, lace, and yellow flowers on the bodice. Then she eyed the tomb and declared firmly, "Oh no, not my style!"

A distant rumble and small cloud of dust signaled the old tomb collapsing in the distance.

"Oh, all right, but I'll look ridiculous."

Just stepping through an amber glowing portal-ring was a golden-haired young man flanked by the dreadful sight of the hulking figure in ebony armor that still haunted Theria's mind. She was frozen like some weak prey-animal once more in presence of the Dragon Master.

"Theramon?" Anya asked tentatively, staring with a faint frown at the young man.

"Yes," the young man replied, "I thought I'd slip into a skin more suitable to some of my current endeavors." He spun about like a boy displaying a new favorite shirt.

"The wise-old-sage skin was necessary for you to believe in me at first, but I think our friendship has passed beyond that now, don't you agree?"

"Of course," Anya replied.

The young man had violet-shaded eyes, strangely vibrant and disturbingly familiar at the same time. Theria felt she should know this human, but whenever her thoughts tried to focus on him, they skidded away in a cloud of confusion. Each time, she ended up with just an image of Scorch for some reason. What did this strange man have to do with her little one?

Other than a small shift of that faint red glow emanating from the visor slit of his full helm, the Dragon Master stood still and silent. His one gauntlet was raised slightly palm-up, fingers bent as if he was gripping something. And indeed, Theria felt the force that held her like a titanic hand.

"You've succeeded in restoring *him*?" Anya asked, glancing nervously at the dark armored form.

"Urekar is still not fully awakened yet. I have enkindled more shards of the spirit clinging to his armor with the power of an elder orb. We just need a real spark to ignite his glorious return. I left the key to that with you, but now I fear she is no longer on this ship."

Theramon still spoke calmly, standing there smiling pleasantly, but there was an ice to his presence that was chilling.

"A minor setback," Anya blustered, trying to maintain her normal aura of arrogant command. "She was broken; we will recapture her shortly."

"Broke? Who told you that? Your foolish dabbler?"

The wizard Sigfus bridled as Theramon's disdainful gaze was cast in his direction. He made a move to retort, but the princess' hand stopped him.

"I told you, our lost prize has more layers than that. No, I'm afraid you failed. But it is not all lost. As valuable a pawn as the young dragon was in this endeavor, a far more crucial piece in the grand game was forced to expose herself in the rescue.

Theria strained on the invisible bonds that held her, but although this disturbing young human and the princess were ignoring her, the Dragon Master's attention had never wavered.

Theramon went on, almost more to himself than to the princess. "I can sense my sister's power at work on this ship. There are few who could sabotage the ancient Aerde Crystals so subtly that you would not notice until miles away."

"Who?" Anya asked sharply.

"No one you need to concern yourself with," he said, still seemingly musing to himself. "A near-perfect precog is a difficult opponent to pin down. You must make sure that all outcomes lead to your eventual victory, but that is a longer game than this."

"And you have more pressing challenges to deal with," Theramon went on, looking out over the ocean waters. "You have at best two days before your escaped dragon reaches the Queen."

"To great-grandmother?" Anya asked, a slight glimmer of outward nervousness starting to peek through her confident shell.

"You are missing quite a few greats," Theramon pointed out with cold amusement. "You of all people know the Eternal Queen Amerelis is more than she seems. If you ever want to be queen yourself, you need to get better at following my advice, Your Highness."

"This is just a minor setback," Anya said, gesturing toward Theria. "We can use another as a key to awaken him."

So that was why Mallona wasn't here!

Hearts of fire know no fear, but they know burning rage. They know revenge. Theria would use that rage to break the bonds that held her, if only for an instant. That is all it would take to snuff the life from this foul woman and her abhorrent ally. Perhaps the Dragon Master would slay her then, but it wouldn't matter.

Theramon sighed quietly and gave an almost imperceptible nod. The black gauntlet of the Dragon Master closed into a fist, and Theria's body fell to the deck with a resounding thud. Her breathing failed in her crushed chest; her heart-fire suffocated to a mere fading ember. Through the white failing of her sight, she saw Theramon step forward, and over the ringing in her ears she faintly heard his voice.

"This one has no value," he said, somehow looking down on her from his small stature like an insect he was considering if it was worth the effort to crush.

"She's still a valuable asset to my forces," Anya stepped forward nervously.

"Your forces?" Theramon turned his cold, superior smile toward the princess. "Do you really believe you could ever truly control her with just your power and the shard? The only thing that's held this one in check is an aberrant flaw in her psyche that causes actual devotion for her offspring. I found it fascinating how a fire dragon could have such a deficiency as maternal instinct. Completely unique, in an otherwise total spirit of destruction. That is why I restored her spawn to her and brought her here. But now," Theramon turned his head to Anya with a look of mock sympathy, "you've sent that little wyrm to its death in a vain attempt to spy on your escaped guests."

A veil of deep crimson descended on the world. The deck groaned, and the heat-blackened wood splintered with Theria's titanic efforts to launch herself at these foul creatures. She could see the armored form of the dark master shift its stance, its arm quivering slightly with the first signs of effort to hold her. She redoubled her struggle, forcing her head up a small margin from the deck.

Anya backed nervously away, her sycophants forming up around her. But Theramon just looked back and forth between her and the Dragon Master with calm interest.

"Maybe some small value in a test," Theramon said to himself, then turned to Theria with his piercing violet eyes. Something in that look made the flames of Theria's heart flicker with dread. He was only a fang's length from her quivering jaws, his skin beginning to flush from the heat. But his cruel smile was unwavering and his cold eyes showed no signs of fear.

"The story will be told how the vile little wyrm was cleverly ambushed by the brave and noble spiritblade, his powerful blades cutting through the young flesh in an instant. And before it could cry more than once for its fiendish mother, it was gone. Good cheer was passed all around, with comrades patting each other on the back at vanquishing the beast before it could ever grow into a threat."

Scorch! She stopped her struggle for a moment and reached out for the eldritch mark she had lovingly placed on him. He was nowhere. Gone! Even dead, she should be able to track his body by that mark.

"Such fine, bright crimson scales the little one had," Theramon went on, no amusement left in his tone, just pure cold calculation as he watched Theria closely. "The heroes stuffed the carcass gleefully in their portal-bag next to their trinkets and turnips.

Theria grew still, her anger growing first cold, then into an inexplicably quiet inferno. But instead of releasing it, she held it in and let the fire build in pressure.

"The hide of dragon-young is the best for human footwear, you know. What better use for the remains of such an ignoble creature than on the prancing feet of a bard on stage. The scaled hide of the creature forevermore part of a motley uniform for the entertainment of jeering humans."

Theramon began walking away, nodding slightly to the dark form of the Dragon Master as he passed. He then turned and continued. "Such is the way of *heroes*; those brave valiant souls so lauded in song. Heroes like those who hunted and slew your parents, and like these current heroes, the so-called Heroes of Ravenford!"

Theria erupted in a fiery explosion as her soul burst with her anger and sorrow.

Uncle Vic was clearly more than just skeptical of the fortune teller. His distrust of her was deep and personal. And Merry thought she saw an occasional haunted expression on his face when he thought she wasn't looking. What had happened to him all those years ago as a result of some dark prophecy Elistra gave?

So, he had them hustle up that steep hill at a frantic, driven pace. In spite of his burned shoulder and the obvious pain, he climbed like a mad man. And Gully virtually bounded up the incline, with his normal limitless energy. As Merry watched them both from increasingly further behind, she began to wonder, between huffing breaths, if she spent *too* much time reading books.

Staring into the crystal to learn that pattern was impossible while climbing. Trying, she tripped twice, smacked her shin on roots thrice, and nearly slipped back down the leaf-covered wooded slope more times than she could count. She finally gave up, placed the crystal carefully in her pouch, and tried to catch up.

Gully bounded back down to her, as surefooted as a goat.

"Give me the crystal," he held out his hand. "I can be up there and throw it *way* before you get there, slow-poke."

Merry had a sudden image of Gully gleefully throwing away the most magical object that she had ever seen before she had a proper chance to study it.

"Not a bad idea," Uncle Vic called from where he had stopped a dozen strides upslope.

Looking at the strain in his face, she realized he was even closer to his limit than she thought.

"No, we stay together," she declared firmly, trying to channel Ma's voice so the two of them would listen.

She caught up to him and said, "Let's take a break and then make one last push to the top."

"That airship could be almost on top of us," Uncle Vic said, watching the leafy canopy above them with nervous concern.

"No," Merry stated confidently.

She reached her hand into her bag and gripped the crystal, then closed her eyes, spun slightly, and pointed downslope and a little to the left of the path they'd taken upward.

"It's down that way. It stopped moving away, but it's coming no closer."

She opened her eyes and saw Uncle Vic watching her with fearful concern.

"The sooner we toss that thing into the sea, the better," he stated resignedly.

Considering his current frame of mind, Merry didn't want to mention that the fortune teller was right; they could certainly find this crystal again once they start looking. It was attached to its eleven mates by lines of power linked to one symbol. That was the pattern that tied them all together and unified their power for the airship's flight, and it was wickedly complicated.

Merry remembered one of the Lanfor stories she read where the hero was amazed by an eight-crystal ship. Synchronizing more than that was supposed to be impossible, according to that old tale. Apparently not, as that ship had twelve. She was very certain they would be after this crystal soon.

Merry took the opportunity of the brief break to dive deep into the crystal again, tracing the pattern with her eyes and building a picture of it in her mind. She burned the lines into the image, snaking them around. But every time she made it halfway through, the part she picked for the beginning began to crumble away.

"Alright," Uncle Vic grabbed her shoulder. "Enough of that. Let's go."

She hadn't realized how intently she was sitting there frowning into the crystal, and maybe muttering to herself until he snapped her out of it.

They tripled their pace in a frantic scramble to reach the top. Even Merry, who was dreading having to cast away the precious crystal, was starting to feel the urgency. *How long until the powerful owners of the airship began following the telltale lines to their missing crystal? What could be distracting them from that all-important task?*

They reach the top of the climb in a gasping tumble, settling for a moment in a small field of wildflowers at the top. Even Gully appeared winded slightly.

The far side of the clearing was just sky as if the world fell away at that point. At the end was an old stone platform about twice the height of a man. From this angle, it looked like little more than a carefully laid pile of rocks, twined with rose bushes gone wild. There was a weed-covered and crumbling stairway leading to the top of the platform.

Regaining his breath first, Gully bounded over and up the stairs.

"Wow, you can see forever up here!" they heard him call. "There's the cove! And the airship's landed in the ocean!"

"Just a moment," Uncle Vic gasped, laying in the meadow flowers and waving weakly in that direction.

Merry had neither the breath nor time for reply. She took out the crystal and prepared to trace that pattern once more. But she found she couldn't keep her eyes open in her exhaustion. She would close them just for a moment.

It was a shame; she was so close. But there was no time left; they had to throw it away now.

She traced the pattern again, not realizing her eyes remained closed, so clear was the vision of the pattern in her mind. The lines flowed through each other in interlocking loops. In her visualization, it occurred to her to think of it like a knot. Then the snaking lines kind of made sense. Suddenly the whole pattern snapped into place with glowing cerulean threads in her mind.

She gasped, realizing she knew instinctively what it did.

At her gasp, Uncle Vic snatched the crystal from her slack hand in concern. "We're getting rid of this thing now!"

Merry panicked for a brief second until she realized that even without the crystal in her hand, the pattern was still there. Like the one for light, it was part of her now. Indelibly burned into her mind.

She glanced at the stick slipped through a loop in her pouch strap. It wasn't magic, no more than any piece of natural wood, it just faintly echoed the magic previously cast on it, making it easier to do so again. Even the pattern wasn't magic, it was just a way of directing and controlling a natural force. The power came from her, and through her from the world around.

She stood in the field of flowers, at one of the highest points on the coast, and felt it all around her. She felt like spreading her arms to the magic of the world and spinning and dancing. But she just smiled at Uncle Vic and said, "Okay, let's do this."

Tossing the crystal into the sea was a shame, of course, but she felt that one symbol was all she could hold at the moment. She had read of the tiers of magic spells, and she was certain that the one she held was the only one of the first order on that crystal. There was no way she could learn the others now, even if they had hours.

Looking at the size of those other patterns, she couldn't even begin to envision them fully in the space she held the other patterns. She felt she had to somehow expand the canvas of her mind. But others had done so, and so could she. Merry just needed time to study, and she was *very* good at studying.

When she was ready, she would find another crystal, she promised herself and began to imagine it. Maybe she would travel across the channel to the magical Kingdom of Lanfor someday. There were other crystals there, not tied to such a dangerous ship. The stories claimed that the Queen's knights placed single crystals into boards of wood that they rode across the skies like the southern island natives were said to do on the waves of the oceans.

All in all, she was riding a magical high herself, feeling that new symbol burning inside her. And she practically pulled her confused uncle up the rough stone steps to the top of the world.

The lookout summit was a circle a half-dozen paces or so across. Faint traces of rough cobblestones set in a starburst pattern peeked out below the blanket of creeping flowers gone wild. Four stone benches sat in an inner circle around a center-mounted sundial.

Surprise gripped Merry's chest as her sun-dazzled eyes saw another figure standing there near Gully. But it passed as she realized it was a finely carved statue of a man set upon the southeast cardinal of the burst.

Looking about, you could see the knife-edged ridge marching in a serrated climb out of the rolling foothills to the west. It reached its apex here, at this grand peak above the sea. Seaward to the east, the spent remains of the ridge plunged rapidly down, to be swallowed by the water. To the southeast, it was a sheer cliff straight down to the waves of an inlet below. And to the northeast, the inclines they had just climbed fell in steep, undulating tiers of forest to the valley that ended in Fisheye Cove.

There, just outside the cove, the grand airship had landed upon the sea. At this distance, the ship looked like a toy, and the people tiny ants crawling on it. So far away, even the huge crimson dragon perched on the deck looked small.

She forced her gaze away from that dangerous ship to examine the statue. It was a man with a stone vase or pot of some kind in the crook of his left arm. It was filled with dirt that small yellow sun-drop flowers improbably still grew from. Some had escaped the pot and also grew where soil had gotten caught in the folds of the stone arms. The statue had an amazingly expressive face. Its gaze looked longingly out over the cliff to the inlet with what Merry imagined was love and sorrow.

Carved at the base of the statue, the following lines could still be made out through the tangle of yellow blooms.

Her beloved flowers shall bloom forever with the memory of her passing. I shall await here until that glorious day when the Lady Magdeena sails again.

The feeling of surreal peace and safety Merry hadn't even realized she felt standing on this ancient platform was tinged with mournful sorrow and unending love. She now knew it was radiating from this statue.

There was a real-looking spyglass in the statue's other hand, with actual lenses. Gully stepped onto the statue's base and pulled on the spyglass determinedly, hanging his weight on the unmoving brass to no avail. He stepped down, disappointed.

A distant rumble faintly reached them from across the inlet, and their stony lookout seemed to shake in response. Merry reached out her hand, grabbing the statue to steady herself. Her hand grasped the spyglass and it came away, slipping easily from the statue's now-loose grip. Something had changed. The stone face now seemed weathered and worn, its longing somehow seemingly relaxed.

Following the lifeless gaze of the now-ancient-appearing statue, Merry could just make out the white speck of a tiny sail on the glit-tering waters.

A quick, gentle buff on her skirt-hem left the spyglass surpris-ingly clear. Following the statue's gaze, the first thing she saw was a cloud of dust not quite settled from a recent rockfall across the inlet. Moving down, she focused on the small sailboat moving away from that fall toward the cliff below them.

Her breath caught and relief flooded over her, as the view of Pa at the boat's tiller swung into the glass. Then toward the mast, she saw Uncle Wex working the lines. Standing at the prow, she saw a slight blonde girl. The wind was blowing her fair hair, and she wore a pretty white dress. The yellow flowers on the girl's bodice were unmistakably sundrops like the statue held. Was this young girl, the Lady Magdeena, mentioned in the inscription? But that was so old!

It was only when the girl stepped casually off the edge of the prow and a glittering bronze-scaled dragon danced like a dolphin around the boat's wake that Merry realized her mistake. She hadn't recognized that brightly smiling girl in the sunlight and pretty dress as the grimly determined dragon-girl in dark leathers from the shadowy chamber.

The bronze form of Ruka flashed up the coast, only breaching a few more times before vanishing beneath the waves. Regardless, she was too fast for Merry to follow with the glass. The boat continued sailing toward the base of their cliff so that she had to lean way out to follow it.

Uncle Vic grabbed the back of her dress with a "Whoa!"

She hung there for a brief moment, looking over the edge of the high cliff with the new pattern humming in the back of her mind, and realized she wasn't the slightest bit afraid of that deadly plunge. Smiling at Uncle Vic only seemed to make him more worried. How could she explain it?

An amber glow from the deck of the distant airship captured her attention, and Merry focused her new spyglass in that direction. She looked for only a moment. Just a glance at the evil red dragon justifiably sent chills to run up her spine. But she couldn't put a finger on the cause of dread on seeing the dark armored form confronting the dragon. She somehow just felt menace from it, and she believed that if it deigned to notice, it would surely know she had looked upon it.

The air of peace and security had vanished with the spirit in the statue. And suddenly, that airship beyond the cove was not nearly far enough away. All that distance they had exhaustingly climbed and a dragon could fly and be on them in minutes. She felt exposed up here. Passing the spyglass to Uncle Vic, she held out her hand and said, "Let me hold that crystal one more time."

"Hurry," he said, with only a mildly askance glance about what she would do with the crystal, and then he studied the airship through the glass.

Merry held the gem tightly with both hands and focused on it. There was so much she didn't understand about all the rest of those symbols, but there was one thing singing loud and clear from the crystal. It *wanted* to fly.

"Holy…" Uncle Vic's exclamation trailed off in shock.

"Whoa, check it out!" Gully cried, grabbing her arm.

Merry didn't need the spyglass to see the conflagration that engulfed the ship's deck. A vortex of flames was tossed about by titanic forces that she felt even from here. So much power conflicting, and such enmity! Her new senses screamed in silent shock at the immensity of it all. If that attention was turned toward them… she shuddered.

Soar! She cried to the crystal, in that spirit place where the crystal glowed so brightly. It felt like it wanted to leap out of her hand in its eagerness. And with a firm grip, she handed the faintly vibrating gem to Gully.

"Throw it," she urged him, "with all your might!"

Spirit Battles
Chapter 7

As the backlash of Theriaxus' initial assault hit Sigfus' shields, the strain brought him to his knees. As always, he was the only one prepared for the dragon's assault. And he was used to creating a large enough ward to protect, not just himself and the princess, but her entire useless retinue. It was normally no problem, but this time was different. The raw power of this assault was crushing his mystic shields. And the attack wasn't even directed at them!

The outer magic shield buckled, then shattered instantaneously into a thousand triangles of crimson energy under the raging forces without. The next layer lasted only a moment longer, cascading into broken diamonds of glowing orange. The third layer gave him a precious handful of seconds to bring up a reinforcing ward before being crushed into sparkling pentagons of amber.

Thanks to that reinforcement, the emerald layer held long enough for Jesira to finally react and get up a reinforcing ward of her own to buttress his shield.

As a Priestess of Lenara, the Lady of Battle, Jesira's magical arsenal was more physical combat-oriented. But she had a potent ability to channel battle-spirit, and she had linked hands with Delandria the Spiritblade and Oripeah the Mystic Archer, to pump a formidable amount of power into that ward.

It was a little too late, as the next layer finally fragmented into green glittering hexagons.

Even with the multiple powerful reinforcements, the cerulean layer began to buckle, too. The subtle heptagons within complex lines of lattice began to glow an angry electric blue at the excess of enraged dragon spirit assaulting them.

Then Princess Anya stepped forward. As a dragon-blooded sorceress of the royal line of Lanfor, she understood the nature of the draconic magic arrayed against them more thoroughly than anyone. The power of her ward flowed outward and into the barrier like a golden wave, reinforcing it in subtle harmonics in tune with the draconic assault. The shield now held rock-steady around the princess and her retainers. She turned to them with a self-satisfied grin. All four of them would have to bear so much more than embarrassment for their liege having to assist them. Anya would see them pay for that failure in subtle cruel ways.

They couldn't see anything beyond the sphere of their shield as the firestorm enveloped it with primal destructive rage. The ship was strongly warded against fire, of course. But that was normal fire, not flaming explosive dragon-spirit. The scream of heavy copper rigging cables being torn from their moorings overlaid the ping of nails flung from super-heated decking.

Thankfully, their shield blocked the command deck from the worst of the blast—some of the officers there might escape with only minor burns. But any of the crew caught on the main deck were certainly disintegrated, even their bones reduced to explosion-borne ash.

When the pressure of the fiery assault finally began to decrease a little, Sigfus coaxed a gust of sea breeze across the smoldering ship and visibility returned in smoke-strewn patches.

Theriaxus' form seemed to waver in billowing veils of super-heated air—or perhaps she also wavered after that tremendous outpouring of power.

The Dragon Master's armor still stood, although pushed back several feet across torn decking. Its gauntleted fists were crossed in front of it, its head lowered and legs braced.

Theramon's new avatar crouched behind the armor, seeming mildly surprised and impressed with the power of the attack. Although that damnable smug expression never left his face, and he looked satisfied as if this was an unexpected display of his own power, rather than a primal force bent on his destruction.

Sigfus extended a tentative probe out to the battlefield. The draconic inferno had extended multiple layers into the spirit plane, and he had to completely withdraw at the first sign of the burst.

What he sensed made him recoil in shock. Theriaxus was still building dragon-spirit for another destructive assault. How she had power for more was inconceivable. There was a slightly different feel to the energy this time. And even though the dragon's spirit was flickering like a bonfire in a gale, what was growing was still a powerful fire, just of a different color.

Worse, the Dragon Master had raised one hand as if holding something aloft. And indeed, Sigfus could sense the huge, growing ball of captured dragon rage growing above its head. It felt like a colossal spirit hammer poised to fall on the dragon *and* the hapless ship she was standing upon.

"Reinforce the shield again!" he cried.

Jesira looked at him skeptically for a second, but complied instantly when Anya snapped, "Do it!"

Anya had begun bolstering the shield without hesitation. They had survived together through rebellion and bloody purges only through instinctive reactions and trust. Her mask of royalty and privilege fell away, exposing the will of steel beneath the gilded veneer as she focused. It was that which would make her the one to finally break the tyranny of the Eternal Queen.

They renewed the wards just in time. The shield was stronger than ever when the Dragon Master's strike simultaneously hit the second burst from Theriaxus. The shockwave of the impact of those two forces rolled across the deck and shredded the cerulean shield into careening polygons of force.

The last layer lit up in a glowing violet mesh of interlaced octagons. It buckled and resonated with deflected force, the buttressing wards singing with impact—but they held. Barely.

When the reverberation of the colossal impact faded, the ship was left in an eerie calm. The only sound was the faint lapping of waves around the hull. Into that near silence, Theramon's voice rang clear across the desolation of the once opulent main deck with the happy tones of a schoolboy after an interesting play in pitchsticks.

"Well, that was instructive. Fortunately, the assault was diluted with enough rage for Urekar to enthrall it into a shield and strike back before it overwhelmed him."

Sigfus would have called that burst 'pure' rage, so potent and disturbing was that feeling from it. But had there been something else to it? Was there some flaw to this shade of a Thrall Lord's control over dragon spirit? If there was, it might be critical to know. Sigfus had no delusions that their 'ally' wouldn't turn that abomination against them if it suited his purposes.

According to legend, the Dragon Thrall Master could not only absorb dragon-spirit attacks directed against him, he had been able to use their strength as his own and return it back with double the force. Those tales said that few dragons could refuse his commands, and none could harm or stand against him. Yet one had—the storm dragon Yatharia was supposedly instrumental in his original downfall.

Yatharia was known as a berserker, wild and tempestuous even by storm dragon standards. But if rage was a spirit force the Dragon Master could so easily turn to his own power, what had Yatharia used against him? Even the original Thrall Lord must have had a flaw in his complete domination of dragons. And what else was there in Theriaxus' spirit attack, other than rage that Theramon considered dangerous?

The Dragon Master's armor stood motionless. Only a dim ember of light flickering from the dark visor indicated it still held the shade of one of the most powerful beings of this age.

The crimson form of Theriaxus sat on her haunches, still and vacant-eyed, apparently unharmed in the epicenter of smashed ship structure. Sigfus' wizard-sight saw differently. That strike had not been primarily on the physical layer, and most of the destruction was backlash of power through the spirit veils.

The dragon's spirit had been brutally broken. The image of her anima lay splay-limbed in weird contortions, with wings bent and shattered. Her spirit form was beyond beaten—it was totally and completely devastated. Such was the power of even an unawakened Thrall Lord, and Theriaxus was now completely enthralled in the Dragon Master's power.

"Look what you've done!" Anya called as she picked her way across the ruinous remains of her deck.

"The damage is superficial, mostly decking and a bit of rail," Theramon commented offhandedly, brushing idly at a small singed area on the side of his trousers. "If you had a competent wizard, you could have it restored in short order."

Sigfus steeled himself not to react. He knew it was bait, and part of the constant undermining of his credibility. It was a no-win situation. Not reacting would tacitly acknowledge that he couldn't mend this decking.

Anya made a subtle hand motion for him to stand down. Had he stiffened and acted without realizing it, or had she just assumed he would? The latter was perhaps worse. Theramon trying to insinuate himself as the princess' only competent magical adviser had to be obvious, even to Anya.

Pointing out that the spirit of the deck itself was damaged two layers deep was a setup he suspected. Or maybe it was a challenge. He had recently discovered a pattern to pierce the third veil. It was a magus level symbol and took a tremendous amount of energy to power, but he took the challenge and took the spirit plunge through it.

Time seemed to stretch taut past the third barrier; movements on the physical level appeared slowed, and one's spirit form here could move independently of the body in small ways. Although doing so caused a stretched feeling, similar to a green sapling that you could bend away from its position, but would snap back when released. And one felt certain that, like the sapling, moving too far would cause something to break.

Here, as he suspected, the deck still remembered its original form. The dragon spirit had not reached this deep, and the echoes of destruction would take days to permeate so far. But to bring this volume of spirit form up through *three* veils would be impossible!

And then he saw the third-layer form of Theramon and froze. The spirit of a boy was there, blessedly unconscious, but still somehow motionlessly writhing in pain. Silver barbed threads cruelly enwrapped the spirit form. They jerked at the corners of the mouth and pulled at the head as the puppet form of Theramon turned and smiled at him.

This is what Theramon had meant by a 'new skin'!

Sigfus, as jaded as he was by the many acts he had performed over the years in the name of his princess or simply through his own vices, recoiled from the nature of this evil. The perversion of innocent human souls for their own power was the purview of devils, not man nor wizard, no matter how far fallen.

Although not as numerous, or enveloping as on the boy's spirit, threads were attached to the wispy smoke-like form of the Dragon Master. But these were not positioned for direct puppet control; they seemed mostly placed to anchor the spirit as if it would sink down, or drift upward, depending on your point of view, if not held to this world. With the weight of evil on the Dragon Master's soul, Sigfus was certain that direction would be downward.

The Dragon Master's armor here appeared translucent and multicolored. Closer examination revealed a multitude of dragon spirits tangled, stretched tight, and in constant angry motion. The buzz of their rage was a din across the third layer this close to that fell armor.

From the Dragon Master sprang black chains that wrapped the spirit of Theriaxus in tight binds. These chains were not subtle threads as Theramon spun; they were like the anchor chains that great warships used. Nor were they sadistically barbed, but were cruel in their weight and constriction nonetheless.

Nearly a dozen similar spirit chains branched out and vanished into the faded distance of the spirit realm. The number of dragons that the resurrected Thrall Lord already had under direct control, and out in the world doing Theramon's bidding, was unnerving. How much longer would he need Princess Anya's help in his plans? Especially now that the dragon shard she used was sabotaged.

There were broken threads hanging off Theriaxus. Theramon has been influencing her before the burst, but she had broken free of that subtle influence only to be ensnared by the clumsier but more powerful chains of the Dragon Master. The type of influence thread he had used there was not strong and barbed, but subtle and near-invisible wisps, even with third sight.

It was all too much—there was no way to compete with the power of this man who, unlike Sigfus, was a true master. Sigfus had always been a fraud, a boy rejected by masters, kicked out of his school. Only through bumbling luck did he stumble across the princess fleeing the purge and save her with stolen spells. And even in that, he bungled. His constant failures lead to Anya's year of the rabbit, which twisted her psyche and nearly broke her mind. He should just leave her now to save her from further incompetence. He…

Sigfus found the thread yanking on his feelings of inadequacy and broke it.

Anger welled through him at this man, this creature, who thought him a puppet. He was a wizard! And he would give this wretch a proper lesson in that. He ran through his cluster of spell patterns at ready. He would…

And then he broke the thread pulling on his anger and regained full control of himself.

Perhaps not useless after all. The smooth voice of Theramon whispered behind the third veil, where only Sigfus could hear it.

Theramon smiled wider at Sigfus; it was creepy on the physical layer and downright frightening seeing the overlay of his puppeteer victim. Then his smile vanished and he looked up at the sky.

Sigfus saw it, too—how could he not? Not just on the third, but on the second and first spectral levels, the Aerde crystal flashed overhead, lighting the spirit heavens like a brilliant meteor would across a moonless sky. All those with any form of spirit-sight on the ship saw that.

"Our crystal? How dare she?" Anya exclaimed.

But Theramon's gaze was not on where the soaring gem was

heading, but on where it came from. A ripple beneath the third veil, like the roll of water and shadow of a leviathan, passed beneath the surface as his attention focused shoreward.

There was no way he could follow that view—the range of his senses was too limited on this layer. And Anya's voice brought Sigfus' attention back to the physical.

"Theramon! What *is* going on?" Anya barked the name as a command, but the petulant question gave lie to it. She was finally realizing it was too late to control this man, if man he ever was.

"An integral part of your ship was just tossed far out to sea," Theramon waved distractedly toward the ocean, but his attention was directed toward the bluffs.

"Not thrown by her, of course," Theramon mused to himself, "just some local peasants she duped. But best to be sure."

"Theria, my dear firebug," he turned to the enthralled dragon and said in a pleasant conversational tone, "fly up there and incinerate those pesky humans for me."

"Leave them alone, you monster!" A girl's shout was punctuated by a booming thunderclap as a blast of coursing lightning enveloped the form of Theramon. A blackened husk collapsed to the deck in its wake.

Sigfus rapidly began forming another shield as he located the new threat. A slender blonde-haired girl in her mid-teens perched on the one remaining section of railing on the port side main deck. Although screwed into an angry scowl at the moment, her features were clearly similar to Vestiralanna's human form.

With his third-veil pattern still vibrating with remnants of energy, he could sense something more around the girl. So, he fed some precious power to that as well and took another spirit-dive down through the layers. He was surprised to still find a girl rather than the dragon he expected through the first and second veils. Shape changes almost never went deeper than the first.

Behind the second veil, another form stood next to the blonde girl. A raven-haired woman whispered in the girl's ear, pointing at Theramon. Spirits could only rarely interact with people from beyond the veils unless there was some bond. Indeed, this spirit appeared wearing an identical dress as the dragon-girl, except the pale-yellow flowers on the front were glowing like shards of sunlight.

It was apparent from the cast of her eyes that the dragon couldn't actually see or hear the woman's spirit, and perhaps just followed its directions on impulse. The dress was the link between them.

But the spirit definitely saw Sigfus. Frowning at his presence, the dark-haired woman faded easily through the third veil, vanishing from second sight. So, he pushed through.

On the third, he found the spirit of the woman again. Next to the woman was finally the image of the storm dragon he expected, but the girl-form was still there, too. This assumed human shape was superimposed on her dragon form, almost like at the deepest core of her spirit she was both.

Looking at where the corpse of Theramon's avatar should be, Sigfus realized the effects of the lightning had reached all the way through the third veil to here. But the energy of the dragon girl's strike had not burned the spirit of the boy dominated by Theramon. On this level, just those cruel barbed threads that entwined the bound soul were charred. It had almost freed it!

But even as that hapless spirit threw off the last of the cruel thorns, a dozen more barbed threads seemed to flash from the depths to ensnare it.

Immediately, the spirit woman flew across to the boy and began pulling those new entwining strands off.

Magdeena, you pathetic witchling, the voice of Theramon echoed up from the spirit depths, *still doing my sister's bidding even in death? I should have destroyed your spirit the first time, rather than just kill you. I will correct that mistake.*

The barbed silver threads began attacking the woman's spirit, too, but she held up one hand. Attached to the pinky finger of her right hand was a spirit thread of another type. It was red, and softer in appearance like string, but no less strong as it grew taut when she made a fist and pulled it to her heart.

"You still have that fatal blind spot, Xantos," the spirit of Magdeena said. "You could never fathom love. I am not alone in my vows beyond life."

A man sped through the spirit aether, following the tug of the red string which was strung around the pinky of his left hand. He landed on the deck, clasped Magdeena's string-bound hand with his, and drew a slender azure blade of light with the other. A pulse of light passed from the sword, through the man to the woman, and through her to her opposite hand, where a similar blade appeared. Then the lady began to sing, and they both began slashing through Theramon's remaining control threads in rapid order.

The threads stopped forming around the boy and suddenly erupted everywhere around the dragon girl. The man made to dash over to the dragon's aid, but the woman caught him up and shook her head.

"Behold the Aes Aeris, the true heir of storms, and the first sign in the prophecy of your doom, wretched one!" the spirit woman intoned like a righteous pronouncement.

Where the writhing mass of cruelly barbed spirit threads fell on the dragon-girl, they withered and disintegrated. The dragon did nothing to fight them—she, like everyone else rooted to the material plane—was moving in slow motion and had barely shifted from the pose in which she cast the first bolt. The threads were just utterly destroyed on contact with her aura.

No! the psychic shout preceded a surge of horrible malignant rage that began to breach up through the lower reaches of the fourth veil.

The spirits of Magdeena and her partner grabbed the boy and escaped in a different direction through the fourth veil in a flash of light. Instinctively, Sigfus knew they had passed through all the remaining veils at once, and that flash was the brilliant light of piercing the seventh. Depending on one's beliefs, beyond that last veil lay oblivion, reincarnation, or the judgement of the true god. Regardless, they were well beyond the reach of even a monster like Theramon.

Crush that dragon and bring her to me! the command vibrated across the threads attached to the Dragon Master.

It gave Sigfus great satisfaction to hear that tone of desperation creeping into Theramon's command. With his local avatar gone, he no longer had an anchor to this place. The fourth veil was holding, and this was their opportunity.

Coming back out of the spirit dive was even more jarring than usual. Going so deep was a serious strain on its own, but now he was trying to keep half an eye on the spirit realm down through three veils while focusing a shield against any lightning attacks.

"Come here, little one," the Dragon Master's deep voice flowed out of the dark helm with a muffled, empty-sounding echo.

One armored gauntlet made a grasping motion toward the girl on the rail as he said it, and five heavy spirit chains shot out to enwrap the dragon's spirit. They held for only a split second, never having a chance to tighten, then fell off their target as her spirit form flowed from dragon to girl and back again.

"Why don't you bite your own tail, kettle-face!" the girl exclaimed as she launched herself backwards off the railing. In midair, the girl exploded in a flash of electrical energy and a bronze-scaled dragon hit the ocean waters below.

"Bring her to me," the burned throat of the boy's corpse croaked the command past blackened lips.

Sigfus hadn't seen the one taut thread grasping up through the veils to manipulate the abandoned body of the boy. He dropped the now-unnecessary shield and prepared the pattern for psychic shards.

A flick of the Dragon Master's finger and Theriaxus was forced to leap into the ocean after the storm dragon.

"No," Princess Anya cried, "You idiot! Fire dragons can't swim!"

Anya ran up and kicked the burnt corpse in frustration, saying, "That was my dragon!"

Sigfus didn't dare contradict his princess and point out that Theriaxus was certainly no longer 'her dragon.' When he saw the heavy chain from the Dragon Master to the dragon go slack and vanish, he felt considerable relief to have the flaming menace of *that* dragon good and drowned.

The Dragon Master turned toward Anya as she kicked the corpse again to make sure she got the point of her displeasure across.

In a flash, Delandria stood with her blades just inches from the armored throat. It was a flash, literally, and very annoying to Sigfus' spirit-strained eyes. As was the high-pitched humming sound emitted by the golden dagger shards of Jesira's Hundred Blade Assault, which now hovered about the armored form waiting eagerly to strike. The name was a lie—there were only forty-eight blades. Sigfus had counted them, although he doubted any opponent would live long enough to point it out to her. And he certainly wasn't going to.

Oripeah was at the rail, scanning the ocean for targets. The barbed point of her nocked arrow was tipped with dragon's blood and gave off the faint wisps of black smoke that indicated her slayer curse was on it. Sigfus avoided looking at that with spirit sight—the whirling vortex of malignant evil attached to the arrow always made him slightly queasy. Or maybe it was knowledge of whose blood it was.

He had spent many an hour staring longingly at the beauty of Vestiralanna during the few nights she was their 'guest.' The thought of Oripeah using Ves' own blood to slay her upset him greatly, for then he would never get a chance to claim her. But the arrow might also be very effective on Ves' sister dragon. In that endeavor, he wished the archer the best of luck.

"Bring her to me," the corpse croaked again, and Sigfus realized that parroted phrase was all a single control thread could make it do.

He looked from the corpse of Theramon's puppet to the Dragon Master's armor, which was also effectively his puppet. And then to Anya.

"Shall we take the armor as recompense for the lost dragon?"

Anya matched his wry smile with a wicked one of her own.

"Siggy, I like the way you think!"

He invoked the psychic shards pattern and thoroughly bombarded the armor to sever all the binding threads at once. The multiple dragon chains pulled taut as the spirit tried to summon its thralls to fight back. *Not good!*

Sigfus redoubled his efforts, overloading the pattern. He was rewarded with a sharp headache and the empty armor falling lifeless to the deck. The dragon chains thankfully went slack. The spirit of Urekar was still attached to the armor by bonds Sigfus could not sever, but it once again slumbered.

He also cut the fell thread from the corpse and proceeded to burn it even more thoroughly with fire, just to be sure.

"We should recover our emitter crystal before it attracts some sea-creature we don't want to deal with right now," he advised the princess.

"Make it so," Anya agreed, then added, "Oh, and send Irovnia to deal with whoever threw the crystal."

Sigfus glanced at his princess in surprise. Her eyes were calculating and worried. If they had lost control of their dragons, it would be better to find out now before the next disaster struck. And their control on that one was the most questionable after Theriaxus, for totally different reasons.

He bowed to her. "As you wish, Your Majesty."

So, half-crippled, the once glorious airship hesitantly lurched into the air and floated slowly out over the sea. They skimmed the waves at a painfully slow and somewhat sideways crawl. There would be no problem with the ice dragon catching up.

If she came back at all.

———

"We've got to move!" Uncle Vic commanded. "Back down the hill."

He lowered the glass; it was sadly not needed with the rate that white form was closing on their vantage point.

"No," Merry said, "we'll never make it that way. It will just pick us off."

It was several hundred yards downslope before the trees became thick enough to effectively hide under. They'd certainly be spotted by the dragon's sharp eyes. And once spotted by a hunting dragon in the wilderness, there was little hope of escaping.

Besides, she already knew the way they had to go. But Uncle Vic was *not* going to like it.

"So, we fight!" Gully exclaimed. He had already unwrapped Inazuma and was holding the short sword in a ready two-handed grip.

"No!" they both declared simultaneously.

Uncle Vic looked at Merry and said, "If you have a plan, make it quick."

"Climb down behind the lookout," she instructed Gully and Uncle Vic. As they scrambled over the edge to the small lip of stone between the lookout and the cliff edge, she commanded, "Inazuma, project our images running downslope."

"My range is limited," the sword replied.

"Fine, just have them duck behind the farthest tree you can reach with your illusion and vanish."

"That's great, kid, but now we are stuck here." Uncle Vic gestured to how the narrow two-foot ledge dwindled to sheer cliff to their right, and their left would just bring them around to clear sight of the dragon again. "And all it has to do is fly once around the lookout and pick us off."

"We jump."

"Cliff diving," Gully exclaimed. "Awesome!"

"We'll never clear those rocks, and even if we do, we'll break every bone in our bodies when we hit the water at this height," Uncle Vic countered. But then he muttered quietly, "might be a better end than the dragon."

"We'll float down," Merry stated. She held out one hand to each of them. Gully gripped her fingers eagerly, and with Inazuma in his other hand, gave her a smiling salute.

"What? Look, I don't know what hocus pocus has got in your head, but…"

"Yes, it *is* in my head! But it's *magic* in my head. And it *will* work!" Merry declared forcefully, then added pleadingly, "just trust me. Please."

"It's a leap of faith," Gully added, helpfully echoing the Seeress' words.

"A leap of…" Uncle Vic trailed off, smacking his forehead. "Gods! I hate that fortune teller!"

Then he grabbed her hand and they all jumped.

Invoking the pattern was instantaneous; as soon as they began to fall through the air, it activated and Merry poured energy into it. And poured, and poured. There was so much of it! So many loops and turns and knots of pattern. And she had to light all of it three times!

When she felt she couldn't push any more energy into it, she realized it was done. The pattern for floating was overlaid onto all three of them.

She felt exhaustion overcome her. Tiredness worse than the climb up the hill, more like she had run all day up that slope. But she had done it! They were floating like the down of a feather.

"We're flying!" came Gully's joyful cry. And Merry was too tired to shush him.

"Quiet!" Uncle Vic ordered, and then declared, "It's not flying, it's more like falling with… Oof!"

Like a feather, they were at the mercy of the winds. And a mischievous gust decided to push them into the cliff face at that point. They lost their grips on each other, and Merry had a panicked moment until she realized the pattern held on all of them even without her touch.

Gully kicked off the cliff, sword out, point-first. And with his legs together and other arm pulled close to his side, he managed to fall faster and sail out toward the inlet waters. There below, she saw what he was aiming for—the ship.

Uncle Vic managed a similar feat of dexterity. But he sported a grimace of pain instead of a grin and was gripping his wounded shoulder where he had struck it on the cliff.

She tumbled gracelessly at least three times before she was finally able to kick off a little and cartwheel slowly in that direction. Merry really hated being the agility-challenged member of the group, and she just gave up trying to maintain her skirt direction. There was no one here to care if she flashed her knickers.

By the time they reached the bottom, Gully had gotten so good he was actually able to land in the small boat. Merry was a little annoyed; she wanted to see Pa's amazed face up close as they floated in from the sky. And she wanted to be the first to feel his crushing bearhug at their return.

Uncle Vic almost made it inside, too. He caught the deck rail and floated down next to the boat while they pulled him in.

Merry, of course, splashed down head-first a dozen feet short of the boat and had to be fished out. All her ire at that ignoble landing left, along with all her breath, as Pa hugged her for a glorious minute, disregarding her drenched state.

Gully was already showing off pretend fencing moves with Inazuma to Uncle Wex, probably telling of some improbable sword fight that never happened. But who would disbelieve him after swooping out of the sky like that?

Merry nearly jumped back out of the boat when a small lizard creature with dark goggles appeared out of the bilge. It tugged on Pa's shirt and said something urgently in sharp, high-pitched tones. It was obviously pointing repeatedly to a partially submerged cave in the cliff.

"Oh no," Pa said, "we'll never fit between those rocks."

"Sure, we will," Uncle Vic had taken over the tiller and was pointing their boat toward that dangerous opening. He motioned upward with his chin while keeping both hands on the tiller, declaring, "We will because *we* are properly motivated."

Looking up, they saw part of a white wing and tail sail around the cliff summit as the ice dragon circled. Perhaps it had not looked beneath the cliff on that first pass. But they needed to get out of sight now!

Uncle Wex and Pa rapidly took down the sail, and whether by luck or Uncle Vic's sailing, they cruised into the cave on momentum with barely a scrape of the hull.

The cavern inside was larger than it looked from without, and it was blissfully cool. Strangely, there was a piece of ice floating in it, almost as big as the boat.

Merry untangled the driftwood club from her pouch strap. She was glad it had miraculously stayed secure during her careening decent; it was easier to impose the light pattern on this wood that remembered it so well.

She then reached out in that place beyond to gently touch the spirit of the sword and tried to project words to him like he had done with her earlier.

Inazuma, can you... she motioned with her club to the opening.

Of course, he seemed to pick up on the idea before she finished projecting the words. And he immediately projected the illusion of boulders perfectly filling the cave entrance. The illusion fit so well that it blocked the late afternoon sun completely and they were plunged into darkness.

She was still mentally exhausted from the air-floating pattern, but light was much simpler and used so much less power, that she was able to have the club alight with nary a thought.

"We should be safe now," Merry said tiredly, leaning on the railing.

"What?" Uncle Wex stammered, "H-how did you do that?"

Merry stared around at her family from under drooping eyelids that just wanted to close for a minute, and wondered why they were all looking at her like she was a stranger. It probably didn't help that she held a magically glowing stick. And that she had her back to a glittering mound of ice that cast a constellation of reflections around the room.

"Oh, that was the sword," she motioned to the blocked entrance, causing the reflective lights to dance and form new constellations. "It's just an illusion."

"Hey!" Gully looked accusingly down at Inazuma in his hand like they had been conspiring behind his back. Which, she supposed, they had.

"I just made the stick glow, that's all."

"*Just* made a stick glow?" her father repeated.

"And made us fly," Gully exclaimed, spreading his arms.

"Not fly, float on air…" she corrected, but trailed off, seeing the look on her father's face. She couldn't recognize it in the shifting light.

"Pa, I just… learned a… a little magic," she said hesitantly.

He looked at her closely for a second, then smiled and grabbed her in a hug. Not as crushing as the first one, but no less sincere.

"Of course," he said softly in her ear, "you've always been my magical girl. And I am so proud of you!"

The Ice Dragon
Chapter 8

When this new group of Fokari dropped from the sky, Ratnosk had thought they were attacking, and so he hid. But it was quickly apparent that these two groups were from the same nesting circle, although obviously from multiple hatchings. The one holding that annoying light, he suspected might be a female. It was hard to be certain with these creatures since they didn't have tails. If a female was out of the nesting caves, she must be either a powerful priestess or sorceress.

And, as one would expect, this female was obviously their leader. It was not just her light-magic that gave it away; she was the only one of them wearing a proper kilt rather than the trousers of a servant. So, he approached her and bowed.

"Oh, illustrious sorceress of light and sky, do you also serve the magnificent incarnation of storms, Rukastanna?"

The female seemed taken aback by his approach. Had he overstepped? Was the bow not severe enough? A lowly trap-jack such as himself, daring to speak to a mighty sorceress, would normally be unthinkable. He steeled himself under her appropriately wide-eyed gaze at his affront; wasn't he now a chosen servant of a mighty dragon? But what if he inadvertently insulted a powerful ally of his glorious mistress?

The entire group moved protectively around the female, proving that she was obviously their leader. The littlest, and most belligerent, of their group, actually came at him brandishing a sword! He fell backwards with a panicked cry.

One of the two who had traveled with him earlier—*Vexil*, his benevolent mistress had named him—put a hand out, stopping the little one. Vexil said something in the disturbingly rolling speech of the Fokari. The only thing that Ratnosk could make out was a slurred mangling of his own name and a fragment of his mistress'. He hoped that Vexil was extolling what a diligent and valued servant of a powerful dragon Ratnosk was.

The sorceress spoke in a questioning tone, and an unknown voice answered her out of thin air. He felt his heart sink—this sorceress was powerful enough to command spirits! Who knew what other forces she had at her beck and call? Was it a mistake to treat her with only the third-degree of supplication?

After conferring with her nestmates, the sorceress spoke a few words directed at Ratnosk. He thought for a second that she had forgiven him, then she bared her teeth in a sign of third-degree aggression and he knew he was doomed.

He forced himself not to slip into the stance of trepidation, for he was now a draconic servant. And, while he was awaiting his imminent annihilation with as much stoic fortitude as he could muster, the magic voice spoke to him in high-draconic.

"Miss Meriwynn says that she and the entire Fichgotz clan are forever in Rukastanna's debt, and would render whatever service to her that is in their power. If you feel the same, then we are allies."

The sorceress still had her mouth with ends upturned and teeth slightly showing. But the words sounded friendly, and her posture didn't match any of the seventeen aggression stances. How was he supposed to read sincerity on these odd creatures with their chaotic, tailless posturing? And it was impossible to tell emotion on such disturbingly flat-snouted faces.

Ratnosk pondered for a moment and came to the only possible

conclusion. It must be that he was being spared the sorceress' ire only because he was held in high regard with his glorious mistress. And then it further dawned on him that she must be jealous, thinking that Ratnosk was vying with her for chief servant position.

He shifted to second-degree supplication; he would not do first-degree for her. That was reserved only for the Most Glorious One.

"Oh, mysterious spirit-voice, please announce to your master that I am pleased to meet the mighty sorceress, Meriwynn. I am Ratnosk, trap-jack third-class, and just a humble servant that defers to her in how to best serve our mutual magnificent mistress."

As he said his introduction, he realized with a pleased tingle that he was no longer really just a trap-jack third-class, he was now a first-tier draconic herald! But he could not bring himself to assume a stance of pride and say that to such a powerful and quick-tempered sorceress.

"I shall do so," the voice responded, "but I should clear up several misunderstandings. First, I do not serve Miss Meriwynn, nor any of the Fichgotz. I serve Rukastanna, although not in the way I think you mean when you say it. But she has directed me to protect them. That is her most sincere desire, in which I hope we may share a common goal.

"Second, I am not a disembodied spirit. I am Inazuma, the sword, and the spirit in the sword. You see me now being wielded by young Master Gulhawk. I should apologize in advance; the boy's enthusiasm knows no bounds, and I am not fully in control of how I may be swung."

Ratnosk pondered those revelations while the sword-spirit spoke to the Fichgotz clan, hopefully relaying his message with the proper degrees of meaning.

Apparently not, for the warrior Gulhawk fell to the ground with little yipping noises and was pointing at the sorceress. He was trying to say something, but the strange sounds he was making kept him from speaking properly.

The sorceress had been offended! But since she could not strike at a first-tier servant such as Ratnosk, she had obviously taken out her anger on one of her second-tier servants with a dreadful spell.

He needed to tread carefully around this one! So great was her anger that her face was turning a ruddy color.

"You didn't repeat it correctly!" Ratnosk complained.

"I did," Inazuma replied, "Master Gulhawk just found great mirth at the appellation 'mighty sorceress' applied to his sister."

So, he was mistaken and that was the Fokari equivalent of laughter? This was all so confusing. The warrior Gulhawk stood up, wiping moisture from his eyes, and gasping in what he now suspected might be chuckling. And the sorceress' face turned even more red in shade.

This was dreadful! He had impinged the sorceress' abilities by using just a single honorific-descriptor when she must warrant so much more. And her denigration caused amusement with a close hatch-mate, compounding the insult! He was so dead!

Prostrating himself in first-degree supplication, he cried, "Tell her that this unworthy one begs her mercy, she is obviously the glorious mistress of a thousand spells and powers too grand to contemplate."

"I really don't think that will improve things, and politely decline your request to repeat it," Inazuma stated firmly.

"I think we have a cultural chasm of misunderstanding." The sword-spirit went on, "For now, please be at ease knowing that Miss Meriwynn is not the mighty sorceress you imagine her, she is not angry with you, nor is she truly displeased with your words. I would like to focus, if we could, on our mutual mistress' desire of protecting the Fichgotz clan."

"Yes, oh diligent sword-spirit, the last command from our glorious mistress was for me to assist these Fichgotz in any way possible," he sat up in second-degree attentiveness.

"Very good, we could sorely use your assistance, for we are being hunted by an ice dragon," Inazuma stated simply.

"Because you stole some of his ice?" Ratnosk gestured to the rough sphere floating in the center of the cavernous inlet. It was much diminished from when he first saw it, but still almost as big as the boat. He shivered, not just with the cold permeating this chamber from it, but from the thought of the dragon that created it.

"I believe it is because we have become accomplices in the sabotage of an airship belonging to the dragon's master."

"Dragons don't have masters, they are mastery itself," Ratnosk intoned firmly.

"If only that were true," the sword's spirit-voice sounded sad when it said this. "Unfortunately, it is not; there are very dangerous individuals who certainly can. And I believe *that* is the origin of the conflict we are caught up in."

"The Dominus Draconis!" Ratnosk gasped. It could only be that dark bogey from stories used to terrify nestlings. It was the abomination that turned nature upside-down, subverting the natural order of draconic supremacy. It corrupted the very spirit of the universe!

"Perhaps," Inazuma admitted, "or some incarnation thereof."

"Regardless," he went on, "what we have is an ice dragon that seeks us. I am using precious energy to maintain our illusionary cover. I cannot maintain it for long. And what energy I have left will be sorely needed if we must confront this dragon.

"So, we need you to scout and determine if that dragon is still out there. Only you, brave Ratnosk, worthy servant of a glorious dragon yourself, can safely do that. You know all the small tunnels and caves that must permeate this cliff, and can creep out from another entrance to spy without revealing our location."

An involuntary meep escaped from Ratnosk's snout at the thought of him trying to spy on a dragon, let alone one that may be under the sway of the Dominus. He began to cower in second-degree anxiousness at the thought of it.

"It is what Ruka would want," Inazuma said softly.

The mentioned of his glorious mistress' name, shortened with base familiarity, shocked him upright. This sword-spirit claimed to be a first-tier servant, yet he didn't even know the proper forms to address her, the most glorious of incarnations!

But regardless, he was right. This would be their mighty mistress' wish. And only Ratnosk could do it, not this sword-spirit, nor even that formidable sorceress. This was his moment to truly serve!

"For the glory and power that is the magnificent Rukastanna, I shall not fail!" he declared in the posture of first-degree pride, actually daring to invoke his mistress' name in his pledge.

A few minutes later, Ratnosk peeked carefully out of a small hole on the beach, then shot back in. He repeated this several times, but there was no sign of anything living. Thankfully the sun had moved far enough west that the bottom of the cliff was plunged into blissful shadows.

As he finally came fully out and looked around, he caught a glimpse of white a short way down the shoreline and jumped back in. He scrambled a hundred desperate strides back up the tunnel and sat cowering for several moments. There was not a sound but his ragged breathing and the calm surf. There had been something strange about that white object. It was moving with the rolling waves. So, he steeled himself and moved to a different opening, further up the cliff, and very slowly crawled up to peer out.

There, bobbing slightly in the surf, was a huge chunk of white ice like the one in the cave. Was this another remnant of the ice dragon's spirit magic? It was floating very close to where Inazuma's illusionary boulders blocked the cave inlet; perhaps that is just where the current was inclined to take such things.

Stretching his neck as far as he could, Ratnosk peered up the cliff, but it was no good. From this vantage, he could not see the cliff top. Even the other hole, down on the rocky beach, would not be far enough away from the base to see the top.

So, steeling his courage, he went down to the first hole and stepped out carefully, scanning the sky and cliffs. Nothing moved on the beach except some gulls and crabs. He ignored the tasty snacks and moved out to the waterline to peer up at the craggy heights. Thankfully, nothing more than a hawk circled above.

Ratnosk straightened himself back into a less cowering stance and allowed himself a sigh of relief. He had succeeded!

Looking at the floating boulder of ice, he admired how it seemed to almost glow in the shadows as a stark reminder of draconic power. It was somewhat translucent, and looking into it, Ratnosk caught a glimpse of what appeared to be a pair of light blue gems…

With a panicked scramble, he dashed back toward his hole, but not fast enough. The remnants of a thousand crystal shards burst outward as the dragon broke from its icy cover and leaped. It sprang with winged grace not onto Ratnosk, but onto his escape hole.

She was brilliantly white, with tiny glistening gems of ice on her scales that caught the light with thousands of rainbow flashes. Those shimmering crystals floated off with the faint mist that her cold scales radiated in the summer heat. The eyes that regarded him were a pale blue that still looked vivid against her white countenance, like sparkling sapphires in a snowbank.

A single claw snatched him up, with almost casual gentleness, and brought him close to those terrible jaws.

"Greeting, little one. Irovnia, I am." Her voice was quiet but chilling, the kiss of a mild breeze in the deepest winter. She spoke slowly, stumbling, with a strange accent and wording, her disjointed phrases sounding oddly more akin to the low draconic spoken by non-dragons.

"Searching for Sorceress, I am; most grateful would I be for your help."

Cold penetrated deep into his body from those frigid claws, and from the certain knowledge that this dragon could see right through him. She knew! And he couldn't lie to a dragon!

"Oh, chilling incarnation of winter's killing beauty, I fear I cannot serve you, for I am already sworn to serve the most magnificent incarnation of tempestuous power."

Ratnosk was proud of his speech, it was only slightly wavering with the shivering chill of terror and cold he felt.

"Dragon of storms, you know? Wonderous luck," the ice dragon exclaimed. "Meet her, I could not. Separate, she was kept. But sorceress friend, she must be. Speak to sorceress, I must."

Her broken way of speaking, and the nonsense she spouted, was starting to make his head hurt. Or maybe it was the cold creeping into his brain.

Miraculously, she put him down. With a wave of a claw, the sheen of frost that had started enveloping his whole body fell away, and he felt the blissfully warm air of summer around him again.

"Tell where Sorceress is, you must," the dragon commanded.

A brave servant would die here, with joy in having served his mistress in his death. Ratnosk found that even in performing that final service, he was a failure. So, he steeled himself for the unthinkable—he must try to lie to a dragon.

"The mighty sorceress has left; she is far from here now."

He could not meet her eyes, and involuntarily averted his snout. Under the dragon's right wing, he caught sight of where the inlet waters met the illusionary rock. It was so close, just a stone's throw away. And then he saw the mistake in the sorceress' magic. His eyes widened for a brief second, and he quickly looked away.

"Mistress of icy…" he began trying to distract her. But a raised claw in front of his snout radiated waves of pure cold that seemed to freeze his voice. Or that might just have been his fear.

The dragon had followed his gaze and was studying the fake rock blocking the inlet. Her head was tilted in intense study for a few moments while he forgot to breathe. Then she turned to him.

"See it now," the ice dragon stated brightly. "No splash. Through rock, waves roll."

Rather than the sly satisfaction of a huntress resuming the prowl, the dragon radiated simple, tail-twitching joy. She was looking at Ratnosk like a young nestling that had solved her first twist-stick puzzle and was hoping for a snout-rub as reward.

Then she reared back on her hind legs, spread her foreclaws wide, and a small but dense blizzard of snow swirled around her. It heavily stuck to her until she appeared as a dragon shaped of snow like something nestlings might build from winter's first fall. The snow-dragon burst in a gentle flurry, falling in a semi-circular drift around her new form, that of a very young and pale Fokari.

In this form, the dragon waved one small hand, and most of the snow blew away toward the cliff. It stuck to the rock everywhere except for the illusion, leaving a powdered white outline around the inlet cave opening.

She stepped casually across the remaining snow on small bare feet and held out the crook of one arm to the shocked Ratnosk.

"To see Sorceress?" the dragon asked pleasantly, with a quizzical tilt of her head.

Even appearing as this small Fokari child, those icy blue eyes pierced his spirit. Like all dragons, this one was both terrible and strange.

"I am sorry, oh chilling mistress of ice," Ratnosk gasped, collapsing in the final degree of despair, fighting the natural compulsions of draconic servitude. "I cannot help you in this."

"Already have, you did."

"It's here!"

The first warning they had was a cold breeze that carried faint white flakes through the illusionary rock that blocked their cave. Merry was the only one who felt it. Everyone else was in the water, trying to maneuver the boat around to face outward.

The three men, more through determination than strength, had nearly managed it. Gully, of course, would not be left out; although, with what little he contributed, he might as well have stayed warm and dry. He had made a large whoop—that they quickly shushed—when plunging into the ice-chilled water. But he persevered, as they all did, after the first cold shock.

Merry wisely stayed on the boat, moving about to hold the light where it would do the most good for the struggling men.

When that first wayward flake was carried by a chill breeze to land on her hand, Merry was toward the fore of the boat. Uncle Vic was in the shallow water just below, trying to guide the bow safely past a particularly difficult submerged rock. Pa, Uncle Wex, and Gully were swinging the stern around to line up with the entrance.

It took Merry only a moment to realize what that breeze meant and to whisper her sharp warning.

With a great shove, Uncle Vic pushed them past the last rock. He maintained his grip on the side rail and scrambled over. Rushing past Merry to the mainline, he called softly, "She's clear. Heave now!"

Very slowly, their little ship started moving forward. Holding her light up as they moved toward the cave entrance, Merry could see a faint pattering of snow outlining the rock around the real cave mouth.

"Inazuma, drop the illusion," Merry commanded. "We're found, and we need to see the real rocks now."

She looked down at the lightning sword lying on the deck. He was back in the sheath that Ruka had discarded along with her old, ruined clothes.

Merry really didn't care for swords, and the whole cult-like obsession boys had with them, but Inazuma was different. His spirit was both gentle and powerful at the same time and infused with draconic wisdom. His magic shone brightly in her new sight, and she could almost make out the symbols of storms engraved throughout his bronze blade. Inazuma was much more than just a weapon to cut at flesh, he was both an ally and a magic catalyst of unfathomable tempest power. So, she really wished she could wield him, or at least that Gully was here holding him now.

Uncle Vic obviously agreed. With a grimace of pain from stretching his burned shoulder, he hauled Gully up in one smooth motion and dumped him onto the desk. "Protect your sister," he commanded.

Rolling to his feet, Gully weaved across the deck like he was dodging imaginary archers. He did one final roll, and came up in a crouch next to Merry, while somehow having unsheathed Inazuma, and holding him in a dramatic battle stance. This time, Gully's usual fanciful playact reassured rather than annoyed her.

Even though the late afternoon sun was behind the cliffs, casting the shoreline in shadow, the sudden transition from dark was still enough to dazzle their eyes. Merry, who had been holding her magic light, was the first to recover. What she saw perplexed her.

Instead of the fearsome ice dragon, what stood on the shore of the inlet was a small albino girl who looked younger than Gully. Clutching the girl's leg was Ratnosk. Even though he was no smaller than this slight child, it looked like he had been dragged behind the girl in a futile attempt to keep her back from the inlet.

This child was obviously the ice dragon, but Merry had not realized how young she was. And she was just standing there in human form, watching their boat warily.

They were drifting very slowly forward and had no choice but to pass close by the dragon girl's position. Uncle Vic stood ready to unfurl the sail, but the sea breeze was in their faces and being scattered by the looming cliffs. In these conditions, there was little chance of making much headway until they were clear of the inlet and could tack properly.

Pa and Uncle Wex hauled themselves aboard and grabbed a pair of boathooks hung on the inner railing, and pushed the boat along. A quick look at the child on the shore and their worried faces indicated that they knew what that creature really was.

Gully, also coming to the realization, raised Inazuma and pointed at the disguised dragon.

"Hold on!" Merry whispered urgently, pushing his arm down. "Don't anger her."

Something was not right. Why had the dragon chosen to appear like this? She had seen the massive ice boulders that dragon's breath left behind. It could have frozen their whole boat with her entire family in one blast. And Merry suddenly realized she hadn't seen it attack *anyone* in the cove, either.

Seeing Merry's actions, the watching girl suddenly smiled. She grabbed Ratnosk by the shoulder, easily breaking his grip on her leg to haul him up. She pointed directly at Merry and said something excitedly. Ratnosk just closed his eyes and gritted his fangs determinedly.

The dragon-girl shook him crossly, and Merry could see tendrils of frost creep across the poor little kobold from her grip. Finally, with an anguished yip, Ratnosk nodded and gave an affirmative whimper.

Their boat had almost drawn even with the girl, so she dropped Ratnosk and stepped into the surf. Immediately, the water around her ankles flash-froze, and a large tendril of white shot out toward the boat. In seconds, their forward motion stopped with a frozen crackle.

The dragon stepped easily up onto the ice, the area initially holding her legs breaking into fine powder. She walked casually across the frozen path, in bare feet and with no sign of slipping. When she reached the boat, the ice pushed upward with a great creak. It raised her to the level of the railing, which she stepped nimbly over.

Merry felt Uncle Vic's hand on her shoulder, steadying her, and she suddenly remembered to breathe again. His other hand had Gully's sword arm held firmly. Pa and Uncle Vic stood to either side, holding their boathooks at ready, but not threatening.

"Hello, how can we help you?" Uncle Vic said with a friendly smile. And Merry couldn't believe his casual and easy tone.

"Oh, thank the Eternal, you speak common!" the girl exclaimed happily. "Trying to talk draconic was giving me a headache."

"You don't speak dragon?" Uncle Vic asked.

"No, sorry," the girl replied, "my name is Irovnia, and I'm a Lost Egg."

Uncle Vic looked a little confused at this. But Merry had read many stories of dragon eggs stolen from their nests to be raised in secret by foolish and greedy people. Those stories all ended in disappointment or outright tragedy. Most kingdoms hunted out these 'Lost Eggs' to free the enslaved dragonlings, and to punish the transgressors, hopefully, before enraged dragons themselves got involved.

"That must have been terrible," Merry couldn't help speaking up.

"I… don't really know," Irovnia said tentatively. "Everyone tells me so. They also tell me I'm not much of a dragon, especially Theria. But I think being *rescued* by Princess Anya was more terrible. Don't you? Isn't that why you broke her dragon crystal, freed your storm dragon friends, and sabotaged her ship?"

"I didn't…" Merry began when Uncle Vic's firm squeeze on her shoulder stopped her.

"*Elistra* is way too modest," Uncle Vic said smoothly while looking meaningfully at Merry, "claiming she didn't do it on her own. But we helped very little, it was mostly her."

"You're the Heroes of Ravenford?" Irovnia asked dubiously.

"Of course, we are!" Gully exclaimed with utmost sincerity, eagerly joining Uncle Vic's lie. Although with him, he probably really believed he was a hero of Ravenford.

"We're in disguise, trying to avoid an unpleasant encounter with the Princess of Lanfor," Uncle Vic confided. His friendly smile never flickered once while perpetrating such a bold-faced lie on this dangerous dragon-child.

With a sudden ripple, Uncle Vic's bare chest and trousers were covered in heavy red leather armor over bulging muscles. A pair of ridiculously big swords poked over his shoulders. Gully was dressed in black, and had hairy feet, while both Pa and Uncle Wex were wearing azure armor and carrying halberds instead of boathooks.

Uncle Vic's face only flashed briefly with surprise, then his grin returned. His grinning features on that overly musclebound body were so ridiculous that Merry almost laughed aloud. He looked just like he had stepped behind one of those fancifully painted wood cutouts that the Rovers put out for festivals. Then she looked down at her curvaceous form, with bare midriff beneath a pair of bulging boobs, and blushed instead.

"We better not let anyone see us like this," Merry said quickly. And then sent a mental *please* to Inazuma.

It was not just to save herself the embarrassment, although that was part of it. Merry was not sure an illusion could fool a dragon for long at this range. Even such a young dragon as this had powerful senses.

She made a waving motion with her hands and the illusions faded away.

"You *are* her!" Irovnia cried in childish glee, "the Fate Weaver! I got your secret note. Please tell me more of the Whitelands."

Merry unintentionally winced when ice-cold hands reached out and grabbed her own.

"Oh, sorry," Irovnia said, seeming truly remorseful, "I forget sometimes when I get excited."

The small hands noticeably warmed in Merry's grip, and although still cool to the touch, were no longer unpleasant to hold. And Irovnia looked up eagerly at Merry with that small, pale child's face she had assumed.

Uncle Vic also looked her way expectantly for a second, and seeing her freeze up, began explaining with a smile, "Now is not a really good time to…"

Merry's brain engaged again, and she recited, "North, even farther than the Ice Plains of Niracrom, where summer's grasp still reaches for a few brief weeks a year, past the Icy Reach, where the sun itself fears to roam, lies the Whitelands of eternal winter.

"Snow falls endlessly there, building in great magical mountains of elemental ice, called glaciers. Only the barrier of the Reach keeps these glaciers from marching south to crush the frail lands of summer beneath their frozen boots.

"It is upon these mighty glaciers that the ice dragons mate and hatch their young. And it is beneath the greatest of the glaciers that the elder wyrm, Crustallumax, father of all ice dragons, has his vast crystalline hall."

Uncle Vic looked impressed; maybe spending all those hours in the library had been worth it.

Irovnia sighed longingly, "That sounds so wonderful, like a blissful dream. A place where snow falls naturally from the sky onto all the lands, not just on mountain tops."

She's never seen even normal winter or snow! Merry suddenly realized. *How far south was this ice dragon forced to live?*

Of course, it wouldn't do for a fortune teller to have to ask such questions. Merry needed more information, so she instead asked, "What are your thoughts on my note?"

"I don't know, do you really think Crustallumax will be able to tell me my progenitor flight? Can I really meet them? Be accepted by them? How can I dare go north, like you say? I don't even speak proper draconic! I've always been told that I'm tainted by humans, and that proves it. I will be driven out or slain by true ice dragons!"

The dragon's feelings seemed to be coming out in a torrent like some ice dam had broken.

"But I can't stay with humans. The best I could hope for would be another luxurious basement prison keeping some other summer palace cool. But most probably, like Theria says, they will just see me as an evil enemy no matter what I do. I will be reviled, hunted, and slain just for the color of my scales, and my ancestors from a millennia ago being on the wrong side of some war.

"But I can't be like Theria, I can't just hate humans. I can't wage war to hunt and kill them, as the code of the Quinary says. And I certainly can't *eat* them!" At that last point, Irovnia made the same disgusted face that Gully did when confronted with broccoli.

"There is truly no place for me!"

Irovnia's childlike form looked on the verge of tears; in fact, a few flakes of snow fell from her eyes. Merry wanted to just reach out and hug her, but the icy chill that began radiating from her hands as she got upset reminded Merry of what this 'child' really was. Would an ice dragon even like warm hugs?

In the ensuing silence after Irovnia's rant, both the dragon and her whole family were looking at Merry expectantly. She felt like she was tightrope-walking a razor.

Merry remembered clearly the time she found a baby bird fallen from its nest and brought it home. Pa said that they couldn't possibly care for it, and it would most likely die in their care. He also told her that by picking it up she had doomed it as the bird's parents would no longer care for it. The best they could do would be to put it back in the nest and hope for the best.

When she saw a similar-looking bird flying around the following season, she was overjoyed that it had survived. That is, until her brother told her, with typical Gully glee, that it had died and Pa had secretly buried it. Merry vowed to herself to at least try and save the next fallen baby bird.

But that analogy failed in the simple fact that a baby bird cannot freeze her entire family to death. And although she had a pang of guilt in lying to a child, Merry also didn't want to get her family killed in a childish tantrum if this 'baby bird' got too upset.

Uncle Vic was making a subtle *move on* gesture with his hand and clearly mouthing *go north* out of the corner of his mouth. Merry sighed inwardly but outwardly projected what she hoped was a confident visage.

"If no matter what you do, you will most likely encounter heartache or failure, why not do what your heart most desires, and go north?" Merry said. "At the very least, you'll get to see the lands of snow."

"Snow," Irovnia said wistfully, her face lighting up with simple delight at the idea of it. "Yes, I will."

"Thank you," Irovnia declared, climbing to the railing, "not just for freeing me from the princess, but for your wise advice. You are a true dragon-friend! Farewell, sorceress and heroes!"

Then she stepped off the railing into a blinding blizzard of snow that was blown apart by flapping wings. And the white ice dragon, Irovnia, flew north, over the cliff.

When the dragon was out of sight, all the strength left Merry's legs and she sat down hard in the middle of the deck.

"Well done." Pa put his hand on her shoulder and smiled down at her.

"Get comfortable," Uncle Vic said, looking over the railing at the ice, "We're going to be here a while."

"Can we blast it?" Gully asked eagerly.

"Sadly, it would not be as effective as you think," Inazuma responded.

"I'll try breaking up some of the ice, and maybe I can save a bit of it," Uncle Vic mused. "There's always a rube in the market who'll over-pay if we tell him it's dragon-ice."

"It is," Merry pointed out.

"Still just frozen water," Uncle Vic replied.

"I'll go check on Ratnosk," Uncle Wex said.

"Really?" Uncle Vic raised an eyebrow at the thought.

"Yeah, the little lizard has kind of grown on me."

A half-hour later, they spied Ruka slowly approaching their beach. She was swimming backwards, struggling and hauling something large. Looking through the spyglass, Merry gasped, "The dragon!"

"Yeah, we know Ruka's a dragon," Uncle Vic pointed out.

"No, she's got the fire dragon! Look." She handed the spyglass around.

Everyone was equally stumped, and they had to wait another half-hour for Ruka to make it to the beach. It was nearly full dark, with the retreating sun only painting faint pink traces on some high, wispy clouds. Merry once again evoked light upon her club, and they all cautiously made their way down the beach to where Ruka was. She lay panting, with her head laying just out of the surf. Next to her was the crimson head of the fire dragon. It was covered with large spines, and its jaws were half again as large as Ruka's.

Ruka raised one claw weakly in their direction as they approached and gasped out, "No, don't bother lending a hand, I got this. She only weighs three tons, and *doesn't* float."

"Why?" Pa asked the question they were all wondering.

"Good question! Not only don't they float, but I think fire dragon muscles are made of solid rock. And who needs that many spines? It's like hauling a sack of boulders, but in a porcupine sack!"

"No, why did you…"

"Why is a beautiful dragon, dragging a dragon onto your beach? I bet that isn't something you get to ask every day. And now I've beat you to it."

It was strange hearing that sarcastic girl's voice coming from that serpentine throat. Merry was certain there was some kind of magic to it. But it made it clear enough for them all to catch the faint, desperate dodging behind her attempts at humor.

"Unfortunately, it looks like it was all for nothing, she's mostly dead already. I don't know what to do… but I'll think of something…"

"Ruka," Uncle Vic said quietly.

Ruka suddenly rose from the surf and scrambled up to Uncle Vic so quickly that everyone else took a step back. She stopped with her jaws only inches from his face. And sniffed.

"Vic?" she asked in a soft, tentative tone.

"Yeah."

They were all shocked when he reached out to cradle that deadly jaw against his chest, and even more surprised that she let him.

"You just can't watch anyone die," Uncle Vic said quietly.

"No, never again," Ruka's reply was just a soft rumble, almost lost amid the sound of rolling surf.

It was a long, tiring climb back toward awareness, punctuated by little jolts. And the only reward for the climb was terrible aching pain that permeated her whole body. Theria had just decided that it was not worth it and began to sink back down when she heard the voice.

"Ha! Foul beast, there will be no mercy for you!"

Everything was still fuzzy. She had no clue how she came to be bested by some knight. Despite the pain, her body seemed distant, and she couldn't move a single claw. Her hearing was warped; the knight's voice sounded strangely high, even for a puny human speaking the common tongue. Just opening an eye was beyond her. But she struggled with titanic effort to do so.

Slowly she finally managed the exhausting task of forcing up the lid of one eye. Focusing seemed to take even longer, but eventually, she made out the form of a skinny man-child. He stood upon her shoulder, holding a wooden stick like a sword. The boy wore no armor, just a garment around his loins. And so cold were her scales that he could stand upon her in bare feet without burning. They seemed to be on a beach of some kind, with glistening stars partly blocked by a dark looming cliff, and icy lapping water nearby. And it was cold, *so cold!*

"Once again, Gulhawk the Mighty is triumphant," the boy crowed, brandishing his fake sword aloft. As he did so, he turned slightly and Theria saw the scar that ran across his chest.

She recognized this boy. It became clear that she was in purgatory and the spirits of those she had slain had come to torment her. But she didn't mind so much. The boy's weight was unnoticeable. She only felt the faint sparks that traveled down the stick from the boy's hand when he struck her scales. But they were almost pleasant pricks of pain, compared to the constant soul-freezing torment that was her existence.

In fact, the tiny spawn's antics of busily trying to behead her with a stick reminded Theria of her little Scorch. He would play such games, jumping at her with delightful viciousness.

She saw with terrible clarity now that her Scorch was dead, killed long ago by his cruel sire. In her grief, she had fled the molten lands and been ensnared by the Dragon Thrall Lord. Worse, that monster known as Theramon had clouded her mind, making her believe that another orphan dragon, controlled by Princess Anya, was her Scorch.

Neither of her Scorches had lived long enough to get their true dragon names. You don't give little fire embers their names until they make it into their second decade because so few survive that long.

And she couldn't fault that fake little one. He had been dear to her, regardless of the lie. And the deception was only possible because it was what she most fervently wished. Theria had deceived herself. And she couldn't let him go to the fate that the master of lies claimed was his.

Maybe there was a chance if she recovered his body, and begged Princess Anya, that they could restore him. She had seen the priestess Jesira do it with humans but wasn't sure it could be done with dragon spirits. And the cost would be terrible. But it would be worth it.

Of course, if she were truly dead herself, that was impossible. But why couldn't she travel from this purgatory to unite with the spirits of her lost ones? With a sinking feeling, she realized that she had died in the water, and so was eternally damned.

"Gully, get away from there. It might not be dead!" a familiar girl's voice called.

So, another slain spirit had come to torment Theria and tease her that she might still be alive.

"It *will* be dead when I'm done with it," the boy responded.

Oh, what splendid ruthlessness! She was beginning to like this one. There were worse things to spend purgatory with than a little scorchling.

The girl brought a light over with her; it glowed on the end of a familiar-looking stick. Theria found the energy somewhere to shift her eye and focus on her. This was *that* girl alright, Meriwynn Fichgotz, the storybook author. The light she carried was enough for her to see Theria's one-eyed gaze.

"Gully, run!" the girl Meriwynn hissed urgently.

The startled boy leaped off Theria with a gasp and ran to his sister. She placed him behind her and raised her glowing club. Was she going to try beating on her with a stick again? Theria wished she had the breath to chuckle.

The boy recovered slightly and moved to stand next to his sister, his little stick-sword held forward in both hands. There was only the slightest tremor to it. Looking through the veil, she could see his spirit encompass the stick with a very minor aspect of lightning. So, he was some fledgling spirit-blade? He probably would have grown up to be a dragon slayer, so it was just as well they were all dead.

"Ruka!" Meriwynn called out the side of her mouth in a nervously rising pitch trying to be heard without making too much noise, "it's alive."

They back out of Theria's sight. She didn't even consider moving her head to follow their movements. All that talk about her being alive was giving her a headache. So maybe it was true. So what? Theria found she had little interest in continued existence, one way or the other.

There is no fire. Some small, faint voice from within told her. *I need to relight it.* She looked deep to find her flames. There should be a roaring inferno spread throughout, but there was not even a small candle's flicker in a corner.

Searching for a spark, she came upon the image of herself as a tiny wyrmling shivering in the cold and snuggling up to the still body of her mother, who would never shed heat again. She had hidden when the knights came, obeying her mother's command, and believing her lie that everything would be all right. All that was left to her then was a cold corpse and a torn pennant of a rose.

This was one of her first and most powerful igniters of inner blazing rage, yet it only left aged, cold sadness now. *Where has my fire gone?* Even the memory of her poor dead Scorch, doubly lost to her, did not bring healthy bitter fury, it only invoked staggering sorrow.

She tried to clear the miasma from her mind and remember what happened. After Theramon had goaded her with Scorch's death and desecration, she had found the strength to briefly break free of the Dragon Master. She fought him with every ounce of her spirit and got totally thrashed.

Theria felt betrayed at the failure of her own power. She had been defeated before, but always knew deep down that she could overcome anything with a heart of fire. This defeat went deeper. It was a rape and plunder of her spirit such as no creature should endure. And then she drowned.

She faintly heard whispering voices over the ringing in her ears. At least her draconic hearing was still working.

"It's not dead! You said it was dead," Meriwynn's voice was an accusatory whisper.

"First of all, *it* is a *she*," a new girl's voice replied calmly. "Seriously, you fish-guts need to work on your pronouns. Second of all, I said she was *mostly* dead; that's a critical difference."

"Okay, but what're we going to do about *her*?"

"*We* are going to nothing," the new girl replied. "*You* are going to get on the boat and tell your dad to set sail. The moon will be up very soon; the airship is long gone and the coast is literally clear.

"Sail up to Fisheye Cove and I'll catch up to you there. And just in case, I'll lend Gully Inazuma once more, now that he's fully charged again."

"Awesome!" This excited cry was voiced by that wonderfully wicked little scorchling again.

"No lightning unless necessary," the new girl said firmly, "I'll sense it, come fast, and it had *better* be serious trouble, or there will be."

"Oh, all right."

Several footsteps moved hurriedly away with a final whispered "Be careful" from Meriwynn. A single tread approached Theria confidently.

"Not dead? Good, I wouldn't want to go through all that work just to haul a corpse here. You're heavy!"

The dragon approached her in the form of a girl. Looking through the spirit veil, Theria could only see the girl. But she knew this one. She wasn't sure why the storm dragon bothered with a disguise so deep, or what game she played. The obvious answer was to better torment Theria in the form of the most dangerous and hateful of creatures.

She knew this game; she was kept alive to be tortured and then killed later. It was something Garrikon had taught her. She had escaped then, but she had a hard time generating any real interest in her fate at the moment. It was best to just get it over with quickly. So, she struggled to gather a little puff of air in her once-mighty bellows and play the game.

"Who?"

It was a ragged, faint whisper that would have ended in coughing from her seawater-burned throat if she had the breath to do so.

"Me?" the pretend girl casually walked over and crouched on her haunches near Theria's head. Her tormentor was well within striking distance of her jaws; perhaps to demonstrate her current weakness.

"Hmm," she seemed to seriously consider the question. "Formally as written in the Gol Draconis, I am Rukastanna ga Yatharia, et cetera and yawn all the way back to Leviantianus. You've heard it all before from my sister.

"In my dad's culture, I'd be Rukastanna Greymantle. I usually go by the latter, although I've recently discovered that isn't really his surname either, but a title. So, I'm just me; and I'd rather be called Ruka, by both friends and enemies."

Theria tried to gather the breath for a formal reply. It was compulsive even in her present torpor; the proper forms had been literally beaten into her. Her traitorous lungs took that opportunity for the coughing they so desperately needed. A half-ocean of seawater seemed to come out as well.

"Whoa," Ruka said, standing and stepping back from the spray. "Don't hurt yourself."

"Let me help you out. You're Theriaxus, something, something, of the Ignoramus clan, right? You shouted it pretty clearly across the cove, but I was busy being on fire at the time." She rolled her shoulders with a grimace. "So, hopefully you'll forgive me if I didn't memorize it."

Theria was fairly certain that the mangling of her ancestor's name was an insult in the common tongue. If she had even the slightest flicker of fire left, it might have enraged her.

But this was just the expected next play. The first stage to breaking a captive's spirit was to tear down their pride. Her tormentor apparently didn't know her spirit had already been thoroughly crushed.

"Why?" Theria wheezed out. She might as well prompt the process on to the monologue stage, which leads to the ensuing torture and her eventual blissful oblivion.

"Why save you?" Ruka said with a shrug. "No reason really, it's just something I do—I save the weak and helpless who can't save themselves. Today, that was you. Think about that the next time you have the weak in your own claws."

Not quite the megalomaniac bragging of a conquering dragon that Theria expected, but rubbing her snout in her own weakness and dangling false hope for future victories was a good play.

This was such a young dragon, standing here pretending to be an inoffensive human. Yet Theria had seen her shrug off both Theramon's subtle influence and the Dragon Master's massive power. And even more impossible, this little dragon had casually broken her own spirit chains as well. Theria still felt the pain of that grip of iron that sent her to a drowned doom, and how those chains snapped like brittle bone at this dragon's slightest touch.

"How…" she started but broke into a fit of coughing again. This one was thankfully somewhat dryer than the last. Between hacking, she could only get out, "resist…Dragon Master…"

"Wow, nasty cough," Ruka mocked, "that's what you get for smoking too much."

Theria just glared at her as best she could with only one eye available. Her tormentor knew it was vile water, not blissful smoke that she choked on.

Ruka looked at her for a moment, then sighed and shrugged, saying, "Just don't use dragon spirit, he can own that. Oh, and it helps to be mad." She grinned and tapped her head at the last part.

That made no sense, what power could a dragon use but dragon spirit? She didn't buy the insanity claim either. Ruka was obviously unwilling to share the actual secret. For the first time since she awoke, Theria truly wished she had her fire back. She would beat the answer out of this smug human-loving dragon.

A faint sound reached them, and Ruka looked behind her.

"Oh good, they're here."

Another light approached—this one, she sensed long before seeing it, was a flame. A small figure holding a torch came into view. He was a tiny bipedal lizard-looking creature that Theria was sure must be one of the Daiamanus. They were actually relatives of sprites who had taken on a draconic cast a few millennia ago due to some ancient vow or curse or something. They lived to serve dragons, and in the common tongue, they were known as kobolds.

"Oh, glorious mistress of prodigious power, the tribe is prepared," the creature said in a high-pitched and strangely accented version of high draconic.

"Good job."

"I could never dream to comprehend your incalculable brilliance, oh glorious mistress of inscrutable wisdoms," the kobold went on nervously, "but surely the humble Bendtail tribe could provide better tribute than what you requested."

"Don't worry, Ratnosk, it's not for me, and it's exactly what's needed." Ruka cast a sly human smile at Theria when she said it. It might be the flickering torchlight cast from beneath her face, but she really did that creepy-looking-human thing well.

"Send them in," Ruka commanded Ratnosk.

"As you wish, oh magnificent…" Ratnosk began, but Ruka cut him off.

"Just go!"

He scampered away with a 'meep' sound and Theria watched the open flame of the torch go with sad longing. It wasn't for the light she pined; her vision was fine, the beach crisp and clear in the black and white of draconic darkvision. It was the glorious reminder of heat and fire she missed.

A horde of kobold poured from caves out onto the beach. Three ostentatiously, but cheaply, jeweled ones approached Ruka first.

"Oh, glorious and powerful master of spirit and elements, we have no greater wish…" all three began in unison.

"Whoa, whoa, whoa!" Ruka stopped them, "not to me!"

She walked over to Theria, and in a theatrical flash of lightning and deafening rumble of thunder, she assumed her true form. Theria had forgotten how small this dragon was, her spirit just felt so much more immense than her physical size.

"Here is the mighty Theriaxus," Ruka boomed in full draconic volume. "As you can see, she is a far larger and more glorious dragon that I. It is to her that the Bendtail should swear!"

"But you must first prove your worth," Ruka went on to the rapt crowd. "Bring forth your tribute!"

There were well over a hundred kobolds, the vast majority of which had large bundles of sticks or small logs on their backs. These they began placing reverently around Theria's body. A large number had sacks that they disgorged coal from. And about a dozen had small casks of oil that they poured on the wood and coal.

As they were about halfway through, Ruka leaned down and whispered, "You'll either be cured or burned alive—either way, you'll be a true fire-dragon again."

The kobold Ratnosk approached Theria, bowed, and said, "I am sorry, oh glorious mistress-who-could-have-been, but I am already sworn to another and must leave with her."

Ruka added still in a whisper only for Theria's draconic hearing, "Just one is a headache, a hundred may actually *make* you insane."

With that, the dragon Ruka carefully picked her way through the throng. Turning back only once, she called out in common, "Good luck, I'm bailing on this barbecue!"

As she left, she partially unfolded her wings as if stretching and Theria could clearly see the blackened burn holes on the shimmering bronze surfaces. That movement was no accident, but Theria had no clue what it meant. This dragon had great cause to hate Theria, yet she did all this to save the enemy who hurt her so.

Perhaps Ruka *was* insane. But *she* was the only one who held the secret to stand against the Dragon Master. It was something to ponder during the long, slow burn it would take to restore her spirit.

Ratnosk solemnly passed the torch to the clan elder, bowed, and ran to catch up with his mistress. As the elder placed the first lick of fire to Theria's pyre, the chanting began.

"Oh, glorious and powerful master of spirit and elements, we have no greater wish, and there is no greater fulfillment than to serve you in both our life and our death. Take of us what you will and we will give you our all."

A funeral pyre and a fanatically chanting cult? Theria supposed this could be the start to a glorious rebirth!

They sailed out from beneath the starlit shadow of lover's over-look just at moonrise. The sultry summer moon crept up over the ocean, swollen, orange, and at least to Merry's imagination, fraught with a promise of danger and romance.

She found herself at the tiller, as the menfolk fumbled jovially with the best way to set the unfamiliar rigging in the wan moonlight. The small but dramatic silhouette of Gully was at the prow, centered in the rising moon, eagerly scanning the sea and sky ahead with 'his' mighty sword Inazuma in hand.

When Ruka had inevitably taken her sword back, Gully neither pouted nor sulked, neither action was in his nature. He immediately found the most appropriately sized stick and continued practicing his pretend sword moves. And what shocked everyone but Gully, both figuratively and literally, was that he could still shock people. It was a small minor charge, to be sure, little more than that generated walking across a thick rug. But he could generate it at will and force it down one of his pretend stick-swords.

When Inazuma told him that was the basis of spiritblade magic, and if he practiced for many years, he might eventually evoke true tempest power on a sword, there was no stopping him. After Pa made him stop shocking her, Gully ran around the beach practicing his idiotic blade technique. It should have been obvious where he'd end up, and Merry could only fault her exhaustion for not realizing it sooner. Only Gully was crazy enough to shock a *mostly*-dead dragon awake.

As they cleared the headland between the inlet and Fisheye Cove, Merry turned the boat from east to north, swinging the ever vigilantly posing silhouette of Gully out of the rising moon. Just before they rounded the ridge, a bonfire flared to life on the beach behind them. It was huge, to be seen at such a distance, a small but bright flare of light in the looming dark shadows of the cliffs behind them.

Looking at the far-off conflagration, Merry imagined she saw great infernal wings spread out from the flames in rapture. Then in another moment, they were behind the promontory, and Merry wasn't sure what she saw. No one else on the boat had noticed it—or at least they didn't mention it.

They tacked north along the coast on the nightly land-breeze, back toward Ravenford.

The pale sands of the cove clearly caught the moonlight, so it was an even better landmark on a night such as this. As they were coming abreast Fisheye Cove, she began to hear a faint screaming.

The sound was growing louder and was definitely approaching from the aft. Scanning the glittering waters behind them, Merry could see a wake of white heading directly toward the boat.

Everyone could hear it by this point. The menfolk stopped their debate on the best set of the foresail and looked to each other nervously. Gully came bounding back across the ship in a nimble leaping dance around mast and men.

"What is that?" Gully asked, pointing the sword toward the approaching creature.

"Don't know," said Uncle Vic who stood on the starboard rail to try and get a better view. He was leaning out, holding a line with his good arm for balance.

It sounded like some high-pitched banshee. They could now make out a small figure near the center of the wake. And it was approaching fast.

"You two get in the hold," Pa said as he came back to take the tiller from Merry.

After everything they had been through and done, Pa wanted to protect them? They should be the ones protecting him. She was at a loss of how to say it without hurting him.

Gully, of course, had no such restraint, declaring, "Stand back, I'm going to blast this creature out of the water."

Uncle Wex cried, "Wait!" at the same time that Inazuma commanded, "Hold!"

A familiar dragon head rose out of the water as Ruka slowed and pulled up behind the boat. She plucked the now-silent Ratnosk from her back and deposited him gently but unceremoniously on the deck, where he promptly collapsed.

"You brought *him*?" Uncle Wex asked, sounding both surprised and annoyed.

"Tried leaving him," Ruka said with a rise of eye-ridge and tilt of the head that Merry interpreted as a dragon shrug. "He's *insistently* dedicated."

She could tell that Ruka was trying to sound irritated, but was in too good a mood to pull it off. In fact, her voice sounded happy now, and Merry took her first real good look at their benefactor in dragon form.

The moonlight made her emerald dragon eyes seem to glow with an inner luster. And her lively serpentine form beneath the waves also caught the moon's radiance and reflected it back in sparkling flashes through the water. They had a magically shimmering dragon-wake as Ruka easily kept up behind the boat.

As beautiful a sight as that was to her eyes, when Merry looked beyond sight through her new magical senses, her breath failed her in a quiet gasp. Ruka's spirit-form glowed with a blinding radiance and hummed with a happy tune that resonated with the joy of the open ocean under the moon. Here, she had relaxed enough for the full nature of her dragon-spirit to shine through.

It was something that Merry knew she would never forget. She longed for ink, paper, and the elusive words to try and capture the feeling it evoked in her. But she knew that even if she had her book, she wouldn't dare to look away for fear of waking from the dream.

"Wow," Merry whispered to herself when she remembered to breathe again.

Ruka seemed to notice Merry's scrutiny of her unguarded spirit. And in a second, she clamped down on it. But like a shuttered storm lantern, some of it could not help but leak out. It was still powerful as you would expect a dragon-spirit would be, but just a dim reminder of the unfettered glory of a moment before.

"Anchor at the cove," she commanded their little group, "and let's scavenge as much of your gear as we can."

"It's too dark," Uncle Wex pointed out.

"Oh," Ruka winked one glittering draconic eye at Merry, "from what I hear, we have a *mighty* sorceress. Light will not be a problem."

Merry's light, although useful, was one of several, and secondary to the bright glow of two moons. The real one, now risen completely above the waves, and an illusionary one. The false moon was a silver disk which glowed brightly a dozen feet over Gully's head. For a sword, Inazuma seemed to have an artistic streak; the dragon-in-the-moon image on it was subtle, but distinctly beautiful.

"Behold the legend of *Gulhawk the mighty*," Gully intoned.

Having his own personal moon caused what would have been endless 'chosen one' posturing by Gully. Ruka had to rap him on the head with one claw-knuckle to get him back on track.

"Focus," Merry admonished him.

There was one more light for their party—Ruka made the spines down her back glow. Although not the brightest light, to Merry it was the most dazzling. Illuminated with a soft multi-hued glow, Ruka had her spines raised nearly straight up. Looking closely, Merry could make out the pattern for light on each. But it was subtly different; the loops were shifted slightly, creating a different color and warmth to the light. And they were shifting more as she watched.

She could almost envision how pattern variations like that could create a multitude of colors. It would take a phenomenal amount of power and control, but from just that, could you form intricate illusions like Inazuma's old-man ruse? Looking inward to that place in her mind where the light pattern was stored, she wondered what would happen if she just altered this or that strand a little…

A very light tap on her head brought Merry back to awareness.

"Focus," Ruka made an excellent attempt at echoing the scolding tone that Merry usually had for Gully. And, although it wasn't physically visible in her draconic visage, Merry envisioned a friendly, ironic smile from her.

So, they split into two groups to begin their salvage. Ruka, Pa, Uncle Wex, and Gully worked on the main wreck of the Foam Lady. With a dragon hauling gear up in great bundles from underwater, the two uninjured men sorting and untangling lines and sailcloth, and Gully providing Inazuma's light and hopefully staying out of the way, they began making quick work of it.

Uncle Vic and Merry were delegated to search the beach for any useful flotsam. Rather than head along the waterline, Uncle Vic made a beeline for a shadow up on a small dune that was a good distance from the water and the area of the wreck.

When she got closer with her light, Merry realized it was the picnic basket that Ma had packed for them. How Uncle Vic had spotted the basket in the moonlight from such a distance was almost as big a mystery as how it got over here. But Ma always said Vic's one magical power was never missing a meal.

The sand across a good portion of the beach, including most of the way over here, was churned by heavy dragon claws. But in this area around the picnic basket, there were no dragon tracks. And other than theirs, there was just a single set of human-size tracks going to and leaving this otherwise pristine area of beach.

"All the fishcakes are gone, but the honey rolls and jam are still here. Awesome!" Uncle Vic declared after a brief search of the basket. "And your sunhat is also here, with the brim pinned politely under the basket so it won't blow away."

"Irovnia?" Merry guessed.

"No, it was a woman who sat here," he stated, pointing to an indentation in the sand next to the basket.

"You can't tell anything from that," she held her light closer to examine the amorphous marks in the sand.

"I'm a studied expert in the shape of woman's rears, and this one was certainly endowed."

"Gross, you pig."

"Maybe, but I'm not wrong. It wasn't that little dragon-kid sitting here."

"Who then, someone from the ship? Maybe the princess? Can your pig-powers tell if it was a *royally endowed* posterior?"

Uncle Vic just flashed his most irritating smile at her, grabbed the basket, and placed the sunhat on her head.

"Come on, we have a lot of beach to cover."

It was kind of sad to find the guts of their trusty old boat strewn down the beach, with a lifetime of old tackle and fishing gear mixed in. They found so much, they had to make piles, and return to the boat for something to carry it all in. Luckily, the old three-handled fish basket was among the items recovered from the wreck.

Ruka was recharging Inazuma; his bright moon illusion had depleted a large amount of his power. Gully was standing nearby, disappointed that he wasn't allowed to hold the blade while it was being blasted with dragon lightning.

As the men hauled the large basket, filled with the flotsam of their life, back to the new boat, Merry took the opportunity to head out on the south breakwater. She wanted to look once more on the place where mighty dragons had raged. It seemed like a lifetime ago, rather than just this morning.

The stones were fire-blackened across most of the large end-boulder. Only an area near the center was clear of the burn marks. Merry imagined she saw the outline of a valiant and noble little dragon that had shielded a pair of kids with her body. Ruka had refused to show Merry her wings, but even folded, they looked terrible.

A reflected flash caught Merry's eye, and she saw the broken remains of her ink bottle on one corner of the stone. It was the symbol of her art and love, smashed there on the rocks. An even blacker mark than dragon fire upon the stone.

Then, near it, she saw the book, and her heart leaped with joy. Somehow, thank the gods, it was securely wedged between two rocks, and well above the tideline. As she snatched it up and held it to her breast, Merry felt a tingle like magic in her old worn tome. The feeling was gone in a flash of her over-wrought imagination.

Perhaps the pouring of her heartfelt stories had charged the book with spirit, and she never had the power to notice it before. She was standing there, leafing through her book, and organizing the thoughts of what she needed to write as soon as she had ink and quill in hand again, when a familiar voice cried out from behind her.

"Don't worry, Princess. I, Sir Gulhawk, will save you from that tome of dark, incomprehensible, inky words!"

"Sir Gulhawk is mistaken," Merry intoned, while striking a grand Gully-pose back at him. "It is not a lowly princess you face, but the mighty sorceress, Meriwynn!"

Epilogue
Erik P. Wenson

Irweena absently seasoned and breaded the raw fish, preparing it for the oil. It was a process she had once done with love and attention. Now, while the resulting taste was hardly any different to the average patron of the Corner Tavern on Calipherus Street by the wall of Ravenford, there were some who would know the difference. The Baroness was one. The others were all gone. It was the fishcakes that had kept her from them on that fateful day, and it was the fishcakes that allowed her to continue afterward.

Irweena had heard the stories of what had happened. The Drellers had seen it from afar, and sailed back to warn the town. It was so like the stories her young Merry had written in her journal. Dragons locked in some mortal battle, for reasons no mere mortal could possibly fathom. Fire, frost, and lightning wielded carelessly, like her Gully flailing about with sticks. But, as always, when the great do battle, the small are wounded the worst. The tale ends with all of the dragons leaving—harmed, but alive, and all the people in the cove gone without a trace. The people… her family.

A tear formed in Irweena's eye and she knew that she had better go out of the kitchen. Her departed father's old friend, a man she called uncle, watched her leave and continued helping his customers, letting them know that their fishcakes would be delayed slightly.

Irweena sat on the steps that faced the yard behind the shop. She cried for a minute softly, then began looking around at the buildings and the wall. This was where she had grown up. What fun she had with her playmates after the chores were done. There was a puppeteer who practiced two houses down, and they would sneak into the yard next door to take turns peeking through a hole in the fence to watch. There was a stray cat they had named Mr. Sniggerbottoms that was as tame as tame could be with them, because they fed him fish scraps after the soup was cooked. He was very fat, but they would pick him up and dance with him and tell him all their deepest secrets because he would listen, but never tell. Eventually, the now much-older Irweena would look at the herb garden and collect some fresh dill or basil. She would then go back to her fishcakes and the patrons would not be displeased.

It was mid-afternoon, just after the midday meals were served. There were still a few of the regulars who always came by when it wasn't busy, enjoying their meal and discussing the gossip of the day. Mrs. Gottermot was expecting, but wouldn't admit it yet. Clive Durncastle was arrested again for punching a carriage horse that he said insulted him. Arigorn Schwartz had moved off to Dunwynn, to no one's surprise and to everyone's delight. And then a new voice was heard. It was the voice of a lady, but it was young. She said that she had heard tales of there being delicious fishcakes here, so she had to try one. When Irweena turned her head, she saw that the girl had taken a corner table by the window and was looking out at the street. She was dressed in fine clothes, but they were for travelling, not for taking in a day in Ravenford. She turned back to the hot oil and placed two cakes into the pot. After a few moments of looking at the flour bucket and measuring in her mind how long it would be before it would have to be refilled at Mr. Froddleskin's grain wheel, she looked at the cakes. She was looking for the skin to crack just slightly and there, they were done. With hands that knew their trade without their owner's attention, the cakes were out and draining in an instant. Once the excess oil had dripped off, the cakes were dusted slightly with sea salt, put on a wooden plate, and Irweena headed off to the corner table. The girl said, "Thank you. I've heard so much about them. I can't wait to try."

She motioned for Irweena to stay while she tasted the cake. She took a bite that was not quite as dainty as Irweena had expected, for the Baroness had always taken dainty bites. After swallowing and drinking some water, she smiled and said, "That was really good. But if I'm not mistaken, this was made with river trout?"

"Yes, m'lady. It calls for yellow jumpers, but they're scarce this time o' year," Irweena said with a curtsy. Irweena, when she was young, had once been distracted by a fire in another part of the royal kitchen and the Baroness' cake had been slightly overcooked. When the Baroness made a peculiar face, the head cook had told her she would receive no pay for that day and that she would also have to peel dragonfruit for the rest of the week.

The panic of imperfection must have shown on her face, for the young lady said, "Well, for a trout-cake, it is extraordinary, and you are truly the finest at your trade!"

"Oh, thank you, m'lady," Irweena said with obvious relief in her voice.

"Are you the owner of this place?" the girl asked taking another larger than necessary bite of the cake.

"No, my uncle…" Irweena said meekly.

"Where is your uncle?"

"He takes a nap in the afternoon while it's slow."

"Well, you simply must have yellow jumpers for your cakes, and there is a man out in the street with a basket of them looking for someone to buy them."

"Oh, m'lady, my uncle handles all the money. I can't possibly…"

"Here, I think this will buy the whole basket," the girl said handing her a coin of platinum. "Now hurry before they're all gone."

Irweena was befuddled, to say the least. She was sure the whole basket wasn't worth more than a few silvers, and no fishmonger could make that kind of change. As a fishmonger's wife, she had never seen so much as a piece of gold. However, the young lady had a compelling tone in her voice that seemed to give Irweena no choice but to attempt to buy the fish. Irweena walked out of the door and into the street. The platinum coin was immediately dropped and forgotten as she saw—each holding one handle of a three-handled basket of full-size yellow jumpers, packed in ice no less—her brother, her brother-in-law, and her lovely, bearded, sunburned, leatherhanded, smiling husband. To their side were Merry and Gully.

The young lady watched the Fichgotz family's hysterical reunion from the window, hearing the screams, and almost feeling the crushing embraces Irweena Fichgotz gave to her loved ones, not noticing or caring how unkempt they were nor how badly they smelled. She also noticed Merry, who, as instructed, picked up the platinum coin and placed it in her pocket.

"Mummy, I've written it all down, everything," Merry said to her mother. "I can read you the whole story if you like."

"Oh, yes, yes my dear. I want to hear every word, over and over," Irweena stammered through her joyful tears.

The young lady sat at her corner table and ate the second fishcake. "I think I might even prefer the trout," she said to herself. Then she put her hand on a long, purple velvet bag and held one end as one might a sword hilt and said, "We've done well. They're so happy. Doesn't it make you feel so good all over? I'm positively tingling. Now don't start complaining again. The job I gave you was extremely important, just look at them. I know you don't have eyes, but you know what I mean…"

HERE ENDS TALES FROM THAC.
FOR MORE ADVENTURES FROM THIS
MAGICAL LAND, PLEASE READ
HEROES OF RAVENFORD BOOKS 1-5.
ALSO, THE STORY CONTINUES FOR
THE STEALLES, DONATELLO, SEISHIN,
KORTIAMA, VES, AND RUKA
IN A NEW SERIES,
RISE OF THE THRALL LORD.

ABOUT
F.P. SPIRIT

F.P. Spirit writes high fantasy fiction inspired by the likes of Tolkien, Eddings, Brooks, and Piers Anthony. An avid science fiction fan, he became hooked on fantasy the moment he cracked open the Lord of the Rings in high school. When he is not writing, F.P. is either spending time with his wife and sons, gaming, doing yoga, Tai Chi, or walking their dog.

A long-time lover of fantasy and the surreal, he hopes you enjoy his fun contributions to the world of fantasy and magic.

Other Titles by F.P Spirit

The Heroes of Ravenford
The Ruins on Stone Hill
The Serpent Cult
The Dark Monolith
The Princess of Lanfor
The Baron's Heart

You can learn more about F.P. Spirit by visiting his website at:
Fpspirit.com

ABOUT SHANNON PEMRICK

USA Today bestselling author Shannon Pemrick is a full-time slow-burn romantic fantasy author, fuller-time geek, and unrelenting dragon enthusiast. She owns too many novelty mugs, not enough chocolate, and maintains a forbidden love-affair with all things shiny. When she's not burning her fingers across a keyboard handing out adventures and HEAs, she's rolling dice and getting lost in RPGs or searching for brides for her dragon overlords.

Other Titles by Shannon

Experimental Heart
Destiny
Pieces
Secrets
Exposed
Surrendered
Reborn

Oracle's Path
Prophecy of Convergence
Prophecy Tested
Prophecy Chosen

You can learn more about Shannon by visiting her website at:
Shannonpemrick.com

ABOUT
K.J. FOGLEMAN

Keeper of dragons and lover of coffee, Kathryn always has some devious plot brewing in her cauldron and any number of bad ideas hidden under her pointy wizard hat.
Be sure to catch her online and follow her crazy antics!

Other titles by K.J. Fogleman

Tales of the Wovlen
The Dragon's Son
The Dragon's Due

You can learn more about K.J. Fogleman by visiting her website at:
Kathrynjfogleman.com

ABOUT
Timothy P. DORAN

A lost dream-walker along roads of fantastic and alien worlds, Timorthy P. Doran, whom some call Tim, only occasionally finds his way into this one. On those rare moments when he does, he happily finds himself to be the husband of a wonderfully understanding wife, and father of three imaginative and clever children.

In addition to having an insatiable appetite for fantasy and science fiction, Tim is an avid gamer with a particular focus on fantasy RPG, turn-based tactical and old-school pen-and-paper role-playing games. Tim played Dungeons and Dragon, from a very early age with a close group of friends, who, many decades later, still get together to roll the dice whenever they can.

While introducing his children and their friends to the wonders of worlds previously lost in the mists of fancy, Tim encountered an individual of kindred imagination. This individual not only had the sense of adventure to walk those dream-roads, but the resolve and fortitude to actually chronicle some of them. And, through cajoling and determined prodding, F.P. finally got Tim to break his vow to write a thousand stories, and never finish one. So here we are.

Although Tim consoles himself with the knowledge that Merry and Gully's story is far from over…

ABOUT
Jeffrey L. PRICE

Jeffrey L. Price has been a has been a science fiction and fantasy fan long before it was cool to be a geek and still has a fear of being pushed into lockers to prove it. He began his career as journalist before transitioning into the IT field. He still keeps his toe in the writing world as a frequent commenter on the iO9 website, through his blog, The Blue Scream of Jeff and by working on his own novel which he's sure will revolutionize the genre if he could just finish it.